"… Sassy! Ridgway Rocks!"

Susan Andersen

Also:

THIS PERFECT KISS

WISH YOU WERE HERE

"Ridgway's smart, peppy style is reminiscent of Jennifer Crusie, but her…heroines stand on their own."
Publishers Weekly

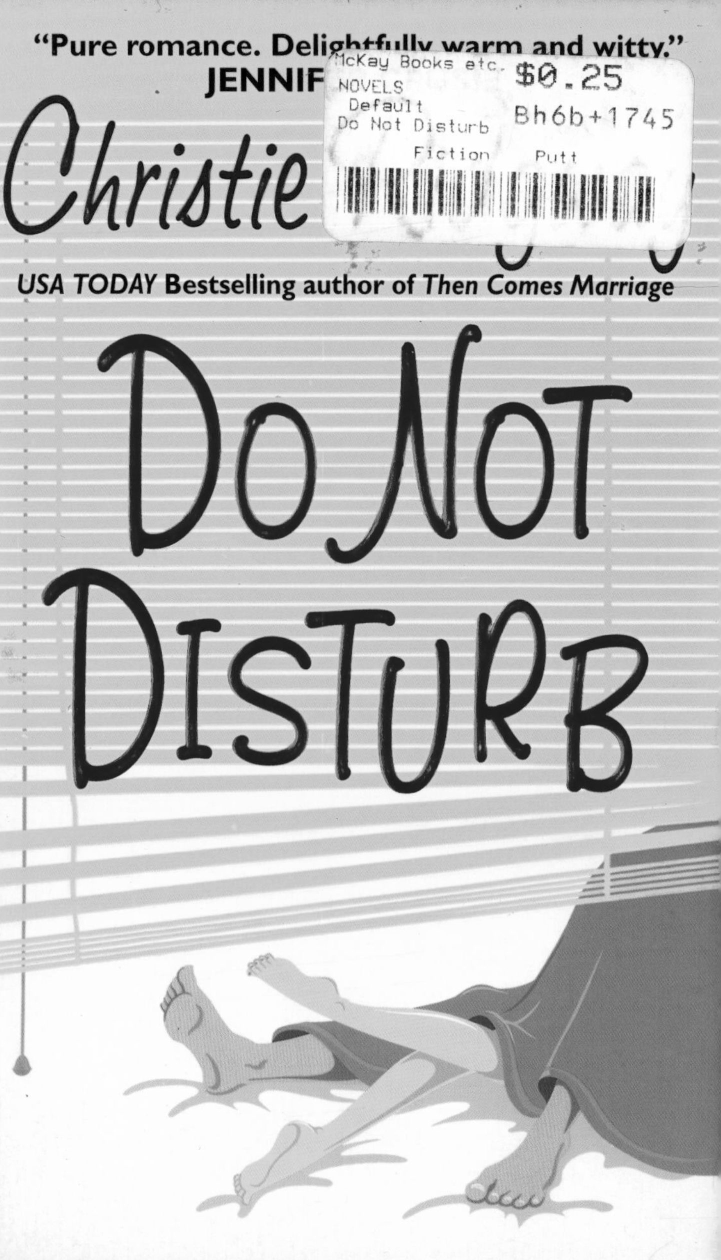
"Pure romance. Delightfully warm and witty."
JENNIF
Christie
USA TODAY Bestselling author of Then Comes Marriage
Do Not
Disturb

"Who are you?" Cooper asked again.

Lifting her chin, she matched him stare for assessing stare. "I'm Angel. Angel Buchanan."

A magical creature, all right. *An angel.*

For a weird instant he wondered if he'd actually died. But then he sucked in a breath of air, inhaling a heady shot of her perfume with it. The sophisticated fragrance sparked the memory of her skin beneath his hand—his palm actually tingled—and he decided it was a safe bet that his first thought in heaven wouldn't be about stripping naked one its winged residents.

Then she smiled at him, and it was so sweet that he thought *angel* again until he caught the amused glitter in her eyes.

"And," she added, all moonbeams and sugary whipped cream innocence, "I'm also the woman who's going to be living with you for the next few weeks."

Avon Contemporary Romances by
Christie Ridgway

Do Not Disturb
Then Comes Marriage
First Comes Love
This Perfect Kiss
Wish You Were Here

Christie Ridgway

Do Not Disturb

AVON BOOKS
An Imprint of HarperCollins*Publishers*

This is a work of fiction. Names, characters, places, and incidents are products of the author's imagination or are used fictitiously and are not to be construed as real. Any resemblance to actual events, locales, organizations, or persons, living or dead, is entirely coincidental.

AVON BOOKS
An Imprint of HarperCollins*Publishers*
10 East 53rd Street
New York, New York 10022-5299

ISBN: 0-06-009348-X
www.avonromance.com

First Avon Books paperback printing: January 2004

Printed in the U.S.A.

10 9 8 7 6 5 4 3 2 1

For Marlene and Jasper DiGiovanni,
my Tante and Uncle Jay,
who always made me feel loved and special

Acknowledgments

With thanks to author and San Franciscan Candice Hern for her help with details about "the City." More gratitude to Michael Pundeff for providing answers to my attorney questions.

Elizabeth Bevarly and Barbara Freethy are wonderful people to bounce story ideas off of . . . thank you! Barbara Samuel and Teresa Hill continue to provide the kind of support every writer needs.

As always, my husband and two boys deserve much credit for providing me the opportunity and the understanding to pursue my dream.

Christie Ridgway
www.christieridgway.com

Prologue

"He's dead." Angel Buchanan stared at the television mounted above the bar. Her whole body sagged, her high-heeled foot slid off the rung of her tall stool. "He's *dead*."

"Huh?" Angel's intern-assistant paused in the act of wiggling her own stool closer to the marble-topped cocktail table where the pair were sitting and glanced up. Her gaze followed Angel's over the heads of Ça Va's noisy postwork crowd to the news ticker creeping across the TV screen. "Oh. That 'Artist of the Heart' guy. So?"

Angel didn't answer. Instead she gripped the solid table edge to anchor herself as the chatter of the restaurant's upscale clientele, and even the presence of her curious intern, receded. Her eyes tracked the crawl.

Stephen Whitney, the self-dubbed "Artist of the Heart," had been hit by a truck while walking in the predawn dark. Though it was clearly an accident, the famous painter was dead all the same. A memorial service was scheduled for the following week in Carmel, California, near the place where the artist had lived for the last twenty years.

"Twenty-*three* years," Angel muttered, correcting the newscaster.

Already the holy and the holier-than-thou were weighing in on the loss of one of America's "great visionaries." One claimed that not only had Whitney's paintings celebrated home and family, but so had the way he lived his life. Both the National Choral Ensemble of the Baptist Church and the Harlem Boy's Choir had promised to sing at the memorial service. A representative from the White House was planning to attend. The public was "stunned" and "saddened."

Angel didn't know what to call the ball of emotion suddenly expanding inside of her.

"She's here," the intern hissed in her ear. "Miss Marshall's coming this way."

Despite the warning, it still took a sharp elbow jab to jolt Angel's attention back to the present. San Francisco. The popular Ça Va Restaurant. That she was here as a writer for *West Coast* magazine because her latest story needed Julie Marshall's reaction to the fact that her boss was a two-faced charlatan who had swindled investors in a classic Ponzi scheme.

The thin, fiftyish Miss Marshall was settling on the barstool across the table. She looked at Angel with anxious eyes. "I know something's wrong, Ms. Buchanan. Something about Paul. What is it?"

Angel's gaze flicked back to the TV, that unnameable

emotion roiling again in her belly. Something was wrong, all right. The world was getting ready to beatify Stephen Whitney, the man who Angel knew was no saint.

Later, though. She'd have to think about that later.

She forced herself to refocus on Miss Marshall. Though Angel knew from a previous interview that the older woman was head-over-girdle in love with her boss, she wouldn't let anything as useless as a soft heart soft-pedal the bad news. In her experience, the baldest truth was always healthier than the most handsome lie.

"It *is* about Mr. Roth," Angel began, slipping her hand inside her purse to bring out the wad of tissues she'd stuffed there before leaving the office. "You told me last week that you believe he's innocent and that your house is on the market to pay for his defense. But I found evidence during my investigation . . ."

"Wh-what are you saying?" The older lady's voice trembled.

"I followed the paper trail." Angel placed the tissue wad on the tabletop and pushed it forward. "He bilked all those investors, every one, including your mother's church circle. Don't sell your home for him."

The lady licked her pale lips. "Perhaps . . . perhaps you're mistaken?"

God, why did women do something so foolish—dangerous, even—as putting their faith in a man? Shaking her head, Angel gave the tissue wad another nudge across the table. "He isn't the man you think he is."

Her hand closing around the tissues, Miss Marshall slowly, ever so slowly, rose to her feet.

Swallowing, Angel stood too. *Here it comes,* she thought, steeling herself for the sick panic she always felt when a woman cried.

The older lady sucked in a sharp breath. Then her eyes narrowed. "That bastard!" she spit out.

Angel stared.

"That slimy, lying bastard!" Instead of tears, Miss Marshall's pale eyes were filling with something else, something that looked a lot like that emotion coiling and writhing inside Angel herself.

"Promise me it will all come out in your article," Miss Marshall demanded. "Promise me that the whole world will know the kind of man Paul Roth is."

"I always tell the whole story," Angel assured her.

"Good." There were spots of color on the woman's cheeks. "I thought, we all thought, he could do no wrong. The world should know the truth about men like that!"

Before Angel could say any more, a waiter paused at Miss Marshall's side, the small tray balanced on his palm crowded with martinis and highball glasses. "Ladies, I'll be with you in just a moment."

The older woman rounded on him. Angel guessed it happened because the poor guy did bear a slight resemblance to Paul Roth, the "rat-faced, smarmy-smiling, hell-bound seducer of hearts" that had done Miss Marshall wrong. Whatever the reason, following that damning pronouncement, the betrayed woman threw down the tissues and lifted a martini glass off the waiter's tray to dash the contents into the unsuspecting man's face.

Then she stormed away.

Not until Angel handed over that wad of tissues and a massive tip to the dripping waiter did she finally put a name to the emotion that had been radiating off the older woman. It was outrage. And Angel recognized it as the same feeling burning inside of her at the idea that Stephen Whitney would be remembered as a noble family man. A hero.

But she didn't devise a plan of action until later, after she'd returned home to her apartment, her dry cleaning in one hand and a tiny bag of groceries in the other. Outside her door, she dropped them both when her neighbor's oversized cat, Tom Jones, demanded his customary belly rub.

Of course, the instant another set of footsteps sounded on the stairs, the philanderer abandoned her.

Isn't that just like a male.

With a sigh, Angel walked into her apartment and immediately crossed to the TV, filling the silence with the voice of the evening anchor on the all-day, all-news channel. Now she learned that even more were mourning the "upstanding" Stephen Whitney, whose paintings "captured so many precious moments of the American family experience."

The flames of that hot, angry emotion inside Angel leaped higher. *They're wrong, all wrong!*

The upstanding Stephen Whitney, who the world thought knew so much about family, was the same man who'd fathered Angel . . . and then forgotten her. It was then that Miss Marshall's exhortation blazed in Angel's mind.

The world should know the truth about men like that.

Chapter 1

Inside Carmel, California's largest church, the unseasonal early September heat opened the pores of the one-thousand-plus gathered for Stephen Whitney's memorial service. The mingled scents of deodorant, aftershave, hairspray, and perfume rose above the crowd to hang like a thick cloud over the pews, making each of Angel's breaths a struggle.

Add to the cloying humidity yet another piercing *Hallelujah!*, followed by the droning voice of yet another moralistic muckety-muck at the podium, and Angel wondered if she'd made the short drop to her own personal hell instead of the short drive from San Francisco. Her scalp itched beneath her broad-brimmed black straw hat. She pressed the fingertips of her black cotton gloves to her upper lip to blot the moisture gathering there.

She needed air.

She needed out.

But she could hardly retreat now.

Not after pitching the idea of an in-depth profile on Stephen Whitney in such winning tones to her editor, Jane Hurley. Not after following that up with an interoffice e-mail inquiring if Jane had any contacts that might be helpful.

Jane herself proved to be that—Angel had counted on it. While her editor was the woman who had turned *West Coast* magazine from a monthly filled with decorating tips and regional recipes into a nationally read and respected political and cultural journal, she was also Hearst-rich and maintained a second home on the famed Seventeen Mile Drive. So thanks to Jane, Angel had scored one of the scarce press passes to this memorial service, and her name was on the short list of guests for a much more private ceremony taking place later that day.

Nevertheless, Angel couldn't quash her serious second thoughts about digging into Stephen Whitney's life. In the past, she'd made it her mission to ignore anything having to do with the "Artist of the Heart," just as he'd ignored her when she'd so desperately needed him. Maybe she shouldn't—

Oh, stop being such a sissy, the journalist inside her interrupted, *there's good stuff here. A story worth telling.*

But even as another choral ensemble trooped up to the front of the church, Angel continued to waffle. So she settled her latest dilemma the same way she'd settled nearly all of them since she was a lonely twelve-year-old hooked on the video of *All the President's Men.*

WWWD? Angel asked herself. *What Would Woodward Do?*

And the answer was obvious, of course. Woodward would work the story.

Without delay.

Inhaling a deep breath, she glanced left and appraised the person nearest her in the second-to-the-last pew. Middle-aged lady, politely interested expression, quiet mauve suit. A likely source for some basic info.

Abandoning her niche at the outside corner of the pew, Angel slid closer. The filmy chiffon overlay of her sleeveless, little black dress floated up around her knees and she settled it back down before catching the lady's eye.

"Excuse me," she murmured. One of the very few things Angel knew about the artist was that he'd married. "I wonder if you could point out the widow."

Ms. Mauve took her time giving a less-than-neighborly once-over, which made Angel sorry she'd tucked her hair beneath her hat. She had yards of the curly blond stuff, and though it was a real pain to manage, it did take ten years off her age. *That* was a real blessing in the news-gathering biz, because people tended to trust those who looked more vulnerable than they.

It was another long moment before the woman finally spoke. "Stephen Whitney," she said in a biting whisper, "didn't believe in black."

Angel glanced down at her dark dress. "Oh." That explained why she was the lone beetle among the throng of butterflies in the room. She'd thought it was the heat that had everyone wearing pastels. "How, uh . . . colorful of him."

When her comment did nothing to endear her to Ms. Mauve, Angel gave up and slid back toward her corner. But instead of the outside of her right leg finding the inside edge of the wooden pew, it found the long, hard thigh of a man.

"Oh!" Angel exclaimed again, scooting away to stare at the person who had invaded her corner when she wasn't looking. "Pardon me."

He glanced at her. Well, she supposed he did. It was hard to tell exactly *what* he was looking at when his eyes were hidden behind the dark lenses of Armani sunglasses.

"Don't mention it," he said in a low voice, his attention returning forward.

For some odd reason, Angel's attention stayed on him. He must have known Stephen Whitney better than she, because the man beside her was dressed in a butter-yellow linen shirt and a light olive suit. Both the suit and the shirt looked a little too big on him. He was very tan—oh, like, for sure, the tan, the expensive suit, and those fancy shades just screamed Malibu Beach—and his shiny dark hair untidily brushed his collar in an I-don't-give-a-damn sort of way.

As if sensing her continued regard, he turned his head her way again.

A sharp jolt of something—something like . . . like . . . uh, recognition?—straightened her in her seat and stirred a sexy little tickle low in her belly. Angel barely suppressed the sudden urge to squirm against the wooden bench as her hormones said, *Hell-o! You gotta check this guy out!*

But then, thank God, in dour, sensible tones, her head reminded the rest of her they were at a funeral. Stephen Whitney's funeral.

Feeling an embarrassed flush rising up her neck, she tried glossing over the awkward moment with a warm smile. It rarely failed to disarm men, because to go along with that curly mess of hair she had one of those skinny, frail-looking bodies too. Despite nature, despite nurture, the whole package just oozed take-care-of-me innocence.

"Did you want something?" he asked.

"Uh . . . well . . ." *Why not?* She always figured that if she had to go through life looking like a creature who needed a knight in shining armor, she might as well get something out of it. "Perhaps you *could* help me out," she said softly, inching closer.

He edged away.

Hmmm. Angel turned down the wattage this time, but gave him another of her unsullied smiles. "Don't worry, it's just a little thing."

"The Vice President is about to speak." Sunglasses Man had a husky whisper that set her scalp prickling again.

Ignoring the sensation, Angel gave a tiny shrug.

"The Vice President of the United States," he clarified, nodding toward the front of the church.

Though she kept her bottom glued to the pew in order not to spook Sunglasses, she leaned confidingly close. "I haven't listened to him since he ordered plastic pasties and weatherproof fig leaves for the nude statuary in the White House garden."

When she saw Sunglasses' lips twitch, she knew she had him. She smiled again. "I just wondered if you could point out Mrs. Whitney."

"Excuse me?"

Uh-oh, Angel thought, her smile dying. His wasn't one of those innocuous I-didn't-quite-hear-you excuse me's. Instead, it smacked of the protective, guard-going-up, excuse-me-why-the-hell-do-you-want-to-know sort. Worse, Angel had taken a crash course in smelling trouble when she was five years old and all at once her nose was twitching at the scent.

Making a quick, dismissive gesture with one hand, she slid as far away from the mystery man as the crowded pew would allow. The move accidentally jostled Ms. Mauve's elbow and the lady took the opportunity to slice Angel with a glare, adding a hissing "Shh!" for good measure.

She had to force herself not to cringe. With hostility on her right and suspicion on her left, those second thoughts from before swiftly returned for a third, fourth, and fifth round.

You're a journalist, she reminded herself. *And so, accustomed to being the unwanted guest.* It was no big deal. All she had to do was stay neutral. Dispassionate. Detached.

But Angel didn't bother scouting the church for the Whitney widow, or even attempt another mental pep talk. As the virtues of the artist continued to be extolled from the podium, she found herself hugging her elbows against her ribs, trying to become as small as possible in the hot, suffocating atmosphere.

Eventually, though, the final sanctimonious speaker wound down. There was more singing, an orgasmic organ chord or two, and then, without warning, the church went dark. In the next instant, a close-up photograph flashed onto a huge screen. A man's face, framed by gray-blond, lionine hair, took over the room.

Stephen Whitney.

It was as if a hand had found Angel's throat and squeezed. Erupting from her seat, she didn't think of anything but getting that air. Of getting out. Somehow she scuttled over Sunglasses' knees and then bounded toward a narrow side door. As she pulled it open, another body joined hers and they burst into the sunlight shoulder to shoulder.

As the door swung silently shut behind them, Angel sucked in several long breaths of fresh air. Then she glanced over at her fellow escapee. It was a teenager, her dark hair in one of those ballerina-buns that young girls favored. She had on a light blue cotton sweater set and a matching teensy-weensy skirt that high schoolers always wore with chunky shoes.

"Stuffy in there, huh?" Angel said, feeling a thousand times stronger now that she was outside, more than strong enough to feel sorry for the kid someone had dragged to such an event. "Not just the air, but all those old white men talking at the podium. I wish I had an M&M for every time I heard the phrase 'American values.'"

The girl's eyes widened. A single note of laughter bubbled out of her, then she clapped her hand over her mouth.

Angel felt sorry for the kid all over again. To her mind, a little irreverence was as necessary to survival as venti lattes, juicy half-pound hamburgers, and quest-for-justice movie marathons on the Lifetime channel.

She gave a wondering shake of her head. "And what do you think about that boys' choir? I know they say their voices will change with puberty, but have you ever met even a *little* boy with a voice that high? I'm thinking there are girls under those coats and ties."

The teenager choked off another laugh. "You don't really believe that."

Angel's spirits lifted higher with the simple task of lifting someone else's. Smiling, she shrugged. "It's possible."

She should know.

The girl released another half-laugh, then looked around guiltily.

Poor thing, Angel thought, *her folks should have left her at home.* "Go ahead, hon, it's all right. You're not dead."

The teen's eyes focused over Angel's shoulder, then widened. Angel felt a sharp kick of awareness, then her nose twitched, itching at that unmistakable sense of trouble. She didn't turn around—or move, for that matter.

She didn't need to, because she already knew who was behind her. His voice confirmed it. Even though he wasn't whispering now, she recognized the voice of Sunglasses Man.

"Your mother's looking for you, Katie," he said. "We have to get going."

The teenager—Katie—bobbed her head. "All right."

The girl brushed past. It was then that Angel finally turned, steeling herself to meet the man's suspicious gaze, eyeballs to eyeglasses. But he was looking down at Katie instead, easy-to-read love on his face.

Angel breathed easier. Then Katie looked over. "This

is my uncle, Cooper Jones," the girl offered. "And I'm Katie. Stephen Whitney's daughter, Caitlyn."

Whitney. Stephen Whitney's daughter. His other daughter.

Stunned, it was autopilot that had Angel shaking the slender hand that was proffered. *Damn, damn, damn, damn,* she scolded herself. If she hadn't been such an ostrich about the artist, she would have known that as well as being married, he'd fathered another daughter.

"I'm . . ." Angel's mind whirled through all the names she'd used in her lifetime. The identity she'd inexplicably chosen for herself when she was fourteen years old didn't immediately present itself.

"Let's hurry, Katie," the girl's uncle—he must be the brother of Katie's mother—urged. "The family limousine is out front."

With a farewell nod to Angel, the girl hurried away. The man turned to follow, but then he paused to cast one dark-lensed, enigmatic look over his shoulder.

Angel couldn't miss it, because she couldn't take her eyes off the both of them. The uncle. The girl, especially the girl. Katie *Whitney*. Stephen's daughter, going to take her place in the family limousine.

After a few more minutes absorbing her surprise, Angel took off toward her own car. There was no turning back now. She *had* to find out—find out everything about the man who hadn't bothered with her since she was four years old.

The world should know the truth about men like that.

Chapter 2

Angel knew Cooper Jones—Katie Whitney's uncle—was stalking her.

Not physically—she stood apart from him and the fifty or so others waiting quietly on the oceanside bluff where the private farewell ceremony was to take place. But behind his dark lenses she felt his gaze following her, the sensation of being closely watched as tangible as the Pacific-cooled breeze tugging at her hat.

Pulling the hat's brim lower on her forehead, Angel kept tabs on the dark-haired figure from the corner of her eye. He was standing by himself on the other side of the small crowd, his arms crossed over his chest, bodyguard-style. When a gust of wind flapped the hem of his suit jacket and whipped his too-long hair over his face, he shook it back with a single toss of his head.

Obviously a guy who didn't waste movement. In

general, she liked that in a person, just as she, in general, wasn't averse to intense scrutiny from attractive men. But it was vibes of distrust, not desire, she was picking up from this one, so she figured it best to stay out of his way.

"Hello, there," a voice from behind her said, its friendly tone loud enough to be heard over the unceasing rush of the ocean. "Are you a friend of Stephen's, or a relative?"

Angel froze. *It's just a casual question,* she assured herself. *Nothing to feel jumpy about.* Her name was even on the guest list—her legal name, although it wasn't the one she'd been born with. Lifting her lips in a polite smile, she turned to face the—

Priest? Friar? What did you call a man wearing an ankle-length brown robe and heavy silver crucifix with Berkenstock sandals?

The stranger smiled gently back. "Friend or relative?" he asked again.

And should you, could you lie to such a man? Angel swallowed. "Neither, I suppose. I'm an, uh, observer."

It was true enough. Biology aside, nothing had connected her to Stephen Whitney in well over twenty years, not since he'd dumped her and her mother for his muse and free rent in an artist's colony in Big Sur.

"I'm Angel Buchanan," she added, holding out her hand.

The robed stranger shook it. "And I'm Brother Charles, from the monastery over the hill."

She blinked. "I had no idea there was a monastery nearby." Though her intern at the magazine, Cara, had gathered a copious amount of information on the artist as well as the area where he'd lived, Angel had stashed the files in the trunk of her car without glancing through them.

"Ah, well, the Sur holds several surprises."

Angel could only nod in agreement to that.

"Much of the land is under federal protection," Brother Charles went on, "but there are also private residences scattered around, as well as our monastery. Even a fancy inn or two like that one." Brother Charles gestured up the zigzagged flights of steps they'd taken to reach the bluff. At the top was the elegant, Victorian-style Crosscreek Hotel.

Angel's gaze lingered on the place. Cara had booked her at an inn farther south on Highway 1, closer to the Whitney compound. Angel hoped her accommodations would be on par with the well-appointed luxury the Crosscreek Hotel promised. Even now she could almost taste steaming breakfast muffins, thick grilled steaks, luscious pillow chocolates.

She'd reward herself each day with a bit of pampering, she decided, because surely Cara had selected an inn that would offer the most up-to-date spa services. Floating off on daydreams of herbal wraps and aromatherapy sessions, it took her a moment to register that the man in the robe had half-turned and was beckoning someone closer.

"Brother Charles, what are you doing?" her voice croaked out.

The man glanced over. "I want to say hello to Cooper. Cooper Jones," he explained. "Stephen's brother-in-law."

She was already shuffling backward, trying to look

casual as the soles of her black pumps slid along the gritty sandstone.

"Don't run away." Brother Charles reached out, looping his elbow through hers to lasso her back. "I'll introduce you."

"We've already met," she demurred. "And perhaps this isn't the best time to further our acquaintance." Not to mention that she was planning on avoiding Mr. Cooper Jones and his patent mistrust for the rest of her life.

"Well . . ." Brother Charles looked back toward the other man, then dropped her arm. "Never mind. Lainey, the widow, is coming down the stairs. She'll need Cooper now. You can see that they're a very close-knit family."

Angel squinted to study the small group descending the final flight of steps from the hotel. There was the girl—Katie—close beside a dark-haired woman in her thirties.

Angel frowned. "Wait. There are two women. Twins."

"Mmm-hmm." Brother Charles nodded. "Elaine and Elizabeth. Lainey was Stephen's wife and Beth was Stephen's business manager."

That's what you get, Angel thought, annoyed with herself again. If she'd prepared like she would have for any other story, she would have known about the twins. About the daughter. But no, for all those years she'd resisted even submitting her father's name to an internet search engine, which forced her to play catch-up now.

As a matter of fact, Angel had never walked into one

of the Whitney Galleries—as common in American malls as Starbucks and multiplex theaters. The only thing about Stephen Whitney she hadn't been able to evade was the knowledge of his mass popularity and his goody-goody reputation.

But all that was going to change.

Studying the women walking toward the crowd, Angel noted their similar-but-not-matching knee-length suits, one in a soft yellow, the other in green. Their hair was styled differently as well, a layered style for the twin in yellow, a sleek bob for her sister.

"The widow, Lainey, is the one in the green, I assume," Angel said. Even from this distance, she could tell the woman had been crying.

"No, that's Beth." Brother Charles's voice filled with concern. "I hope Judd is keeping a close eye on her."

Angel didn't look away from the small group. "Is Judd another brother?"

"A family friend. Judd Sterling is the gray-haired man just now putting his arm around Beth's waist."

The family friend was forty-something and prematurely gray, with handsome, chiseled features. He continued to support the widow's sister, while the worrisome Cooper character wrapped one arm around Katie and the other around Lainey Whitney.

So that's what it looks like when a man comes through for a woman in a time of need.

Startled by the stabbing thought, Angel took a hasty step back. There was no call for bitterness, she reminded herself. She only desired the truth.

"It looks as if the service is ready to begin," her companion said. "We're being signaled forward."

"I think I'll stay right where I am." As she saw the others drawing together, her throat was tightening, just as it had in the church. "I'm only here as an observer," she said again.

Not as a mourner. Not as a daughter. The fact was, she didn't even have one simple memory of the man who'd fathered her.

Brother Charles sent her a compassionate look. "I understand. Some people find it difficult to face death."

Angel's spine snapped straight. "I don't find it difficult to face anything," she protested, but Brother Charles was already moving away. Her avoidance of Stephen Whitney had nothing to do with fear.

So to prove that to them both, she wiped her palms on the skirt of her dress and without further hesitation made for the circle the others were assembling near the edge of the bluff. Though she quickly found a place, she suffered another pang of—of *something,* when her eye happened to catch Katie's. Edging back again, Angel created a gap between herself and the person next to her.

Of course, she paid for it. *That's what weakness gets you,* she told herself grimly as Mr. Sunglasses-and-Suspiciousness instantly stepped in beside her.

She pretended not to notice his presence, though, as a sudden gust of wind yanked at her hat, forcing her to quickly clap her palm against the straw crown.

"You might want to take that off"—his murmur was a mere notch above the low thunder of the ocean below—"or the wind will do it for you."

And give him a chance to look at her naked face? She

thought not. Now was not the time to throw caution—or her hat, for that matter—to the wind. Without answering, she tugged it farther down her forehead and blessed its elastic band, hidden beneath the hair coiled at her nape.

At the farthest point in the circle from Angel, another berobed man began to speak. It was difficult to hear him over the sound of the waves below, but now and then the wind tossed a word her way. "Nature," "beauty," "reunion."

"Family."

Family. Ducking her head, Angel sucked in a sharp breath. The air tasted salty on her tongue. Like tears.

A large hand closed strongly over hers.

Angel jumped, her chin jerking up. From beneath her wide-brimmed hat, she shot a glance at the dark lenses of Cooper Jones's sunglasses.

"We were asked to join hands," he explained.

She wrenched free of him anyway, then her gaze took a turn around the circle. Everyone *was* linked, except for her. Everyone was staring at her too.

Embarrassed, she instantly thrust her palm toward the woman on her left. She made a gesture toward Cooper with her right hand as well, but only allowed the lightest brush of their knuckles, just enough to make it *look* as if they were holding hands.

When the man in the robe started reciting some sort of benediction, Cooper leaned toward her again. "What's the matter? It's just a little thing."

It's just a little thing. Exactly what she'd said to him in the church, right before asking him about the Whitney widow. Oh, he had suspicions about her, all right. It wasn't likely that she allayed them any either, by jumping about two feet when his fingers happened to brush hers once more. But she didn't want their hands touching again. Once was enough. His palm had felt too warm, too big, too solid.

That was the problem with men. They made you want to hang on to them.

That unpleasant thought caused her to miss the final "amen." The next thing she knew, the leader of the service was directing the group into a single line, placing Angel at its head, with Cooper her faithful shadow.

Once the ceremony was over, she vowed, easing another cautious inch away from him, she'd make sure they were never in the same place at the same time again.

The robed leader was now approaching her, an elaborately carved box in his arms. "One last request to fulfill Stephen's wishes," the man said, his voice carrying clearly this time. "Then we'll return to the hotel for refreshments."

When he stopped at Angel, she turned her back on the ocean to face him. His smile was brotherly as he flipped open the wooden lid. "Take some in each hand," he instructed, "and toss them into the sea."

Angel peered into the depths of the box. Then her stomach cramped. Ashes? *Ashes*. She was supposed to take some in each hand and toss them into the sea.

Her father's ashes.

Her stomach cramped again.

This is nothing to me, she assured herself, embarrassed by her hesitation. *I don't even remember Stephen Whitney, so it's nothing*. The ashes would feel weightless, meaningless, more nothing in her palms. But she couldn't force her locked arms from her sides.

"To the sea," the man with the box urged. "Stephen wanted the ashes of his last paintings to ride free on the waves."

His paintings.

His *paintings*. Her muscles released, and, near giddy in relief, Angel quickly scooped her hands into the box. Then she spun and took a step toward the bluff's edge.

Pausing, she glanced down at her lightly clenched fists, feeling the slick, soft ash inside them clinging to her skin. The giddiness evaporated and her stomach spasmed again.

Now desperate to free herself from the ashes, from the moment, from him, she took a hasty, giant step forward and flung open her hands. As the ashes swirled up, into the air, she felt the ground shift beneath her feet.

Her heart lurched. She twisted, her pumps scrambling for purchase against the crumbling edge of the cliff.

A big hand appeared in front of her. A man's hand.

Instinct and experience warred. But when her heels ran off of solid ground, she ran out of options. To save herself, she was forced to reach for, grasp, depend upon Cooper Jones.

If his brother-in-law hadn't already been dead, Cooper Jones thought, *he would have done the job himself.* Stalking through Crosscreek Hotel's terrace restaurant, he ran his gaze over the small group who had attended the ceremony, the one that had just ended in that ridiculous throwing of ashes. It had almost been like tossing handfuls of cash off the damn cliff.

Jesus, it was *exactly* like tossing handfuls of cash off the damn cliff. Feeling a sharp cinch of his neck muscles, a sure sign of his stress level climbing, Cooper slowed down to take a few deep breaths. Funerals topped his personal "To Avoid" list and he wished he'd done just that.

Then he could have sat at home worrying about what financial stupidity had caused Stephen to sink every penny into a risky marketing venture while leaving the stipulation in his will that any unreleased paintings be burned. A year's worth of the prolific artist's work had been destroyed. Paintings that would have made a hell of a hedge against Stephen's potentially bad investment.

If Cooper had been the Whitney attorney he would have insisted on striking that clause from the will, but since his specialty was criminal defense and not probate law, he hadn't known a thing about it until it was too late. Now his sisters' and his niece's long-term security was rocking on the fulcrum of the artist's popularity.

Perhaps that underlying anxiety was to blame for the way his hackles had risen when he was near the black-hatted female who'd been beside him at the church and then again on the bluff. *Something* told him she was trouble.

He scrutinized the subdued crowd on the patio again, relieved when there was no further sign of her. She'd made herself scarce after he'd hauled her from the edge of the cliff, and with luck she was gone for good. Damn, but he hoped he wouldn't regret rescuing her.

"Uncle Cooper."

At the sound of Katie's voice he swung around. She wore the blank mask she'd rarely let slip since being told of her father's death. More disquiet slicing through him, he reached out and pulled her against his chest.

"How are you doing, honey?" he asked, holding her tight. "I wasn't much older than you when my father died. I remember how hard it is." And in the last year, the memories had only sharpened.

Katie leaned into him for a moment, her shoulders sagging in a soft sigh, but then she moved back again, her expression carefully empty.

Cooper scrubbed a hand over his face. The only occasion she'd shown any natural animation in the past week was outside the church today, when she'd spoken with that woman—a fact that had his hackles rising all over again. He made another quick scan of the patio. "Did you need me for something, sweetheart?"

"Mom wants Aunt Beth. I thought she might be here."

"I think I saw her head inside." Cooper looked back down at his niece and chucked her on the chin. "Go tell your mom I'll round up Beth. Then why don't you get us both a Perrier and stake out the perfect spot for sunset-viewing." During the past year, he'd been learning to count a day a success if he was there at its end to share the sunset with his niece.

As Katie turned to obey, he headed for the hotel's

back door. He pulled it open, then strode down the hall, glancing into doorways right and left. Three down, in a small room that also contained a desk and two pay phones, he found Beth sitting on a couch, crying in the arms of the black-hatted woman.

"Please don't," the woman was saying to his sister, her voice laced with panic. "Please don't cry."

Suspicion once again leaping along with the hairs on the back of his neck, Cooper vaulted into the room. "Beth! Are you all right?"

His sister's face stayed hidden behind handfuls of tissues, but the other woman started, then jumped to her feet.

The movement looked guilty as sin. "What the hell is going on here?" he demanded.

"Am I glad to see you!" the woman declared.

Yeah, right. After their brief conversation in the church, she'd given him the distinct impression they shared a mutual wariness. Crossing his arms over his chest, he lifted an eyebrow. "Do tell."

"I don't know what happened." She glanced down at Beth and patted her shoulder, the gesture awkward-looking, perhaps due to the mammoth snowball of Kleenex in her grip. "I found her like this when I came in to use the phone—I can't get a signal on my cell."

Damn. Apparently Beth had finally fallen off that emotional edge she'd been balancing on all week. He'd seen her struggling to keep calm, and he supposed she'd been hiding her sadness from Lainey, who as Stephen's widow was entitled to the majority of the tears. But now Beth needed Cooper's comfort.

Which he'd supply—right after confronting the black-hatted woman.

Maybe she read the intention on his face, because she suddenly went into action. A shuffle, a sidestep, a murmured "I'll be going now," and she'd ducked around his bigger body to give herself a clear shot at the door.

"Wait just a minute," he said, grabbing for her. He wasn't going to lose sight of her again, not until he'd satisfied his niggling uneasiness by finding out exactly who she was and why she was here. His hand latched on to her shoulder.

Beneath his palm, her bare shoulder stiffened. But that didn't register nearly as much as the satiny feel of her pale skin. It seemed to warm in response to him, and because he hadn't touched female flesh in such a long, long while, his fingers instinctively flexed.

She made a little sound of distress, then twirled on her high heels to face him. "What?" she demanded.

Though his hand still gripped her shoulder, he was too tall, or she was too short, for him to get a good view of her features beneath that wide black brim. Fair skin, rosy lips, some sort of nose. He didn't have a clue about her hair; it was either very short or tucked under that overlarge hat.

His gaze wandered down to the sleeveless black dress she was wearing. It modestly skimmed over breasts and waist, hinting rather than revealing, but ended at a point that barely cleared her midthighs. A knee-skimming filmy overskirt-thing was probably intended to make the hemline appear modest too, but it only served to draw Cooper's attention to her pale, naked legs.

Stockingless, you idiot. Not naked.

But all the same, the "naked" notion started a surge of half-forgotten pleasure in his blood. His heart made an odd *ka-thud* against his breastbone.

And just like that, fear poked its icy fingers against the back of his neck.

Yet somehow he ignored them, his focus concentrated on the sensation of his skin touching hers. The curve of her shoulder molded his hand into a cup, and it was so reminscent of cupping a breast that he automatically caressed the crown of the curve with the heart of his palm. He thought she shivered.

The small reaction made his blood pump faster, and his gaze roamed along her bare legs as he imagined his palms sliding up her inner thighs to open them for his eyes, his touch, his body. His heart lost its rhythm again, only to play catch-up with another ominous *ka-thud,* redoubling the alarm gathering at his nape. When his heart skipped again, it tumbled down his spine in an icy rush.

And still he couldn't make himself let her go.

That's what finally scared the shit out of him.

His release was so abrupt that she stumbled back. He shoved the offending hand in his pocket. It was his left hand, and he squeezed his fingers into a fist, making sure it hadn't gone numb.

"Are you all right?" she asked, taking another step back.

He wanted to laugh, but it wouldn't have been a pleasant sound. "I'm dandy, just dandy," he muttered. "Now go."

He probably imagined her slight hesitation. Because in half a breath she was out the door, leaving only a lingering note of her perfume. He sniffed, surprised that after more than a year away from the city he still recognized a city girl's sophisticated scent—Joy.

Dragging his attention from the woman gone to the woman at hand, he turned toward his sister. "Beth," he said, dropping to the couch beside her. "What's the matter? What can I do for you?"

She shook her head. She wasn't crying any longer, but she shuddered with each indrawn breath.

"Something." Despite all the opportunities life had thrown at him lately, he still had miles to go toward accepting any kind of helplessness. "I must be able to do something, say something."

"I'm sorry, I know this isn't helping." Her head lifted and she swiped at her cheeks. "I keep wondering, thinking, replaying everything."

Replaying the accident that killed Stephen, Cooper guessed. Lainey had talked to him about it too, wondering aloud if Stephen had felt any pain. Well, yeah, Cooper figured it probably hurt like hell to be hit by a truck going fifty-five miles an hour. And he was entirely certain that in Stephen's last moments it only gave him more pain to realize he was leaving behind ones who loved him. But there was no point in telling either of his sisters that.

"We've just gotta give it time," he said, for want of anything better. He let a beat go by, then spoke again. "Lainey's been looking for you."

"Lainey." She swiped at her cheeks some more, even

as fresh tears filled her eyes. "Oh God, Lainey. I . . . I'm not doing right by her again."

A man paused in the doorway, catching Cooper's eye. "Judd," he said with relief. If anyone could soothe his sister, he could.

Without a sound, Judd approached Beth, flowing to her in a smooth motion that looked like one of those tai chi movements he practiced. They all had poetic names like Cloud Hand or Wind Rolls the Lotus Leaves, and as Judd knelt at Beth's feet and linked his fingers with hers, Cooper titled this one Tiger Finding Flower.

Something unspoken yet palpable passed between them. Judd would probably say it was their *chi*—the life energy that moves through all living things. He'd earned the right to call it whatever he wanted, Cooper thought, because with just that simple touch, Beth relaxed. Her tears dried, her color evened out, the next breath she took was long and deep. Oh yeah, Judd's yin was definitely balancing Beth's yang.

Feeling unnecessary—and grateful—Cooper rose off the couch.

"I'll be all right," Beth said softly. "Thanks."

He didn't bother determining if she was talking to him or to Judd, instead leaving the room to them. There was that date he had with Katie and a Perrier. Even on a day like today, surely the sunset would bring him some measure of peace.

But when he threw open the door to the terrace, he knew there wasn't going to be any sunset to enjoy after all. The fog had moved in, and the wet mist was swirling around the tables like the cold, gray breath of ghosts. Several gas patio heaters had been lit against the dampness, and knots of people were gathered beneath each one.

His gaze wandered, then skidded to a halt.

The black-hatted woman. Again. Still. She was standing to the right, chatting with Brother Charles. That odd uneasiness she awakened in him set off another clanging round of warning bells.

So, no sunset tonight, and no peace either. At least not yet. Not until he discovered who she was and exactly how to get rid of her.

With a measured stride, he headed toward that big black hat. He'd been a pretty canny attorney not long ago, so he began concocting a strategy, outlining his cross-examination on a mental legal notepad. But the pages blew from his mind as he watched her lift her hands and remove her hat.

His feet stuttered as she shook out her hair, using one hand to fluff out miles of the stuff that had been confined all afternoon. Under the comb of her fingers, the miles descended, then sprang back up into a shoulder-blade-length mass of blond spirals.

"Jesus," he heard himself say loudly, as he regained the use of his legs and started moving again. "Who—*what* the hell are you?"

She spun to face him. It was as if she'd fluttered out of one of his brother-in-law's more fanciful paintings. Outside of his customary depictions of hearth and home, Stephen had occasionally painted fairies sleeping in the stamens of flowers, elves hiding among the leaves of a tree, pixies peeking from beneath four-leaf clovers. There was something about her appearance that reminded him of magic creatures like those.

He knew he was staring at her, but the woman's looks were nothing short of arresting. Her small size and wealth of blond hair was paired with a heart-shaped—heart-shaped!—face and eyes of a pure, blameless baby blue.

He swallowed. "You . . . you're . . ."

Those remarkable eyes rolled and she released a resigned sigh. "I'm twenty-seven years old."

He wanted to laugh. Apparently the world usually took all that blond fragility for youth. But as a damn good criminal attorney, he'd honed his ability to size up people quickly, and he sensed that beneath all the marshmallow fluff was something much more substantial. No wonder his instincts had been tipped off. This woman looked lethal.

Yes indeed, her sinless appearance couldn't fool him.

So he stepped up to her, the warmth of the patio heater washing over his head and shoulders but doing nothing to dispel his cool sense of purpose. "Who are you?" he asked again.

Lifting her chin, she matched him stare for assessing stare. "I'm Angel. Angel Buchanan."

Shit. A magical creature, all right. An *angel*.

For a weird instant he wondered if he'd actually died this time. But then he sucked in a breath of air, inhaling a heady shot of her perfume with it. The sophisticated fragrance sparked the memory of her skin beneath his hand—his palm actually tingled—and he decided it was a safe bet that his first thought in heaven wouldn't be about stripping naked one of its winged residents.

Then she smiled at him, and it was so sweet that he

thought *angel* again until he caught the amused glitter in her eyes.

"And," she added, all moonbeams and sugary whipped cream innocence, "I'm also the woman who's going to be living with you for the next few weeks."

Chapter 3

Angel thought Cooper Jones was about to have a heart attack. For a moment he stood stock-still, the wind blowing his hair and clothes around him. But then he blinked—without his sunglasses she could see his eyes were greenish brown—and he seemed to recover from his surprise. "You're staying . . . ?" he began.

"At your inn," Angel finished for him. Brother Charles was an easy man to pump for data, and it had taken her all of three seconds to find out that the Jones siblings had grown up in the area and that Cooper ran the place where she'd be staying. It hadn't been a good omen, but Angel refused to let omens, or any men, for that matter, get in the way of her plans.

"My inn," Cooper said slowly.

"Yeah," she said. "Tranquility House."

A pretty corny name if you asked her, but it didn't burst her happy daydreams of salt scrub pedicures and herbal oil massages unless—Oh, God. Unless Cooper Jones gave them, that is.

At the thought, she instinctively scooted a more cautious distance away. When he'd touched her shoulder before, she'd nearly jumped out of her skin.

"So you're staying at Tranquility," he repeated. The wind shifted, blowing his hair back from his face. "Exactly why is that?"

Without the disguise of sunglasses or disordered hair, Angel saw that his face was lean like the rest of him. With his slashing dark brows, high cheekbones, and patrician nose, he looked like an Italian nobleman. An arrogant, suspicious, and . . . somehow familiar nobleman.

"Angel?"

Why, she remembered. He wanted to know why she was staying. Distracted by that odd feeling of recognition, Angel fumbled for a good answer, couldn't quite think of one, had to stall. She gave him one of her best smiles. "Why, uh, why not?"

His eyes narrowed, turning even more watchful.

Oh, sheesh. Her smiles didn't work on him, she had to remember that. So then how was she supposed to play this guy? Men never distrusted her. Usually her hair, a sweet smile, certainly a combination of the two did the job. Her baby face and mop top seemed to make men feel studly, or at the very least it rendered them unsuspecting.

But not this one.

Angel glanced toward Brother Charles, hoping for rescue, but the man of the robe had inconveniently wandered off. Her attention was forced back to Cooper, who was still eyeing her expectantly.

"Look," she said, frustrated. She hadn't planned on getting into this here and now, but she was fresh out of tricks. "I'm a writer, okay? For a magazine."

"A reporter?" His voiced lowered. "No wonder you give me the heebie-jeebies," she thought she heard him mutter.

The heebie-jeebies? Well, that wasn't a good sign either. In general, people were fascinated by the press—unless they had something to hide, of course. But what would an inn manager want to conceal?

Then a likely answer struck. "Oh, hey, don't worry," she said, waving away any concerns he might have. "I'm not with *Vacation* or *Getaway* or any other travel publication."

He blinked. "What? What are you talking about?"

"I'm not here to review Tranquility House," she assured him.

He blinked again. "I'm not the least bit worried about Tranquility House." The wind was blowing all that hair of his around again and with an impatient movement, he raked his hand through it to hold it away from his face with his fist. "I'm worried about *you*."

Angel was hit again with that strong sense of recognition, but she shook it off as his words sank in. He distrusted her, all right. And he was up-front and personal about it.

Sighing, she took a chance on being direct, because God knows her cutie-pie looks weren't bringing down his guard. "Listen, I'm a staff writer for *West Coast* magazine. I'm here to do an in-depth story on Stephen Whitney."

"West Coast?"

If she'd said she was from *Military Times* she didn't think he would look any more surprised. "Yes," she said tightly.

Sure, men often had a hard time believing she wrote for a prestigious publication, but for some reason *his* disbelief was especially irritating. If Cooper wasn't going to be bowled over by her froufrou femininity, the least he could do was believe she had a brain under all that hair. "Is that really so difficult to imagine?"

A smile twitched the corners of his mouth. "Settle down, settle down. Would showing me your Mensa card make you feel any better?"

Shooting him a cool look, she lifted her chin. "I don't carry it with me."

For just a second, he grinned. For that same second, she was *certain* she knew him from somewhere. But then he shook his head and turned away to face the ocean.

She followed his gaze. The terrace hung over a narrow fissure that opened to the Pacific, providing an unobstructed view of undeveloped coastline. When clear, you'd be able to see miles of rugged, ragged cliffs—it was a pictorial California landmark nearly as famous as the Golden Gate Bridge. But even now, with the colors and the distant vistas painted out by the fog, it was Ansel Adams–beautiful.

Angel supposed the majestic scenery could provide an artist inspiration. But not an excuse to forget the daughter who had needed him.

Her grip tightened on her hat. "Maybe you could introduce me to your sister. I can run the idea by her, or even you could, if you'd like. You see, I—*West Coast* wants to explore Stephen Whitney's world and bring it to our readers. If you're familiar with the magazine—"

"I know it." He turned back to her, then stepped closer. Too close. "And it seems to me it does a better job of *exposing* people rather than exploring them."

Angel managed to deflect the hit with a friendly smile. "The magazine prints plenty of other types of stories too."

"Yeah?"

"Yeah." She mentally thumbed through her recent tear sheets. "I wrote a story on a philanthropist who promised to put a kindergarten class through college." No need to mention she'd also reported that the dirty old man had reneged on the promise and spent the dough on his fifth Bunny-turned-bride.

"And last month I did a feature on the national women's curling team." A completely innocuous, though inspiring piece, if she did say so herself. "The sport, I mean, not hair."

"I knew what you meant." But despite that, he reached out and twirled a lock of hers around his index finger.

"Well, then." She couldn't feel his touch. Hair cells were dead, she reminded herself. Like fingernails or . . . horses' hooves. Maybe that was why her heartbeat was starting to gallop like a mare trying to elude the domineering stallion.

Oh Lord, she thought with disgust, what was wrong with her? Mares and stallions! *Get a grip on yourself, Angel.*

But Cooper did that, holding tighter as she tried to move away from him. The tug on her scalp didn't hurt, but it did make her reckless.

"Is there some problem with the idea?" she asked baldly. "Why would you object to a story on your brother-in-law?"

"It's not that." He looked over her head, fingering her hair absently. "It might be good, as a matter of fact. Helpful."

Helpful? Angel puzzled over that for a moment, but then decided to let it go. "So we're set, then. You'll talk to your sister about me?"

"You?" His gaze shifted back to her. "Oh, that's right, there's you," he said, as if she were a bad taste in his mouth.

Angel had had enough. She grasped her hair above his hand and yanked. Free of him, she stepped back.

Then, remembering that artless charm had always been her friend, she gentled her voice and smiled up at him again. "Come now, you've certainly heard of freedom of the press. I don't need your permission to write a story about Stephen Whitney."

His eyebrows rose. "What do you know about the Sur?"

She shrugged, vowing to look through the intern's research as soon as she checked into her room.

"It's a reclusive area," Cooper said. "Private. Its people are even more so. If we ask our friends and neighbors to shut you out, they will."

Angel stifled her sigh. While she didn't doubt that she could wheedle her way past a lot of ill will, it was so much easier when people *wanted* to talk. "I don't understand what you're being so cautious about," she grumbled beneath her breath.

He heard, though, because he swiped a single fingertip along her cheek and asked, "Don't you?"

The question hung in the air and the oxygen backed up in her lungs. Oh God, had he sensed that momentary flash of attraction she'd felt toward him in the church? The way his palm on her skin had made her quiver?

But before she could determine the answers, he turned abruptly away. "Reporters are . . . intrusive."

"Yeah," she admitted, breathing a little more easily. "*Nosy* might be a better word. But people like to talk about themselves and we writers are good listeners."

"Too good, sometimes, at asking questions."

Angel's eyes narrowed. If she wasn't mistaken, there spoke a voice of experience. Interesting. Very interesting. Mr. Inn Manager must have had some former run-in with the press.

Cooper swung around to face her. "How would you like someone probing into your life, your past?"

Without hesitation, Angel shrugged. "My life's an open book."

"Is that right?"

"Sure." The gesture of her hand was carefully careless. "Ask me anything you want."

"All right." He settled back on his heels and crossed his arms over his chest again. "Where did you go to school?"

"Graduated from Bay High School in San Francisco." No need to mention the seven elementary schools she'd attended before she and her mother had escaped to Europe. "I majored in journalism in college. When I graduated I'd already been interning at *West Coast* for two years. The magazine hired me and I've been working there ever since."

"Family?"

She'd been skating over this forever. "It was just my mom and me for a long time." Truth. "Now she's remarried and lives in Paris."

"Do you get along with your stepfather?"

She shrugged. "Sure." At least he hadn't abandoned her mother like Stephen Whitney. Or hurt her mother like the other bastard she'd hooked up with.

"And you like your work?"

"Love it." When he didn't say anything for a moment, she pulled out another of her trust-me smiles. "See how easy it is to answer questions? Piece of cake."

"I'm not through yet." He let her stew through another beat of silence. "Are you married?"

Funny, how the simplest question stumped her. When it came to this particular subject, she had nothing to cover up or cover over, but suddenly she wasn't sure that telling Cooper Jones the truth was such a good idea.

There was that strange sense of recognition. That sexy little shimmy she felt inside just looking at him. "Uh . . . no," she finally confessed.

"Engaged?"

Given that the fourth finger on her left hand was as bare as a baby's behind, she didn't think she could pull that one off either. "No."

"Dating, then?"

"No," she said a third time, staring down at her shoes and feeling like an idiot. The closest she'd been to male companionship lately, if you didn't count Tom Jones the cat, was the articles on dating she read in *Glamour, Mademoiselle,* and *Cosmo.*

"Then this definitely isn't going to work," Cooper muttered.

Angel's head jerked up. "What do you mean?"

"Someone else, maybe. Another reporter. But not you." He started to move away.

Angel grabbed his arm. He'd taken off his suit jacket and she was diverted for a moment by the warmth of his skin and the fine linen of his shirt. Expensive duds for a guy in the service industry, she mused, tightening her fingers around his hard arm. "Another reporter from *West Coast,* another reporter from any publication, won't tell the story that I will."

"Angel—"

"An extensive, in-depth exploration of the art and the man. What's the source of his immense popularity? What inspired him? What motivated him? I'll write about his life."

She hoped her voice didn't sound as desperate as she felt. "And I'll write about what he left behind." She swallowed. "Who he left behind."

"No—"

"—way will we turn her down just like that," a feminine voice finished for him.

Angel whirled. It was Lainey Whitney. The artist's widow gave her a small, tired smile. "I had a call from your editor—I've known Jane for years. She says you'd do a good job on the story."

* * *

Trying to ignore the woman trailing him on the path through the woods, Cooper shifted the luggage in his grip and cursed the kindness of his sister. Not only had she practically agreed to cooperate on Angel Buchanan's story, but she'd volunteered *his* services in guiding the woman to Tranquility House. Angel had appeared thrilled with his sister's help on both counts. She'd still been smiling when they'd climbed out of their cars in the Tranquility parking lot, and though he should have known better, it had worked a spell on him. He'd offered to help her with her bag.

She had a bag, all right. Bags. Luggage. He had three bulging totes cross-strapped over his chest and a briefcase in each hand. The weight of them kept his pace along the softly lit path slow and steady. Behind him, she trundled a suitcase the size of a steamer trunk on wheels.

"Wow, she said. "It smells so good here. The trees, right?"

He didn't bother to answer, because over the rich scent of ferns and redwoods, what *he* was smelling was her city-girl perfume. It caused old memories to surface, the sharp sound of ice striking a rocks glass at a cocktail party, the gut-tightening anticipation he'd felt in the crowded elevators that took him to a courtroom and his next case, the casual pleasure of a beautiful woman passing him on a city street, her hurry affording him glimpses of her rounded ass shifting beneath an austere business suit.

For the first time in months, the craving for a cigarette pierced him.

Biting back an oath, he picked up his pace.

So did she, her mouth speeding up along with it. "I've never been to this area before. It's almost as if nature has swallowed us up."

That had been his grandparents' intention, to make their guests realize that they belonged to nature and not the other way around. But he didn't want Angel appreciating what Tranquility House and the Sur had to offer. Not when he had good reasons for booting Ms. Buchanan out of his family's business.

"Growing up here must have been something out of *Huckleberry Finn* or *Treasure Island*. Pirates and shipwrecks and mermaids."

He grunted. It *had* been idyllic growing up with the woods and the ocean as his private playground. But then Cooper had become the man of the family and play had been supplanted with twenty-hour workdays fueled by too much coffee and too many cigarettes. All three had become a lifelong habit.

"We'll get some great photos of the area for the article." Angel was still chattering away, fueled by who knew what. Nerves, maybe, because he could feel something waving off her whenever they were alone.

Something. Hah. He wasn't so out of touch that he couldn't remember what mutual sexual awareness was like. That and his lawyer's inherent distrust of the press were the reasons he didn't want her doing the story, even though the family was in no position to turn down the publicity.

But sex in the air would distract him from the serious business of making sure any press would depict his brother-in-law in just the right manner. Stephen's licensing venture included the trademarking of the "Artist of the Heart" phrase and the use of certain Whitney images on everything from Christmas decorations to floral arrangements.

It was imperative to keep the Whitney name untarnished, and to keep it in the forefront of the public's mind. Otherwise, no one would call FTD for an "Artist of the Heart" bouquet, no one would buy the "Artist of the Heart" bed-in-a-bag set at Macy's.

No income would be generated for his sisters and his niece.

"You know, I keep thinking that I know you."

Angel's comment jerked his focus back, and he stumbled.

"Do you think it's possible we met somewhere?"

Without turning to look at her, he shook his head.

"Are you sure?"

The landscape lighting was bright enough for her to see him, so he merely shook his head again.

They reached the first buildings of Tranquility House. The "house" was actually comprised of two dozen stucco cottages tucked for privacy among the trees, yet all within walking distance of a grass-covered clearing and an adjacent communal structure that housed a kitchen, dining room, first aid area, and office space.

"Are these the housekeepers' units?" Angel asked, slowing. "I like extra pillows. Will I need to call for them, or can we just stop and gather them up? And what about dry cleaning?" Her chin tilted toward the trees towering over them. "You must need a satellite dish for television. Shoot, I was having trouble using my cell phone at the inn. How does yours do out here?"

Cooper halted, turning to stare at her. Extra pillows. Dry cleaning. Cell phones and satellite dishes. Then he grinned to himself. Oh, this was going to be good. Better yet, easy.

Angel Buchanan wouldn't be staying long.

"Well?" she said, sounding half-puzzled and half-impatient. "Are you going to answer my questions or are you just going to stand there looking silently amused?"

Though darkness ringed them, the light from the outside fixture of a nearby cabin made perfectly legible one of the several signs posted around the Tranquility property. Angel's expression wasn't quite so readable as he dumped her stuff at his feet and then approached her.

She made a muffled noise when he detached her grip on her rolling suitcase, but she didn't protest as he used her shoulders to push her toward the wooden sign that depicted the "Tranquility House Tenets."

Perhaps she couldn't believe her eyes, because she spoke the painted words out loud. "'Please respect nature's noise. No radios. No TVs. No phones.'" Her head whipped around to stare at him as she read out the last rule. "'No *talking*'?"

He only smiled in response.

It was either her surprise or his smile that kept her quiet until he got her into her cottage. That's when the fun really started. After showing her in, then shoving her stuff over the threshold, he stepped inside and shut the door behind him.

He watched as her gaze roamed over the unadorned white walls, the simple woodburning stove, the stack of wood beside it, the narrow bed made up with white sheets and a gray wool blanket. One pillow.

Several silent moments went by. Finally, she looked at him, her expression full of hope. "The magazine will pay for a room upgrade," she tried.

He shook his head.

"This is all there is?"

He nodded.

"No salon services?."

He shook his head again.

"And I . . . and I can't say anything to anyone?"

She looked so dejected it was hard to keep a straight face. "Not in the common building or on the grounds of the retreat. But you're free to speak in the confines of your own cabin."

"Retreat." She rolled the word in her mouth as if she'd never heard it before. "This isn't a resort, it's a *retreat*."

He tried not to laugh. "Right. Definitely not a resort."

She narrowed her eyes. "Hey, you're enjoying this."

Immensely. It meant that all his worries were for nothing. No doubt the spartan atmosphere would send her hightailing it for home, tomorrow probably, or at the very least she'd hie herself to some *resort* that would keep her at a safe distance from his family and from him.

Still, he made an effort to wipe the smugness from his face. "Don't worry, all is not lost," he said, crossing to the tiny closet to pull open its door.

From the top shelf he snagged something, handing it

to her as if it were a special prize. "Your extra pillow, Ms. Buchanan," he said solemnly. "Accept this as your official welcome to Tranquility House. And please don't hesitate to call on me if I can assist with any of your other needs."

Her eyes narrowed on him again. There was something on her face; speculation, maybe. Or maybe it was sex, because suddenly he replayed what he'd just said—*call on me if I can assist with any of your other needs.*

Damn. Though it was surprising the hell out of him after all this time, the one with needs was him. His blood moved heavily toward his groin while his brain went off on its own, fantasizing an image of her on the bed, that angel hair spread across the first pillow, the second shoved beneath her naked hips. He saw his mouth trailing from the pulse at her throat down to—

"You know, there's something about you . . ." Speculation filled her voice.

Yes, it was definitely speculation, not sex, and it chilled his blood and slowed his heartbeat and probably saved him to see another day.

"I'll be going now," he said, quelling the worry that she'd recognize him by reminding himself he was about to get rid of her. "Though there's just a few more things . . ."

"Tomorrow's menu?"

Poor kid was still thinking resort. "Meals are served in the community building. It's the largest one and you should have no trouble finding it. But I'm afraid Judd handles all the culinary details, so I don't know what's being served."

She sighed, her expression glum. "Okay. I can take it as it comes."

He cleared his throat. "Well, speaking of, uh, taking . . . Tranquility House has an ironclad policy. All its guests must relinquish anything that runs on batteries or electricity." With a nod, he indicated one of the briefcase-sized bags he'd set down. "Like your laptop there."

"No! Not my computer."

"I'm sorry," he said. "Those are the rules, and have been since my grandparents built this place. If you need writing implements, we have paper and pens available."

She scowled. "I have paper and pens." After a moment's hesitation, she waved at him with a hand. "Go ahead, fine. It's all yours."

As he bent to lift it, she turned away to push her big suitcase into the corner with her foot. "Is there anything else?" he asked her.

"No, only the one laptop."

"I mean, anything else that runs on batteries or electricity?"

"Nope." She wasn't looking at him.

He cleared his throat again. "I believe you mentioned you have a cell phone."

She froze, muttered, "Me and my big mouth," then stomped over to another bag to retrieve it. She slapped it into his outstretched palm. "There. Satisfied?"

"As long as that's all you have." His eyebrow lifted. "Is it?"

"Yes."

He lifted his other brow.

"Yes!"

"Uh, Angel, I may be a man, but I grew up with two sisters."

"I don't know what you're talking about." Her gaze slid off his face.

Sighing, he prompted her. "Come on, every woman I know uses one. You must have with you—"

"Well!" Her eyes widened in offended embarrassment. "I can't believe you'd have the nerve—the *nerve*!—to mention it."

He blinked. "It?"

"You know . . ." Her expresson was all innocence. "My vibrator."

Her *vibrator*? Shock quickly rolled through him, pushed out of the way by another hot wave of lust. A vibrator. Those naked images started piling up in his mind again, making him feel hard and hot and . . .

And stupid.

"I almost fell for that," he said, shaking his head. "You almost distracted me."

She opened her mouth.

"Don't bother denying it." He pointed at her. "As I'm certain you're aware, I was talking about a blow-dryer. Give it up, sweetheart."

When she opened her mouth again, he wagged his finger back and forth. "N-uh-uh-uh-uh. Those are the rules. Take them or leave."

Making a disgusted sound, she threw up her hands. Then she marched over to another suitcase and from its depths removed the largest blow-dryer he'd ever seen, its nozzle as big as a head of cabbage. "Jesus," he said, staring at it. "That's not a hairdryer, that's a weapon of mass destruction."

If looks could kill, he would have been vaporized. "Don't mock the hair tools," she hissed, shoving the dryer at him. "I'm going to get you back for this. Just you wait."

Yeah, baby, punish me by debarking. Then his family, his identity, and his health would be a lot better off. "Why don't I give you directions to the nearest resort," he offered.

She was a breath away from taking him up on it, he could tell.

So, relaxing, he smiled at her. Everything was going to be just fine. "Or I can tell you the quickest route back to the highway and the city."

Angel bristled. "What? And let you win? I don't think so—" She broke off, staring at him.

"Wait a minute, wait a minute. Wait a darn minute." She strode closer to him, her curly hair floating off her shoulders, her perfume floating through the air to dizzy him.

So dizzy that he didn't see it coming.

"I know who you are!" she exclaimed, all angel crowded out by the devilish delight in her eyes. "The day just keeps getting better! *This* is where you've been hiding the last year. You're the so-called 'Trial Dog.' You're C. J. Jones, San Francisco's most tenacious, most relentless, and most winning criminal defense attorney."

Chapter 4

Angel lay on the skinny but surprisingly comfortable bed and listened to nothing. To her mind it was as loud as a dripping faucet, and the inky blackness of the little cottage was just another distraction from sleep. The dense surrounding woods made the whole place look and smell like a giant's version of the Delancey Christmas-tree lot she visited every December, and the trees even muffled the sound of the nearby ocean.

"I'm a city girl," she admitted aloud, because it seemed wise to make sure that it wasn't sudden deafness that accounted for the thick silence.

After another few minutes of unrelieved quiet, she gave up on trying to sleep. She couldn't, not with her mind fixed on the discovery that Cooper wasn't the simple but suspicious resort manager she'd first presumed.

He was C. J. Jones! She gave a little bounce against the mattress, thrilled that she'd stumbled upon the elusive partner in the prestigious firm of DiGiovanni & Jones. Her menopausal editor, Jane, would have one of her notorious hot flashes when Angel called in with the exciting news.

When she called in from a pay phone. She sighed. It was inconvenient to lose her cell and all her other tools of civilization, but it was a fair price for the unexpected twofer. *Two* stories, one on Stephen Whitney and the other featuring the now-reclusive C. J. Jones.

She hadn't broached the idea of interviewing Cooper yet. He'd managed to duck out of the room right after she'd made the I.D., muttering something about locking away her possessions. But he couldn't get far.

What annoyed her was how long it had taken her to figure out who he was. But he *had* been wearing those sunglasses in the church—was it in order to remain anonymous?—and it wasn't as if she'd been looking for him.

Or ever actually *met* him. Her previous contact with C. J. Jones had come in the form of what she'd read in the newspapers and then what she'd seen for herself a number of years ago. Early for an appointment at the courthouse, out of curiosity she'd ducked into a courtroom that was filling with an unusual number of onlookers.

She'd sat in the back row just as C. J. Jones began his closing argument in an infamous assault case. Within minutes, she'd been transfixed by his clipped voice and its leashed passion. He'd been heavier then, she remembered, his hair much shorter, his movements explosive.

Recalling that, it wasn't as surprising that she hadn't

immediately seen him in the lanky, long-haired Cooper with his cool, calm air.

But it explained that prickly, tingly sense she'd experienced around him. Why, it was nothing more than her reporter's intuition at work, trying to tell her to pay attention because it had already recognized the man.

She relaxed against the soft sheets, comforted by the rational explanation. Not that he wasn't attractive enough to make a woman prickle and tingle. As a matter of fact, that day in the courtroom she'd developed the teeniest, tiniest of crushes on him. There was no shame in admitting it. She'd been young, impressionable, and, well, starstruck.

But she'd always been old enough and wise enough to put the story ahead of any female silliness. So she'd gone on to her meeting that day just as she would go on tomorrow, focused on the job.

Which led her right back to wondering why Cooper had left *his* job in San Francisco. She yawned, her eyes closing. Tomorrow she'd find out all she wanted to know about him.

The racket of the birds was loud enough to awaken her. Angel lay in bed, her eyes closed, and wondered if robins had made a nest under the eaves of her apartment building like they had last spring. But this wasn't spring, and—

Her eyes popped open. And this wasn't San Francisco anymore, Dorothy.

Sunlight had found a knife's-edge opening in the drawn curtains. It was certainly past dawn, but beyond that Angel couldn't guess. At home, she had her bedroom TV programmed to wake her at seven A.M. with the world and national news on MSNBC.

But without the customary rumble of the morning anchor announcing the time, she was forced to fumble for her watch on the wooden nightstand. In the dim light, she brought it close to her face to read the hands.

Nine A.M. Late, but not so late that there wouldn't be coffee available, yes? Though at home the stuff would be auto-brewed, waiting for her the instant she opened her eyes, today she'd have to shower and dress before caffeine.

In an amazing ten-minute speed record, which attested to (a) her eagerness for coffee and (b) how much time she usually spent on hair care, she soon wore jeans and a T-shirt and was lacing up her Gatorade-green hiking boots. Without her precious blow-dryer and its "patented curl control" diffusor, it seemed safer to skip her usual daily shampooing. Instead, she went for a 1960s flower child look by tying a bandanna around her head.

The walk between her cottage and the main building passed in a blur of clean air and leafy scents. The guest accommodations were spaced among the immense redwoods and other semi-tamed vegetation, but the communal building sat at the head of an oval-shaped, grass-covered clearing. Unshadowed by trees, the outside of the door marked "Dining Room" felt warm beneath her hand.

Inside, she didn't smell coffee.

But surely that couldn't be right. She gazed about the empty room, taking in the simple picnic tables, the chafing dishes sitting on another long table against the far wall. As she walked farther into the room, an interior door beside the buffet swung open. A man stepped in.

Judd Sterling, Angel recalled. Family Friend. Close up he was definitely handsome, but even more interesting was the graceful way he moved—as if he'd found a current of air that she couldn't see or feel.

She sent him the best decaffeinated smile she could muster up. "Coffee?" she asked. "I'm desperate for coffee."

Smiling back in a friendly manner, he shook his head and pointed to her left.

Angel's gaze followed his finger to a sign on the wall. " 'No'—" She swallowed her next word, grimacing. *No talking*.

Sorry, she mouthed. Taking a deep breath, she mimed gripping a mug. *Coffee?* she asked, just moving her lips.

He shook his head, giving her another warm, soothing smile.

She might have to strangle him. *Caw. Fee.* She exaggerated the movements of her lips, shifting her imaginary grasp so that she pretended to hold a handleless take-out cup rather than a mug.

Neither seemed to help. He shook his head again, but that might be laughter lurking in his gray eyes.

Listen, pal, she hoped her stomping footsteps communicated as she approached him, *you don't want to get between me and my ground beans.*

Maybe he saw her annoyance, because when she was close enough to use her nails on him he slid out a small notepad and pencil, wrote, then passed the page to her.

Angel stared down at the words. Oh please, it couldn't be, she thought. It couldn't. It was his bad handwriting. Those neat block letters didn't say . . .

"No caffeine?" she spoke out loud. So give her ten demerits, but they had to be absolutely clear on this.

He handed her another page with more of his neat handwriting. NO CAFFEINE, ALCOHOL, OR TOBACCO ON THE TRANQUILITY GROUNDS. ALL FOOD SERVED HERE IS ORGANIC.

Worse and worser. No coffee, no diet Pepsi, no nice five P.M. glass of pinot grigio.

And there would be bugs in her food! She'd eaten at a natural food restaurant in Berkeley once where her chopped salad came—free of charge, the waiter had tried to joke—with chopped caterpillars.

Judd touched her arm. Sunk in disappointment, it took a moment for her to notice his sympathetic expression and to realize he was directing her attention toward the chafing dishes. As he lifted each lid with a little silent *ta-da!*, Angel morosely inspected the offerings.

Gloppy, fiber-filled oatmeal. Scrambled eggs—from free-range chickens, she was sure. (Did anyone ever bother to find out exactly *where* those liberated chickens had been ranging?) Finally, he revealed some sort of cold dish that appeared to be tofu squares floating in unflavored yogurt.

Stomach going queasy, Angel averted her gaze. To her mind, if God had intended humans to eat tofu, he wouldn't have made it resemble congealed kindergarten paste.

Stifling a sigh, she allowed the man to serve her some of each dish. Then she sat down on one of the picnic benches, turned her plate so that the tofu was as distant as possible, and resorted to a childhood method of dealing with unpleasantness—she pretended it away.

She was falling into a decent apricot-danish daydream when Judd set a steaming cup beside her elbow. Her hand made an instinctive grab for it, and though her sense of smell rebelled, her brain didn't catch up quickly enough to stop her first sip.

"Ggh." Her throat refused to accept what was swishing around inside her mouth. "Ggh. Ggh."

My God, what can it be? Breathing in and out through her nose, she felt her face go red as her gaze lifted to Judd's. Was he trying to poison her?

He grinned and held out a piece of paper that she snatched from him, even as she tried not to gag. YARROW TEA, it read. AIDS DIGESTION. YOU'LL GET USED TO IT.

Squeezing the note in her fist, she forced the pungent liquid down, then gasped in a breath of palate-cleansing air. "I'll *never* get used to that," she choked out.

She didn't imagine anyone else could either. As a matter of fact, she had a sudden, sneaking suspicion the "yarrow tea" was a special concoction created just for her. Same with the awful, organic breakfast fare.

Her eyes narrowed. While Judd Sterling had a peaceful, benevolent air about him, there was someone else in charge of this whole operation. Someone who didn't want her at Tranquility House.

Why, it made perfect sense.

Cooper Jones was planning on starving her out.

* * *

It was the stomach-turning breakfast that decided Angel's first course of action for the day—well, that and the dearth of newspapers, apparently another Tranquility House no-no. Without anything worth eating or reading, the next logical step was to work on Cooper. Both the Stephen Whitney and C. J. Jones stories required his cooperation.

While it hadn't gone well between them so far, she wasn't really worried—she had a knack for making people comfortable. Her first journalism course had been Interview Techniques 101, and she'd never forgotten the professor's three-pronged strategy for warming up a subject.

1. Conduct a short exchange of pleasantries
2. Proceed into some casual conversation
3. Conclude with a sincere compliment

The formula never failed to ease the initial stiffness between herself and an interviewee. So though she and Cooper might have gotten off to an awkward start, in no time at all she would have him eating out of her hand.

Though Judd couldn't provide the other man's whereabouts as anything more specific than SOMEWHERE AROUND, Angel set off to locate Cooper, taking the first path she found leading away from the cottages.

The trail meandered eastward, up rolling inclines of dry, nutty-scented grass and down into shady notches with trickling creeks and arthritic-looking oaks. A girl from hilly San Francisco should have been able to manage all the ups and downs with one high heel tied behind her back, but within ten minutes the new hiking boots were pinching and the warming air made her wish for shorts and a tank top instead of her long pants and T-shirt.

Pausing beneath a group of trees at the base of the next hill, she plucked her shirt away from her sticky torso and moved it back and forth to fan her skin. Though she'd yet to catch a glimpse of Cooper, or any other human life for that matter, she couldn't suppress the hope that any minute now she'd stumble across civilization—specifically, civilization in the guise of a Peet's Coffee Shop. As if jeering at her fancy, a blue jay on a nearby branch screeched down at her.

"Fine," Angel retorted, scowling at the headache starting to throb at the base of her skull. "Give me a Starbucks, then, I'm not picky. Even that ulcer-inducing stuff they serve at 7-Eleven will do."

From behind her, someone spoke. "Sorry, kid, but we don't do trademarks around here."

Cooper! Her first jolt of surprise dissolved as she recognized his voice. *Okay,* she reminded herself, willing the headache away, *here's your chance. Put him at ease.*

"Well, hello, there." Her back still to him, Angel mentally checked off *exchange pleasantries,* then moved straight on to *casual conversation.* "What's that about trademarks?" she asked, turning to face him.

"For the hundred miles of Big Sur coast, you won't find a single national chain—not fast food, bank, or supermarket."

Under other circumstances, his words might have made her groan in disappointment. But now they barely sank in, distracted as she was by Cooper himself. His hair was damply slicked back, and instead of yesterday's almost sloppy-sized designer suit, today his body was wrapped in exercise gear that clung to, well . . . well . . . everything.

Wow. She swallowed. *Wow.*

Those loose-fitting clothes had hidden a hard, sculpted body that was cut and rippled in the most intriguing places.

Suddenly aware she was staring, she felt her face go hot and dropped her gaze to her feet. "So, um . . ."

Oh God. Though she remembered she'd been bent on winning Cooper over, now the thread of their conversation was completely burned from her brain. Floundering, she returned to the top of Interview 101's formula.

1. Conduct a short exchange of pleasantries

"Hello, there," she said brightly. The greeting rolled off her tongue with a stomach-sinking familiarity. Hoping she wasn't making too big a fool of herself, she continued her inspection of the dusty toes of her boots. "So, uh, whatcha been up to this morning?"

"It isn't obvious?"

His amused tone made her glance up again and she allowed her eyes another moment of free rein. There was a big metal contraption leaning against his right thigh.

His long thigh. His hard thigh. His long, hard thigh. The quadricep muscle seemed carved out of rock, and she followed it with her eyes as it curved from his lean hip to wrap inward at his knee.

South of Angel's belly button, things clenched. It was *her* muscles, she realized as they tightened again, the ones that *Cosmopolitan* magazine recommended women routinely exercise in order to drive men wild.

Her face went hotter, but she couldn't stop looking. His inner thigh was well defined too, she discovered, all firm as it led up to—

Eeek. She jerked her gaze up to his face, passing over the big plastic hat he held in one of his gloved hands as she tried remembering his last remark.

"Sure, sure, it's obvious." Assuring herself she sounded casual, possibly even intelligent, she made a vague gesture at the metal contraption against his leg. "You've been, uh, exercising with that, that thing there."

His brows lifted. "It's a mountain bike. But I'm betting you've seen a bicycle before."

A bicycle? Angel blinked, then glanced downward again. Oh heck, it *was* a bike! And then, under her gaze, one of his big hands tightened on the handlebars, flexing a tendon running up his forearm.

She stood transfixed, that below-the-belt *Cosmo* area of hers contracting again. As a journalist, she considered herself a keen observer, but who had ever noticed that men had muscles like that in their *arms*? Sinewy, long muscles that—

"Angel?"

Jerked from her fascination, she shuffled backward, tripped on a root, and fell on her butt in the dirt.

In a blink he'd dropped the bike and the helmet and was squatted beside her. "Are you all right?"

"No." Because on top of humiliation, now his hard

thighs were near enough to touch. To stymie temptation, she lifted an inch and sat on both hands. "No, I'm not all right."

He shifted closer. "Where are you hurt?"

Shaking her head, she scooted back, refusing to admit it was her pride, her professionalism, that was taking the hit. She was supposed to be thinking about the all-important story, for God's sake, not the intriguing specifics of sexual differentiation.

"Sit still a minute and take some breaths," he advised, moving forward to close the gap between them. "Deep breaths."

His short-sleeved shirt was made of a stretchy, satiny fabric that fit closely at the neck and then molded itself to his chest. It clung so snugly, she had no trouble appreciating the wide planes of his pectoral muscles, each ridge topped by the tight buttons of his— *Stop!*

Wrenching her gaze away, Angel again struggled for control of her thoughts. She'd seen bikers wearing this same getup millions of times. Just because Cooper was wearing it was no reason to allow that tingling awareness she'd finally been able to dismiss as recognition-gone-awry to rebloom.

Anyway, women didn't switch from fine to fascinated, from neutral to sexual with a glance, did they? The female of the species wasn't visually turned on, she'd read that fact in an article in *Men's Health* as recently as last week.

Not that she didn't have previous experience to rely on too. She'd had relationships with men. She'd had sex on occasion. But the guys always had to sort of . . .

rub her toward response. Never, not once, had she seen a particular man's form and been instantly enthralled.

Realizing she was staring at his legs again, she choked back a mortified moan.

"Angel, what the hell's wrong?" Putting one hand on the ground, he shifted nearer.

"I don't know," she answered, trying not to think about the way his arm's movement had caused his biceps to bunch. "I don't know what's wrong with me."

Then, finally, gratefully, she made the connection. When she was eight, she'd wanted to be a boy, a big, strong boy, more than anything. There had been a gang of bullies at her new school and she'd wished every night to wake up with the height and the muscles to save herself from the next round of intimidation. She'd already given up on her father rescuing her.

Maybe, probably—for *certain*!—Stephen Whitney was responsible for this temporary fixation. Past feelings and fears were resurfacing, that's all. She wasn't lusting after Cooper Jones. In a flashback to her past, she was lusting after his *muscles*, the physical symbol of the strength to take care of herself that she'd longed for so many years ago.

Relieved, she managed to smile and rise to her feet. "I'm fine. It's just that . . ." Cooper's eyes were that hazel, greeny-browny color that could appear light one moment and dark the next. They were dark now, and watchful, and sighing inwardly, she remembered that she was supposed to be inspiring his trust. "That I haven't had my coffee this morning."

He stood too. "I've seen some strong reactions to caffeine withdrawal before, but this seems pretty extreme."

"You're telling me," Angel muttered. She gave herself some additional recovery time by bending over and brushing the dust off her jeans. *Get back to the point,* she told herself sternly. *Focus on those interview warm-up techniques. Concentrate on getting Cooper to relax.*

As he turned and stepped toward his bike, she straightened. "Which reminds me . . ." She kept her voice light, trying for a smooth segue into some more casual conversation. "You'll have to tell me your secret."

"*What?*" His voice sharpened and his spine stiffened.

"Your secret," she repeated. "You know, where you've hidden your stash of those three banned substances: caffeine, alcohol, and tobacco. Around the courthouse you weren't famous for your abstinence, you know."

"Ah." Cooper's shoulders relaxed and he wheeled the bike around to face her. "Now I get you."

She figured she was making progress with him, because his eyes had lightened and there was a tolerant half-smile on his face. Smiling in return, Angel sauntered closer, thinking good ol' Professor Brown had been proven right once again.

"So, see," she said, close enough now that she had to tilt up her face to look into his, "I'm guessing you have some triple roast hidden somewhere, right alongside a carton of cigarettes and a bottle of scotch."

"What would you say if I told you I don't smoke or drink—alcohol or coffee—anymore?"

"I'd say . . . I'd say . . ." Angel couldn't think what she'd say because she was astonished. C. J. Jones had a reputation for playing as hard as he worked.

His laugh was short. "You'd say what?"

There was something in his eyes now, some kind of pain, that made her break their gazes. She let hers slide down to his neck—another strong, manly column—then on to his wide shoulders and long, lean body. God, he looked good.

"Angel?" There was a husky note in his voice. "What the hell are you thinking?"

What the hell *was* she thinking? She was supposed to be working. Getting Cooper to eat right out of her hand. Looking away, she ran through the preinterview formula again.

Pleasantries: Check. Casual conversation: More than enough. Her eyes drawn back to him, she realized that only the sincere compliment was left.

And for some impulsive, mindless reason Angel blurted out the first one that came into her head. "I'm thinking that abstinence gave you one awesome body."

In the same time it took for her to absorb her own words and then to cringe with humiliation, she saw the leap of embarrassed color on Cooper's face, his leap onto his bike, the leap the metal contraption made down the path toward Tranquility.

If that wasn't proof enough that her warm-up technique had failed, the hasty manner in which Cooper pedaled off made it very clear she'd done anything but relax his guard.

"I'm an idiot," she said aloud.

The blue jay above her jeered in agreement. Cursing the bird, the renewed throbbing at the base of her skull, and most of all herself, she hurried off in the opposite direction of Cooper.

At the top of the next rise though, her feet stuttered

to a halt, the view below freezing her movement. The trail she'd taken had apparently wound north, because the dark-forested Santa Lucia Mountains were at her right. Looking to her left, her gaze flowed down gently rolling hills to miles of staggered bluffs that dropped into the ocean. On the nearest of the headlands, in the midst of all that natural wonder, sat a cluster of buildings that appeared enchanted.

Angel blinked, certain they were the figment of someone's imagination—but not hers, because she hadn't daydreamed fairy tales since she was four years old. Dominating the clearing was a huge three-story house with deep eaves and a rustic rockwork foundation. It was painted a pale gray, with a bright blue door that was flanked by flowering shrubs in pinks and red. Between the house and the ocean stood a tower, faced with the same rough-hewn rock.

Nestled in the curve of a small stand of pines, Angel glimpsed a portion of a pool and the roof of a poolhouse. Farther away from the big house was a cottage, one that Hansel and Gretel might have wandered from. It too was painted gray, but the trim was a triple threat of colors: salmon, saffron, and sapphire.

Angel realized she was holding her breath, as if the simple act of taking in oxygen might disturb a pretty vision. But then the toylike figure of a man appeared on the edge of the trees and strode toward the front door of the little house.

It was only then she accepted this was no hallucination. Because even from this distance Angel recognized Judd Sterling, and she knew he was flesh and blood. He knocked on the door and in a moment it was opened by a dark-haired woman, a cat at her heels. Beth Jones.

Which meant that the little kingdom below had been Angel's father's.

Chapter 5

Judd paused in Beth's foyer, still somewhat hesitant to follow her into the kitchen. He hadn't stopped by her house for his customary midmorning break since her brother-in-law Stephen's death—though he'd wanted to. But Taoism taught that one planned in advance and carefully considered each action before making it, and he hadn't thought Beth was ready to reestablish their normal routine until today.

She looked over her shoulder at him, her brows lifting over her brown eyes. "Don't you want coffee?"

He had to smile then, because it brought to mind Angel Buchanan's desperation at breakfast that morning. Stifling a small pang of guilt that he was going to assuage his own greed for freshly ground beans, he nodded and gestured Beth forward.

Her turquoise-colored pants were cropped at the ankles and left her slender feet bare. She wore a platinum chain around one ankle, and though he couldn't see it from here, he knew that dangling from it was a diamond-encrusted *E*, the anklet one of a pair that Stephen Whitney had presented to his wife and sister-in-law the Christmas before.

Beth's cat had been Judd's own gift to her. During their short procession to the kitchen, the sleek, black-haired Shaft carried on a one-sided conversation in loud meows. He determinedly twined his mistress's ankle too, rubbing against it as if he, like Judd, wanted to break that chain.

"Silly cat. He's been sticking close for days," Beth said, reaching down to stroke the animal's head.

Judd, on the other hand, had given her space. He'd been with her briefly at the memorial service and then at the reception afterward, but other than that he'd kept his distance from the family.

She placed his coffee mug on the small table across from hers, the San Francisco paper between them. Reading the news while drinking coffee together was the morning ritual they'd established sometime during the five years he'd been living at Tranquility House. Nominally an employee of the family, he'd found himself with a place in their lives. He and Beth had been comfortable, fast friends from the first.

He didn't want Stephen's death to change that.

Judd took his usual seat and watched her fill his cup from the pot, then her own. She turned her back to him and replaced the pot on the burner. "I've missed you," she blurted out.

His chair scraped against the floor as he started to rise, but she shook her head.

"No, don't," she said. "I'm a mess right now, I know that."

The cat jumped onto the countertop, butting against her. She lifted Shaft against her chest, then swung toward Judd. With her eyes closed, she rubbed her cheek between the animal's ears. "How could this have happened?" she whispered.

Judd shook his head, taking a long, assessing look at her. Beth's face was pale and her skin appeared tightly stretched across her cheekbones. But even obviously exhausted, she looked a decade younger than thirty-four. He'd always wondered if her glow was the result of the sea air or the spell of Stephen Whitney.

After a moment she sighed, then set the cat on the floor and dropped into her chair. She doctored her coffee with a generous dollop of cream, and then pushed the pitcher toward Judd, as she always did.

He ignored it, as he always did.

She laughed, the sound forced. "Why do I always do that? I know you drink yours black."

He decided against pointing out the obvious—that it was *Stephen* who took his coffee with cream.

Before he could even take a sip from his mug, she popped up from her chair. "I have a million things to do. List upon list. Look!"

She hurried over to the counter to grab a sheaf of papers, her movements jerky. "But I suppose it will be good to keep busy, don't you think? Lainey says Cooper will help her with Stephen's personal things—they'll do that as soon as Katie goes back to school. I said I'd take care of the art show and I'm sure it will be twice as much trouble to cancel as it was to put it on."

Judd nodded. Each September, Whitney showed his year's worth of paintings. But those canvases had been burned and, yesterday, the ashes thrown into the sea.

Beth frowned down at the papers in her hand, chattering away in a manner totally unlike herself. "This would have been the twentieth year. We only canceled it one other time, when there was a wildfire in the Lucias and everyone in the area was forced to evacuate. Lainey was six months along with Katie and I . . . I wasn't well."

She whirled back to the counter. "But you don't want to hear about all that. Excuse me, excuse me a moment." With that, she threw down the papers and disappeared from the kitchen. He heard the bathroom door slam shut.

Staring after her, Judd rose from his chair. *Damn it*! What was he supposed to do now? Go to her? Leave?

It flooded him then, a hot rush of the kind of frustration he hadn't felt in years. His fists clenched, and he struck out with his foot, kicking the leg of his empty chair. It skidded wildy across the floor . . . and did nothing to calm his mood.

Damn, damn, damn it! Already he was losing what he'd worked so hard for.

His mornings with Beth, more important Beth *herself,* had become integral to the life he'd built for himself here. She was part of the cure that had healed his soul, she was part of the balance he'd finally found with the universe. He'd accepted that the artist's death would upset that equilibrium some, but he wasn't prepared for things to change with Beth.

He'd been so content with how it was between them.

At the back of the house, he heard the door reopen. Beth's footsteps were usually light and steady, but now they dragged—as if grief, or maybe Stephen, were holding her back. The sound pulled at him—no, it tore at him—and he started for the door. He needed to get away, he thought with sudden anxiety. He needed to do anything but witness the misery on her face.

Maybe through some meditation he could recover—

"Judd. Judd, please. Please, don't go."

Her voice stopped him before he made it out of the kitchen. He gripped the doorjamb, struggling with himself. He'd miscalculated her readiness to get back to normal, that's all. If he went away now, if he came back another day, a later day, then they'd be able to regain their comfortable harmony.

"Judd, please," she whispered.

But he couldn't leave her, not when she said his name like that.

He turned. From across the kitchen, she was looking at him, her eyelashes spiky and wet. She was so beautiful.

Following her lead, he retrieved his chair, then sat back at the table and cradled his mug in his palms. What was he supposed to do now? Comfort her? He supposed he could tell her that Buddhists think the soul is not extinguished at death, but passed on like a candle flame to an unlit wick. That Hindus believe a person must die for them to discover their deathless, Supreme Self.

But then again, maybe he should offer nothing. The Shoshone Indians said that grief was a landslide the griever had to work through alone, one rock at a time.

After all, he'd been out of the advice game for five years, and inside him, some cautious, wise voice of his own warned that inviting discussion would only further upset the peace between them.

He glanced up, and caught her swiping a trembling hand beneath her nose.

That broke him.

Grabbing up the pen and paper she always had on the table, he quickly blocked out the question. After all these years of self-selected silence, he could be pretty damn pithy with a pen.

WHY SO UNHAPPY?

"I—" Beth broke off, swallowed. "I can't stop thinking about the past. Oh, Judd, I hurt so much."

She hurt.

He sucked in a sharp breath, and then another, her out-loud admission striking hard at the unprotected and tender belly of his heart. He rubbed his chest, trying to remind himself that the first of the Four Noble Truths of Buddhism was the universality of suffering. That he should be able to understand and accept her pain.

But it was impossible, because another truth, maybe not as noble, but certainly as elementary, was suddenly staring him in the face. *Breathe slow and deep,* he told himself, *because you'll definitely have to understand and accept this.*

There would be no denying it, no turning back, that's for certain. Not when he practiced *wu wei*—the Taoist art of letting nature take its course.

And that course had led him to here, he saw now. To Beth. To the realization that he was in love with her.

And nothing would ever, ever be the same again.

* * *

It was very late afternoon when Angel wound the curly telephone cord around her fingers. "Yeah, yeah. They took my laptop, my cell phone, everything."

At the other end of the line, her intern, Cara, was properly astounded.

"But I'll survive," Angel promised, keeping her voice low. Especially now that she'd discovered the deserted room marked "Infirmary" and its old-fashioned rotary telephone. She didn't feel the least bit guilty about making the long-distance call either. For one thing, the charges were going on her credit card, and for another, she figured it had a medical purpose. Access to regular inoculations of Real World would keep her sane.

"But listen, Cara, I don't have much time. I've been going through the files you sent down with me. But I need something else. I need you to mail me a package. No, not more research, not right now." Angel lowered her voice to a whisper. "A jar of instant coffee, okay?"

She rolled her eyes when Cara demanded she speak up. "Coffee. Instant coffee," Angel said more loudly.

A rustling down the corridor made her freeze. "Shh!" she hissed into the receiver, listening intently. After a few moments of unrelieved silence, she dared to go on.

Turning her back to the door, she hunched her shoulders and cupped her hand over her mouth. "And Cara," Angel said into the phone, "the issue with the story on Paul Roth hits the stands today. I want you to call Miss Marshall. You know, just to check on her."

Cara made some squeaky protest noises.

"Listen," Angel replied sternly. "This isn't an easy job. If you want to be a journalist, a good one, you have to ask the hard questions and you have to write the hard truths."

On the other end, the young woman responded a bit sharply that then you got to order your intern to make the hard phone calls.

Cara was smarter-mouthed than she looked.

But Angel kept both her smile and her sympathy out of her voice. "Hey, think of it like this. You get to learn the easy way not to give your heart or place your faith in a man. That's worth dozens of uncomfortable conversations."

Suddenly the little hairs beside the scarf-knot at the base of her neck prickled. Angel slammed down the phone and whirled in one quick movement. Uh-oh. Caught by Katie Whitney.

Angel cleared her throat, not knowing what to say to the girl. "Well, uh, hi. How ya doing?" The last time they'd spoken Angel had made irreverent comments about old white men and choirboys who were really girls. She'd also found out they shared the same father.

Pushing the thought from her head, Angel stuck out her hand and hoped Katie wasn't a stickler about the Tranquility rules. "I didn't introduce myself yesterday. I'm Angel Buchanan."

The girl's grip was brief. "Nice to meet you." She hesitated a moment. "Are you . . . are you ill?"

Angel blinked. "Me? No." Then she belatedly remembered they were standing in the infirmary. "I was . . . I was just . . ." She sighed. "Look, I'm a journalist and I needed to check in with my assistant."

Katie nodded. "My mom mentioned you're here to do a story on my father."

"That's right," Angel agreed, ignoring the "my father" and focusing on the fact that the comment was a natural, even lovely lead-in as lead-ins went. She could take the opportunity to ask the girl a few questions about the kind of father Stephen Whitney had been. Casual questions.

There was no sensible, rational reason to feel squirmy about it either, not when Lainey Whitney had almost guaranteed the family's cooperation. And after all, WWWD? What Would Woodward Do?

That decided it.

"Listen, Katie," Angel said. "If you wouldn't mind, I'd like to talk with you. About . . . about your dad."

The teenager stiffened.

Guilt gave Angel a nasty pinch. "Not if it makes you uncomfortable, of course," she added hastily. "But your perspective would add a lot to my understand—my story."

Katie was shaking her head now, her eyes widening.

Oh, blast. She'd scared the kid off. "Katie, I—"

Before Angel could get out another syllable, the girl grabbed her by the arm and hustled her through the door on the other side of the room.

Angel suddenly found herself outside. "Hey—"

Katie put a finger over her lips and tugged Angel toward the woods. As she let herself be guided away, she looked back. Through the infirmary window she could see Judd and Cooper step into the room.

Oooh, close one. Especially since she was still mortified by what she'd said to Cooper that morning.

Katie didn't stop moving until they were a good distance from any Tranquility buildings. Then she dropped Angel's arm.

"Sorry," the girl said. "I thought I heard someone coming and Judd takes his silence seriously."

"Can there be a punishment worse than yarrow tea?" Angel murmured, grimacing. There'd been more of the stuff served with the food-fit-for-rabbits lunch.

Katie glanced around. "If you do want to talk, we should move farther off. We're still too close to the path to the hot tubs."

"Hot tubs?"

Katie put her finger over her lips and then started off again. Angel had to quicken her footsteps to keep up with the girl's longer legs. A low hum became a low roar and the warm, green-scented air started to smell saltier. Then they broke free of a tangle of trees and Angel found herself on a promontory overlooking the ocean. Hundreds of feet below, water churned and swirled, creating latte froth at the base of the cliff.

"God," Angel said, looking around her. The beauty of the spot was astounding.

"Uncle Cooper always says that if He's anywhere, He's here." Katie sat down on a long flat rock, and the late afternoon breeze snatched her ponytail, flying it behind her like a flag.

Angel dropped beside her, dumbfounded by the unspoiled wildness of the view. She stared down at the jagged sea cliffs, then up at the blue sky, then back at the forested mountains gathered behind them like a column of brawny men standing shoulder to shoulder.

Her gaze returned to the ocean below and the unforgiving boulders it pounded against.

From Cara's research, Angel had learned that the Spanish explorers hadn't dared landing their ships along this treacherous coastline. They'd continued north to Monterey, calling the inaccessible area they'd passed El Sur Grande—the Big South. Though the Spanish had eventually discovered the Indians who lived in El Sur Grande as well as its ferocious grizzly bears—and depleted the population of both—they'd maintained a superstitious dread of the area, whose name was later bastardized into the English-Spanish Big Sur.

"It makes me feel small," Angel murmured.

Katie glanced over. "You said you had things to ask me?"

Ask Katie. Ask Katie about Stephen Whitney. "I . . ." As Angel tried formulating her first question, the wind slapped at her cheeks. "I . . . um . . . I . . ."

But words refused to take shape in her mind. Looking into the girl's face, Angel knew she'd only feel smaller if she pumped the kid for information on the day after the memorial service. But Katie was still looking at her expectantly, so Angel finally forced something out.

"Hot tubs?" she asked. "Did you mention something about hot tubs?"

Hours later, lying awake in bed, as Angel was longing for resort surroundings and a Swedish masseuse named Inge, that conversation with Katie drifted into her mind. A little water therapy might work the kinks from her back, the knots from her calves, and the disturbing image of Cooper Jones and his gorgeous body out of her head. She could sit in the warm water and make believe it was Swedish Inge's big, warm hands.

Katie had said the tubs were three separate pools fed by a natural spring overlooking the ocean. The bathing area was open twenty-four hours a day and the path leading to it was lit all night long.

Angel pushed back the covers, ignoring a quick jitter of city nerves, reminding herself again that Cara's exhaustive research claimed that the ferocious bears were long gone from the Big Sur woods.

Cooper leaned the back of his head against the lip of the redwood tub. He'd dimmed the nearest lights and had chosen the darkest corner of the third bath. The hot spring provided the heat, but enough cold water was added to this particular tub to keep it at a temperature he could stand for a long soak.

It was a long soak kind of night.

As usual, he was having trouble sleeping. When he'd lived in the city, there never seemed to be enough hours between dark and dawn. Wired by caffeine and nicotine and whatever case he was working on, he'd pulled hundreds of all-nighters, preparing motions or preparing to face judge and jury the next day. And if there wasn't work, then there was play to pursue just as vigorously.

It wasn't until this past year at Tranquility that he'd come to understand just how long twenty-four hours could be: 1,440 minutes; 86,400 seconds.

Though you'd think a man in his position would

revel in the slow hands of time, there were moments when he thought he'd die of boredom before anything else.

In search of sleepiness, he closed his eyes and tried letting his mind drift. When he heard the sound of someone singing, at first he thought it was part of a dream.

But a breathy rendition of Helen Reddy's "I Am Woman" didn't seem a song even his subconscious would throw at him. He opened his eyes just as the gate to the baths squeaked and Angel Buchanan danced in.

Damn.

She assumed she was alone, that was obvious. Without even glancing toward his dark corner, she continued warbling away, bare feet cha-cha-ing along the deck. Cooper silently sank lower in the water, deciding to hide in the steam and the shadows until she went away.

Like her, he'd come out here counting on being alone.

Then Angel threw off her robe and tossed it to a nearby bench and he released a silent, relieved breath. Thank God. Unlike him, she'd decided to wear a swimsuit for her solitary soak.

He watched her cross to the first hot tub, the meager starlight caught in her blond hair and the glow from the low fixtures washing up her bare calves. She was still singing Reddy-style as the toes of one foot dipped toward the surface of the water. "I am stro— *Eek*!"

She jerked her toes away. "Not that strong," she muttered. "Too hot."

The next tub was closer to Cooper, but she remained

unaware of her audience as she headed for it, singing again. "I am invinc— *Ack*!"

Not so invincible either, Cooper thought. She leaped away from the tub and rubbed at what must be a major case of goosebumps. If he'd left more lights on, she would have seen that the middle pool was labeled "Polar Plunge."

"Too cold," she muttered.

Then, though he saw her backing toward his tub, he didn't have the time to wish her away or even warn her of his presence. With a defiant, "I am wo-man!" Angel whirled, then hopped in.

Eight feet across the water from her, waves lapped against Cooper's chin. Uncertain what to do now, he watched as she sank low into the warmth. Her butt gave one wiggle against the submerged redwood bench and her eyes drifted shut.

"Just right," she murmured, then sighed.

After a moment, he sighed too. "Sorry to have to break it to you, Goldilocks. But Papa Bear's already home."

Angel apparently saved her *eeks* and *acks* for extremes of temperatures. For him, she merely appeared to stop breathing for a moment. Then, sighing again, she opened her eyes.

"It's you," she said, her voice resigned.

"In the flesh." Though he was certain his shadowed corner protected his nudity.

Nothing protected her expression, however. She was clearly annoyed to find him here and probably a little bit embarrassed too. Then he saw the steel inside her sugar-cookie exterior harden and she sat up straighter in the water.

So what that she'd paid him a compliment? he could almost hear her thinking. So what that he'd reacted by riding off like death was on his heels? She tossed her head and the top layers of her hair floated behind her shoulders, leaving one long, wet squiggle plastered to her throat and chest.

Though certain it would only add to his insomnia, Cooper couldn't stop his eyes from slowly following its curving path. Surely a man could take a harmless look, he excused himself, especially when he hadn't been this close to anything so tempting in so very, very long.

And it wasn't as if he could get up and leave, not when he was butt-naked beneath the water's cover. So he indulged himself a moment by tracing with his gaze the corkscrewed lock of her hair. It meandered down the pale skin of her neck to make an interesting pattern over the modest amount of plump cleavage revealed by her swimsuit.

The perusal was all fairly clinical, he told himself. Just a man observing the pretty rise of a pretty woman's breasts. It wasn't even offensive, not really, not when the darkness hid the direction of his gaze.

Except maybe she could feel it, because as he watched, she backed farther away from him, nervously pressing her spine against the side of the tub. He swallowed, telling himself to look away. But he didn't.

Instead, he saw her fidget again. She now sat taller, the movement drawing her breasts out of the water. Her nipples reacted to their sudden exposure to the cooler air by gathering, tightening, standing hard and small against her wet swimsuit.

Jesus, he thought, the sight thickening his blood. He felt his heart begin pumping heavily to push it through his body, its work made even more difficult because lust kept drawing it back toward his groin. Even then, though, he couldn't look away from Angel. She squirmed some more, and the water lapped against her hardened nipples, then rippled in his direction.

Reaching him, the little wave curled up and licked the underside of his chin. He jerked, then tore his gaze from her.

"One of us should leave," he choked out. And it wasn't going to be him—not naked and now more than half-erect. He knew he sounded rude, but hell, she'd probably thought worse of him after the clumsy way he'd ridden off that morning.

There was a moment's offended silence, then she spoke, enough chill in the words to cool the water several degrees. "Well, go right ahead, then." He wasn't dumb enough to look at her, but it was clear by her voice that she'd rooted herself to the hot tub's bench.

Gritting his teeth, he wished like hell there was a way to get out of the tub without exposing himself—and his arousal. There was another tense moment of silence, then he finally spoke. "Listen, Angel—"

"No, no, wait. You need to listen to me," she said, waving her hand to halt his spiel. The frost in her voice had thawed. "I've been thinking about this all day and I . . . I have to apologize."

Apologize? "For what?"

"For this morning, of course." Squaring her shoulders, she cleared her throat. "For what I said to you. Believe me, the last thing I wanted to do was make you uncomfortable."

He groaned. "You didn't—"

"Let me finish. Please." She made another quick gesture that sent drops of water flying. "I don't do coy well, so I'll just lay it out on the line, okay?"

"All right."

She cleared her throat. "It, uh, it must be clear to both of us that for some odd reason I'm attracted to you."

He decided to let the "odd reason" go. "So?"

"So, um, that still doesn't excuse my behavior this morning. I shouldn't have embarrassed you like that. So I apologize and I assure you, *assure you,* that even if the attraction ran both ways, I wouldn't act upon it."

He stared at her. Even *if* the attraction ran both ways? She thought he'd run away that morning because he didn't feel that sexual pull too? She thought she'd *embarrassed* him?

For God's sake, Angel might not be coy, but she sure as hell wasn't smart at deciphering sexual vibrations. "I—"

Almost too late, he swallowed the words that would set her straight. "I . . ." he restarted, rubbing his hand over his chin. He could play it this way. Sure. Her misunderstanding would serve to keep her at a distance from him.

"I accept your apology, and I'm feeling, uh, much better now that we've cleared the air."

"Really?" Her shoulders relaxed and she slid closer to him. "We're okay now?"

"Yeah," he lied, "okay." Because with her nearer he

could smell her hair, the warm steam releasing its alluring, sophisticated perfume. It didn't make him okay in the least. It unfortunately made him feel a year younger—when he'd still been so stupidly sure he was invulnerable.

"Well, great," she said. "That's just great."

"Great," he echoed, trying to relax by leaning his head against the edge of the tub and half-closing his eyes.

But the ensuing silence was just as awkward and tense as before. She'd have to be dense not to realize the air between them was charged with sex and getting heavier by the second.

He shot a glance at her. Her new position in the tub cast most of her face in shadow, but he could see her mouth, see it clearly, and he watched as her tongue slipped out to moisten her bottom lip.

When her tongue darted out again, stroked her puffy bottom lip again, it was *his* mouth that went dry.

"Just great," she muttered.

The disgruntled tone might have made him laugh, but he was too distracted by another wet glide of her tongue against her lip and the slow chug of his blood sliding south once more.

Then, between the space of one breath and the next, the heavy tension in the air pushed the darkness down, closing it around them. Instead of the wide-open night, it was a private, intimate darkness. And in it, just Cooper and Angel. The sound of her breathing was loud in his ears and the air was thick with perfume-scented steam.

He sucked in more of it, felt his pulse throb, and

wondered now if Angel could possibly miss that the sexual current was running from him to her and back again.

"Maybe you were right," she said hoarsely. "Maybe one of us should leave."

"Yeah." But God, he'd forgotten how good it felt, that slow build of pressure, of pleasure.

"But, um . . ." He heard her swallow. "I didn't think . . . I didn't know . . ."

"I didn't want you to," he murmured, wishing like hell he'd been able to pull it off. A year ago he would have been enjoying the buildup—this ascent from attraction to awareness to arousal. If this was a year ago, he would move toward her now, stroke her bottom lip with his own tongue, tug on those hard little nipples. He would kiss her and touch her and take her to bed, then wake up in the morning with a smile on his face.

Instead, tonight he'd go to bed alone.

Because he felt so damn sorry for himself, he reached toward her. Just one touch, he promised himself, just one. The swish of the water sounded loudly, an alarm that he ignored.

His hand inches from his target, his target's hand clamped down on his wrist, held on. "Hey, hey, hey. What's going on here?"

He laughed, though the need to have his skin on hers still clawed at him. "You're not that naive, are you?"

Her fingers tightened. "I was a cynic by six."

"Then you've figured out that I think you have a pretty awesome body yourself." What the hell, he'd taken it this far, hadn't he? "You've got to realize now that the attraction isn't one-sided, Angel."

He heard the quick catch of her breath. "Then I think we have a problem."

"I don't see why." He was done with worrying, for the moment. All he wanted right now was a little contact: her wet, satiny skin against his palms, her wet, satiny lips on his. Just a kiss. "You have self-control, don't you?"

"Of course I have self-control," she snapped. "I can't speak for you, though."

"Oh baby, I have very good reasons not to let this go too far."

"Mine are better." She dropped his hand and in the same movement slid out of reach. "It's against my journalistic ethics to get involved with the subject of a story."

"You're doing a story on Stephen Whitney." He stood and stepped toward her, the surface of the water lapping at his chest. "Not me."

She put up her hand to halt his progress. "Stephen Whitney *and* you. Two stories. Now that I know who you are, I want to also write about C. J. Jones."

It was the name that finally knocked some sense in him. That and the determined expression on Angel's face.

Lust cooled. Desire expired. Regret and that sense of doom that he was trying to become accustomed to rushed into the void.

"You *can't* do a story on C. J. Jones," he said grimly, for the first time moving into the dim light.

"Oh, c'mon," she replied. That coaxing tone of hers, paired with her youthful, innocent appearance, was probably lethal to the usual man, woman, and liar. "C. J. Jones is news. . . ."

Her gaze dropped from his face to his chest. *Ah, she sees it now,* he thought. The nine-inch scar bisecting his rib cage was darkly purple and fresh-looking. Her eyes widened and her mouth fell open.

Her visible shock sent him vaulting from the tub, no longer concerned about his nakedness. She'd seen the worst of him already. Without another word, he located his towel, wrapped it around his hips, then walked toward the gate. Finally glancing back, he caught her still looking at him, her expression still stunned.

"You see, Angel, you can't do a story on him because . . ." Cooper hesitated, then decided there was no point in trying to make it pretty. "Because C. J. Jones died."

Chapter 6

The next morning, Cooper was standing at the breakfast buffet in the communal dining room when something blond and wild burst through the door. The retreatants in the room gasped, their collective breaths loud in the usual silence. The two-legged wild thing came toward Cooper at a slow stalk, the soles of her shock-green boots making heavy thuds against the terra-cotta floor tiles. He cautiously set his bowl of oatmeal aside, then braced himself as he watched her determined approach.

Obviously, Angel—the wild thing—had gotten over her surprise of the night before. He'd known she would, and also known that then she'd come after him for answers. What he didn't know was if she'd accept coronary bypass surgery as an excuse for the way he'd dumped the information on her. And for the way he'd been reacting toward her too—cold one minute and hot the next.

She came to a lurching halt mere inches from his chest, her baby-blue eyes hidden under an untamed tangle of hair that was standing out around her head. He could feel the heat gathering on her tongue.

When her mouth opened, he clamped a hand over it.

"Mm!" Although muffled, her protest was clearly outraged.

With his free hand, he pointed to the nearby sign requesting silence. Though she followed his gesture, he could sense the words still boiling up inside of her. And he was certain this little teakettle had one hell of a whistle.

To save all their hearing, he made a hasty grab for one of the pads and pens that lay scattered about the room. He thrust them into her hands just as they appeared to be reaching for his throat.

Angel snatched the writing implements and he thought better of leaving his palm over her mouth. In this mood, her bark was probably less painful than her bite.

Though his hand was no longer clapped against her lips, she didn't speak, just moved her hand deliberately across the page. Cooper waited, prepared for her to take a layer off his skin. He'd mismanaged things with her, he had to admit it. Sex had been absent from his priority list for so long that he'd been knocked off his feet by its unexpected reappearance.

Riiiip. The bad-tempered sound of paper being torn from the pad made him wince. She shoved the sheet into his hand and, bracing himself again, he gingerly turned it over.

The handwriting was passionate and so were the words:

My hairdryer! I'm begging you!

Astonished, he looked at the paper another minute, and then at Angel. She shook back the mess of curls and he could see her eyes now. They weren't angry, but they weren't quite alert either.

She scribbled again.

Begging you!

At the near desperation on her face, he was forced to swallow his laugh.

What had he been so afraid of? He'd spent the night awake in bed, his ear plastered to the pillow, reassuring himself with his heartbeat and reciting all the reasons why he should keep clear of Angel. He'd vowed again to get her off the story and away from him.

But looking at her now, rumple-headed, heavy-eyed, and on Day Two of serious caffeine withdrawal, he thought she looked . . . manageable.

And hell, why not admit it? He thought she looked adorable too.

Turning away, he grabbed a mug and filled it with hot water from the nearby carafe. Then he took her hand and started towing her out of the building. She stumbled along behind him, admirably keeping her mouth shut until the dining room door slapped closed behind them.

"My hairdryer?" she asked, voice full of hope.

"Shh!" From the corner of his eye he could see one of the regular visitors coming their way, her hand-carved walking stick poking into the dirt with each step. Mrs. Withers would whack them both with it if they dared to disturb the quiet.

As the old lady passed, they exchanged nods, and then he rushed Angel around the corner of the next cottage and toward his own. "No hairdryer," he said to her under his breath. "But coffee. I can get you coffee."

Her fingers tightened on his. "Coffee," she repeated, in the same tone he'd heard the Benedictine brothers up the hill use during prayer. "Real coffee."

He didn't go so far as to commit to that. But at least it kept her quiet until he got her inside his cottage. A quick rummage in a cupboard produced a tiny bottle of crystals that had hardened into instant-coffee clay. He managed to scrape off enough with a spoon to color the hot water in the mug a muddy brown.

"Here." He passed it to her.

Holding a clump of curls off her face with one hand, she brought the mug to her lips. Drained it. Then she blinked a couple of times, looking around her as if coming awake from a long sleep. "What day is this?"

His lips twitched. "Tuesday." Oh yes, she was manageable, all right. And still damn adorable, with her baby blues now clearing and that hair of hers waving about as if half-electrified. If somebody was going to do a story on Stephen—and under the circumstances

Cooper could only welcome good publicity—Angel might very well be the best for the job.

"Tuesday?" she echoed.

Nodding, he reached for the mug. "Let me take that from you." Then he shooed her toward the loveseat and easy chair that were angled beside the window in the front room. A plan was forming in his mind, one that would keep all the cards in his hand.

She obeyed, the overstuffed, denim-covered chair nearly swallowing her up. "Tuesday, you said. That makes last night—" she broke off, narrowing her gaze at him.

Yep, she was waking up, all right.

"*Last night,*" she repeated.

The ominous way she said the words made him guess she was remembering the night before and how he'd tried to let her think the sexual pull was on her side only. How he'd let her apologize for it.

He dropped onto the sofa. "I was wondering when you'd get to that."

She was still staring at him, narrow-eyed. "I . . . you . . ." She sputtered, her hand lifting. "You . . . me . . ." The hand dropped.

"Yeah." Whatever he was admitting to seemed to satisfy her, because he waited a moment and she said nothing more. Hoping they'd left that topic behind for good, he continued talking. "I'd like to talk to you about something else."

He paused, giving her a chance to light into him if she must. But when she merely lifted her eyebrows, he finished his thought. "I have a proposition for you."

Her eyebrows rose even higher, and then she settled

back onto the cushions and crossed her arms over her chest. "A proposition?" she repeated, her voice oh-too-cool. "What kind of proposition?"

"So suspicious."

"So wise," she retorted.

He shrugged. "Whatever. Here's what I'm offering. The cooperation of our family and friends, complete cooperation, on your story about Stephen."

"I already have that. Your sister—"

"Will change her mind if I ask her to. You can figure out why she'd be interesting in keeping me happy."

"Hmm." Angel crossed her jeans-clad legs at the ankle and pursed her lips, obviously considering all the angles.

Cooper knew the plan was perfect. With the hairdryer and caffeine as last-ditch leverage, keeping her on the story would be a safer bet than some unknown reporter. They could end up with a writer bent on a hatchet job, instead of one who admitted to usually writing pieces on philanthropists and little-known sports.

Oh yeah. The Angel he knew was preferable to some devil he didn't.

She was still eyeing him suspiciously, though. "And in return for all this cooperation, what, exactly, do I give up?"

Smart woman. It had taken her less than ten seconds to smell a catch. "In return," Cooper said, "you *offer* up your promise not to write about C. J. Jones."

She offered up nothing right away. A moment passed, then her gaze dropped from his face to her lap. "You said he died."

"Thanks to the miracle of modern science," he replied lightly, "they managed to bring me back to life. Twice."

Her lashes rose and he was looking into that heavenly blue of her eyes again. "There's more to it than that," she said.

"Sure. You've seen the scar." He stretched his legs out in front of him, pretending a casualness he'd never feel about it. "I had an acute myocardial infarction."

"Heart attack."

"Right." Though *attack* didn't come close to describing the long minutes when pain rolled over his chest like a two-ton Ford Ranger and more agony had sliced like a butcher's knife along his left arm. He ran his hand over his face, remembering how the sweat had poured off of it. "And then I had coronary bypass surgery."

"You said they saved you twice."

"I don't remember the second heart attack. I was on the operating table."

"And since then . . . ?"

"Since then," he replied, "I've recovered, stopped smoking, learned to eat differently, exercised a lot, managed my stress." And waited to die.

"But Cooper, it would make a great story . . ." she began, but the wheedle in her voice was halfhearted and she left off altogether when he started shaking his head.

"You get Stephen," Cooper said. "Or you get me."

She rose to pace back and forth in front of the window. "I don't like it," she muttered to herself. "I just don't like it."

He stood too, and on her next pass grabbed her hand to halt her. "I prefer to keep my health issues private."

Her chin edged higher, her cheeks going pink. "You make me sound like a gossip."

He just looked at her.

She whipped her hand from his. "What if I called *you* an ambulance chaser?"

He shrugged. "I don't apologize for seeking justice."

"And I don't apologize for seeking truth!"

He had to smile at her passion. "So we're a matching pair of idealists." But then he sobered. "Seriously, though, Angel, who really needs to know about my heart attacks and surgery?"

Her gaze slid away.

"Who?" he insisted.

"Nobody," she finally admitted. "Not when you put it like that. But my slant would be C. J. Jones and his most important, albeit out-of-courtroom, battle."

"*No.*" God, no. Because both C. J. Jones and Cooper liked to win, and he planned on going out a winner, at least in the eyes of the public.

She studied his face. "All right," she finally agreed. "On one condition."

He set his jaw. "The hairdryer's still out. And I can't promise the coffee'll get any better either."

She shook her head and he watched with wonder as her hair lifted a couple of inches and stayed there, suspended in midair. "It's not that. I want you to reconsider the story once you come back to San Francisco."

"Huh?" He blinked away his distraction and refocused on her face. "What?"

"When you go back to work at your firm, at DiGiovanni & Jones, I want you to reconsider letting me interview you."

"When I go back to work. At the firm."

She nodded. "Just think about it, okay? A story like yours could inspire people, you know."

He wanted to laugh again. "Man smoking and working himself into an early heart attack? What's inspiring about that? We could add that since my father suffered the same fate I should have known better."

She ignored his protest. "Tell me you'll consider it."

He sighed. But then, since he would never practice at DiGiovanni & Jones again, he decided it was simplest to agree. "Fine."

After a moment more's hesitation, she shoved out her hand. "Then you've got yourself a deal."

Her fingers were warm and small in his. He held them a second. Two. Too long. Because then it happened again, that undeniable yearning to touch her further. Touch her more. Hungry for the long-lost pleasure of female skin, he found himself succumbing to it, his thumb smoothing over her knuckles.

So smooth, soft. His muscles tensed, his blood went predictably thick, and his free hand found its way to her cheek.

The skin warmed beneath his palm. Then his thumb moved of its own volition too, brushing across her lower lip.

Her breath rushed over it. Hot, quick, nervous.

He'd forgotten that about women. The first time an encounter turned from flirtatious suggestion to blatantly sexual there was always that brief hitch, that vulnerable moment when they revealed their lingering doubts, and yet didn't move away. It used to make him wary, he remembered, as if he were taking advantage somehow. As if a woman's trust put too much expectation on him and what they might be to each other.

But Angel's stillness, *her* final decision to trust, made him feel surprisingly smug. He smiled to himself and drew his thumb over her mouth again. Then he froze, recognizing his own gesture as a possessive one.

Possessive. *Jesus.*

He had no business wanting to hold on to anything. Any woman. Her.

Lifting his hands, he stepped back.

They stared at each other.

"Well," she said after a minute.

"Well," he echoed.

"I suppose there's that attraction thing again."

The offhand way she mentioned it worked like a charm to relax him. He found himself smiling, because he was beginning to enjoy her I'm-no-good-at-coy directness. "Yeah."

She nodded slowly. "And though you tried to make me believe otherwise, you say it does go both ways?"

"Obviously." He was still smiling. See? He'd been right. The lust was controllable. *She* was controllable.

She nodded again. But then she stilled and her eyes went wide. "Hey! Wait a minute! It occurs to me that since we've just agreed you're no longer the subject of a story . . ."

He felt his smile fall from his face.

". . . there isn't a reason in the world we can't pursue that attraction now, is there?"

His perfect plan wasn't so perfect after all.

* * *

Men!

Angel damned the entire gender, even as she delighted in the look of dismay on Cooper's face. That's what he got for playing games . . . with the truth, and with her.

Like any man, he probably avoided revealing his health issues whenever he could, as long as he could. Males invested so much ego in their image. To greater and lesser degrees, they'd do anything to keep their armor untarnished.

Her mother's first husband, he with the especially shiny armor of the Homicide Division, Oakland PD, had been of the former degree. Angel and her mother had spent years running from him—and from what he'd threatened he'd do if they ever told anyone that he battered her mother.

Angel shook herself free of the memories and focused on the man before her. Cooper wasn't Captain Brendan Colley. But still, she didn't appreciate the casual—no, almost cruel—manner in which he'd told her about his illness the night before.

"He died" was the way Cooper had put it, and her stomach had shrunk to a cold, leaden ball. She couldn't let him get away with playing games with her like that.

Tucking her hair behind her ears, she took a cocky step forward. "So what do you say, Cooper? Should we see where this little . . . pull takes us?"

He shoved his hands in his pockets. "I, uh . . ."

She didn't feel an ounce of guilt over his discomfort. Nuh-uh. Because she'd felt uncomfortable herself, foolish even, when she'd admitted her interest in him. When she'd *apologized*!

Curse him for that. And herself too, while she was at it. She knew better than to give a man the upper hand.

Determined to take it for herself, she moved closer to Cooper and with her forefinger lightly touched a button on the soft cotton shirt he was wearing. "What do you say?"

He stared down at her finger as if it might sting if he breathed. "I say this isn't a good idea."

"Oh come on. I won't bite." Now tracing a little circle around the button, she smiled up at him with what she hoped was the right combination of insistence and flirtation. She respected his resistance, was glad of it, but she didn't mind giving him a taste of the same kind of foolish feelings that he'd served up to her. "At least not right away."

His expression lost some of its alarm. Oh, maybe she *wasn't* doing this right! Between work and wariness, her physical relationships with men had been few and far between. The truth was, about three years ago she'd decided the tepid night befores weren't worth the awkward mornings after.

If you didn't put your heart into sex—and she never intended to—then what was the point?

Cooper placed his hand over hers, flattening her palm to his chest. "What maneuver is this, Angel?"

"No maneuver," she retorted, trying not to take notice of the heat of his body coming through his shirt. Trying not to be distracted by the heat, by his body. This moment was supposed to be her payback, her way of regaining control, not the time to succumb to more rash and irrelevant lust.

With her other hand, she reached up to toy with the

ends of his shaggy hair. "But it could be fun, though. Wouldn't it be fun?"

His gaze narrowed. His fingers folded over hers.

She tried to suck in some air, but her lungs seemed already overfull. *Breathe out, Angel, breathe out.* "We could—" She cleared her throat, trying to make her voice stronger, more confident. Bravado had always worked when she was a little girl, scared and lonely. "We could start with a kiss."

Beneath her hand, she felt the quick jolt of his heart. "No—"

"Unless you're afraid."

Be afraid, Cooper! She willed it, willed him to back away and admit that she'd won. That he shouldn't ever underestimate her again.

"'Afraid'?" His voice roughened. "Of you? How could I possibly be afraid of a woman who looks like I should put a hook through her hair and hang her from a Christmas tree?"

Then his free hand clapped against the small of her back to jam her against the front of his body. His mouth fell against hers.

Angel's mind slid from "tree" to torch to fire. Oh wow. *She* was on fire. But she opened her lips to its source and let him try to cool her with the stroke of his tongue. More heat sprinted down her body as he thrust it inside. Her fingers speared through his hair to keep his head bent to hers.

He curved his forearm around her waist to haul her up on her toes and even closer against him. His body was Grade A, she'd seen that, but now she felt it, hard to her soft, protrusion to her intrusion. She wiggled against the firm plane of his chest and felt his groan through her hand that still covered his heart.

She slid her hand out from between them and used it to touch him everywhere she could reach, racing it across his shoulders, his biceps, the granite wall of his back. He was all lean muscle and hot skin, and she couldn't get enough of it.

His mouth moved across her face and she turned hers against his neck, running her tongue over the faint stubble and the tangy taste of man. Everything inside of her was liquid, it was only Cooper who was holding her up, and when his lips found hers again she leaned into him, to absorb more of the flavor and feel of his body.

It's a delicious weakness, she realized, widening her mouth to take the heavy thrust of his tongue. *And only he can save me from it.*

The thought, the fear of it being true pierced the hot haze. Locking her knees, she shoved against Cooper. Then, standing alone, standing straight, she took a step away.

They stared at each other, and she was gratified that at least he was panting like she was.

"What the hell was that?" he demanded, raking his hand through his hair. "What the hell was that?"

Her revenge, her payback, her countermove, her way of keeping things cool between them. God, he would laugh her out of the room if she tried those out now. Angel scrubbed her hands over her face to hide how they trembled.

"My mistake," she finally said. Though it chagrined her to admit it, she'd underestimated *him*. Without thinking, she touched her fingertips to her mouth, and finding it still burning, jerked them away.

He was still staring at her.

"I . . . I'm sorry." She rushed toward the door, opened it, was almost all the way through before he spoke.

"Me too, Angel," he called to her. "Me too."

It took Angel several hours to recover her equilibrium. But in the early evening, she ventured into the woods surrounding the retreat, eyeing the untamed environment with a new interest. Her last meal had been two bites of an unappetizing tofu-and-sprouts sandwich, so her grumbling stomach had her wondering just exactly what parts of the forest *were* edible.

She splashed through a trickle of stream, disturbing a frog. It hopped off a few feet, to the camouflage of a feathery fern, and watched her with a nervous air. *Like chicken,* Angel remembered, assessing the plump little creature. She'd eaten frog legs on occasion during the six months she and her mother had lived in Paris.

Her foot took a stealthy step forward.

Good Lord! She jerked her boot back and her mind away from the tantalizing memory of meat in a delicate white wine sauce and a fluffy side serving of garlic mashed potatoes swimming in butter. "You're safe from me, little buddy," she reassured the frog.

At least for now.

"It's this place," she muttered to herself. It brought out the weirdest impulses in her. She hadn't wanted a man in ages, and she'd never before wanted to capture her own meal either.

At the moment, she wasn't sure which worried her more.

She tramped onward, following the sound and smell of the sea. A few minutes at the spot Katie had showed her yesterday might clear her head.

But she missed the route they'd taken and was forced to backtrack. By the time she reached the edge of the trees, the sun was hovering just above the horizon and the spot was already occupied.

Cooper and Katie sat silently side by side, their backs to Angel. For a moment she didn't move, because it was such a pretty image with that backdrop of setting sun. The man's hair fluttering back in the wind, his shoulder brushing the young girl's. Katie's knees were bent, her arms wrapped around them. She stared out at the sky.

The sun slipped another notch and the breeze died. In the well of quiet it left, Angel heard the girl's voice. "Mom wants me to go back to school tomorrow."

Cooper didn't move. "Are you ready?"

She shrugged, one of those teenage gestures that conveyed nothing at all.

They were silent again, and even the sea went quiet enough that Angel didn't think she could creep off without detection. So she stood where she was, surrounded by the smell of pines and salty air.

Cooper raked a hand through his hair, revealing his frustration. She could feel his question in the air, her own mother had said it to her a thousand times. *Are you all right?* he'd ask any moment now.

And Katie would answer as only such a question could be answered, the only answer the questioner wanted to hear.

Instead of crying, yelling, railing against fate and fathers and fear, the girl would say the same words Angel had answered a thousand and one times herself. *I'm fine.*

Cooper's hand speared through his hair again. "It sucks, Katie. This sucks."

Both Angel and Katie jolted. The girl took a quick breath, but didn't give her uncle a glance. "No, no. I'm fine," she said quickly. "Just fine."

The words, the way they were said with so little emotion or inflection, poked at Angel like a dulled pin.

Cooper reached over to rest his hand on the crown of his niece's head. "I've been fine before, sweetheart," he told her. "Just that same kind of fine. And it sucks too."

Angel's throat squeezed at the bittersweet feeling in the words. Then it squeezed again when Cooper's hand fell to Katie's shoulder and drew her closer against his side.

The girl didn't protest, but she didn't snuggle either, and that stiffness pricked at Angel again. She remembered Cooper with his arm around the girl and her mother at the memorial service and it had almost hurt then too, that sign of a man's support. But now the pain she felt was for Katie, that the teen couldn't, wouldn't let herself be comforted by him.

Little girls needed someone to stand between them and the big, bad world.

She didn't hear Cooper's sigh, but she saw the way his shoulders moved slowly up, then down. "It's a pretty good sunset, though, eh?" He reached up to fluff Katie's hair. "Some days that's all we have, so we might as well enjoy it."

Angel's throat tightened again and the wind whipped up so that it stung her eyes, even in her sheltered hide-away. A clear signal for her to get a move on, she repri-manded herself. She'd been stalling, just as she'd been doing since her arrival at Tranquility House.

As silently as she could, she headed back for her cot-tage. As soon as she got there, she'd develop a list of questions for her first interview with Katie's mother. Though she'd pretended to herself for two days that she'd been soaking up atmosphere, she'd really been putting off interviewing the new widow. But the only thing that stalling had bought her was trouble with Cooper and this uncomfortable empathy for Katie.

So Angel steeled her spine. If Katie's mother thought Katie was ready to go back to school, then Katie's mother was probably ready to talk about Stephen Whitney. She'd agreed, after all. She *wanted* Angel to do the story.

The truth would set them all free.

So, yes, it was time to put scruples, sex, and sisters aside. Especially since, so far, they'd only brought her trouble. WWWD?

What Would Woodward Do? He'd get on with the story and then get out of here.

Chapter 7

For her meeting with Stephen Whitney's widow, her first actual interview relating to the story, Angel dressed carefully. The September sun was searing hot again, so she selected a filmy, flowered dress. Her mother would have called it a "lady dress" and Angel thought a lady-like image would work well for her today.

The night before she'd written a thorough list of questions, and then added several more this morning. Though her goal was to make the interview an extensive one, she'd try to let the other woman feel as if she were leading the conversation. People always revealed more when the questioning didn't feel like an interrogation.

Her hair was an untamable mess, but short of begging the widow for twenty minutes with a hairdryer and an electrical outlet, she was going to have to live with it. Sighing, she slipped on a thin, bead-and-wire headband to keep it out of her eyes.

And last, for luck, for remembrance, and mostly because she was going nuts in the prevailing silence of the retreat, she latched her gold charm bracelet on her left wrist. The links bore a keepsake from each of the cities she'd lived in while on the run. Though they'd always been low on money, her mother had insisted on buying the charms. Angel suspected her mother had hoped it would make their secret life seem more like an exciting adventure than a life-and-death necessity.

It was the thought that counted.

She strolled toward the common building, in search of directions to the Whitney house. She hadn't been face-to-face with Cooper since their kiss the day before, so she was just as happy to find Judd presiding over the breakfast buffet. And then even happier when he offered—via paper and pen—to not only show her the shortcut through the woods, but go with her himself.

In less than half an hour, they found Lainey Whitney behind her house, on the flagstoned surface surrounding the pool. In a sundress, large hat, and gardening gloves, she was plucking withered pink blooms from a flourishing geranium. With a farewell wave, Judd disappeared.

"He visits my sister at this same time every day," Lainey explained.

Angel was still trying to grasp what she'd learned about the man on the way over. "He doesn't talk," she said, looking again at the scrap of paper he'd pressed into her hand. "Not just at Tranquility, he doesn't talk anywhere."

With the back of her wrist, Lainey pushed up the sagging brim of her sunhat. "He came to the retreat five years ago for a couple of weeks. He's never left, or spoken, since."

Shaking her head, Angel shoved the note into the satchel she carried. "Weird."

"Maybe only because you don't know his reasons why."

Reasons why. The innocent comment snapped Angel's focus back to her purpose. She was here to find out another man's reasons why. "You're right, of course. And I'm sorry, Mrs. Whitney, for barging in on you like this. But since I don't have access to a phone, I couldn't determine if you had time to talk to me any other way."

"Time?" The other woman let out a strained laugh, even as her eyes went wet. "I wonder what I'm going to do with all the time I have."

Tears, Angel thought, her stomach clutching and her grip tightening on her satchel. Why hadn't she thought to bring Kleenex? "I'm, uh, I'm so sorry for your loss."

"Lainey, you don't have to talk today if you don't feel up to it," a voice called from behind Angel.

Cooper's voice. Annoyed with his interference, she turned.

And forgot why she was irritated with him. He had gloves on too, leather ones, their saddle-tan the color of his bare chest. His scar drew her attention, of course, but not any more than his wide shoulders and the heavy bands of muscle that rippled toward the low-slung cutoffs he was wearing. She'd termed his body Grade A before, but now she knew it was just plain great. So great, in fact, she had a sudden urge to run her tongue along—

Shocked by the foreign craving, Angel stumbled back.

"Watch out!" Cooper started for her.

Which only caused Angel to retreat another step. But her sandaled foot only found air—the air over the surface of the pool—and she knew she was tipping. Then Cooper clamped on to her wrist and hauled her away from the edge.

She yanked her arm out of his grasp, stroking the place he'd touched. "Ouch."

He rolled his eyes. "Most women would thank me for saving them . . . again."

Determined to keep herself from further danger, she turned her back on him to address his sister. "But truly, he's right. If this isn't a good time . . ."

There was a different gleam in Lainey Whitney's eyes now. "How about you? You look a little . . . flushed."

"She needs coffee," Cooper put in, striding past them to retrieve a pair of long-bladed hedge clippers.

Lainey frowned. "It's too hot for—"

"Coffee," Cooper asserted again, attacking a nearby bush. "You won't believe what it awakens in her."

Angel shot him a dirty look even as she felt her face going redder. "Coffee would be great, if it wouldn't be too much trouble, of course." She refused to enjoy the play of muscles along Cooper's back. "Maybe in the kitchen?"

To her relief, the widow went along with the plan. Within seconds Angel was away from Cooper's distracting presence and sitting at a long pine table in the expansive Whitney kitchen. Painted in a wash of pearly pastels, the walls and the country-style cabinets glowed in the morning light.

Certain that by now they'd passed the greeting and casual conversation stages, she tossed out a polite compliment to finalize the interview warm-up. "It's a lovely room, Mrs. Whitney."

If you liked Easter eggs and Italian sugared almonds.

"Please, call me Lainey." The other woman moved between the pantry and countertop with practiced ease. "I love this room too. After *An Invitation Home*, of course."

"Huh?"

"That's the first of Stephen's paintings that gained him national exposure. I'm sure you must have seen it. . . ." She crossed quickly to a towering bookcase, then crossed back to slide a hardbound coffee-table book in Angel's direction. "Here. It's on the cover."

It was a book on Stephen Whitney's work. The glossy image on the cover was a kitchen, like this one painted with colors usually exclusive to the Easter Rabbit. No modern appliances in sight, but flowers spilled out of an old-fashioned milk bottle sitting on a gleaming countertop. A child's shoes were tumbled in a corner as if just tossed there by their owner. On a center table, old-fashioned canisters marked "Flour" and "Sugar" were opened, some of their contents dribbled onto the surface. Beside them was a bowl of dough with a wooden spoon stuck inside and a heavy platter filled with cookies.

The only things missing were Aunt Bea, Opie, and any sense of reality.

"Nice," Angel said, as her gaze snagged on the signature of the artist. It read "Stephen Whitney," all right, the *W* larger than the rest of the letters and sort of scallop-edged. Bothered by it somehow, she looked away. "Very, um, nice."

"Can't you just see it?" Lainey asked, pausing to admire the image herself. "Whoever received the invitation home has just rung the bell and the family has rushed out of the kitchen to greet the arrival."

"Sure." It was hard to argue with a woman wearing that sentimental half-smile. Still, it was time to get their little show on the road. "Lainey, would you mind if I record our conversation?"

The other woman agreed, but there was a hesitation to it, so Angel decided against immediately retrieving the small recorder from her satchel. Instead, she tapped the book cover with her fingernail. "Is this your favorite of your late—of Mr. Whitney's—paintings? *An Invitation Home*?"

"Oh, that's hard to say." Lainey slid a sugar and creamer onto the table. "By the way, where's your home, Angel?"

She blinked. "My home? I live in San Francisco. I have an apartment on Sacramento Street in Pacific Heights."

"Do you enjoy living in the city?" Spoon, saucer, and cup clacked onto the tabletop.

Angel leaned back in her chair. "Yes. I've lived in cities, some bigger, some smaller, all my life." In a city, a woman and child could blend in. Be anonymous. Be forgotten. She fingered a charm on her bracelet, the St. Louis arch, sandwiched between the Eiffel Tower and Big Ben.

Lainey scraped out the chair across the table. "You never lived in a small town?"

Angel lifted the cup the other woman had placed before her, sipped. "Well, one summer we lived in a tiny village in northern Germany. I was horribly bored. Though there was a VCR and a large video collection, I didn't know a word of German. My mom finally managed to find the only English language video in the area. It was *All the President's Men* and I must have watched it a zillion times."

"Ah-ha! And a reporter was born."

Angel nodded, then caught herself. Wait, wait, wait! She was supposed to be interviewing Lainey, not the other way around. Taking another bolstering sip of her coffee, she tried thinking of a way to segue to Stephen Whitney. Her gaze drifted out the window, and then her focus drifted too, because Cooper, biceps bulging, was trundling by with a wheelbarrow of trimmings. Maybe she sighed.

"He's a good-looking man," Lainey said softly.

"Oh yeah," Angel said, watching him pass. Her gaze traced the long line of his naked spine. The waistband of his shorts had slid below the curve at the small of his back and now rode on the high swell of his buttocks. Her lower body did that odd little *Cosmo* clench again. "Oh *yeah*."

Then, hearing herself, she started, flushed, stuttered. My God, she was going to have to get her thyroid checked or something! "I mean, uh, well—"

"I'm sure all reporters notice things like that," Lainey offered mildly.

Angel grabbed at the excuse. Hadn't she told herself something similar? "Right. That's it." Still feeling all goofy and girly, she lifted her coffee cup again.

"So, after watching that movie, you became a journalist to uncover political scandals?"

"Not really." Angel's attention snagged on the cup in her hand. It was decorated with Whitney renderings—who else would come up with the schmaltzy border of pastel-colored teapots?

"So what did you want to uncover?"

Angel jerked her gaze from the cutesy drawings to Lainey Whitney. The woman looked sincerely interested, not at all suspicious or alarmed.

"In general, it's the job of reporters, the entire Fourth Estate, to keep watch," Angel answered, hoping that a few points from her schoolkids' lecture would satisfy the other woman. "The media provides people with the information they need in order to make decisions about the world and their lives. It's information—the truth—that's the cornerstone of a free society."

"Told you she's a romantic." It was Cooper, behind her. Again.

Angel ground her back teeth together. *Romantic*. That's the last thing she was. The very last. But she ignored him and instead used the comment to redirect the conversation.

"And speaking of romance, Lainey"—because

Cooper was lurking, Angel slid her hand stealthily into her satchel, and after some fumbling around emerged with a pad and pencil—"why don't you tell me how you met your husband?"

Finally, the interview commenced. The next minutes went smoothly enough, even with Cooper's tall figure in the periphery of her vision. He'd pulled on a T-shirt—*thank you, God*—and lounged against the nearby countertop as if he had nothing better to do than watch over his sister.

Or watch Angel.

For half an hour Lainey seemed comfortable talking of the past. Stephen Whitney had arrived in the area twenty-three years before, just as the hippies were clearing out and a more mainstream colony of artists and New Age types were moving in. The old-timers, the descendants of the area's pioneers, were firmly entrenched, of course, including the Jones family. During her senior year in high school, Lainey had caught Stephen's attention and they'd fallen for each other.

"He said he'd never loved anyone before me," the artist's widow said, her eyes misting over.

Angel froze, and another piece of sage advice came to mind, not from a professor this time, but from her mother. *Don't ask a question unless you're prepared to hear the answer.*

But she *was* prepared, she told herself fiercely. She was a journalist, an objective professional who had never shirked either the hard questions or the unpleasant answers. "He, uh—" Cursing herself, she had to break off and clear her throat. "Stephen Whitney was older than you by several years, though. Surely another woman"—*a daughter, even*—"might have meant something to him."

Lainey shook her head. "Not anyone, he said. He was a romantic too, you see."

Or a cold, selfish SOB. But Angel couldn't let the thought show on her face, so she made an agreeable "Hmm" and moved on to her next line of inquiry, which was . . . was . . .

Only a single thought came to mind.

He'd never loved anyone before. Not anyone.

Ruffling the pages of her notebook, she searched for the list of questions she'd written the night before. But her fingers, crazy things, were suddenly so clumsy that she couldn't seem to find her place. "If you'll just bear with me a moment, um . . ."

From inside her satchel, Angel heard a tiny click. She stilled, then latched on to the sound as a signal to let herself off the hook for the day.

Trying to appear casual, she shoved back her chair. "You know, it's better if we do this a little at a time," she said.

It was a lie. If a subject was willing, it was best to keep the subject talking. But at the moment, Angel's journalistic powers were fraying around the edges. "May I come back again tomorrow?"

Lainey, thank goodness, seemed willing to allow Angel the reprieve. With fake smiles for both Jones siblings, she made a hasty escape.

Stewing over the morning's events, she took the path back to Tranquility at a headlong pace. Though she'd cut the interview short, it had been a success, wasn't that right? She'd wanted information and she'd gotten information.

It was patently clear Lainey didn't know her husband had lived with a woman before her. She certainly didn't know he had another daughter.

It shouldn't surprise Angel, it didn't, but to know for a fact that her father had never acknowledged her to his second family made her feel . . .

Not disappointed, no. Not sad! That burning ache in her chest was something else entirely.

Her footsteps ate up the path, distancing her from the place where Stephen Whitney had lived, worked, *loved*.

"Whoa, whoa, whoa." A hard hand clamped on her arm to halt her. "Not so fast, kid." Cooper swung her around to face him. "Don't think I don't know what you're up to."

Angry, Angel decided. That was exactly how she felt. *Angry*.

"Don't call me kid," she hissed, wrenching out of his grasp. "I'm not anybody's kid."

Cooper made another grab for Angel's arm and caught the strap of her leather briefcase instead. They played tug-of-war with it for a minute before he ended the game by using his superior strength to haul both bag and woman close.

Ignoring Angel's alluring city scent, he dug his hand inside the leather case and pulled out her mini tape recorder. "*Tsk, tsk,*" he said, smiling at her outraged expression. "Remember the rules."

Narrowing her eyes, she snatched at the recorder, but he held it out of reach. "Nothing that runs on batteries or electricity can be used at Tranquility," he reminded her.

"Your sister agreed," she said through her teeth. "And this is important."

"So's the letter of the law." He smiled at her again, even though she looked ready to breathe fire. She looked damn delicious too. She'd abandoned her camper-chic for the day—his retinas were grateful for a reprieve from those green boots of hers—and her dress seemed to float over her slender body. Buttons marched down one side, and he let his gaze linger on them, not as worried as he might have been about the brief, prurient fantasy he had about unfastening them one at a time.

With his teeth.

Though virtually unspoken outside of mutual apologies, he figured they'd buried the sexual issue for good yesterday. As wild as the pleasure could be, neither one of them wanted to burn like that again.

She made another swipe at the recorder. "Give it back."

He held it higher. "Not a chance."

She stretched for the little device again. "Don't you want the quotes to be accurate?"

That gave him pause. After a moment, he shrugged, then held the recorder out to her. "Fine, you can use it for your interviews."

She wrenched the machine from his hand. "Gee," she grumbled. "Thanks for understanding."

"Just don't play the tapes in your cottage. Old Mrs.

Withers can detect the use of contraband kilowatts from a hundred yards."

"As you command." She jammed the device into her briefcase.

For someone who'd just gotten her way, she wasn't very gracious about it. "I can't stand in the way of the story, I know that. After all, 'it's information—the truth—that's the cornerstone of a free society.'" He knew that would get her goat.

As predicted, she glared at him, her eyes blue-hot flames. "That's not a joke, though maybe it is to someone of your . . . your . . ."

He waited, expecting an attorney crack. "Occupation?"

"Gender." She flung her briefcase strap over her shoulder and stalked off.

Staring after her, he didn't move.

Gender? *Gender?*

As he watched her stomp off, he realized it said volumes about the long, unfilled hours of his day that one, two-syllable word could arouse such instant curiosity inside of him. Down deep, Angel was obviously simmering, and the object of her ire was the XY half of the world.

But what had triggered the eruption? His mind ran through the men she might have encountered at Tranquility or its vicinity besides himself and Judd. Had someone bothered her? Made a pass—or . . . ?

The back of his neck heated—a sure sign of his stress level starting to rise—and he took off after her. Reason told him there was no one at Tranquility to worry her—and that she could take care of herself if someone did—

but something about that stormy look on her face didn't sit well with him.

He didn't catch up to her until she stepped onto the lawn beside the common building. "Angel—"

"Shh!" Her finger stabbed the air in the direction of a "No Talking" sign.

Rolling his eyes, he tried again. "Angel—" But he caught himself this time, because Mrs. Withers and her walking stick were exiting her nearby cottage.

Duty bound him to take a minute to smile at the elderly lady and help her down the porch steps. She'd spent a month at the retreat every year since before he was born, but he suspected this visit would be her last. The arthritis that gnarled the hand he held would soon make it impossible for her to get around on her own.

On impulse, he leaned down to kiss her thin, powder-scented cheek. He'd miss her and he knew she'd miss her independence. What if you could choose between years of life and quality of living? Would you willingly shave some off as payment for good health?

He shook the moot question out of his head as Mrs. Withers went on her way. And, looking around, realized Angel was gone.

But his concern for her was not. He didn't want to examine that either, so he strode to her cottage instead. It was just his tenacious personality reasserting itself—the "Trial Dog" in him—he told himself, that could never let things go.

When he rapped on her door, she opened it quickly enough, but just as quickly exited the minute she saw it was him.

"Wait—"

She shut him up with a finger across his lips, then she pointed to her watch. Both hands were straight up. Lunchtime.

Grinding his teeth, he followed her to the dining room, where many of the other retreatants were already gathered. He followed again as Angel moved through the buffet of vegetable soup, organic greens, and crusty, eleven-grain rolls. Then he took the spot beside her at one of the long tables and watched her pick morosely at one of the sprouted seeds in her bread with a perfectly manicured nail.

The manicure said city to him again, city woman. In his mind's eye he saw, with a strange longing, a feminine forefinger on an elevator button, playing swizzle stick in a martini glass, pointing out an error on a motion to suppress. He heard city noises in his head too, the hum and clatter of traffic that had operated like white noise in his offices on Montgomery Street and the courtroom sounds that had been the pulse of his previous life: the nearly mute click of the court reporter's keys, the clack of the judge's gavel, the collective hiss of indrawn breath the instant before a verdict was read.

It took the very real thump of Angel's glass of water against the tabletop to bring him back to the present. Even forgoing the bitter iced yarrow tea hadn't cheered her up. With her still-troubled expression nagging at him, he reached for the nearest pen and some sheets of the scratch paper lying on the table.

Then he wrote *What's the matter?* and passed it to her.

She quickly scanned the note and, with barely a glance at him, shook her head.

He used another piece of paper. *It's not nothing.*

She shook her head again.

Talk to me, he wrote on the last sheet of paper.

She crumpled it up unread.

His frown had no effect on her. Frustration growing, he sat back and studied her. It was that fragile outward shell, he told himself. That was what was getting to him. In that flowered dress and with that candy-floss hair, she looked as if she bruised too easily.

But he was adept at reading people, he reminded himself. It was the most necessary yet undervalued aspect of being an attorney. People thought good lawyers needed sharp minds or aggressive personalities, but what they needed most was the ability to look past appearances and see what was underneath.

On the first day they'd met, he'd detected that beneath Angel's baby-soft skin was steel.

But now, damn it, underneath *that* he knew Angel was holding tight to some private misery. He sighed, annoyed at his sudden drive to change her mood. But hell, a man in his position would be smart to spread a little sunshine whenever, wherever he could, right?

Without a second examination of his motives, he picked up the pen again and went to work.

She sent him little sidelong glances, he could feel them, but he turned slightly away so she couldn't see what he was doing. Her charm bracelet jingled as she gathered up her dishes in preparation for leaving. He rushed to finish, just managing to complete the job as she rose.

He clamped his right hand on her thigh, pushing her back down. She made a tiny sound of distress, but he ignored it and swung a leg over to straddle the bench seat, facing her.

He slid a scrap of paper toward her: *Play the game and win a prize.* Then he presented her with his left fist, knuckles facing forward.

She read the piece of paper, then switched her gaze to what he'd written—upside down—on the back of his hand. *Press me,* was circled to imitate a button.

Her eyes flashed up to his, narrowing in assessment. *So cynical,* he thought, not for the first time. *What makes someone so young so wary?*

When still she hesitated, he pushed his fist practically under her nose. *Press me.*

After a last glance at his face she obeyed.

At her light touch, his fingers shot out.

She jumped. Then, frowning, studied the rest of his hand.

Backward again, he'd written a different number on every middle knuckle, upper knuckle, and fingernail. *Choose,* he mouthed when she looked up, indicating his middle knuckles.

Oh, he'd caught her now. Smiling to himself, he remembered distracting a cranky Katie in just such a manner a few years back. He watched Angel reluctantly indicate the number "7" on the knuckle of his forefinger.

In pantomime, he counted the number out, touching each of his fingers in turn to stop on his ring finger. *Choose,* he said again silently, wiggling his ring finger under her nose. There was "4" written on his upper knuckle, "3" written on his fingernail.

Her pretty manicured nail tapped his and again he

counted out the number, ending on his forefinger. Curling the rest of his fingers under, he flipped his hand to show the prize he'd written along the inside of his finger.

Congratulations! Your prize: access to our secret beach.

Then, crooking that finger, he signaled her to follow him from the dining room.

Oh, he was good, he thought smugly, as she obeyed without protest. He might not be up to practicing law anymore, but he was still damn good at reading people. Could any curious reporter ignore the word *secret*?

Once they were safely away from the common grounds, he wasn't surprised that Angel went into demand mode. "What's this all about?" she said, trailing him through the trees, graceful even in high heels. "What secret, what beach, why the game?"

"Shh." He turned to her, walking backward a few paces. "It's a *secret*, remember? Just because you're a journalist doesn't mean you have to give them away to everyone."

He spun forward before she could retort.

"I don't like this," she grumbled all the same. "I don't like this at all."

What he didn't like was the way something had tamped down the I-am-woman attitude that lent that tough-girl spine to her Tinkerbell looks. "Come on, babycakes," he said, knowing the endearment would piss her off. "Just follow studly Papa Bear through the dark tunnel up ahead. He'll keep you safe."

"Oh, Papa Bear," he heard her murmur behind him, "what a big ego you have."

"All the better to make you smile." But it was he who

was smiling when he grabbed her hand as they breached the entrance to the narrow thirty-foot tunnel his great-grandfather had blasted through a granite outcropping in the early 1920s. Legend had it that a man had died during the explosion, but the family didn't keep the path a secret for that reason. Because the small cove and even smaller beach it led to weren't safe on a year-round basis, it seemed prudent to keep it off-limits from visitors.

As they reached the tunnel's far exit, Cooper put his hands on Angel's shoulders and pushed her out, onto the sand.

He grinned when her feet lost their momentum as she caught her first sight of her fellow visitors to the cove. Though he hadn't been certain they'd be there, they hadn't failed him. Floating on their backs in the relatively calm waters, they lifted their heads and looked back at Angel, curious and friendly, cautious but unafraid.

"Sea otters," he whispered into her ear. "They say, welcome to their world."

She sank down to the damp sand, ignoring her pretty dress. The breeze blew its fluttering hem around her bare legs and whipped color into her cheeks and the tip of her nose. But her eyes were only for the otters, who after a few minutes went back to their usual behavior. At this time of day it was all about siesta, siesta, siesta, with an occasional vigorous scratch or sleek dive thrown in.

From personal experience, he knew it was impossible to be anything but charmed in the presence of the otters. One wet head popped up beside another drowsy basker, and at the lazy, playful cuff the second gave the first, he heard Angel softly laugh.

His own mood lightened too.

"My work here," he murmured to himself, "is done."

"What?" She tilted her head toward him, but didn't take her eyes off the otters.

"You feel better now." He let himself brush a hand over the tickly ends of her seemingly weightless hair.

A smile curved her mouth. "Gotta admit it's some prize. Thanks."

Then, frowning, she turned her head toward him. "Hey, what were the others? Prizes I mean?"

He ran his tongue over his front teeth, wondering how much to reveal. *Oh, what the hell,* he thought. Turning up the thumb of his left hand, he read what he'd written. " 'The latest editions of the L.A. and San Francisco newspapers.' "

She winced, then glanced over at the otters. "Never mind. I still came out ahead."

He held up his forefinger, with the prize she'd ended with. "Then the beach." His third finger came out and he hesitated.

"Go on," she prompted.

" 'A night in my bed.' "

"What?!"

He loved the outrage on her face. "Hey, I look real cute rolled over on my back too."

"Oh, please," she said, shaking her head. "Go on."

It was tough to break this one to her. " 'Beef jerky.' I know where I can get my hands on some home-smoked, home-dried slabs of honest-to-goodness beef jerky."

Her pupils dilated. "Beef. Beef jerky. You don't mean salty, chewy, bad-for-you beef jerky?"

"Yep." His lips twitched and he tried to remember the last time he'd felt this good. "You can get it in town at Pop's Tobacco Shop—though you have to tell Pop I sent you."

She nodded, then her lashes squeezed shut, as if bracing for more bad news. "All right. Go ahead, hit me with the last one."

"Ah. Well. That's when I ran out of ideas." He hesitated. "It's a repeat. 'A night in my bed,' again."

Her eyes popped open. "You stacked the deck!"

"With the best prize of all," he defended himself, straight-faced. "I'd think you'd be grateful."

Her jaw fell, but then she collected herself and whacked him on the shoulder with the flat of her hand. He'd been swatted by his sisters often enough to know she wasn't really mad.

And a sister seemed a fine way to consider her.

With one last censuring shake of her head at him, Angel returned to watching the otters and he returned to watching her. That's how he caught her smirking—a sort of suppressed-giggle smile.

"What are you thinking about?"

It was a full-on smirk now. "Nothing."

"Come on." He jabbed her ribs in a friendly, *brotherly* way.

Angel gave him one of her devil-woman looks from beneath the lashes at the corners of her eyes. "Oh, only that the joke's on you. If you'd kept your jerky source to yourself, I just might have spent that night in your bed to get the information."

Chapter 8

Judd had just settled into his chair at Beth's kitchen table when her sister Lainey walked through the back door, a cardboard box in her arms. Automatically rising, he took it from her and kissed her cheek in greeting.

"Good morning, Judd." Lainey patted his face in return. She was a tad shorter and a tad softer-looking than Beth. The family joke had always been that Beth got the elegance and Lainey got the artist. She turned to her twin, who was already reaching for a third coffee mug from the cupboard. "Morning to you too, Beth."

The corners of Beth's mouth lifted briefly. "Hey, Lainey. What's in the box?"

"Samples of the latest Whitney products from the licensing company." She took the proffered coffee and pulled out the chair beside Judd's. "I kept some of each and thought you might like the rest."

Beth turned her back and refilled her own coffee cup. "Sure. Thanks."

Judd couldn't help but notice the new, tense set to her shoulders. He'd been hyper-aware of her every breath, move, mood since that fateful morning when he'd reinstated their coffee routine the week before. He'd visited every morning since, seeking acceptance for these feelings he had for her, seeking the answer to what he should do about them.

First and foremost, he knew he didn't want to cause her any more hurt.

Lainey took a sip of her coffee. "I spent an hour with Angel Buchanan this morning. That's the fourth time we've talked," she said, then turned to Judd. "She said she interviewed you, as well. She still can't get over that you choose not to speak."

He shrugged his shoulders. They'd done well enough with paper and pen.

"Well, *I'm* not going to talk to her!" Beth abruptly exclaimed, whirling to face her sister. Then, looking away, she lowered her voice. "Questions, all those questions about Stephen."

Judd hadn't wanted to talk about the artist either. Stephen had always rubbed him wrong, no matter how hard he'd tried to pretend otherwise.

Lainey reached over to pat her sister's arm. "You don't have to talk to Angel. It's up to you." A little smile warmed her face. "But I like her, and Cooper does too. I think she likes him back."

Beth's mouth dropped. "Really?"

Judd rolled his eyes. You only had to see the two together to know that there was a whole lotta liking going on.

"She told me he showed her the beach access," Lainey said, nodding. "You know what *that* means."

As if stunned, Beth fumbled for a chair, pulled it from the table, sat. Lainey followed suit and they both took bolstering swallows of their coffee.

When the silence continued, Judd broke down. He grabbed up paper and pen. BEACH ACCESS? He knew of it himself, of course, but the significance of Cooper showing it to Angel escaped him.

Beth read the note, then looked over. "We used to tease him when we were teenagers about Cooper's Secret Love Cove. We were sure he was bringing his girlfriends there to, uh, uh . . ."

I GET IT, Judd wrote, stifling a grin.

"Well," she continued, "we told him we better agree on some sort of sign that would let us know if he was on the beach with a girl." She smiled, and it was the first real, really amused smile she'd worn since Stephen had died. "We had several suggestions, remember, Lainey?"

"Oh yeah," Lainey agreed. "Everything from cryptic chalk messages on the rocks at the entrance to the tunnel, to boxer shorts left like a signal flag on one of the pine trees."

Beth took up the story now, falling into a rhythm with her sister. "But Cooper didn't appreciate our teasing or our suggestions. As a matter of fact, he said it was his special, secret place, all right, but he wasn't going to share it with any woman outside the family."

It was Lainey who put in the last word. "Except, someday, the woman he was planning to marry!"

Apparently stunned all over again, the twins turned their heads to stare at each other. "Could it be?" they said together.

Judd had no idea, and, sympathetic to Cooper, wasn't going to speculate. But he didn't regret the speculation and the amusement on the sisters' faces. It reminded of earlier times, happy times, and it gave him hope that they could all recapture the warm, relaxed sense of friendship and family that had existed before Stephen died.

Though Lainey and Beth's worlds had revolved around the artist, the man himself had given the majority of his energy and attention to his art. He'd spent much of his time locked in his tower with his paints, leaving the rest of them to enjoy their corner of paradise without him.

The women sipped their coffee again, sighed, then Lainey looked expectantly at Beth. "Aren't you going to open the box? I'd like your opinion."

The cardboard container was in front of Judd, so when Beth turned her gaze on him, he was forced to stand and open it for her, scoffing at his sudden sense that there was trouble inside. He wasn't Pandora after all.

And the first item he pulled out was innocuous enough. It was a package of eight pencils, each painted a different pastel color and decorated with tiny book covers of fairy tales. He passed them to Beth.

"What do you think?" Lainey pressed.

Her sister shrugged. "I guess they're all right." She

handed the package back to Judd. "Why don't you keep these? You go through pens and pencils all the time."

Judd stuck them in the back pocket of his jeans without another glance. Oh yeah, he had a use for them. He was always in need of kindling for the woodstove in his cottage.

The next item that came out of the box was one of those fancy soaps that his ex-wife used to pile up in the guest bathroom. About as big as his palm, and white, it was molded into a strange shape that appeared kind of . . . feathery.

He handed it to Beth. Her puzzled expression cleared almost immediately. "Oh! It's a *W*, see?" She flipped it over, then held it up for Judd's inspection. "Stephen's *W*, the one he used when signing the paintings."

Now cradling it in her palm, she stroked the surface with her fingertips. Then she lifted it to her face and sniffed. "It doesn't smell like him, though."

Unable to help himself, Judd leaned across the table and snatched the soap from her. Beth flashed him a startled look, but he ignored it as he shoved the soap into the box. Then, with a quick, fury-induced snap of his hand, he let it fall to the bottom.

Broken in two.

The next product would have rendered him speechless, if he wasn't already. Trying his damn best to keep a poker face, he handed the shrink-wrapped roll of toilet paper across the table.

Beth blinked. The paper's background was white, then printed with Whitney drawings, all of them ocean images like shells, dolphins, and California gray whales.

With a wince, she looked over at her sister. "Don't you think this might be in poor taste?"

Gee, ya think? Judd never bit back laughter, but this time he swallowed what he knew would be a snicker.

Lainey sighed. "That's what I thought too. I hoped I was overreacting."

"I thought you had control of the products," Beth said.

"Yes, but Stephen had already agreed to this lot." Lainey sighed again. "And Cooper's telling me that with the last paintings gone and all our money invested in the licensing, I should agree to whatever is suggested. I imagine it can't get much worse, can it?"

Beth handed the TP back to Judd with a shudder. "I don't know. I couldn't have imagined *that*."

The twins' shoulders sagged. Judd barely kept his from doing the same. Finances were sticky at the moment, for both women. Beth had acted as Stephen's agent for the paintings, but with no more Whitneys, she had no more income. The income she *had* collected over the years—a very tidy amount, he knew—she'd thrown in with her sister and brother-in-law when they'd invested in the licensing deal.

He'd bitten his tongue at the time, wanting to scream out, *Diversify!* And now, damn it, he realized it was one of the few times that speaking would have been better than silence.

"You'll like the last one, though," Lainey assured her sister. "It's just the kind of thing that those who love Stephen's work will find irresistible."

Judd obediently rummaged in the box and pulled

out a tissue-wrapped parcel. He passed it to Beth and watched her slowly unwrap it. Then her breath caught.

"You're right," she whispered, pulling the item free of the paper. "It's wonderful."

It was a suncatcher, no bigger than Beth's slender palm. In glowing shades of stained glass, it was a graceful, fairyish figure in flight.

"There's a collection of them," Lainey said. "One for each month—that one's January. They're all the same blond sprite, but in a different pose and wearing different garments."

In a petallike dress of blues—from sapphire to almost turquoise—this one was poised on tiptoe. With her arms raised over her head and her hands together, fingers pointed, the figure appeared to have been captured midsoar.

Sometimes even Judd had to concede Whitney had talent.

Beth pushed out her chair and rose to her feet, then half-turned to hold the delicate piece toward the light coming through the window over the sink. "It reminds me of something," she said slowly, her voice almost as thin as the glass. "I don't quite know what."

"It reminds me of why I married Stephen." Lainey closed her eyes. "That's how he made me feel, from the first time we kissed. As if I could fly."

"Yes," her twin murmured. "Just like that."

At the dreamy tone, Judd's heart dropped like an anchor. He watched as Beth, obviously mesmerized by the sparkling fairy, drew closer to the window.

Lainey released a small, sentimental laugh, her eyes

still closed as if she were replaying memories in her mind. "We would meet at the cove, you know. I never told anyone, not even you, but when you and I were still in high school it became Stephen's and my special, private place."

Beth froze, her spine rigid, her expression set.

"He used to tease me, saying he was afraid he'd go to the beach someday and you'd be there instead of me. He was afraid he might mistake us for each other and kiss you, giving our romance away." She laughed softly, as if her husband kissing her sister were the silliest of ideas.

"But of course that was just a joke. He always knew which one of us was which, even when we used to dress alike. As an artist, he would never make that kind of mistake."

At that, Beth jerked, the glass fairy in her hand falling, then shattering against the porcelain sink.

Judd leaped to prevent her from picking up the glass with her bare hands, but she was just staring at the mess.

It looked like a rainbow of tiny teardrops.

"I broke it," Beth said hoarsely.

Unmoving, he watched her, though he wanted to comfort her. He wanted to say that the damage had already been done.

He also wanted to shove his fist through the wall. His world kept getting worse. Whether he burned those pencils, or busted that soap, or wiped his ass with Stephen's toilet paper, what Judd couldn't do was break Beth's ties to the artist.

He forced himself to breathe slowly in and out of his

nose, struggling to achieve the peace he'd come to the Sur to find. All his reading and all his hours of meditation had helped him learn to see and accept the true nature of things, hadn't they? But damn him, at the moment deep breathing and deep study weren't worth shit.

Accepting his feelings for Beth—that had seemed doable. But he'd never be able to accept what he had to face now.

Not when he knew there was no place, absolutely none, for him to go with what he felt for her.

Not when it was obvious that Beth was in love with her brother-in-law.

There was even a punch line to the cosmic joke. The situation meant that Judd didn't have to worry anymore about hurting her—*he* couldn't break Beth's heart.

Stephen had already done that.

In the vicinity of the tiny hamlet of Big Sur, at a local watering hole known as The Well, Angel stood in the narrow hallway leading to the restrooms, tethered to the pay phone by a silver snake cord. Waiting for her intern's voice-mail greeting to complete, she tapped her toe and peered around a doorway to the tiny, table-ringed dance floor and scarred bar beyond.

She'd placed an order for the Well Special, a half-pound hamburger with the works, and she wanted to be there the instant the juicy patty and crispy side of fries were served. The decent meal was her reward for ten days of sticking to the story and sticking to her objectivity too. Yes, indeed, tonight she was celebrating the triumph of her reporter's skills.

At the tone, Angel leaned her shoulder against the scratchy, resawn wood-paneled wall. "It's Angel. At the editorial meeting in the morning, please report to Jane that I'll wrap up my interviews in the next couple of days." She'd spent several hours speaking with Lainey Whitney, less time with Cooper and Judd, and then she'd gone farther afield to talk with the locals who'd been Stephen Whitney's longtime neighbors.

"I'd still like to have a conversation with the widow's twin sister," Angel said into the phone. "And Katie, Stephen Whitney's daughter. But tell Jane everything is going fine. Just fine."

Fine covered it, she thought, hanging up the receiver. It was fine that following her first interview with the widow, Angel had managed to recoup her journalistic detachment. It was fine that she'd breezed through the last ten days, working up a comprehensive profile of the painter, all the while successfully separating herself from the fact that the painter was her father. And it was just fine that Angel hadn't uncovered a single thing in the last twenty-three years that spoiled the family-first, Windex-clean image of the "Artist of the Heart."

It seemed that the only person he'd ever failed was her.

She shook her head, refusing to let the thought take root. She was a journalist, Stephen Whitney was the subject of a story. Nothing more. Hadn't she proved that over the last ten days, not to mention during the last hour? It took a wealth of professional detachment to calmly sit through a graphic blow-by-blow from the first person to arrive on scene at the accident that had killed the painter.

Okay, her insides might have wobbled a time or two,

but she'd overcome the weakness by mentally repeating a short, soothing mantra. It only went to show that she had a cool reporter's mind—not to mention an iron stomach, she added—hurrying toward the bar as she saw the matronly bartender slide a thick white plate at her place. Her side of fries!

Sliding onto her stool, Angel breathed deep. The delicious, decadent smell of greasy potatoes sent a shiver of ecstasy down her spine. She pinched one french fry between her thumb and forefinger, moaning a little when she found it gritty with salt and almost too hot to handle.

Perfect, she thought, wiggling against the vinyl cushion in anticipation. Closing her eyes, she lifted it to her mouth.

"Did I tell you about the carnage in '52?"

Angel opened one eye. The man she'd come to The Well to interview, Dale Michaelson, had wandered away after her questions and the two mugs of beer she'd bought him had run dry. But now he was back, stroking his palm down his grizzled, foot-long beard.

"Carnage?" Angel echoed, still holding on to her fry. "Exactly what kind of carnage?"

"Flock of gulls," Mr. Michaelson replied. He reached for one of the hand-rolled cigarettes tucked behind his ear. "I'm an explosives expert, you know, came to the Sur as a young man to work on the highway."

Well, then. Angel bit into her fry—*nirvana*—and made some fast calculations. Highway 1 had been built with prison labor and completed in 1937. If Mr. Michaelson was speaking the truth, he was well into his eighties and a former convict to boot.

"What exactly does it take to be an explosives expert?" she asked, reaching for another fry.

In blatant disregard for California's no-smoking laws, Mr. Michaelson pulled out some matches and lit up. "Can't be afraid of fire, young lady," he said around his cigarette, then drew deeply on it.

Angel glanced over, then stared as bits of flaming tobacco and cigarette paper fell, catching on his beard. The grizzled hair started to smolder.

"Uh . . ." She gestured toward the smoke.

He cackled and casually batted at the tiny blaze. "See what I mean? You can't be afraid of fire."

Someone slid onto the empty stool on Angel's other side. "Are you trying to impress the women again, Dale?"

Cooper. At the sound of his voice, Angel's breath caught. Determined to hide her reaction, she gave him a mere glance. But that's all it took for something—okay, lust—to hit her bloodstream like a jolt of adrenaline. The rush made her light-headed, but she couldn't look away.

She was accustomed to seeing him in the usual Sur-wear—jeans or baggy shorts, T-shirt, heavy boots. But this evening he was dressed city-slick, in a pair of black slacks and a form-fitting pullover that was summer-blue and just had to be out of a silk Italian knit. Post-heart-attack clothes, was her first thought, because they fit him to a T.

Her second thought was that he had a date.

Dale Michaelson leaned around Angel to talk to Cooper. "Is this your woman, then, Cooper? You scared of a little competition?"

Angel frowned, turning away from Cooper to draw her plate of fries closer. "I'm my own woman, Mr. Michaelson."

The old man cackled again. "There. She told you, Coop. But me, I was telling her about that flock of seagulls we accidentally bar-bee-cued in '52. They started one of our big wildfires too—not as big as that one just twenty years back, but almost. But boy-howdy, did those birds smell good when we cooked 'em."

He broke off and pointed with his cigarette at the bartender, who once more pushed through the door from the kitchen, Angel's burger in her hand. "Better than Maggie's Fourth of July chicken special," he said.

Eww. Angel allowed herself a small shudder, but then drummed up her reporter's objectivity and forced the image out of her mind as the fat, juicy burger was set in front of her. Stacked with lettuce, tomato, pickles, and onions, then cut in half, the burger's meat steamed with fragrant, flagrant temptation. Angel lifted the top bun to add a helping of ketchup and mustard.

"That'll kill you, you know," Cooper said, leaning close to her ear.

The skin on the side of her neck goosebumped. "But whatta way to go," she retorted, without lifting her gaze from her food. No sense in giving herself another chance to stare at him, or Cooper another chance to see how he could so easily capture her.

"Now, I heard that, Cooper," Maggie-the-bartender scolded. She leaned one ample hip against the counter behind her and gave him a mock frown. "There's no call for you to discourage business."

He grinned. "Maybe I just want a partner in my new misery, Mag. Who was always your best customer?"

"You," she said. "When we could pry you away from the city."

"And that's exactly where I found Coop," Mr. Michaelson put in, ash drifting from his cigarette to the bartop this time. "Just like I told you, young lady. The first person I called after the sheriff was Cooper's big-city law office."

"What?" Cooper folded his arms on the top of the bar and squinted through the cigarette smoke at the old man. "What is it you told Angel?"

Maggie answered for Mr. Michaelson, thankfully keeping it short but sweet. "About Stephen."

Ignoring a little clutch in her stomach, Angel clapped the top of the bun on one half of the burger, then went to work on the other.

"Told her how the truck blew him right out of his shoes," Mr. Michaelson said. "Pair a size-eleven Nikes."

Her stomach clutched again and she fell back on her little mantra.

subject of a story subject of a story subject of a story

Breathing deeply, steadily, Angel picked up her hamburger.

"Recognized all that blond hair of his, course," the old man continued. "But not much else."

Her fingers tightened on the burger, squirting ketchup out the side.

subject of a story subject of a story subject of a story

"Jesus, Dale," Cooper muttered. He leaned closer to Angel. "You all right, honey?"

subject of a story subject of a story subject of a story

"You all right?" he asked again.

"Of course." She jerked a shoulder, hunching it to create a barrier between them. "I'm a journalist. Details are my job."

"Angel—"

"Don't you dare think I can't handle it."

In third grade, the other boys at her new school had tortured her for months by scaring her at every opportunity. They'd said she screamed like a girl, so she'd toughened up, learned not to make a sound, not to blink, even when she found crickets in her lunchbox and snails squished between the pages of her binder.

Angel put her elbows on the bar and brought her sandwich to her mouth.

"I told her I think he must have flown forty feet."

She closed her eyes, not sure whether the old man had actually said the words again or if she was just recalling them. It was her father who had been hit by the truck. He'd flown forty feet through the air, flown right out of his shoes. Blond hair. Her father. Blood.

Tired of the penny-ante stuff, one day the third-grade bullies had cornered her on the walk home from school. They'd grabbed her backpack, stuffed what they claimed was a dead, bloodied cat inside, then shoved it back into her arms.

Now, like then, she'd heard herself screaming, high and girlish. Now, like then, the sound was only in her head. On the outside she was calm, cool, collected, just as she'd been that day. Tough. Strong. She'd rescued herself.

"Angel?"

"What?" She knew she still held the half-hamburger a few inches from her mouth, but she couldn't take a bite quite yet.

"Honey," Cooper said. "You're white as a ghost."

"Ghost," she echoed. Suddenly the word made her want to giggle, but Angel Buchanan was too tough to giggle. That's right. She was as tough as she needed to be.

The "cat" had turned out to be a bundle of dirty red rags dipped in molasses, but it was one of her ghosts, a part of her past that wouldn't quit haunting her. That "cat" and the man, the father, who had died a few miles from here. She couldn't forget him either.

But had he ever remembered her?

Her fingers loosened and her hamburger dropped to her plate.

"Maggie." Cooper's hand clamped on Angel's upper arm and he spun her toward him. "Bring tea. Hot tea with lots of sugar."

Then he shook her arm. "Are you sick?"

"Of course not." She stared at the middle of his chest. Right there, under that pretty-colored Italian knit, he had a scar, because Cooper was tough too, too tough to die, despite two heart attacks. "I don't want tea. Sick of tea."

"We're getting out of here, then." He hauled her to her feet, his touch not the least bit gentle. She stared down at his shiny loafers.

Nikes. Flew right out of his size-eleven Nikes, she thought.

And swayed.

"Christ," Cooper said under his breath. He shifted to slide his arm around her. But he was tall and she was short and so his hand brushed against the side of her breast. "*Christ.*"

More prickles, hot, skittered toward her nipple, snapping Angel out of her strange reverie. She pulled free of Cooper's hold and shoved her shoulders back. "I'm fine. I—" Turning to find her purse, her gaze landed on the abandoned, ketchup-drenched hamburger instead.

Her stomach rolled. Then, though he hadn't said a word, she forced her gaze toward Cooper. "Don't you dare think I can't handle it."

"Of course you can handle it." His voice was soothing and he slipped his hand beneath her elbow as if he could tell her knees felt mushy.

Which they didn't.

"Just let me help you—"

"I don't need any help! I never need any help." She put her hand on her forehead. "I have a headache, that's all. Too many vegetables give me a headache."

He had her purse. She snatched it from him, the abrupt movement nearly overbalancing her. He caught her again, pulled her toward him. "Let's dance. Someone just put a quarter in the jukebox. It's my favorite song."

Angel listened for a moment. "'Hakuna Matata' is your favorite song?" she asked, incredulous. "'Hakuna Matata' from *The Lion King*?"

"Shh." He pushed her head against his shoulder. "It's our song now."

"Our song is a duet by a rodent and a pig," she muttered. "That's perfect, just perfect."

But she leaned into him because, after all, she had that headache. Not to mention that "Hakuna Matata" had an engaging beat and she didn't remember the last time she'd been dancing, or the last time she'd smelled a delicious man's cologne on real male skin instead of on a peel-and-sniff sample in *GQ*.

Holding her close, his chin against her cheek, Cooper began to hum. He was a hummer! The slight vibration of it buzzed against her temple.

It made Angel snuggle closer. She was a whistler in the dark herself, so she felt a certain kinship to hummers. Though she bolstered her bravado with a Seven Dwarves–type tune in times of trouble, hummers did their thing to express their contentment.

Angel closed her eyes. It was kind of nice to think Cooper was contented with her in his arms.

Shutting off everything else, she floated on that thought, nearly slumping in his arms, as he did all the moving for them both. In that warm haze, a sudden slap of cool, fresh air came as quite a shock. Her eyes popped open and she realized he'd hustled her outside and was now unlocking the passenger door of his SUV.

She blinked. "What are you doing? I—I have my own car."

He took her purse from her and threw it inside. "We'll get it tomorrow."

"No— What the *heck* are you doing?" Instead of listening to her, he'd picked her up and placed her on the seat. "I have my own—" The door slammed in her face.

She was more puzzled than angry when he slid into the driver's seat. "What's going on?"

"When was the last time you ate?" he demanded.

"The last time I ate?" She shook her head. "I don't know. What does that—"

"I have a wet sock that weighs more than you do," he said, his voice tight, almost angry. "I didn't see you in the dining room for breakfast or lunch today, and then you almost fainted back there. You were nearly comatose on the dance floor, for God's sake. I'm taking you back to Tranquility and getting you something to eat before you fall on your face."

She pointed back toward the tavern. "I have a meal—"

"No."

She tried again. "My hamburger—"

His impatient gesture cut her off. "Don't play games with me. You don't want to eat that."

"But—"

"For God's sake, give a little here, Angel. Let me take care of you. If just this once."

If just this once. Angel eyed his determined expression. If she looked at the situation objectively, she *was* hungry, and tired, and tired of fighting. Him. Herself. "All right."

Letting someone else take the reins for a short while didn't mean she would lose complete control.

Together, they raided the Tranquility kitchen. Well, Cooper raided and Angel was waited upon. It was nice, she decided, and even nicer when he was sitting across the narrow table from her, sharing eggplant lasagne leftovers. When she pushed her plate away, he did too.

Lulled by a full stomach, she smiled at him.

"We forgot something," he said, his voice soft.

She gave him a lazy smile. "What's that?"

He reached out with both hands, fisting them into her hair to draw her forward. Her reflexes had been lulled too, because they didn't even protest.

"Dessert," he said against her mouth.

Chapter 9

Yes, dessert, Cooper thought, as Angel's mouth softened beneath his. She tasted hot and sweet and like something he didn't want to skip. Not tonight.

He lifted his head to catch his breath. Her eyes were heavy-lidded, her lips already reddened by his. She'd been driving him nuts during the last week, coming and going from the retreat in her city dresses and city skirts, looking purposeful—God, how he envied her purposefulness. And looking pretty. Looking so damn pretty.

He'd stayed away from her, telling himself to accept his monklike existence and refusing to indulge in fantasies of laying slabs of beef jerky at her high-heeled feet. But hell, he'd given up nicotine, caffeine, and the adrenaline of his work. Surely that proved he had enough control over his appetites to safely allow himself a longer taste of her.

"Come here," he said, drawing his fingers through her hair. "Come over here to me."

"To you," she echoed, blinking slowly.

"Here, to me." He wouldn't risk anywhere more comfortable, because he was giving himself permission for just a taste, after all. Her hand lay limply on the tabletop, so he took it and tugged. "To me, honey."

Even as she rose, a wrinkle appeared between her golden, feathery eyebrows. "I don't know if this is a good idea. . . ."

"Don't worry about that," he said, knowing he would only go so far and no further. "Remember, just this once you're letting me take care of you."

With a little sigh, she allowed him to draw her down onto his lap. Even after he'd fed her, she weighed nothing, and her fragrant hair was just more weightlessness that tickled his chin. For a moment he was still, merely enjoying the warmth of her in his arms. He breathed in and out steadily, keenly aware of the moment. Of living in this warm, woman-in-his-arms moment.

It was almost enough.

But then she shifted and the slinky skirt she was wearing edged up on her knees. His pulse jumped and he ran his hand down her thigh to find her bare skin.

Her breath caught and she looked up, and then he had to kiss her. He intended to take it slow, to give himself plenty of time to enjoy her before drawing the interlude to a close. But Angel was the very devil of a temptation. Her mouth opened beneath his, and he had to steel himself not to give in and plunge inside. Instead, he kissed the corners, the bow of her upper lip, the tender center of the bottom one.

She moaned, but he shut his ears to the demand in the sound and repeated the baby kisses, lingering on that bottom lip, then drawing it between his to suck. His hand was cupping one of her bare knees, and as he sucked more strongly, her other knee clamped tight, trapping his fingers between her legs. Oh, she liked that.

But she wanted more, he knew it, because her fingers speared through his hair, her nails scraping erotically against his scalp. She drew his head closer and he surrendered, releasing her lower lip to slide his tongue into her mouth.

Now they both moaned.

Reminding himself he was supposed to go slow, that he was supposed to savor the little he was going to have of her, he rubbed his tongue against hers, then lifted his head.

"No." Her fingernails bit into his scalp.

He smiled. "I'll do it again, don't worry."

"I'm not *worrying*." Apparently even tough girls could sulk.

He laughed, then fisted his hand in her hair and drew back her head. "You have the prettiest neck," he said, nuzzling along the line of her jaw, then licking toward her pulsepoint. "I've been wanting to taste it since the day we met."

"Mmm." Her eyes closed.

He smiled against her skin, taking his time to reacquaint himself with female flesh, how smooth it was, how his attention warmed it, how that warmth deepened the scent of enticing, feminine perfume. He explored Angel's throat until his chin brushed the little ruffle around the top edge of the lacy sleeveless top she wore. Lifting his head, he tried not to notice the line of buttons that ran toward her waist.

That way led to disaster.

He'd learned a lot about settling for less in the past year. Though he was still working on total acceptance, he was accustomed to paring down his expectations. So he knew this would have to do. Little touches, little tastes, just enough to keep the hunger at bay and not enough to make him greedy for more.

He kissed her bare shoulder, her chin, then allowed himself her lips again. Angel instantly widened her mouth, but instead of taking all that was offered, he just dipped inside.

Little touches, little tastes. Satisfied he was under control, he ventured a bit farther.

Then Angel sucked on his tongue.

He groaned. Oh God. God. *Good good good.*

As her mouth was taking its pleasure, her hand slid down his chest. He didn't have the will to stop her from finding her way beneath his shirt. His stomach muscles jumped as her warm hand slid along his ribs. He tried to ignore the way his heart jumped too.

But the unsettling sensation made him desperate to distract her, so he covered one of her breasts with his palm. She froze, then her mouth released his. Gazes locked, they stared at each other. Both of them were breathing hard, and each of her quick inhales pushed her soft flesh into his hand.

Then *her* hand moved, sliding down his bare back, around his ribs toward his chest. His mouth dried. He knew where she was heading. Tit for tat.

He might have laughed at his own bad pun if he weren't so afraid she'd have her way. Shifting his fingers across the lace of her top, he unfastened the first button.

Thank God, once again she froze.

That's when he knew what he had to do. If she didn't move, if *he* only touched *her,* he would survive this pleasure. Steadying his breath and ordering himself to think of England, he slowly began unfastening Angel's buttons.

She lay passively in his arms, her face flushed, her breathing shallow.

"You're so beautiful." His voice was rough, unsteady. "Like an angel."

She smiled, then lifted her hand to his face. He caught it, kissed the fingertips, then placed it safely back at her side. "Let me," he said to her. "Just be still and let me touch you."

He'd only managed to undo the buttons to the point below her breasts, but he couldn't wait any longer. Pushing the lace edges apart, he created a gap that revealed the first rise of her breasts beneath a glossy pink bra.

Lust beat like a fist inside his chest. Cooper sucked in a quick breath, beating back the sense of almost-panic. The overly rapid thrumming eased, and he lifted his hand to the bra's front clasp.

Where he fumbled.

God, he never fumbled! But the fingers that had

once—and, as far as he knew, still—held the dorm record for one-handedly unclasping twenty-five different bras in fifteen seconds were so unsteady that he couldn't do the deed. Granted, the bras had been strapped to chairs instead of warm-skinned women, but he'd had plenty of opportunity to practice his technique in the flesh since that time.

She started to squirm. "Cooper . . ."

Hell, hell. There was a hint of trepidation in her voice and he didn't want to stop now.

"Cooper." One of her hands rose to the edges of her blouse as if she wanted to draw it together. Her face flushed brighter, and he knew her embarrassment was about to ruin the mood.

Damning his clumsiness, he blew out a calming breath and smoothed her protective arm away. Then he kissed her again and, giving up on the damn bra clasp, slid his hand between the open edges of her shirt to cup her bra-covered breast.

She made a sweet little moan and Cooper glanced down. What a sight. Almost as much a turn-on as that sweet, warm weight in his palm was the vision of his heavy wrist disappearing inside her lacy clothes.

His heart was pumping easily now and he decided it was because most of his blood was staying south. He was hard as stone and he went even harder as he rubbed his thumb over her stiff nipple.

She made another little sound, but he didn't look away from her lace-covered breasts. It was too good to see how she was trembling and to feel the fluttering of her heartbeat against his fingertips as he wandered toward the other breast. He weighed this one in his palm too, then stroked the side of his thumb back and forth to bring the nipple to a tighter, harder point.

"Cooper," she whispered.

He glanced up, saw her nostrils flare and her tongue dart out to moisten her bottom lip.

Watching her face, he lightly pinched her nipple. Her eyes closed.

So he snuck up on her then, in a quick move pulling his hand away to put his mouth there, right over her clothes. Ignoring her little jolt of reaction, he wet the fabric with his tongue and felt her nipple go stiffer. His tongue flattened over it, getting the material wetter, until it was plastered against her skin. Then he took her breast into his mouth, pushing that sweet tight nipple to the roof of his mouth. Sucked.

She bowed in his arms, her thighs shifting against his erection. The sweet, unconscious stroke made him suck stronger, made her shift again.

But he couldn't have her moving like that. No.

Transferring his attention to her other breast, he circled the fabric over that nipple with his tongue. Like before, this new touch rendered Angel motionless. So he circled it again and again, feeling her tense as she anticipated that soft sucking she'd liked so much.

When she was trembling with eagerness, he covered her breast with his mouth and bit down.

She cried out.

He lifted his head, pretended concern. "Did I hurt you?" He knew he hadn't. He knew the cry had come out of pure pleasure.

"No, I . . ." She shook her head, her hair floating

away from her shoulders, then falling to settle over her half-buttoned blouse. "No."

"Then . . ." Keeping his smile to himself, he very deliberately brushed the back of his hand across one breast, moving the blond curls that were in his way. Then he stroked across the other, brushing her nipple with his knuckles. He heard her breath catch, and ran his knuckles by the nipple again. And again.

"Cooper." This whisper was agonized.

He glanced up, reading the desire, the need, on her face. "Let me," he said, suddenly knowing he couldn't, wouldn't stop unless she wanted him to. His original intention had been nothing more than high-school-level experimentation, but now he wanted to go beyond that.

A last taste for himself. Relief for her.

"Let me." Without waiting for an answer, he bent his head to her breasts again.

They smelled like her perfume, and even through the wet blouse and bra, they tasted sweet and warm. They fit perfectly in his mouth, and when he sucked them, the little sounds she released made him think he still served some purpose in the world.

She made him feel like more than half the man that he'd been.

Her body was vibrating, trembling with arousal. He tried to soothe her by stroking his hand down her thigh, but she flinched at the touch, her skin hypersensitive.

"Cooper," she whispered.

He kissed the very tip of her nipple and he could feel her heart racing against his cheek. It was life in his hands, life under his control, and he knew, now, how very precious that was.

"Cooper . . ." she said louder, putting a hand against her temple as if she were trying to pull herself together.

Ah, but he was after making her fly apart.

"Shh," he said, kissing her mouth softly. "Don't fight it."

He stroked down her leg again, ignoring another small jerk. He ignored the next, bigger jerk too, when he began to draw up the hem of her skirt. It was full enough to move easily along her thighs. To divert her attention, he kissed her mouth again, then ducked his hand beneath the ruched fabric to slide his fingers to the warm mound covered by silky material.

His hand resting there, he kissed his way down her chin and throat to take her nipple in his mouth once more. Sucking strongly, he eased his fingers beneath the panties and cupped her. Her moan was long and sweet.

She was hot. So wet that his fingers slid easily between the folds of her sex. Her clitoris was like her nipples—hard, and eager for his touch. He brushed his thumb across it once, and her body went rigid. Eyes squeezed tight, she was soundless now, totally focused on his hand.

He brushed her lightly again, and then, in one deliberate coordination of movement, he slid his tongue over her nipple, he slid his thumb over her clitoris, he slid his two longest fingers inside her tight body.

The moment stretched as her body bowed against his lap, went taut.

He nudged her once more with his thumb, and her inner muscles clenched hard. Clenched hard again. Releasing her breast, he lifted his head to watch the climax roll through her, even as he felt every wave of it through his invading fingers.

It was the most erotic, beautiful thing he'd ever seen. All that delicate blond prettiness splayed across his body, her clothes half-on, shoved up. But even more erotic, more beautiful was that, for a few moments at least, it was Cooper who was controlling every breath, every response, of a woman as complex and independent as Angel.

God, he thought, amazed at the pleasure of giving pleasure. He could die at this moment and die happy.

Even before the aftershivers of pleasure had played out, Cooper had Angel's hem back at her knees, her blouse rebuttoned, and her two feet flat on the ground. Swaying a little, she blinked down at him. "I . . . um . . ."

She should say something, really she should. And as soon as she figured out exactly what that should be, she would. But no other man had ever managed to bring her to such a state and she was still befuddled by it.

He unfolded stiffly from the seat, not quite meeting her eyes. "It's late. I'll walk you to your cottage."

She blinked some more, trying to reconcile his brisk tone with what had just happened on that bentwood chair.

"Ready?" he asked politely. "It *is* getting late."

Since she assumed he didn't have a curfew, she caught the clue and figured out their little interlude was going to end just like this. He didn't want to come into her cottage tonight, much less into her bed.

Good Lord. She didn't know whether to feel rejected or relieved, but she'd been left out of pleasure enough times herself to know that *he* couldn't be feeling very cheerful at the moment. So what was she supposed to do now, apologize?

Ignoring the hot flush of embarrassment rushing over her face, Angel crossed her arms over her chest. Wasn't this always the way of it? Though tonight the "before" hadn't been half-bad—okay, it had been great—the "after," as usual, sucked.

"It isn't fair," she finally muttered.

He shoved his hands in his pockets and glanced away. "It doesn't always have to be fair."

"I'm not talking about *that,*" she said, rolling her eyes. "I haven't even gotten to *that.*"

"Then what are you talking about?"

"I just hate all this." Her hand waved to indicate him, her, the chair.

"You hate to come?" he asked, his tone amused.

Oh, curse him, Angel thought, narrowing her eyes. He'd decided to cover the clumsy moment by being cool. Cool and detached and amused.

It only added a layer of irritation to her mood. "I hate after," she clarified.

"Well—"

"What are you supposed to do, after? Can you tell me that?" She allowed righteous indignation to plow right over her discomfort. "I've read a thousand articles on how to get a man in bed, how to keep a man in bed, how to make a man breakfast in bed, but I've never read a word on how to gracefully pick up right where you left off with a man after . . . well . . . you know."

His eyebrows lifting, he rocked back on his heels. "Is that what you usually do? Try to pick up 'right where you left off' after you've had intercourse with a man?"

Her jaw dropped in disbelief. How had she let this man, this man with the annoyingly calm voice and irritatingly superior expression, touch her? Was he really the one who, just minutes before, had one hand down her blouse and the other up her skirt?

She pointed her finger at his chest. "Don't do that. Don't give me that assessing, amused look while asking me questions. That's lawyer hoo-doo, and you're using it to avoid this discussion."

"Angel—"

"And then there's that word. *Intercourse.*" She was on a roll now, and he wasn't going to stop her. "What kind of word is that? It sounds like something cars travel along—you know, 'take a left at the first intercourse'—not something a man and a woman do together. Which, by the way, we did not. Perhaps you'd care to elaborate on that, counselor."

Hah. Let *him* take the witness stand for a minute.

"Whoa, whoa, whoa. You're moving too fast for me."

"Uh-huh. Yeah. Sure. Let me slow it down for you, then." She sucked in a breath. "The fact is, we didn't—"

"I don't think we should go to bed together."

"Hey, I don't recall favoring the idea either!" She tapped her toe, impatient with his maddening sangfroid and her just-as-maddening lack of it. "But see, well . . . the kissing was nice and then . . . and then . . . and now . . ."

"Then? Now?"

She threw up her hands. "Now I don't know what to do or what to say."

"Why don't you just say thank you?"

At times like this it was hard not to believe that men were truly the inferior sex, Angel thought, staring at him and shaking her head. After thousands of years, they'd yet to figure out that reason and logic had no place under certain circumstances.

"Look," she said through her teeth. "I feel . . . I feel as if I've done you wrong."

"Come on, Angel, it's not that big a deal." Shoving his hands in his pockets, he spun away from her. "Hasn't any man ever done you right before?"

That was such a good question—and on so many levels—that she should be laughing hysterically. But instead there was something about his abrupt about face that made her pause. That made her see there was a ruddy flush crawling up the back of his neck.

She wasn't the only one embarrassed.

She wasn't the only one who was wishing this awkward moment away.

Well.

"I think we should blame it on the eggplant," she suddenly announced, walking over to Cooper to tuck her hand in his arm. She ignored his quick flinch and started strolling toward the door, tugging him with her. "I read all about it in last month's issue of *Vegetarian Times*."

She peeped at him from beneath her lashes and saw the frown between his eyes ease.

"Eggplant?" he echoed.

"Eggplant." Without a thought for the truth, she

launched into an extensive, detailed account of how the purple properties of eggplant led people to do all sorts of out-of-character things. "It affects a person's decision-making process," she concluded, when they were outside her cottage. "The fact is, it's the anti-garlic."

"The anti-garlic."

She waved a hand. "That's right, anything good that garlic does, you know, like heighten the brain's focus or whatever, eggplant *un*does."

"In some cultures garlic's considered an aphrodisiac."

"Well, there you g—" Looking up, she broke off, her tongue tied by the half-smile on his face and the look of understanding in his eyes.

His expression was so warm, so . . . *honest* that it almost had her begging to bring him inside. Angel Buchanan, nearly begging a man to join her in bed.

What was wrong *with her?*

He left before she came up with an answer.

Only later did she fall upon something that satisfied her. Lying in bed, trying not to think of what she'd let Cooper do, she realized that it was the "letting" that had gotten her into trouble.

Let me take care of you, he'd said.

She knew better than to fall for that! A woman had to take care of herself, and take care not to give her heart.

But the very fact that she *had* fallen for that line, and then that she had abdicated even a tiny, purely physical bit of herself to Cooper, made it all the more important that she finish up her interviews and get back to the city. Coupled with instant coffee, the eggplant—organic fare in general—was making her soft.

Dangerously soft.

* * *

The next morning, straight from the shower, Angel showed up at the Whitney house unannounced. "I want to finish my interviews ASAP," she blurted out the instant Lainey opened the door. "I was hoping I could talk to Katie."

Lainey acted as if wet-haired women with urgent voices showed up on her porch every day. "Surely you'd like a cup of coffee first," she said.

Just like that, Angel found herself following the other woman into the kitchen, cursing her own frailties all the way. If she didn't get back to the city, and soon, her self-command would be completely eroded. Not only did Cooper make her weak, but she couldn't say no to Lainey's coffee.

The mug the woman handed her was filled with a dark brew that smelled of French-roasted, freshly ground beans. Angel liked Lainey's coffee. She took a deep breath of its scent. Really, really liked it.

One cup couldn't destroy her objectivity, could it?

Telling herself to gulp it down and then get on with her job, Angel lifted the mug to her mouth. With it halfway there, she froze, gawking at Lainey.

The other woman was warily approaching a cardboard box sitting on the kitchen table, a sharp knife in her raised hand.

Angel set her mug on the countertop. "Shall I arm myself with a frying pan?"

Lainey started. "What?"

"You look as if you're afraid of what's inside that box," Angel said, nodding at it.

"Yes, well . . ." Lainey shrugged, then used the knife

on the tape binding the cardboard flaps. "It's from the licensing company. More of the Whitney merchandise."

Angel already knew of the licensing agreement, but Lainey's odd manner aroused her curiosity. It only grew stronger as the widow reluctantly peeled back the box's flaps and then, taking a deep breath, looked inside.

"Well?" Angel asked.

Flicking her a glance, Lainey drew from the box a cardboard, accordion-style car windshield visor. As she slowly unfolded it, a colorful, typical Whitney image was revealed—a drive-in movie theater at dusk, circa 1950s.

Angel tilted her head. There was something part Norman Rockwell, part Andy Warhol about the artist's work. Every one of the old-fashioned, sentimental scenes were as brightly colored and as marketing savvy as a soup can.

Lainey set the item on the table and reached inside again, this time bringing out a bundled trio of small, shaggy rugs, all three printed with the same bucolic washbowl and pitcher filled with wildflowers. It took a moment for Angel to discern that while two were indeed rugs, the third of the set was actually the furry cover for a toilet seat.

"Oh, Stephen," Lainey whispered helplessly.

Angel shook her head. The "Artist of the Heart's" latest endeavors were going to give the art critics—who unanimously abhorred the Whitney paintings—a field day.

"A chance to get in their potshots," she murmured to

herself, as she watched Lainey unfold one of the matching rugs.

"Oh no," the widow said in stunned tones. "It only gets worse. Look, this one goes beneath the toilet. My husband approved of his art on a shag rug that surrounds the base of a *toilet*." Lifting it up, she peered at Angel through the distinctive cutout.

Oh my. Lainey's pretty face and horrified expression, framed by the little rug, were suddenly too much for Angel. Biting down on her lower lip, she spun toward the countertop.

"What's the matter?" Lainey asked, crossing toward her. "Are you all right?"

Hastily nodding her head, Angel waved the other woman back. "Mmm, mmm." She pressed her lips together harder.

Lainey halted. "Why . . . why, you're laughing."

Feeling lower than a rat and all humor evaporating, Angel spun back, ready to apologize. But Lainey was looking down at the rug in her hand.

Then her serious gaze lifted to Angel's. "Short of the 'Artist of the Heart' toilet paper," she said, her voice glum, "this *is* the tackiest thing I have ever seen."

"T-toilet paper?" Angel echoed.

And then, God forgive her, she burst out laughing. And then, disaster upon disaster, Lainey joined in. To make matters worse, as the widow continued to laugh, she clutched Angel's arm as if they were truly sharing something—as if they were friends.

"Why?" Lainey finally choked out, still holding on to Angel with one hand and shaking the offending rug in the other. "Why this? Why toilet paper? What was he *thinking*?"

Angel couldn't help herself. "That he wanted to be on the minds of men everywhere?"

That set them both off again. When the laughter died down, it was Angel who poured coffee for Lainey. Then she freshened her own mug and joined the other woman to sit at the kitchen table.

Pushing the bath items aside, Lainey frowned at them, then sighed. "One of my bigger regrets is that the last work Stephen gives to the world will be these."

Angel took a swallow of her coffee. "So you didn't want to burn the new paintings?"

Lainey shrugged. "That was his wish, that the unfinished work be burned." Then she sighed again. "Which meant all the past year's work was lost. It was his habit to leave a little piece of each painting undone. Then, come the month before his annual show, he'd paint like a maniac to finish them. I'd bring food to the tower, but half the time he wouldn't eat it."

Lainey's expression turned bleak and Angel heard herself rushing to reassure her. "I'm sure you took very good care of him, Lainey," she said, though she was keenly aware it wasn't objective reporter-speak. The trouble was, she not only liked Lainey's coffee, but she liked Lainey too. "I'm sure you did."

"That was my job. To make his life comfortable so that he could concentrate on his work." Her gaze met Angel's. "But what am I going to do now?"

Angel instantly pretended an interest in the inside of her coffee mug and wished herself in a galaxy far, far away. "Well, uh, I don't know." This was what she got for staying past her one-coffee limit: emotion-heavy, teary-eyed questions. "What did you want to do before he came along?"

Lainey laughed again, but this time there wasn't the smallest grain of amusement in it. "I wanted him to come along."

Angel jumped out of her chair. The other woman's answer cut too close to what she'd wanted when she was a little girl. It was also what she'd vowed never to want once she was old enough to understand why her mother had married—disastrously—on the rebound from Stephen Whitney's defection.

Because by then Angel knew it was the very worst kind of dependence, tying your happiness to a man. Tying yourself to a man at all.

"May I see Katie now?" She took her mug to the sink. "If she becomes upset, I won't push."

At the mention of her daughter, Lainey's expression shifted from sad to worried. "Talking might do Katie some good, actually. I can't seem to get anything out of her—the rest of the family either. Go on up the stairs, her room's the first door on your left."

Angel nodded, turned.

"She hasn't cried since her father's death," Lainey added. "A friend sent me a book on children and grief and it says she should cry."

In one swift *woosh,* Angel's stomach tightened.

"Maybe you can do something about that."

"Um, maybe." *Right after I poke myself in the eye with a sharp stick.* There was nothing, *nothing* Angel wanted to avoid more than a girl crying over her missing daddy.

Chapter 10

Thank goodness Katie did not appear the least bit teary-eyed when she responded to Angel's knock on her half-open door. Nonetheless, Angel tried to establish a lighthearted mood by striking a melodramatic pose, the back of her hand pressed against her forehead.

"Please, please. It's an emergency. I'm desperate for a blow-dryer and some quality time with an electrical outlet."

Hair was a sure way to any female's heart. Within seconds she was standing in the bathroom adjoining Katie's spacious bedroom. And within another few her hair was looking slightly better than it had in weeks. After returning the blow-dryer to its place on a shelf, she took a deep breath and pretended she was hair-fluffing instead of heavily stalling.

You can do this, Angel commanded her reflection.

Was she, or was she not the professional, Fearless

Girl Reporter that she'd fantasized about becoming since she was twelve years old?

Sure, she could write a story about Stephen Whitney without interviewing Katie. There was no guarantee she'd get anything worth using, after all. But she'd had other opportunities to talk to the teenager over the last couple of weeks and she'd ducked every one of them.

Angel Buchanan did not duck opportunities. Or hard truths. Or even the other daughter of her father.

And while she could hair-fluff with the best of them, she didn't stall either.

Sending herself a hard-eyed look in the mirror, Angel allowed one more second of delay. Then she reemerged into Katie's room to find the girl lying on her bed, reading a magazine.

Angel cocked her head, recognizing *Teen People* by its Clearasil ad and white-toothed celebrity shots. "They're not back together, are they? Britney and Justin?"

At a noncommittal hum of reply, she shrugged, then spun a slow 360, taking in the room's bookshelves, entertainment center, computer, and printer. One wall was dominated by a bulletin board crowded with the usual stuff—photos, certificates, a recent report card that was all A's except for a C in PE.

She glanced over to catch Katie looking at her. Angel put on a smile. "How's it going at school?"

"All right, I guess."

She nodded at the report card. "Mine looked just the same. Physical fitness test nailed me every year. Push-ups, pull-ups. I have zero upper body strength."

Katie shrugged, her cool expression unchanging.

Geez, I'm dying here. Angel usually did well with children, because, she suspected, she'd yet to stop looking like one. But she wouldn't give up quite yet. That first day, outside the church, hadn't she managed to get a few laughs out of the girl?

She crossed toward the bed and perched on the lower corner. "I'm leaving soon. Going back to San Francisco the day after tomorrow."

Katie's gaze flicked to Angel's face again. "You're done with your story?"

Angel shook her head. "I'll write it when I get back home. But I've pretty much talked to everyone around here who knew your dad."

She paused. *Wait for it.*

"Not to me."

There. It was so much better for the first move to come from Katie herself. Angel didn't feel nearly as guilty that way. "Well, I did ask your mom if we could talk. She said it was up to you."

Now the girl looked away, closed off again. "I don't know what I'd have to tell you."

What it was like to have a father who stayed.

The thought wrapped around Angel's throat, squeezed. Digging her fingernails into her palms, she forced it free. She was too tough to wimp out now, too strong to let the old pain hurt her.

Just ask a few commonplace questions about their relationship, she bargained with herself. Then she'd cut ties with these people forever.

"Is *your* father still alive?"

Startled by the sudden question, Angel whipped her

head toward the girl. "What?" It came out like a croak, so she swallowed and tried again. "What did you say?"

"Is your father still alive?"

"Um, well, no. No, he's not."

Katie sat up straighter on the bed. "For how long? I mean, since you were how old?"

A little spooked by the conversation, Angel dropped her gaze, watching herself draw an imaginary circle on her denim-covered knee. "My parents split up when I was four years old. I never saw him again."

"Did your mom . . . did she marry a second time?"

The urgency in the question caught Angel's attention. Looking over, she saw that the girl's wooden expression had livened up—with a distinct spark of anxiety.

Poor thing, Angel thought, helpless against a sharp tug of sympathy, *she's already bracing for more changes to her life.*

"My mother married a couple times after she was with my father," she answered. "Now she lives with her husband in France, just outside of Paris."

"Paris." The expression on Katie's face returned to its previously frozen state. "My mom and I met my dad there once, when I was eight."

Angel again tried smiling. "EuroDisney?"

The girl nodded. "We were only there for a few days. My dad went to France a bunch of other times, though."

Angel felt her insides go still. "A bunch of times, you said?" She tried to keep the question casual, even as she calculated the exact years she and her mother had hidden in Europe. "Do you remember when?"

The girl shrugged. "I'm pretty sure he hadn't been outside of the States until that first time when I was eight. After that he traveled a lot more."

Angel's blood started pumping again. For a minute she'd thought Stephen Whitney had gone looking for them. For her. Stupid. Stupid, how she could still hope after all these years that he'd given her a second thought.

She jumped to her feet and walked around the room, determined to distance herself from the old bitterness. Pausing at the bulletin board again, she stared at Katie's report card. "Yep," she said, to prove to herself she sounded normal. "My report cards were exactly like this."

She looked back, steeling herself. It was time to forget about PE and Paris and the kid's obvious misery. It was time to get on with the interview.

Angel opened her mouth, but found herself hesitating again. And then again. *Get on with it, Angel.*

Why was she letting the girl get to her? Why did she feel this crazy need to protect her? Biology aside, she wasn't this kid's family! She didn't owe her a thing! She didn't owe anyone a thing!

But that didn't stop Angel's feet from walking back to the bed. She sat down again, closer to Katie this time. "I know . . . I know what you're going through is hard."

Fine, it was a lame remark, as even those kinds of remarks went. She was admittedly lousy at airing out feelings and actually preferred bottling them up herself. But she'd had years more practice than Katie.

"Really hard," Angel added, shifting uneasily. "But you'll be all right."

She said that last part brightly.

God, she was an idiot.

Truly an idiot, because her mouth was moving again and she was continuing to speak in that dumb, cheerful voice. "You'd be amazed at what hard times you can get through."

Apparently Katie thought Angel was an idiot too, because she pinned her with that near-expressionless stare. "What's the hardest time *you've* ever had?"

It wasn't so much a challenge, Angel decided, as a declaration that she and all the other adults in Katie's world didn't have a clue about what the teen was going through.

Fifteen years old sucked.

Remembering that, Angel did her best to answer. "The hardest time for me . . . I don't know . . ." She thought of the stories she'd written over the years for *West Coast* magazine. "I lived on the streets for a week before writing a piece on homeless women."

When the girl didn't say anything, Angel found herself confessing more. "Of course, it was summer, and at night I slept on a cot at one of the shelters." Even to her own ears it sounded like a camping trip, not a hardship.

"And then there was the time I—" She broke off, knowing that crewing a two-day yacht race didn't hold a candle to losing your father.

Sighing, Angel wished she could let this go, wished she did not feel this sudden urge to give the girl some hope—or at least something else to think about. She dropped her head back, inhaling a long breath as she stared at the clouds that someone—Stephen Whitney, surely—had painted on Katie's ceiling. "The hardest time I ever had was the year I pretended to be a boy."

"What?" Katie drew back, her eyes rounded.

Woke you up now, didn't I? Angel sucked in another breath. "I told you that my mother and father split, right? Well, shortly afterward, my mom married someone else, a police officer. He, uh, he wasn't a nice man."

"How wasn't he nice?"

Angel hesitated.

"Yeah, how wasn't he nice?" It was Cooper, shooting her a half-apologetic look as he stepped into the room. "Sorry, but Lainey asked me to check on you two. I wasn't intentionally eavesdropping."

Fear—or something very much like it—made her stomach dip, scooping right below her belly button. This wasn't something to share with Cooper. She couldn't even say why she'd decided to tell Katie.

No, she did know that. She remembered that day at the church. The teen had smiled then. Angel had nearly made her laugh, and now she couldn't shake the feeling that it connected them somehow—like being responsible for a person whose life you'd saved.

But she couldn't do this with Cooper listening in!

"Angel?"

It was Katie's voice and Angel glanced at her, then couldn't look away. "He, uh, hurt my mom," she continued quickly. "But because he was a police officer, she was afraid to bring charges against him."

Katie's eyes had gone wide again, so Angel took that as her cue to skate over the worst details. "We decided to . . . to get away." *Run away*. "He had access to lots of methods of finding us, though, so we hid from him by changing our identities often and moving around a lot."

She could feel Cooper's gaze on her, feel its steady regard, and knew that he could cross all the *t*'s and dot all the *i*'s that she was leaving out.

"So for the sake of putting him off the scent," she said, moving briskly to the point, "I went through third grade as a boy."

Katie appeared dumbfounded all over again. "But . . . you . . . you look . . ." She laughed.

At the sound, Angel's stomach dipped once more, but this time it was a warm, gentle movement. Telling the story was worth just that one moment of real amusement on the girl's face.

"I know," Angel said. "I look like the girliest girl you ever met. I was as girlie and as shrimpie then too. That's what made it so difficult."

"But you managed."

Katie's brief spurt of laughter had brought real life to her blank expression. Angel didn't flatter herself that she'd made a big difference for the girl, but it was a start. A start.

"I did. I made it through my hard time." She smiled at Katie and, without thinking, reached over to take her hand. Their linked fingers rested on Justin Timberlake's pretty face. "A person is tempered in fire. Never forget that. It only makes you stronger."

Then, embarrassed by her hokey homily, she winked. "And I'll tell you something else that experience proved to me."

There was almost a smile on Katie's face. Almost. "What?"

Angel threw a quick glance over her shoulder at Cooper, then leaned forward and stage-whispered. "The fact is, boys really drool. And girls . . . girls truly rule."

Sitting on a blanket stretched on the sand of Cooper's secret beach, Angel watched the sun slip quickly, and without a splash, into the Pacific. The wind instantly quieted, warming the air of the protected cove.

It should have been a calm time of the day. And it should be a calm time for her in the story-writing process, with the data gathered, contacts made, interviews completed. She was about to begin the part she liked best, when she molded the raw input into a form not only to *in*form, but also to ignite a reader's emotions.

But still, she felt jittery.

She flopped back against the blanket and closed her eyes.

Then she heard it, the humming, its echo announcing the progress of someone coming through the tunnel to the cove.

That someone was the source of her jitteriness—Cooper. She'd been hiding from him ever since she'd left the Whitney house that morning. The way he'd murmured, "We'll talk later," as she'd said goodbye to Lainey had warned her that he wanted to rehash what she'd revealed in Katie's bedroom.

That wasn't going to happen. Her past wasn't a weakness, by God, but sometimes it had the strange effect of making her feel that way.

The humming stopped. "There you are."

She didn't open her eyes. It had been pointless to try to run away once she knew he was nearing, but she could get rid of him quickly, couldn't she? "Do you mind? I was hoping to be left alone."

"Sorry, but you'd have to take your bra off for that."

Her eyes popped open and she rose up on her elbows. "Huh?" Certainly he couldn't tell there wasn't one beneath the thick sweatshirt she was wearing.

Dropping down to the blanket beside her, he grinned. "I thought that would get your attention. It's the old signal my sisters told me to use if I wanted uninterrupted time on the beach."

"If only I'd known . . ." Angel murmured, leaning back and closing her eyes again.

"Well, now that you do—"

"Dream on, buddy."

He laughed. "Oh, baby, I am. I do. Every night."

She ignored him, and the little lick of satisfaction his words gave her. He had a way of disturbing her sleep too.

"You missed dinner tonight," he said.

"I couldn't face another helping of tofu surprise, so I'm out here playing fantasy take-out instead." Eyes still closed, she smiled dreamily. "Right now its Der Wienerschnitzel. Two corn dogs, a chili dog with extra onions, a chocolate shake, and a double order of onion rings."

"That's sick."

"Well excuse me, Mr. Nutrition."

"No, it's sick that if you're fantasizing, you'd choose Der Wienerschnitzel over Doc's Dogs."

Surprised, Angel rolled onto her side and propped her head on her palm to look at him. "You know Doc's? Doc's on Ocean Street? I thought it was a secret shared only by me and the kids at the junior high down the block."

He narrowed his eyes. "You haven't told anyone else, have you?"

"God, no. And risk losing my chance at the best fast food in the city? If those pigs in the financial district find out about it, they'll be dispatching their assistants there 'round the clock. It'll be lines out the door twenty-four/seven."

Cooper nodded. "Remember what they did to Stinko's."

Her lip curling, she sat up. "Arranged for venture capital so the place chained up, then went franchise. I weep, *weep* when I remember how good the cinnamon rolls were before they McDonaldized the process."

"It's the new name that gets to me. I'm too much a man to step foot into a place called Cinnie's."

"Hah! I knew it." Angel looked at him with smug satisfaction. "I got stood up once and I've always told myself it was because I'd picked the restaurant. It was a great place called Ribbons and Rhinestones."

He grinned. "Believe it. Only a wussy name like that could get between a man and finding you irresistible." Then his smile died.

Angel looked away. They both knew Cooper had found her quite resistible, of course. To cover the sudden awkwardness, she gestured toward the dramatic view of orange sky and gray-blue water before them. "Well, uh, I've been wondering . . . This is nice and everything, but aren't you itching to get back to the city? To Doc's and coffee and cable TV? We have ocean there too, if you recall."

His ambiguous grunt had her glancing at him.

"Haven't you missed it?" she insisted.

"Yeah." He pushed a hand through his hair. "Yeah, sure. And—" Breaking off, he pushed his hand through his hair again. "Listen, I came looking for you because I'm not going to be around tomorrow. I'll probably be gone all day, so I wanted to talk with you about—"

"I'm going to be gone most of tomorrow too," she jumped in, guessing where he would try to take the conversation now. Doc's Dogs fan or no, she didn't want to reveal any more of her private, personal past to him. "I'm heading south to San Luis Obispo for the day."

"Angel—"

"I have a few things I want to check out there, you see, and—"

"Angel—"

"As a matter of fact . . ." she babbled on, standing up and brushing off her jeans in a businesslike, you're-dismissed manner, "as a matter of fact, I should probably go back to my cottage, gather my stuff together, and then start packing. . . ."

He spoke right over her. "I want to thank you for what you shared with Katie this morning. She means a lot to me and she . . . she'll have more to face ahead. I hope she'll remember what you said."

A fist pressed against the nervous flutter in her belly, Angel turned her back on him to walk toward the surf line, the sand cool beneath her bare feet. "Well, okay, yeah, glad to be of help—"

"And I'm sorry for what you had to go through."

There it was, too personal. She shrugged, drawing near to where the waves washed up on the sand. "No biggie, none at all."

"Jesus, yes, it's a biggie." All at once he was behind her, his hands gentle on her shoulders. His breath blew warm across her temple. "How long, Angel? For how long did you have to hide?"

Way, way too personal.

His thumbs worked gently into her tense, resisting muscles. He rested his chin on the top of her head, his fingers kneading, working, persuading. Making her soft.

"How long, honey?"

"Seven years." Really soft, because she didn't even realize she was saying the words until she heard her own weak whisper. But that wouldn't do. So she said it again, louder. Stronger. "Seven years. Five in the States, the last two in Europe."

The waves washed in four times before he spoke again. "Were you hurt?" he finally said, his hands still massaging. "Did your mother's husband hurt *you*, Angel?"

"He threatened to. He threatened to kill her and then keep me." She fought the shiver that wanted to roll down her back beneath her sweatshirt. "And she believed him. That's why we left."

"But wasn't there someone who—"

"There was no one!" No one who would take her mother's side at the police station. No one, not even Angel's father, Stephen "Artist of the Heart" Whitney, who would help. Her mother had asked him to take Angel, to keep her safe, and he'd refused to be bothered.

She crossed her arms over her chest. "This was twenty years ago, Cooper. Domestic abuse was hushed up all the time. Her husband was rising in the police ranks, becoming more powerful and possessive."

"So you went underground."

Angel lifted her hand. "There were people, secret . . . networks that made it possible. We moved when he got close, or when we thought he was getting close."

"Then what happened?"

She almost smiled, because she'd covered enough trials to recognize lawyer talk. *Then what happened?* That was an attorney's favorite buzz phrase to elicit more of a witness's story.

"Then one night we got lucky. The bastard dashed to the corner liquor store for his next bottle of scotch. Didn't take the time to bring a weapon with him. He happened to walk in on an armed robbery in progress, tried to stop it, and died a hero."

Cooper squeezed her shoulders.

But it wasn't enough to calm the bitterness welling up in her. She whirled to face him, unable to keep it inside any longer. "That's what gets to me sometimes. God, a *hero*. And you know the greatest irony? My mom inherited the medal."

Cooper let a minute go by. "Maybe she should wear it," he said quietly. "Or you should."

The words drained her anger. Staring at him, she laughed. "Yeah. You're right. You're absolutely right."

Leaning close, he cupped her cheek with his hand. "And you're beautiful."

No, no, no. She scuttled back, her heels chasing the breaker that was rolling back to the sea. She couldn't afford to let him touch her, not when talking about the past made her so vulnerable.

His gaze stayed fixed on her face. "Are you still planning to leave the day after tomorrow?"

She nodded. God yes, and it wasn't soon enough. "I have to get back."

"I may stay overnight in Carmel."

Her stomach sliding low, she put two and two together and took another careful step back. The surf rushed over her bare feet and she hardly noticed. "Oh. Well. This is, uh, this is goodbye, then."

"Yeah. This is goodbye."

The words moved like a wave through her, in one fast rush washing away all the emotions of the day to leave her . . . empty. Though now she was instep-deep in the Pacific, the cold wasn't half as shocking as how the idea of never seeing him again desolated her.

"Of course, there's San Francisco," she said, trying to smile. "Hey, what do you bet that when you get back we'll meet up with each other doing the Rice-A-Roni run for the last open seat on a cable car?"

"Maybe." His dubious voice said it was highly unlikely.

"Yeah, maybe," Angel echoed. When he went back to the city he would go back to a life with a zillion women whom he found more irresistible than Angel.

Not that she cared. Why, at home she had men waiting for her, too. Men like . . . like . . .

Tom Jones. Her neighbor's faithless cat.

They stared at each other for another tense, silent moment.

But Angel had never done silent well. So she resurrected that friendly smile and firmly pinned it on her face as she rubbed her right palm on the seat of her jeans. Then she held out her hand to him. "Goodbye, Cooper. Thanks for everything."

He stared down at her outstretched fingers long enough to make her go jittery again. Just as she retracted her hand, he muttered something under his breath. Then he grabbed her wrist and yanked her to him.

"Wh—" He smothered the rest of the word with his mouth.

Angel tried stepping back, but her feet weren't on the ground. He'd lifted her against him and her toes only found air. She wiggled them helplessly, but then he slanted his head, took the kiss deeper, and she lost any desire to get away.

"This is crazy," he said, when he lifted his head to kiss a path toward her ear.

"Of course it is," she assured him, raising her chin so he could follow the goosebumps that were racing down her throat.

"I promised myself to keep away from you."

"Good idea. I made the exact same promise." She threw her arms around his neck. "So do it. Keep away. Move away."

"Me? Why me? Why don't you?"

"Because you're the big strong man." She moaned

when he licked her pulse. "I'm the fragile, defenseless woman."

"You're the devil."

"Angel."

"Devil." His lips tickled beneath her ear. "*Move away,* you said. Are you sure you want me to do that?"

She had no idea what he was talking about now, but his warm breath rushing against her ear made her nipples tighten and her stomach jump up and down. "Yes. Do it. Let's, um, do it."

He groaned. "You *are* a devil. That sounds so good. You don't know how good."

He found her mouth again, slid his tongue in slowly, so slowly that she felt her pulse hang, waiting for the first touch of tongue to tongue.

And when it happened, her blood gushed hot through her body and liquid heat rushed between her thighs. She pressed closer and he hitched her higher against him. But she had to get closer, closer. His hand slid beneath her sweatshirt, running over her bare skin.

She knew when he noticed she wasn't wearing a bra. His hand froze and then he groaned. "Angel . . ."

He shifted her again, his fingers coming between them to cup her bare breast. Moaning, she made it easier for them both by wrapping her legs around his waist.

Oh. Oh. He was hard against her, hard *there,* and she pressed down, letting her weight drag against his erection. His harsh groan tasted sweet against her tongue.

They exchanged dozens of kisses, or maybe it counted

as just one, because while the kisses changed—soft, slow, fierce—their mouths never parted.

Finally he tore his lips from hers, looking at her with an expression almost panicky with desire.

"Cooper," she whispered. "Cooper."

"Angel." His voice was guttural, thick. His eyes filled with an emotion she couldn't name.

Then his knees buckled. One minute she was in his arms, plastered against his warmth, and the next she was tumbled onto the cold, damp sand. He was kneeling beside her, looking at her with those strangely lit eyes and that same panicky expression.

"My heart," he said, falling on his back against the sand. "Oh, fuck. My heart."

Terror clutched at her insides. "What?"

Then the fear slapped her, taking her from paralyzed alarm to keen alertness. Rolling to her knees, she scooted to his side, grabbed his hand, and looked him in the eye. "You're going to be all right," she said loudly, swallowing her own panic. "I know CPR."

With that, she pushed the heel of her right hand to his forehead and used the fingers of her other to tilt up his chin. Then she grabbed both sides of the cotton shirt he wore and ripped it open, buttons popping high into the air. With his airway as unobstructed as possible and nothing between her and evidence that his chest was moving, she bent over Cooper and put her cheek directly above his mouth and nose.

His warm breath brushed against her cheek. In and out. In and out again. The rhythm was a bit accelerated, perhaps, but he was certainly breathing. She lightly placed her palm on his chest, just to make sure she felt it move too.

"You're breathing," she said. CPR wasn't necessary unless he wasn't getting oxygen. "You're conscious."

"No kidding."

Sarcasm was probably a good sign too, but she kept her position curled over him, her cheek near his mouth, her palm lightly covering his heart. "How are you feeling now?"

"About the same," he admitted. "My breathing is too fast, too shallow. My heart is pounding so damn hard I think they must have stuck a kettledrum in there during the surgery."

"Okay, okay." Angel gently rubbed his skin, hoping to soothe. "Is there any numbness on your left side? Can you make a fist?"

"I'm not numb anywhere. Fists no problem either."

Angel bit her lip, wondering if she should leave him and run for help, or if it would be safer to stay in case CPR became necessary. "I'd give my life for a cell phone right now," she muttered.

He managed a short laugh. "Somehow I think that would defeat the purpose."

She thought laughing was another good sign, but what the heck did she know? "What does your doctor say?" she asked urgently, desperate to find some clue as to what to do next. "What are you supposed to be watching for?"

"He says I'm fine. I lost thirty-five pounds. I'm a vegetarian. I gave up cigarettes. I exercise. He says my heart's good."

She'd be relieved as all get out if he still wasn't lying

flat on the sand, his heart beating like that kettledrum beneath her palm. She shoved her other hand under her sweatshirt and laid it against her own heart, to see what a beat *should* feel like.

Like a kettledrum. *Bam. Bam. Bam. Bam.*

His breath continued to rush against her cheek, fast breaths that mirrored her own. She was a bit panicked now, yeah, but they'd been just as speedy when Cooper had been kissing her, touching her.

She slowly sat up, leaving her hand against his chest. "How do you feel now?"

"Less anxious. But about the same."

Her eyes narrowed. His color was good. He was talking just fine. "The doctor says you're cured?"

"*Cured* isn't the word, I don't think." He inhaled a slow, careful breath. "But there wasn't anything obviously wrong when I was in his office last month."

Angel had a fiftyish, casual gym friend whose husband had had a heart attack the year before. It was amazing the kind of things you'd tell a near stranger on the neighboring Stairmaster. Something about the mingled sweat drops on the floor, maybe.

Remembering some of their conversations gave Angel an idea.

She stroked his chest again. "How are you now?"

"Maybe a little better."

Casually, she slid her palm downward. The heel of her hand brushed the waistband of his jeans and his belly muscles twitched.

"Jesus, Angel." He grabbed her wrist.

"Sorry." She gently pulled from his grasp and returned her hand to its place over his heart. Oh yeah.

Just an almost-sexual touch and the beat had sped up again.

"I think I know what's wrong." Angel took his closest hand in her free one and slid it under her sweatshirt.

She pressed his palm between her bare breasts, and then, holding it there, bent over to kiss Cooper gently, slowly, and very deliberately. She kissed through his momentary resistance and then let him really have it. Still gently, but wet and thorough. Plenty of tongue.

When she straightened, they were both panting.

"Breathless?" she asked. "I am."

His eyes widened, his heartbeat still pounding against her palm.

"Feel my heart?" Under her shirt, she pressed her hand against the top of his. "I think it's going faster, even harder than yours."

"You're not serious. . . ."

"Serious as a heart attack." Angel smiled a little, then slid her hand from his chest to cup his cheek. "It's arousal, my friend. Lust. Desire. Nothing more dangerous than that."

Cooper gawked at her, as an embarrassed flush rushed over his face.

Her gym buddy's husband had been terrified to make love. Every time he got hot and bothered, his natural physical responses had scared him silly. He'd been convinced they would bring on a second heart attack. It was a very common problem, her friend had said, but it had taken her husband months to get past his anxiety.

"You haven't had sex recently, right? Not since the heart attack."

The color deepened on his face. "I don't want to talk about it." In one quick move he slid his hand from her skin and sat up.

She looked at his rigidly set profile and wished she could make this easier for him. Curling her fingers into a fist, she lightly punched his shoulder. "Hey, would it make you feel any better if I admit that my sheets have been pretty cool recently too?"

When he still didn't answer, she tried to think of exactly how long he'd been missing from San Francisco. Ten months, maybe more?

"For goodness' sake," she said, still trying to work him past his obvious chagrin. "I was willing to save your life. Share my spit with you doing CPR. Can't we talk?"

He sent her a sidelong look. "You were sharing spit with me *before* I fell onto the sand, clutching my heart."

"I know! You owe me something for that. I thought I'd killed you with my kiss!" She punched him again. "For goodness' sake. This is me, Angel, the woman you're most likely never to see again. We can get past this, can't we?"

Though it was obvious *he* was the one who wanted to be left alone now, she couldn't walk away. This shouldn't be their last memory of each other—Cooper feeling embarrassed and Angel feeling . . . whatever it was.

"Fine." He turned his head, pinned her with his gaze that was darker and deeper thanks to the now-dusk. "You're right. I haven't had sex since the heart attacks and surgery. I haven't had sex in twenty months, sixteen days, and, oh, approximately three hours and forty-one minutes."

Chapter 11

It was nearly night, but Cooper could see Angel's eyes round. "Three hours and forty-one minutes?" she echoed. "You know it down to the minute?"

He put on a show of looking at his watch. "And fifty seconds."

She shook her head. "You made that part up."

"I made that part up," he agreed.

"Why?"

"To *shut* you up."

He heard her huffy sigh, and under other circumstances he'd have laughed. But hell, how humiliating was this? God, he just wanted to sit here all alone and feel like an ass in peace.

"So, um . . ." she ventured after half a breath of quiet. "How long ago was your surgery?"

He jerked a shoulder. "Twelve months, nearly thirteen."

She went silent. Only temporarily. "But you said twenty—"

"Damn it, can't you let anything go?" he snapped. "I had a big case before that. I didn't have a free moment for wining and dining." And screwing. At the time, the dry spell hadn't bothered him. When he'd made it to bed, if he'd made it to bed, he'd been desperate for sleep.

"Okay, okay," Angel said. "I'm sorry if I've embarrassed you."

"Yeah, well I'm sorry that I put you through that . . . that . . ." Words failed him, so he jerked his shoulder again. "Now that we've exchanged apologies, go away."

"You're angry."

At God, at the world, at the way his body had betrayed him a year ago, at himself for being so stupid as to abuse it in the first place. At how foolish he must have looked to Angel a few minutes ago, stretched out on the sand.

"Not at you. Now please, go away."

She only shook her head again, damn her, sending a waft of perfume his way. Hell, why was she here to plague him now? If fate wanted to throw them together, then why not years ago? Why not at Stinko's or Doc's? He could picture it, he could picture coming up behind Angel in line at some San Francisco fast-food joint. That perfume of hers would have instantly snagged his attention, and then he would have noted all that floaty hair and her slender, curvy body.

Maybe he would have struck up a conversation, if he wasn't in a hurry or preoccupied by a case, that is. Maybe he would have parlayed talk into a date for drinks. Then later that week he would have been standing at some bar or other and Angel would have walked in, wearing a pair of those high heels she favored and a smile just for him. What might have happened then?

Of course, it could have gone a different way. He might have hurried up to that line in his usual rush, his brain racing through the details of his next court appearance. Her perfume would have diverted him long enough to give her the once-over, to silently whistle at another of nature's miraculous spins on femininity, but then her turn would have come at the counter, and then his. His focus would have jumped back to work. And in the few minutes it took to order lunch, she would have been gone from his life.

Leaving him never to know the enticing combination that she was—the tough cookie with a marshmallow filling, an angel with devilish sex appeal. But the way he'd lived before—fast, furious, like his life would never end—he might not have taken the time to appreciate her.

Relaxing a little, he turned toward Angel and reached out. "I'm glad I met you," he said, wrapping his forefinger with a lock of her hair.

For a long moment, he thought he'd managed to shut her up at last. "Knock me over with a feather," she said faintly.

He gave a playful tug to her curl, then set her free. The stars were beginning to punch through the dimming sky and he lifted his face to them, opening his mind to the calming beauty of the night, thinking of those books on holistic healing Judd kept shoving at him. Cooper wasn't too great at meditation, but he kept working at it. Focusing on slowing his breathing, he tried to iron out the last of his mental knots: his lust for Angel, his anxiety about his heart, the humiliation of his pseudo-attack.

Maybe it was working. He synced his breathing to the steady *shush* of the waves and tried detaching from himself, from himself as a man, to see his existence as part of the natural world, the natural order. Birth, life, death.

"So, how long were you planning on going without sex?"

Angel's question yanked him right out of his brief state of serenity. "*What?*" God, she was the most irritating woman.

"Sorry, but I guess it's the reporter in me," she said, sounding not the least bit contrite. "I was sitting here wondering how long you planned to be celibate. Surely not the rest of your life."

Terrific. While he'd been making himself one with the universe, nearly achieving all that kung fu, Little Grasshopper shit, she'd been speculating on his sexual future. The knots retwisted with a vengeance.

"Couldn't we just drop the subject?" he asked through his teeth. The fact was, the "rest of his life" wasn't going to be very long. Like Cooper, his father had had an early heart attack. Like Cooper, he'd come home from the hospital, done the whole healthy lifestyle bit, then died from his second attack within a year.

Myocardial infarction #2 had already hit Cooper. He

figured that even now he was breathing on borrowed time.

"I'm just curious," Angel went on, "about how your mind works. A man's mind. I read this article in *U.S. News & World Report* on the near-supreme priority men put on sex. It astonished me. So I'm asking, how long do you suppose before your interest in sex overcomes your concerns about your heart? And if you knew you were going to die tomorrow, would sex be on your 'To Do' list tonight?"

If she talked about sex for two more seconds he was going to drown himself, that's how his mind worked. For God's sake, since the instant she'd slid her thigh against his in the church, sex had made itself a pain-in-the-ass priority for him. But hell yes, he'd reined in his libido, as irrational as that might sound to people who'd never felt the crushing press of an African elephant on their chest while the Grim Reaper's scythe was slicing into their arm.

He'd reined in his libido, because just thinking about sex with Angel set his heart thumping so damn hard that he was afraid it would provoke—

But it didn't.

It hadn't.

Just moments ago, Angel had placed his hand over the smooth warm skin of her heart and proven that the lusty, pounding rhythm of his was the normal, natural reaction of a man to a woman. Of a woman to a man.

Oh, another heart attack was going to kill him soon enough, he was convinced of that. *But having sex wasn't the certain trigger he'd feared.*

"Good God." He grinned, stunned, then exhilarated

by the turn of his thoughts. Grabbing Angel's shoulders, he planted a hard, smacking kiss on her mouth.

Then he held her away, laughing out loud. "I've been an idiot!" He could admit it now, so he shouted the fact to the ocean, the stars, to the darkness that seemed to be lifting from his soul.

Jumping to his feet, he laughed again. "And I've wasted so much time. So much goddamn time."

Angel didn't resist when he swooped her off the sand and swung her around. "You are the smartest and sexiest woman in the world, did you know that?"

Her feet touched down and he bent to kiss her, but she held him off with her hand. "Wait, wait, wait. What the heck has gotten into you?"

He touched his forehead to hers and lowered his voice. "Lust, baby, and I'm not fighting it anymore."

"What?"

Not wanting to fritter away another second, he started pulling her toward the tunnel. "I'm taking you to bed."

Her feet dug into the sand. "I'm not sleepy."

"And I'm not Doc, Dopey, Grumpy, or Sneezy. *We*'re going to bed."

"Then the jury's still out on Dopey," she muttered, still resisting his forward movement. "We are *not* going to bed."

God, what a woman she was, he thought, letting her protest go in one ear and out the other. He caught her free hand and tried to get her going in the right direction. "Angel, it'll be fun. Great. I promise to blow your mind."

"First off, we're going to have to work on bolstering

that ego of yours." She yanked her hands from his. "And second, have you forgotten I'm going back to the city day after tomorrow?"

He grinned, because nothing could get him down at this moment, not with carnal anticipation fizzing through his blood like carbonation. "So? Surely a strong woman like you can take what she wants without worrying about the future."

"I believe I should point out it's what *you* want, right?"

He moved so fast she didn't have time to dodge him. In a breath, he'd snaked his hands beneath her baggy white sweatshirt to cup her bare breasts. "I can prove you want it too." His voice went hoarse at the feel of her warm, smooth skin against his palms, at the undeniable, heavy thrum of her heartbeat.

"Cooper." Her breath caught as he brushed her nipples with his thumbs. "Cooper, we're not going to see each other again."

That's why no one could get hurt. They'd leave each other, a pleasant memory. A man waiting to die couldn't ask for more. Wouldn't risk it.

"Angel . . ." He couldn't keep touching her and keep his sanity too. Sliding his hands to her waist, he pulled her against him. "Wasn't it you who complained about sex changing things? That you could never pick up right where you'd left off? This will solve that problem. From the outset we know it's just two nights."

"*Two* nights?"

"Caught that, did you?" Why couldn't he have the hots for some bimbo-type blonde who couldn't count?

He cleared his throat. "I was staying over in Carmel tomorrow night to . . . to keep clear of temptation."

"Cooper . . ." Her voice filled with doubt.

He was as close as he'd ever been to begging. "Angel, Angel, Angel. You're killing me, baby."

"Yeah, well, it's becoming an interesting habit of mine."

Oh, he had to capture her chin and kiss the sassy remark from her pretty mouth. She resisted at first, but then she leaned against him. "Say yes," he murmured into her ear.

She closed her eyes. "Cooper . . ." Her doubt wiggled on the end of his name like a fish about to free itself from the line.

"Say yes." Certain her resistance was waning, he bent his head to kiss the top of hers.

It suddenly jerked up, cracking him hard on the chin. "One night," she said, ignoring his yelp.

He gingerly touched his jaw. "Huh?"

She broke away from him to stand a few feet off. It was full dark now, and the starlight gleamed against her hair. Starlight on moonbeams. He stared at her, his smarting chin forgotten, as he was struck once again by her otherworldly, fairy prettiness. Standing there in her white sweatshirt and her faded jeans, she might have slid down to earth on the tail of a comet.

"One night. Tomorrow night. The last night."

He was so caught up in the magic of her looks that he didn't immediately absorb her words. And once he had, she was gone. Poof.

Maybe she *was* magic.

Magic enough, anyway, that by the time he followed her back to the retreat he wanted her badly enough to beg. Problem was, there was little a man could do when silence was the rule. He knocked on her cottage door, but she didn't answer. He wrote her a note that made so many sexual promises he could hardly walk when he was finished. But damn, the heavy weather stripping he'd so ably installed in a recent fit of boredom didn't allow a sheet of paper, even one that had to be melting from its heated words, to slip under the door.

He thought about going out, going somewhere and picking up a woman who was willing instead of maddening. But he couldn't.

Not this first time, anyway, he assured himself hastily.

One night. Tomorrow night. The last night.

It would have to be enough.

The next morning, Angel drove toward San Luis Obispo, agonizing over the promise she'd made on the beach the night before. Stephen Whitney had been born in the coastal city south of Big Sur, but her real reason for getting in her car was to put distance between Cooper and herself.

She needed space in order to reconsider her agreement to go to bed with him. It wasn't an easy answer to settle on, and unfortunately, this time her usual aid in decision making—What Would Woodward Do?—didn't apply too well.

If only she'd kept her head about her last night! But

he'd been so relieved when he'd realized his heart was fine. His hands had been so seductive, sliding over her skin. His patent delight at the idea of going to bed with her had been somewhat appealing.

Who was she kidding?

His delight had made her hot.

And it had made her happy.

That's when she should have said no.

Instead, she'd said yes, to tonight, to one night, because even a mushy woman couldn't make something out of a one night stand. Yet she couldn't help worrying. . . .

Oh, deal, Angel! she thought, disgusted with herself. It was just sex! While it had never lived up to its exuberant press, in her previous experience nothing but bodies had ever been tangled up by the event either. This went here, the man went there, she was either mildly aroused or mildly amused, then she waited it out and hoped he'd go home soon.

It wasn't likely to be all that different—better—with Cooper. Why not skip the whole thing and . . . and then disappoint him?

Right back on the pokey horns of the dilemma, Angel spotted an open-air mall up ahead. Deciding an extra-tall latte and a few swipes of the ol' credit card were just the things to give her mind a rest, she switched on her turn signal and crossed the freeway lanes in the direction of the Seascape Shopping Center.

But once there, between a Sam Goody's and a See's Candies, Angel discovered something else to muddle her thinking. A Stephen Whitney Gallery. Clutching her latte, she stared at the storefront, a banner across its window proclaiming it an official home of the work of the "Artist of the Heart."

There were galleries like it all over America, they'd caught her eye dozens of times. And dozens of times she'd managed to walk past, gaze averted, never feeling the slightest twinge of . . . anything. Not in her heart. Not in her head.

But now . . .

"There it is, Ray." An older woman bustled up, her attention focused on the same storefront. She wore a plain blue skirt and a gray sweater that matched her softly curling gray hair. Over her elbow was a bulky navy-blue leather purse that matched the color of the bulky orthopedic shoes on her feet.

"I see it, sweets." Ray was panting a bit, as if Sweets had been rushing him. He adjusted his glasses with one hand and slid the other around the woman. "They promised to put it in the back, no need to run."

Angel smiled to herself. Ray looked quite a few years and quite a few pounds past running.

"I know, I know." The woman sighed. "And we're early. They're not open yet." She looked about, her eye catching Angel's. "Are you waiting for the gallery to open too?"

"Me?"

"Is there a special painting you have in mind?" Sweets's sweet-looking expression turned a bit anxious. "Not *Summer Sidewalk*? When we found out it was up for sale, we asked the gallery to hold it for us."

"No, no." Angel shook her head. "It's all yours."

The only thing she wanted of Stephen Whitney was answers.

That's when it hit her—the reason for her waffling, the source of all this second-guessing about having sex with Cooper.

It was her conscience.

She'd gone to Big Sur for the story—for the truth. How could she be intimate with Cooper, for a single night or a dozen of them, and then blithely return to San Francisco to write a story that might hurt him and his?

A young man was unlocking the gallery doors. As Angel watched, he pushed them open, then smiled and beckoned to the older couple beside her. Ray moved, but then Sweets caught his arm.

"Wait, Ray, this young lady was here first." She smiled at Angel and shooed her forward with her hand.

Angel blinked. "Oh, but I . . . I . . ." *I don't want to!*

"Go on, now. Go on." Sweets smiled at her again. Shooed again. "There's no reason to hesitate."

No reason at all. Except that at the idea of going inside, Angel's skin went clammy, her breath didn't reach her lungs, and her heart banged on the inside of her chest like it wanted out. Was this sick dread what Cooper felt on the beach last night?

But the couple was still looking at her expectantly and Angel couldn't think up an excuse that would satisfy them. She couldn't tell them she was afraid—she wasn't!

Her gait stiff, she forced herself toward the door. The young man standing there nodded at her, and she nodded back, steeling herself to cross the threshold. It was cold inside the gallery, or maybe it was just cold inside of her. When she made it to the middle of the small space, she halted.

Bringing her latte to her lips to ease her suddenly dry throat, she quickly ran her gaze over the dozen or so pieces of artwork mounted about the room, finally settling on a prominent display of three large paintings. They were his, all right, the kitsch, candy-bright colors certifying them as Stephen Whitney's.

Sweets and Ray drew up to her and the older woman followed Angel's gaze. "Lovely, aren't they? Ray and I collect the missing children."

At Angel's blank look, Sweets laughed and shook her head. "I'm sorry, that's what we Whitneyphiles call the paintings like those three. The missing children."

The missing children? "Ah." Angel got it now. Each of the scenes depicted something child-oriented: a metal swing set, a wooden sandbox, a picnic table with a crumpled brown lunch bag on top. In his usual style, the artist had sentimentalized the background with blue skies and puffy clouds, while the foreground was littered with wildflowers and knee-high weeds.

All three paintings gave the impression that a child had just skipped away—the wooden seat of the swing was flying back, there was a half-eaten cookie on top of the lunch bag, a half-built castle was made in the sand, along with the depressions of small feet leading out of the box.

Missing children. Angel shivered. If you asked her, they were kind of spooky.

"Well, uh, nice." She started to scuttle away, but Sweets caught her wrist in excitement.

"Oh! Here's ours."

The gallery's young man was coming out of a back room, a framed painting in his arms. With an awkward flourish, he spun it to face Ray, Sweets, and Angel.

A typical saccharine sky, blue, with fat, pinky-white clouds. There was a dilapidated picket fence that wouldn't hold back a butterfly. In the foreground, vermilion dandelion leaves poked through a long crack in a pitted sidewalk. A pair of beat-up sneakers were tumbled nearby, holey white socks discarded beside them. On a patch of unblemished concrete at the center of the painting lay a red rubber ball and some metal jacks. Again, there was the feeling the player had just abandoned the game.

Sweets sighed. "Perfect. I had a jacks set just like that when I was a little girl."

"So did I." Angel suddenly saw it in her head, recalling the squishy ball and the tinny jangle when the jacks hit concrete. She saw herself trying to play, remembered her frustration with the game, and then a large hand, the back of it splattered with colors, entered the frame of her memory.

Bounce. Grab. Bounce. Grab more. *It's easy, see?*

No. No! Closing her eyes, Angel shook her head to jar the image loose. Shook it again for good measure. Then she cautiously peered at the painting again. Nothing about it seemed familiar, now. Nothing at all. She wasn't sure anymore that she'd truly ever owned or even played jacks. She never remembered her father.

Still, she let out a relieved breath as she watched the gallery worker walk away with the painting, Ray following him to conclude the transaction. Ready to say a polite goodbye, Angel turned to the older lady. "I'm sure you'll enjoy—"

Sweets was crying. Sobbing.

That old helpless feeling clutched at Angel's still-cold insides. "What is it? What's the matter?" She juggled her latte cup, trying to get into her purse and find something to stanch the lady's tears.

"No, no, no." Sweets was already waving around a handkerchief. "I'll be fine. Don't worry. It's just that the painting . . ."

Angel's grip tightened on her coffee, hating that nice Sweets was so upset. The painting was a piece of crap, Angel thought fiercely. A baby step away from Elvis on velvet and weeping clowns. For God's sake, at least the poker-playing dogs showed a sense of humor.

Sweets wiped at her eyes. "I'm sorry, I'm sorry. It reminds me of being a girl again."

"Crying?"

The other lady let out a watery chuckle. "The painting. You probably think me a silly old fool, but when I look at it, at any of my Whitneys, I remember sweeter times, innocent times. At my age it's a long way to look back, but if I just glance at one of my paintings, I'm there again."

"I see."

Sweets chuckled again. "Perhaps you don't. But what you might not understand, and I know the art critics don't, is that the paintings bring me pleasure. I'll not apologize or be ashamed of that."

Angel's conscience stung her once again. And then again when Ray rejoined his wife, the brown-wrapped painting tucked under his arm. He looked so happy that for a second Angel thought *she* might cry.

Now tongue-tied, she parted from Ray and Sweets at the door and turned away from the gallery. But then she found herself looking back at the older couple, who were still smiling over their acquisition.

She'd been toying with the idea of leading off her story on Stephen Whitney with the slams of the critics. While he was beloved by the political and religious "traditional values" crowd, real art pundits savaged the man's work. But now Angel wondered if their opinions were any more valid than Sweets's. What pleasure did *they* offer to anyone with their sarcastic barbs?

Yet if she didn't hook the readers' interest with someone's flamboyant, nasty criticism of Whitney's work, then what? Open with a critique of the artist's character? Tell how the "Artist of the Heart" had turned a cold shoulder when his daughter was in desperate need? She'd been toying with that idea too, of course. First person. A gripping account of how she'd been betrayed.

And thus betray Lainey and Katie, her conscience whispered. And Cooper. Even if she didn't go to bed with him.

Oh hell. Angel scowled at her reflection in the window of another store. *Fine,* she told her conscience, *you win.* Since all she had to bring down Stephen Whitney was her own sob story, then she wouldn't try to bring him down at all.

Let the emperor keep his clothes. Saint Stephen could be canonized, for all she cared.

Unsure if she was disgusted or relieved, she slammed her paper cup into a waiting trash can. The latte hadn't improved her mood, not at all. Now it was up to her plastic cards and her credit limits.

She was hurrying toward the Victoria's Secret across the courtyard and recalculating her clothing budget when a new thought struck her. Her ethical dilemma was solved.

One back-page, tepid story on Stephen Whitney bought Angel that one-night stand. One conscience-free, emotionally uninvolving opportunity to give Cooper Jones pleasure.

Chapter 12

The night was hot and dark and so was Cooper's mood.

It was past ten when he heard the chirpy little knock on his door, and he knew who was on the other side. He considered ignoring her, but then she'd guess she'd gotten to him. So he strolled to the door and pulled it open, then propped one shoulder casually against the jamb.

His body blocking the entry.

Angel's eyes widened. "Uh, hi."

She might be wearing some silky little wraparound number in pale yellow, but all day long he'd pictured her in black leather and carrying a whip.

"You took off so early this morning, I thought you might have left Tranquility for good," he drawled. That idea had been the first to lash at him.

"You could have checked. All my things were in my cottage."

He jerked a shoulder, because he *had* checked and it still hadn't cooled his temper. "Then I wondered"—*all day long, hour by hour, minute by minute*—"when you were coming back."

Her gaze slid away from his. "I, uh, had a few things to do in San Luis Obispo. It's a long drive."

"You returned a couple hours ago." That's when the torture had really started. He'd promised himself to wait her out, and she'd made him wait, all right. "I could sue you for breach of promise, by the way. You said night. It's been night for quite a while."

" 'Breach of promise.' " She shook her head. "It's that kind of stuff that gives lawyers a bad name, you know."

"You said night." He shrugged, then shoved his hands in the pockets of his jeans. "It's night."

She rolled her eyes. "And I'm here, aren't I? So are you going to invite me in or not?"

Or not was sounding pretty damned good. She'd had him in knots for the last twenty-four hours. But, of course, she was the only way to unravel them too. "Not if you're reluctant," he said through his teeth.

"Of course I'm reluctant, you idiot!" Rolling her eyes again, she placed both hands on his chest and pushed him out of the way. "Right now this is starting to feel clumsy and calculated and . . ." Her voice drifted away as she stomped past him and took in the sight of his living room.

"And pretty," she finally said.

"I'm not a complete idiot." He shut the door and

turned to her. "I had dinner reservations for us at the Crosscreek Hotel. We missed them."

She was still looking about. The retreat had a decent stockpile of candles in case of power outages during winter storms. He'd placed them strategically around the living room, and even more strategically—sparingly—in the bedroom. Their flickering flames made the darkness appear to pulse around them.

"Oh, I'm sorry. I didn't know about dinner." Her earlier exasperation fell away and she sent him a sweet, almost shy glance. Then she walked toward the side table beside the couch, where he had a pail of ice chilling a bottle of wine. "It's all so very pretty."

She sent him another little glance, and her fingertip idly trailed down the neck of the wine bottle. Watching that slow, sliding finger, his mood changed too. With her here, close enough to touch, his annoyance and impatience evaporated, leaving only desire behind.

Clearing his throat, he took a step toward her. "May I pour you a glass?"

"That would be nice." Her voice was soft now, and in the shadowy room, she looked like another yellow candle flame. More light against the darkness.

The wineglass was Beth's, and he filled it to the brim. When he handed it to Angel, he thought her fingers trembled.

She stared down at the wine as if it fascinated her. "Thank you. The candles are a very nice touch."

Taking a deep, calming breath, he picked up his bottle of Perrier and tapped it against her glass. "It's too hot for lights."

She sipped at the wine, her free hand once again idly

cruising the neck of the sweating bottle. "Yeah, well," she said, giving a small shrug. "It's been a hot couple of weeks."

"Yeah." He watched, mesmerized, as one of her fingers dipped into the ice bucket's slushy water.

She drew it out of the pail to stroke it slowly down the side of her neck. From beneath her lashes, she glanced at him. "Very, very, hot."

Lust squeezed his throat. "Fire danger."

"Hmm?" Her finger returned to the icy water.

"This much unrelenting heat"—he paused to down a swallow of his Perrier—"means there's danger of fire."

She let a long beat go by, then she flicked him another look from her tangle of lashes. "You should take your shirt off, then."

Despite his recent drink, his mouth went dry. "Huh?"

"We wouldn't want you to burn." Then she opened her eyes wide, all sexy innocence. "*Oh.* You mean there's danger of fire *outside.*"

"Hear you roar," he murmured, shaking his head at the playful turn she'd suddenly taken on him. "Full of surprises tonight, aren't you?"

A smile twitched the corners of her mouth and she lifted her glass again. "Now that I see you went to so much trouble, the candles, the wine, maybe I'll let them all out."

He could hardly breathe. "I gather you're warming up too."

She set her wineglass aside to toy with the bow that

tied her dress at the side of her waist. "Maybe *I* should take something off."

His gaze shot to her face, then back to the bow again. One tug, he guessed, and that little slip-of-nothing she was wearing would fall free.

His pulse leaped and he abruptly dropped to the couch so that he wouldn't grab, pull, take. "We're not in any hurry." He'd promised her something special, not something hasty. "Come sit down."

She sat beside him, but then immediately leaned closer, her hands going for the buttons on his shirt.

He drew back. "What the hell are you doing?"

"I like your body," she said. "I want to see it."

"No, no, no." He caught her hands, pushed them away. "Drink your wine. Take a few minutes."

At the speed things were moving, he was afraid it was going to have to count as foreplay, this first time tonight.

She angled her head. "Are you worried again?"

"About this triggering a heart attack? No." About performing with any finesse, yes. He reached around her to grab her wineglass, then shoved it in her hand. "Here, keep busy."

Her laugh was soft. "You *are* worried. You shouldn't be. I'll take care of you."

Something about that last sentence didn't sit well with him.

He stroked the back of his hand down her face. "You won't be left out, I promise you."

At that, her gaze slid away from his. "Well, uh, listen. Let me tell you my plan."

"Your plan." He ran his thumb along the soft line of her cheek.

"My plan for sex."

Now it was his turn to laugh. "Weren't you the one who was just complaining about how 'calculated' this felt? Why don't we play it by ear?"

"Here's what I think." She still wasn't looking at him as she took a gulp of her wine. "I think we should do it quick."

His hand stilled. "What?"

She edged away, backing off from his touch. "Well, see, I was thinking about this on the drive. The way I see it, this is a hurdle for you. You know, this first time since your surgery. And I'm sure you're a little nervous about it, despite what you say. So we should just, um, do it quick and get it over with."

"It *was* a long trip," he murmured.

"You'll feel much better afterward," she said earnestly.

"If we do it quick and get it over with."

"Right." Her head bobbed up and down in an emphatic, nervous nod. "Then I can go back to my cottage and finish my packing."

He stared at her for a minute. Then he flopped against the sofa cushions and groaned. "Who the hell is spreading rumors about me in San Francisco?"

"What? I—"

"Natasha. It has to be Natasha Campbell. She's been out for revenge for years, ever since I told her I don't date—much less bed—engaged women. Man, I never thought she'd be so vicious as to malign my sexual reputation."

"I haven't heard any rumors about . . . about that. I mean, I heard you played hard, but not that you, uh . . ."

"Don't play fair?"

She shook her head. "I've never heard anything like that."

"So then why all this let's-get-it-over-with-so-I-can-go-back-to-packing?" Didn't she think he could keep her busy all night long?

She huffed at him. "Because I'm leaving tomorrow morning. I told you it would be one time."

"*What?*" He sat up. "One *night,* baby. You promised me one *night.*"

Her hand waved. "One time, one night. What's the difference?"

This wasn't going right. He took some deep breaths, trying to get that vision of her dressed in black leather out of his head. But she was torturing him again! It wasn't as if he wanted to make grand promises that he couldn't keep, but hell, he had grand intentions. Intentions that he at least wanted to attempt.

Most of all, he realized, he wanted her to spend the night, the whole night, in his bed.

"One time won't be enough for me," he finally ground out. He took another deep breath and forced himself to relax. "And what about you? We're gonna be good together, you know that. You know how things heat up between us. Spend the night with me and we'll both greet the dawn wearing smiles."

"That's a lot of pressure—"

"Try me, baby." He shifted toward her and caught the back of her neck with his hand. Their mouths met, fused, and a hot shudder ripped up his spine. "Try me," he said against her lips.

She broke away from him, gasping.

"See?" He reached out to thumb the moisture off her bottom lip. "I'll make it good for you. Every time."

"Don't." She shook her head, her voice a little desperate. "You don't have to do that."

His eyes narrowed. "I don't have to do what?"

"Make it good for me. Worry about me at all."

"What?"

She rose off the couch, extended her hand toward him. "Let's go to bed, Cooper. Now."

"You're really starting to piss me off," he said, ignoring her hand. "If it's not Natasha, then why is it? Why don't you think I can satisfy you?"

She turned her back. "I . . . I don't want you to."

His mind spinning, he could only stare at her squared, tense shoulders.

"I don't want you to worry about that, about me."

He stood, still not knowing what to think, to say, to do. "You're tying me in knots again, Angel." Her back stiffened even more when he brushed his fingertips across it. "Why would I want to go to bed with you and not think about you? Why wouldn't I want to make it good for you?"

She was silent.

"Angel—"

"Because you won't be able to," she snapped out, her voice brittle. "Okay? Happy now? The truth is . . ."

"Yeah, let's get to that."

She took a breath. "The truth is, we might both die of old age if we wait around for me to have an orgasm."

Cooper would have thought the whole conversation was some weird dream if the embarrassment in her voice wasn't so real, so painful. "But . . ." He scrubbed his face with his hands and went over the last two weeks in his mind.

She'd admitted to the attraction first.

She'd kissed him, touched him.

He'd kissed her, touched her.

For God's sake, he'd *already* made her come!

There was no denying that, was there? Yeah, women could fake it, but not *that* well. "In the kitchen . . ."

Her hand waved again. "An aberration. I told you, too much tofu—eggplant, whatever. I don't know. But it's not as if, as if . . ."

He saw her point right away. "As if I was inside you."

She waved her hand again, but said nothing.

Cooper sucked in a steadying breath. If he *hadn't* pleased her in the kitchen that night, he might have room for concern. But as it stood now, the only thing that worried him was how to convince her he was quite capable of taking her to bed and doing his part.

"Angel—"

"Please, Cooper. Please, let's not discuss it."

I-am-woman-hear-me-roar could apparently only take a person so far. He brushed his fingers across her back again. "Tell me that you like my kisses."

"You know I do."

He stepped up behind her and put his cheek against her temple. "That you like me to touch you."

She leaned back against him. "Of course. And I like to touch you too."

He smiled and his fingers found hers, linked them. There was no need to argue with her any longer. "Then let's go to bed."

When he was through, he promised himself, she'd be too wrung out to leave it.

To make sure things went her way, the instant they made it to the bedroom, Angel shed the dress.

Cooper stumbled back, staring at her body in the meager candlelight. "W-what the hell is that?"

"A little something I picked up today." It was a skin tight teddy. White lace. Well, some of it was, anyway. From the sharp V between her legs to a line just below her breasts. But the cups covering them were an almost-transparent, nude-colored mesh.

"Do you like it?" She twirled.

He made a strangled noise. She'd made a similar sound herself when she'd tried the outfit on in the dressing room. The thong-style back of the teddy was nude-colored mesh too. On the modest meter, she registered an unwavering "very" and this getup was beyond daring. It was wild.

It was designed to make a man wild. It was designed to make a man think of nothing but his pleasure.

And she wanted to give that to Cooper. Somewhere between the moment he'd put his arm around his sister at the memorial service and the time she'd stumbled upon him watching the sunset with his niece, she'd lost her first line of defense. Then last night on the beach, without setting off a single warning bell, he'd slipped past her second guard.

And now she wanted to hold him in her arms and feel him lose himself in her.

It was such a dangerous want, though, that driving back from the mall she'd hit upon the one-time, do-it-quick plan. She was leaving in the morning, and with that plan she would make sure she didn't leave any of herself behind. That he didn't take anything from her.

He stayed statue-still as she approached him, except to shake his head. "You're determined to win, aren't you?"

"Mmm." She focused on unbuttoning his shirt. "Is that such a bad thing?" Her hands slid over his bare shoulders as she pushed the fabric away.

He sucked in a harsh breath as she kissed the center of the scar on his chest. His hand pushed through her hair to cup the back of her head. "You're the bad thing."

She smiled against his hot skin, then ran her tongue down the shiny scar. He shuddered and she thought that bad sounded kinda fun.

The idea blossomed in her mind as she ran her mouth over his chest. Bad Angel could take what she wanted, taste what she wanted, push him to take her, quick, like she wanted him to. His belly was flat and hard and she rubbed her cheek against it. Then she dropped to her knees and shaped the erection beneath his jeans with her hands.

He groaned, his fingers tightening in her hair. "Angel, Angel."

She smiled up at him, noting his half-closed eyes, the little jolt he made when she rubbed him with her palms.

On impulse, she leaned forward and pressed her face there, running her chin up and down his hardness.

Her fingers went to the button at his waist.

He jerked her up by the elbows. "No," he said roughly. "It's too good to end that soon."

"But . . ."

He crushed his mouth against hers. Angel felt that "bad" he'd mentioned start to simmer and burn inside of her—that hot boil of lust that kept turning up to surprise her. He thrust his tongue between her lips and she closed her eyes as he stroked against hers, hard and sure.

Then her mouth was left, wet and wanting, as he bent and took her mesh-covered nipple inside his mouth. As he sucked on it.

"Cooper." Maybe she was moaning his name. Someone was.

"You can't come to me, you can't come to my bed dressed like this and expect me to ignore you."

She heard the words but didn't really listen to them, because then he was latched onto her other nipple while kneading the first breast with firm, demanding pressure. Her back arched, and he slid his arms behind her and carried her to the bed, never lifting his mouth from her breast.

Her pulse was thrumming, her body was throbbing. Need shivered her skin, she could see it quivering as he left her on the sheets to shuck his jeans.

His body was so hard, so long and beautiful, carved of muscle. Standing beside the bed, he stared down at her. His palm slid over his erection. "I could do this for myself, Angel," he said, his voice hoarse. "That's not what I want from you."

Her heart stuttered. No! Not anything else. She tried rolling away from him, but he dropped onto the bed and hauled her back. When his hot skin touched hers, she was compelled to reach out, to run her hand over his muscled forearm and then over the long firm line of his flank.

It was the maleness that called to her, she told herself. Not him. Not *particularly* him. She drew her hand up his thigh again as his mouth moved over hers. This time the kiss was soft, sweet, a gentle persuasion.

His touch was gentle now too, gently tracing her shoulders, her breasts, gently running down her arms to link their fingers. He moved above her and she opened her thighs, let him settle in the cradle of her body.

His weight was so good. He flexed his hips, seating himself deeper against her, and she answered with a push of her own. They rubbed against each other like that, and Angel felt the pressure growing. It was that tingly, tense pressure that was so good.

And that no man had ever been able to release for her in bed.

Remembering that, she willed herself to relax. Ordering her body not to move, she mentally forced the tightening arousal to unwind.

Cooper lifted his head. "What are you doing?"

She pushed her hands into his hair, trying to bring his mouth back. "Nothing. Not a thing."

He narrowed his eyes, but let her draw him down for

another slow kiss. It was pleasant, Angel thought, to feel his warmth, to feel his desire pounding at her breast, heating between her thighs. Her body wanted to catch fire again, to make answering moves to his, but she made herself lie passive beneath him.

Groaning, he rolled away from her. "Angel."

"What?" She turned on her side to stroke his cheek. "What's the matter?" She didn't like the frown between his brows. If he moved against her again, she'd take care of it, take care of him by taking him into her body. He'd find his pleasure there.

He caught her hand and pressed his mouth to the center of her palm. "You're the matter. You don't want this."

"I do!" She swallowed. "You do."

"Angel—"

She muffled whatever he had to say with her lips. With a long, sultry kiss. He groaned, then tore his mouth away.

"All right, all right." He was panting. "You win. We'll give it a try."

"Good." She eagerly moved in for another kiss.

But he held her off. "You have to turn off that pretty head of yours, though. There's too many wheels spinning in there. I can hear them grinding as they go 'round, baby."

But her head was what kept her sensible. Unhurt. "No other man has complained about the sound of my brain," she grumbled.

He smiled and brushed her hair away from her face, the gesture so tender her chest ached. "Maybe that's the trouble." Then he lifted her over him so they were nose to nose. "Now, shh," he said, massaging her temples. "Shut this part down. For me. Do it for me."

His kiss was slow, persuasive, drugging. Angel sighed into it, sighed into him, as his hands stroked along her back. It was sweet, really, and her limbs went heavy.

He shifted her legs, moving them to either side of his hips, and she smiled as she felt the press of his erection between her thighs. There was only a thin strip of material between them and it was nice to feel so close to him, to feel him nudging her there.

"Sit up," he whispered against her mouth. "Sit up so I can touch your pretty breasts."

It was as if she were in the hot tub again, her limbs hampered by heated water, but she finally managed. She smiled down at him, running her finger over his lips. "You're handsome. I used to have a crush on you."

"Yeah?" He grinned, then caught the tip between his teeth. Nipped. Sucked. "Now I have a crush on you."

Even hard and hot between her legs, he was sweet, so sweet. She smiled at him again, feeling warm and lazy.

His hands slid inside the mesh at either side of her breasts, the fabric stretching to accommodate him so he could cup her. He caught her nipples between the scissors of his fingers, tightened.

She jerked. Fire flashed up her spine.

His fingers made that scissor motion again.

Her hips moved over him.

He pinched harder. More fire as she rocked again.

"That's good." They said it together.

Cooper's voice went lower, harder. "Let me come inside now." She started to move off, but he shifted his hands to grip her hips, holding her against him. "Like this," he said. "Just like this."

Then he pulled aside the stretchy fabric between her legs. Thrust inside. Thrust smoothly inside.

He grunted. She moaned. The heat, the pressure, twisted quickly, almost viciously, into a tight coil of pleasure.

His fingers tightened on her hips. "Ride me," he commanded. "Ride me."

She had to. She had to move.

It felt so good. Each time he pushed into her she thought he was getting bigger, harder. But when she tried to back off, when she tried to lift herself from him, he pulled her down, his fingers biting into her flesh. Holding her down, against him, making her take the pleasure of each hard thrust.

The tension inside her was twisting tighter and tighter. Their harsh breaths made it twist, his invading thrusts made it twist, his hands holding her down and making her take it, take him, made it twist again and again and again.

Angel dropped her head back and closed her eyes. Cooper's body was moving with more and more deliberation. Harder. Faster. He was getting close, she knew it, and she needed to unwind her desire now. She tried to put it from her mind, go passive, limp, turn off the tension.

"No!" Cooper grabbed a handful of her hair and tugged her head forward. "Don't go away, damn it. Stay. Stay here."

She couldn't. She wouldn't.

He put his hand between her thighs, just where their bodies joined. Through the mesh he touched her there. She jerked at the first contact, tried to jerk away.

His other hand tightened on her thigh, holding her down. "Let me, Angel. Let me have everything."

Let him? No! That was her signal to ease off, to . . .

But he was so big and hard inside, filling her just right, and his fingers were so insistent on the outside, touching her, touching her just right. Not stopping either, not allowing her to pull away, pull back, go passive.

"Let me," he whispered, his fingers on the mesh, over her right *there,* rolling over the wet bud with a sure touch.

And as she started to quake, he pushed himself higher inside her, thrust harder, higher. And for the first time in her life, Angel felt the orgasmic waves of her body bring on the orgasmic waves of a man. Of Cooper, who hadn't had sex since he'd been brought back to life.

They cried out together.

Chapter 13

"Cooper borrowed a wineglass from me last night."

Across the table from Judd, Beth's brown eyes sparkled with speculation. "What do you think that means?" she asked.

Judd shrugged. Grinned.

She made a face. "Oh, you. You know exactly what it means, you just won't say."

He laughed. Trust a woman to distract herself from heartache by speculating on the state of someone else's heart. But it was doing *his* heart good to see the tinge of color in Beth's cheeks. She absentmindedly stroked the cat in her lap, and that made him feel even better.

She was finding pleasure in something he gave her. She was finding pleasure with him.

A few days back, he'd hit an all-time low when he'd been forced to admit he'd been hiding from a couple of truths for years. One, he was in love with a woman he'd been pretending friendship with. Two, the woman he loved had been pretending she wasn't in love with her sister's husband. He'd thought his relationship with Beth was doomed.

But he should have known he was wrong. In the Tao scripture, the *Tao-te Ching,* Lao-tzu had written:

What is firmly established cannot be uprooted
What is firmly grasped cannot slip away

After recalling those lines, Judd had realized that he and Beth had built a friendship that couldn't be rocked—and that could grow to be more.

Buddha said there was a time for everything, so while Judd patiently waited for his and Beth's, he was trodding the Middle Path, living in the harmony that was the Fourth Noble Truth of Buddhism. Through the daily practice of meditation and tai chi, he'd managed to restore a calm balance to his emotions.

The phone rang, and he watched her bend to the cat on the floor before rising to answer it. She was so graceful, he thought. Polished. Her burnt-orange slacks fit close to her slender hips and the loose neckline of the white sleeveless sweater she wore kept sliding to bare a wedge of golden-toned skin across one shoulder.

What would she think if he buried his mouth there?

What would she think if he slid the sweater off? Then he'd unbuckle the rhinestoned thongs she wore on her narrow feet. When she was finally naked, he'd reach down and rip Stephen's ankle bracelet from her. Then she'd be his.

Only his.

All his.

"Judd?"

He jerked out of the fantasy to look up at her. She was off the phone, and looking at him strangely.

"You're glaring at my sandals." She glanced down at them. "They're a little glittery, sure, but I feel a little glittery today."

Judd sucked in a deep breath, clamping down on this latest spurt of anger toward Stephen and the even hotter spike of hunger he was feeling for Beth.

But then she smiled at him, and another breath, not a million of them, could stop his belly from tightening. It was at that spot, at his *tan tien*, that his *chi*, or life energy, was gathered. His belly tightened again and the *chi* was forced outward, rushing through his body in an unchecked flood of heat.

Gritting his teeth, he tried to conceal his reaction by pointing toward the phone and mouthing, *Who?*

"Lainey," Beth answered. "She wants us over at the tower. A surprise, she said, and she sounds excited."

Judd cocked a brow.

Beth shook her head. "I'm just as curious as you. Shall we go?"

He couldn't get up fast enough, hoping the fresh air might level out his mood. Side by side, he and Beth took the short walk toward the tower that had been Stephen's studio. When its long shadow fell over them, they both paused. Though the morning temperature was as blazing hot as every other the past two weeks, Beth shivered.

Without thinking, Judd moved closer and rubbed his palm against the goosebumps on her bare arm. Her head whipped toward his. She stared at his face, then looked down at his hand on her arm, then stared at his face again.

"Judd?" Her dry whisper told him dozens of things.

There must be some new quality to his touch. It was communicating to her, getting her attention, making her aware. She was surprised by what she felt, he decided, but not displeased. He watched another wash of goosebumps run across her skin and then he lifted his gaze to hers. Held it. *Chi* surging throughout his body, he rubbed his palm over her skin again in a slow, possessive gesture.

Her eyes widened in question.

He nodded his answer, letting his gaze drop to her mouth. Could it be this simple? Had Stephen's death brought about something good after all?

"Hurry up, you guys, come and see this!" Lainey stood in the tower doorway, her face almost as flushed as her twin's.

With a guilty start, Beth hurried forward.

But Judd refused to let the moment pass. Reaching out, he clasped his hand around her slender one. She tried to tug free, but ignoring her, he held fast as they walked inside the tower.

What is firmly grasped cannot slip away.

Lainey was standing in the middle of the one and only room of the bottom floor, surrounded by canvases. Beth halted so abruptly, Judd's forward momentum almost yanked her off her feet.

"What's all this?" Her voice was strained and her eyes blinked rapidly, as if she were trying to adjust her vision to the dim light.

Except he could see just fine. The paintings surrounding Lainey were Whitneys, a couple dozen, maybe. Other than the occasional fairy and sprite, Stephen had never painted figures, but these were studies of babies, toddlers, young children. *Maybe the same child?* Judd thought.

"I found them in the walk-in closet Stephen used for supplies." There was a light, an energy about Lainey that made Beth now seem dull and hollow by comparison.

Judd squeezed her fingers, and she glanced down as if she'd forgotten she had hands, and that one of them was joined with his.

"What do you think?" Her sister was almost skipping about the room as she rearranged the paintings, setting them against the wall, against the heavy leather furniture. "Look at this one!" she said, holding a canvas toward them. "Look at the pretty baby."

A round-cheeked, gilt-haired infant, colored in the otherworldly pastels that signified Stephen's work. The baby was reaching for something out of the canvas, its chubby fingers extending toward the viewer.

"Don't you just want to touch her?" Lainey said.

Beth shook her head. "No," she murmured. Then she raised her voice. "Maybe . . . maybe they're not Stephen's paintings."

Setting the canvas down and darting toward another, Lainey laughed. "Of course they're Stephen's. Not only is it obvious, but he signed them."

She whirled, a beaming smile on her face. "I think finding them is a sign. Finding them is Stephen's way of telling me we should have the September show after all."

"What?" Beth's fingers convulsed against Judd's. "We can't. We canceled. We burned the paintings."

"We'll reschedule. We'll reschedule and show *these* paintings." She darted for the door. "I'm going to fetch Cooper. He's got to see them."

Lainey rushed out, leaving Judd and Beth alone.

After a moment, she slowly approached the nearest painting. Her hand was still linked with Judd's, so he followed, but she didn't seem to notice that, or even him, as she stared at the canvas.

"He told me they were destroyed," she whispered. "I begged him to, because I was afraid someday someone would find them and the truth would come out."

She looked at Judd, her eyes wide and dark in her pale face. "Stephen painted them as a comfort, he told me. Though he swore they weren't, I've always thought they were portraits of the child I miscarried. Our child. Mine and Stephen's."

Shocked, Judd turned abruptly away. A violent tide of jealousy swamped him, washing through him, washing over his *chi*, washing away everything but the image of Beth pregnant. Pregnant with Stephen's child.

Stephen. Goddamn it. Always Stephen. His fists clenched.

No. No! Judd struggled to regain control of himself. Taoism taught him to reject violence and envy. Just about every religion in the world—and he'd studied a shitload—preached against hate. But now he was feeling things he'd never gone looking for.

Five years ago, he'd left his shallow existence trading stocks and come to Big Sur to look deep. To find an authentic life—one of harmony, balance, peace!

Not this . . . this confusion of emotion, he thought, dropping Beth's hand. Never this.

"I'm taking off in a few minutes." Turning away from the infirmary's closed door, Angel brought the receiver closer to her mouth and lowered her voice another notch. "Tell Jane I'll be in the office this afternoon. Though I never got the widow's sister to talk, I interviewed everyone else."

Her bags were loaded in her car. She'd double-checked the drawers in her cottage, she'd removed her shampoo from the shower, she'd looked beneath the narrow bed. She wasn't leaving anything behind.

On the other end of the line, her intern said something that made Angel frown. "I haven't phoned in a few days because I've been busy, Cara. Busy working."

What Cara said next had her rolling her eyes. "Where do you *get* this stuff? No, I haven't found myself some mountain man to fall wildly in love with. Not even mildly in love with." She made a sound of disgust. "Is that all you called to talk to me about?"

The squeak of the infirmary door opening made her spin. "Right, right. I called you. Well, I gotta go now."

Across the metal desk, she met Cooper's dark gaze. Everything inside her jumped, and she felt a flush burst across her skin. He looked a little ticked, but she didn't know if it was because she'd sneaked out of his bed at dawn—leaving him sprawled across the mattress in deep slumber—or because she'd been using the forbidden phone.

She decided against finding out which reason it was. Scooting around the desk, she set her sights on the door.

In her hurry, her sleek-soled sneakers lost their purchase on the glossy linoleum. Her balance wavered.

As Cooper's hand shot out to catch her, she lurched back to avoid it. Her hip slammed against the corner of the desk, and wincing, she regained her footing. Thank God she hadn't had to grab him. Hang on.

Taking a deep breath, she forced herself to walk forward again. Heart thudding, she passed him, taking in the smell of his soap and damp skin. Then she was at the doorway, then over the threshold.

He'd let her go.

Of course he had. He'd never been interested in holding on to her in the first place.

Within moments she was heading down the steep, downhill path that led from the cottages to the parking lot. She didn't look back, just breathed in the mingled fragrances of trees, salty ocean, and sun-baked hills.

As last memories went, she told herself, it wasn't so bad.

"Angel."

At the sound of Cooper's voice just a few feet behind her, she jumped. The jerky movement made her sneakers lose purchase on the thin carpet of fallen pine needles that covered the path. She dug in her heels to stop her impromptu slide and her arms windmilled.

From the corner of her eye, she saw him leaping for

her, his hand reaching out to steady her. But another desperate, graceless flap of her arms took care of the job. His hand dropped to his side.

"Are you all right?" he asked.

She didn't look at him. "Of course. I'm fine."

Cursing herself for not leaving while he was still sleeping, she continued on. He didn't want to discuss the night before, did he? Because she didn't want to talk about it. Any of it.

But why else would he be following her?

Maybe he wanted her phone number. Maybe he wanted her address. Maybe he was going to suggest they should get together when he moved back to the city.

In her mind's eye, she could see the two of them in a small city bistro, knees and briefcases bumping beneath a bottlecap-sized table. She'd tell him about her day and he'd laugh at Cara's latest romantic tangle. He'd rant about his current case and she'd lean across the table and kiss the frown from his mouth.

They'd leave the restaurant and head . . .

Home.

God, she could see that too. Tom Jones, her neighbor's cat, would be waiting in the hall. She would lean down to pet him as Cooper opened their door. Inside, he'd stop her from turning on one of the news channels and instead pull her into his arms to fill the silence with the sound of his heartbeat. Later, when he opened his briefcase and spread out his papers, she'd hook her finger in the open collar of his shirt and draw him away from them and into the bedroom.

She was still deep in the feathery depths of the daydream when they reached her car.

"Angel."

She fought her way out of the fantasy, then hesitated. What *if* he asked for her number? What should she do? Should she agree to see him again?

"Angel."

With that lovely fantasy still so fresh, she decided. *Yes.* She whirled toward him. "All right, it's—"

He was holding out a brown grocery bag. His eyebrows rose as she merely stared at him. "It's your stuff," he said.

Her stuff.

"Your laptop, cell phone, hairdryer."

Here's your hat, Angel thought wryly, *what's your hurry*? But it was just what she deserved for flying off on some stupid fancy. She snatched the bag from him and stuffed it in the backseat of her car. "Thanks." Then she slammed the door and forced herself to turn toward him again.

"I guess that's it," she made herself say.

"Yeah." His eyes were serious. Unreadable.

"Cooper—"

"Angel—"

They both broke off. He signaled *Go ahead* with his hand.

Sloughing off the awkwardness, she managed a smile. "Well, then."

"Well," he echoed. "Then."

She nodded, smiled, nodded again. "Have a good rest of your life."

The muscle along his jaw twitched. "Yeah. You too."

Now, she commanded herself, looking down at the keys gripped in her fist. *Say goodbye now.*

But when she lifted her head, the only thing that worked was her memory. As she looked into Cooper's face, she saw it in the candlelight of the night before. Golden flames flickering in his eyes. Golden heat building inside her body. His hands, working magic. Long fingers teasing her where their two bodies met.

She glanced down and saw his hand flex against his jeans-clad thigh. She remembered that hand on her breast, trailing through her hair, sliding down her side and then around to grip her bottom as he pulled her down against him and ground up against her.

"Angel," he whispered. The hand left his side and reached for her.

On instinct, Angel hopped back. The soles of her shoes skidded on the gravel and lost their grip, the world tilting for the third time that morning. In slow motion, she felt herself falling, felt only air beneath her. Then she saw him move for her again, both hands extended to save her.

Closing her eyes, she knew, just like she'd known the two times before, that she couldn't expect him to catch her. The only person who could save her was herself, Angel thought, but this time it was too late.

She braced for the inevitable, unpleasant crash. Then his fingers closed around her upper arms, yanked her upright. Against him.

They both sucked in a sharp breath.

"Thanks," she managed to get past her surprise.

He grunted, not moving. Not moving her.

She noticed her hands were on him too, her fingers twisted in the soft cotton of his T-shirt. *Time to let go,* she ordered, staring at them. *Time to let go.* They slowly obeyed.

Angel made herself look at Cooper one last time. *This is it.* "Good—"

"Cooper!"

At the excited shout they both started. Cooper swung around, swinging Angel with him.

"Cooper! Angel!" It was Lainey running toward them, her cheeks flushed and her eyes bright. "You have to come with me. You have to see this!"

"What?" Cooper asked.

His sister shook her head, smiling. "Come and see. Both of you have to come and see."

He glanced down at Angel. "Do you have time?" His thumbs caressed the inside of her arms.

Something like relief flooded through her. "Hmm, well, okay." And with a little shrug, she made as if she were doing Lainey and Cooper a favor instead of doing what she had to admit she'd been doing since the sun rose—postponing this strangely painful, strangely poignant goodbye.

"She shouldn't have done it." Frustrated, Cooper jammed his hands in his pockets and looked across the room at Angel. They were alone, surrounded by the newly discovered paintings. "Lainey shouldn't have mentioned it."

Angel was staring out one of the windows instead of studying the newfound canvases. "She didn't 'mention' it. She *asked* if I'd stay a few more days."

God, he was irritated with Lainey for putting Angel in such an awkward position. Or maybe it was Angel who was irritating him with her calm, reasonable tone of voice.

He was definitely annoyed that she'd almost snuck away from the retreat without saying goodbye to him.

He was absolutely pissed with himself for being glad she hadn't.

"Still, don't think you have to agree." He made an impatient wave of his hand. "It's gotta be a bad idea."

"To include the art show in my story?"

"No. Yes!" He blew out an impatient breath of air, then shoved his hand through his hair. "How should I know? You're the writer."

What he didn't want to say was that the bad idea was her remaining at Tranquility any longer. He'd been thirty seconds away from getting her safely out of his life. She was trouble. He'd known that from the beginning and he felt it even stronger now.

"I could use a fresh angle, that's for sure," she said slowly, as if thinking the idea through. "Lainey told me she's given other interviews. My story's shaping up to be nothing more than another Whitney requiem."

Cooper didn't like the note of consideration in her voice. If she stayed on until after the show, how would he keep away from her? What would stop him from touching her, getting close to her?

Hurting Angel was the last thing he wanted to do, and that's what might happen if she thought they were heading for a relationship. They'd met at one funeral, and he sure as hell didn't want her saying goodbye to him at another. At his own.

He paced toward her. "I'm sure you can't be away from your job any longer."

"This *is* my job," she pointed out, then transferred her gaze back out the windows. "By the way, did your sister seem a little . . . upset?"

Angel was wearing that sophisticated perfume of hers. He'd smelled it when he'd woken that morning, on his sheets, on his hands. Damn it, he had to make sure she left Tranquility if he had hopes of finding tranquility for himself!

"Lainey didn't seem upset, she seemed wound up with excitement," he said, taking another step toward Angel, taking another breath of her scent. He couldn't help himself.

Angel's eyes flicked toward him, flicked away. Then she sidestepped out of his reach. "I wasn't talking about Lainey. I meant Beth. Is there something bothering her?"

Cooper shrugged, following Angel as she moved toward the center of the room. "She canceled the whole damn show, now she has to scramble to put it together again."

Angel darted a glance at him over her shoulder. "You don't think there should be a show?"

His gaze slid down the line of her spine. She was wearing a rib-sticking T-shirt with hip-hugging jeans. The pants were fringed at the ankle and one of the back pockets was missing. His gaze focused on that missing back pocket and suddenly he wanted to slide his hands there, then under the pants, the panties, to cup that sleek skin he'd held last night.

She'd trembled when he'd touched her there, when he'd held her to him.

He stalked up behind her, so close she had to feel his breath on her neck. He leaned into her, his cheek nearly touching hers. "Why the hell did you run out on me this morning?"

He saw the goosebumps surface on her throat, and then she hurried away from him.

Oh yeah, Cooper thought with a quick surge of relief. His question had popped out unplanned, but her reaction proved he held the trump card. He would get her away from here, he could. Pushing her sexually, even if it was with only talk, would send her running back to San Francisco.

She wouldn't want to risk how intimacy made her vulnerable to him, he knew that now.

Let me, he'd said. Those words, even when he was hard inside of her and she was riding the very edge of orgasm, had nearly scared her into full retreat.

She drifted toward another of the tower windows. "You didn't answer. Is the art show a bad idea?"

"No." He closed in, standing right behind her. "From what I know about Stephen's popularity, newly discovered paintings will have the public slavering. For financial reasons, the family needs to take advantage of that."

"My story will help fuel the interest, especially if I decide to stay and cover the show."

No! Thinking quickly, he put his hands against the windowsill, caging her with his body. Then he leaned in, his breath stirring her hair. "Are you sure you want to do that?"

When she didn't answer, he tried reading her mind by studying her profile, etched in the light coming through the window. Its pure, delicate lines mesmerized him for a moment. His next breath fluttered through her hair again, and an answering tremor vibrated through her body.

She's so fragile, he thought.

But it was all the more reason to push her. They'd both be better off when she returned to San Francisco. Inching closer, he pressed his groin against the pretty curve of her ass. "You're trembling, honey. Are you afraid of me?"

She whirled to face him, though she arched back against the sill to put some distance between them. "Afraid? Of you?"

"Afraid. Of me." He was counting on it. Reaching out, he wrapped one of her curls around his finger. "Of how close we were last night."

She tossed her head, trying to get free of him. "I don't know what you're talking about."

He didn't like to bulldoze women. Hell, he *didn't* bulldoze women. But there was a greater good to this. His smile was slow and full of promises. Threats. "You have to be close with a man, Angel. And honest, if you want intimacy. Satisfying intimacy."

"Our night is over. That was the agreement," she said, shrinking against the windowsill, her heavenly eyes going wide and nervous.

The scared look on her face made him queasy, but this was where he wanted her, right?

Yeah, right where he felt like a sadistic brute. A brute who went around terrorizing sweet young things who had just given him the best lay of his life.

What the hell had he been thinking? He didn't need

to go this far. Angel was a smart woman. She knew herself it was time for them to part. Lifting his hands, he stepped back. "You're right, you're right. That was our agreement. Don't worry, I promise I won't touch you again."

Her relief was so palpable he cursed himself once more, then braced for her goodbye.

Instead of a farewell, though, she whammied him with a saucy smile that swiped the trepidation off her face and slapped it onto his. "Perfect," she said. "With that small obstacle out of the way, I believe I will stay a few more days."

On that note, she flung her hair over her shoulders and sashayed toward the tower door, her hips swinging. At the threshold, she paused, turning to cast him a devilish look. "What's the matter, Cooper? Are you afraid of me?"

No shit, Sherlock. He was very afraid. Because as smart as he was, as experienced with criminals and the law, he kept forgetting that what she hid under that sweet and vulnerable-looking shell was female, fascinating, and most definitely lethal.

Chapter 14

Two days later, Angel lay stretched on a blanket in the shade near the grass clearing beside Tranquility House's common building. Through half-closed eyes she watched a gathering of retreatants, led by Judd, pretzel themselves through a succession of tai chi moves. She was a single boredom straw away from joining them.

She should have left for San Francisco when she'd had the chance. Instead, she'd let Cooper goad her into staying.

No, no. That wasn't right. He hadn't goaded her, she thought, twisting her head to follow as a thirty-something woman struck a pose that looked not only uncomfortable, but downright dangerous. He hadn't wanted Angel to stay and he'd tried to scare her away with talk of sex.

That had goaded her into staying. The fact that he'd tried to scare her into leaving.

She wasn't afraid of anything and it was time he figured that out. The bogeyman had stepped out of her nightmares and into her waking world twenty years ago. She'd dealt then. She'd deal now.

Then, as if thinking of a monster had called one up, a shadow fell across Angel. It took a mere instant to recognize the long, muscled legs of Cooper Jones. As that instant ended, she shut her eyes and pretended to be asleep.

When he shook her shoulder, she lifted her lashes, but when he began to mouth something, she hastily closed them again. Sure, it was an avoidance tactic, maybe even childish, but she was in the mortifying position—as a reporter and as a woman—of not knowing what to say to the man.

None of the zillions of magazine articles she'd read over the years had ever explained why gratifying, satisfying sex could leave a woman feeling so weak. Like a sissy. Not a one had hinted what to do about it.

Or, for that matter, what to do about a man who ignored her ignoring of him and plopped down on the blanket beside her. Before she had a chance to scuttle away, he grabbed her wrist. Before she had a chance to pull free, he tightened his grip on her fingers and wrote on the back of her hand.

She let herself go limp, as if truly asleep. His lean fingers were steady, though, his clasp strong, and it reminded her of his implacable touches in that hot, candlelit darkness. The gentle trace of a pen against her skin felt like the tickle of a tongue.

His tongue.

A shiver rolled through even as the tickle, the clasp, the man disappeared.

She wouldn't look at what he wrote, that's what she decided. She'd wash it off, wash away whatever he might have had to say.

But back in her cottage no amount of soap and water could erase the words. Cooper had marked her—indelibly.

The back of her hand read: *Be at Lainey's, 4:00 pm. If you're sleeping, I'll do what I must to wake you up.*

Though she'd considered refusing Cooper's order/invitation, it was her inherent curiosity and a need for distraction from the breathless heat that had Angel knocking on Lainey's door at 4:02. The day had started off a scorcher, and now the Santa Lucia Mountains were radiating the afternoon sun like the face of a gigantic iron.

When Lainey answered, her welcoming smile flipped almost instantly to a frown. "You're dressed wrong."

Angel glanced at her sleeveless cotton top and the long gauzy skirt she wore with it. "I, uh . . ."

"Brothers." Lainey shook her head. "Cooper forgot to tell you to bring your swimsuit, I'll bet."

Since she was empty-handed, Angel could only nod.

"Cooper, Beth, and Judd were invited too, and I thought we all might like a swim before dinner," Lainey went on. "Don't worry, we have suits to spare."

Swim? Dinner? Even though some lovely, chilly air was beckoning her into the Whitney house, Angel hesitated. She'd quieted her journalist's conscience about going to bed with Cooper by deciding her Stephen Whitney story would be as banal and blameless as his reputation. But she was still here for a job. A job that didn't include more intimacy with Cooper or getting social with the rest of the family.

It was tempting, though. They might let down their guard and she might finally find out something interesting.

On the other hand, they might let down their guard and she might finally find out something interesting. What would she do then?

Stalling for time, Angel shrugged. "Uh, Lainey, Cooper didn't actually mention . . ."

She rolled her eyes. "He didn't tell you about dinner either?"

"No."

Lainey reached out, snagged Angel's arm, and pulled her over the threshold. "Well, you're invited. Judd is barbecuing vegetable kabobs, but I also roasted a couple of chickens this morning. They've been cooling in the refrigerator."

Chicken. *Meat*. Sighing in surrender, Angel allowed herself to be led through the house toward the patio doors that opened onto the pool area. Oh, she *was* weak. Who would have guessed that after mere days of mainly vegetarian fare, her conscience could be compromised by something as simple as a cold drumstick?

"Hey, everybody, look who's here!" Lainey called out to the people on the patio.

Katie, Judd, and Beth looked over. Beth's eyes widened and she took a hasty step back, even though

Angel was yards away. "I thought you said this was going to be a family meal," she murmured, loud enough for Angel to hear.

"Right. Family." Lainey sent her sister a pointed look. "Think, Beth. Remember the cove." Then she turned to Angel. "Cooper will be here any minute."

Impressions and questions rolled through Angel's mind. As usual, Beth was strangely anxious around her. Why had she consistently refused to be interviewed? And then there was Lainey's "Remember the cove." What was the meaning of the cryptic comment?

Before Angel could bring some order to her thoughts, she was ushered into the poolhouse and left alone with a selection of swimsuits. Her head was still processing all the new data when she stepped out again, wearing a modest one-piece, her skirt now acting as a cover-up. Though she wouldn't take a swim per se, sitting on the edge and dangling her legs in the water sounded pleasant.

As promised, Cooper had arrived, and he'd already been cooling off in the water. The pool was a strange, almost V shape, with two symmetrical arms that met at a bottom point, then widely jutted away from each other. Each arm had its own diving board, and now Cooper stood poised on the edge of one, Katie on the other.

Though she knew it was safer to keep her distance, Angel approached the pool's edge, unwillingly drawn toward Cooper. There was that too-long hair, those broad shoulders and lean torso, the muscled legs in cobalt-blue, knee-length swim trunks. The scar bisecting his chest stood out, shining pinkish in the golden darkness of his tanned skin. He said something to Katie, and then the two of them bounced high on the boards and executed identical flips into the water.

Cool drops splashed against the gauze of Angel's skirt. In the next second a wet hand knifed out of the water and grabbed her ankle.

She yelped, but there was no place to go when trapped by the strong, wet vise of Cooper's grip. His head rose out of the water and he shook it, raining more drops on her calves and thighs. It was cooler, here by the pool, but there was something hot in his eyes.

"You made it," he said. "Too bad for me."

He'd promised to wake her if he had to. He'd been teasing, of course, but as they continued to look at each other, his gaze heated and his hand flexed against her bare ankle. Goosebumps crawled up the insides of her legs.

The look in his eyes was so very, very male. And it was so hot that she felt herself warming up. Oh please, she couldn't be developing a soft spot—and if she was, it was minuscule, shallow!—for this kind of he-man, caveman stuff.

Lifting an eyebrow, she refused to let him see he rattled her. Melted her. "How could I refuse such an . . . unforgettable invitation?" She held out her hand so he could see the words still branding her skin.

He grinned.

She nearly risked her life and leaped into his arms.

Maybe he saw the impulse on her face. "Come in for a swim?" he asked.

No. Oh no. She shook her head.

After a moment, he released her with a shrug, then ducked back into the water to stroke toward his niece. For a few moments she watched him try to engage the young girl, flattening his hand against the water to splash her.

Katie's eyes lit for an instant and she almost surrendered to the simple fun, but then her expression closed down and she swam away, her movements efficient and graceful. Angel wondered who had taught the girl to swim. Had it been Stephen? Cooper?

Whose strong arms had held her, whose deep voice had soothed her fears? A sudden image of Cooper, of his arms not around Katie, but around Angel, his voice warm in her ear, sent her spinning abruptly toward the kitchen and Lainey.

Maybe she should make some excuse. Claim a headache, anything, in order to leave.

But Beth and Judd were in the kitchen too, assembling a fruit salad, and once more Angel caught that strange vibe from Lainey's twin. Curiosity piqued once more, instead of excusing herself from the dinner, Angel offered to help.

She saw Beth dart her a nervous glance, but then the other woman started to chatter about the details of the art show as if to give Angel no room for questions.

From what Beth said, Angel gathered that two exhibition tents would be erected on the large lawn beside the retreat's common building—one for the paintings and one for refreshments. Thanks to the hospitality of the Benedictine monks, the retreatants would spend the day at the monastery so their quiet wouldn't be disturbed. Because there wasn't enough parking, buses were scheduled to ferry the guests from a central location in Carmel.

"How many people do you expect to attend?" Angel asked, fishing for a chunk of zucchini from a bowl of marinade. She'd been given the task of threading marinated vegetable pieces onto skewers.

Beth darted a glance at her. "Since Lainey insisted we keep to the original date, only about one hundred fifty. We usually have twice that number, but on such short notice . . ."

Lainey shrugged off the disapproval in her sister's voice. "We always have the exhibit on September thirtieth," she said. "One hundred fifty on that date is better than three hundred on some other."

"It's a special day?" Angel asked.

"It's the day Stephen arrived in the Sur."

Angel's hand slipped on the mushroom she'd just retrieved, nearly stabbing herself with the skewer. "From San Francisco?"

"Mm-hmm." Lainey loaded paper plates onto a tray and headed toward the pool again. "I think of it as the day that life, as I knew it, changed forever."

It was the day Angel's had changed forever too. The day her father had left her mother.

Turning away from Lainey, her eye caught a strange expression on Beth's face. Again, Angel's reporter's antennae quivered.

But the other woman's must have been working overtime too, because she darted a glance at Angel, then rushed to her sister and pulled the tray out of her hands. "I'll take that. You finish up in here." Beth hurried onto the patio, Judd right behind her.

Through the glass doors, Lainey looked after her sister for a long, silent moment. "I still can't believe what's happened to us," she finally said. "How life has changed again, in just one instant."

There were tears in her voice and suddenly Angel wanted nothing more than to escape the kitchen too. She ducked her head, hurriedly skewering. "I'm sure it takes time to fully understand what's happened."

"Oh, I understand." Lainey stayed frozen by the patio doors. "I understand how short life is now. That's why I rescheduled the art show right away. There's no time to waste, Angel. Do you see?"

She focused even harder on the skewer in her hand. "Sure."

"And love," Lainey continued. "Love is a miracle, when you think about it. You find a man who you're willing to throw open your heart to. You shouldn't waste that either."

"Uh-hmm," Angel murmured. As if she'd let any man into her heart. Sorry, but she was keeping that half of the human species where she could keep her eye on them.

Lainey put her hand on the patio door handle, then hesitated. "Listen to me, Angel. Don't let Cooper get away."

She had the door shut behind her before Angel could lift her jaw from the floor. Oh my God.

Oh. My. God.

The reason she'd been invited to this "family" dinner was suddenly clear. Lainey was matchmaking.

As she finished constructing the final kabobs, Angel decided to draw Cooper aside at the very first opportunity and explain things to him. It was his sister, after all, his newly widowed sister, so it was up to him to make sure she didn't suffer another disappointment. He'd have to tell her there was nothing between them, and no hope that there ever would be.

But when Angel brought the tray of skewers outside, she couldn't get to Cooper right away because Katie attached herself to her side. Angel swallowed, unsure what the girl wanted, but sure the kid made her strangely uneasy.

"Uh, hi," she said.

Katie nodded. In the bright sunlight, she smelled faintly of chlorine. Her hair was slicked back in a wet French braid, and Angel saw a sprinkling of cinnamon freckles across the bridge of the teenager's nose.

Angel rubbed her own nose, where gold freckles lay in an identical pattern, and fumbled for words. "I . . . uh . . . uh . . ." Cursing every curious impulse that had led her to the Whitney house that evening, Angel said the first thing that popped into her head. "I've always wanted to wear my hair in a braid like yours."

It turned out to be a lucky remark, because hair once again proved it was the common denominator of femaledom. Some thought women could most easily bond over man trouble, but in Angel's experience, it was coiffure concerns that brought every woman to the table. Literally, this time. Within minutes Katie had installed Angel at a small patio side table with a comb and a mirror. Then she proceeded to try to teach Angel how to French braid her own hair.

Beth and Lainey drifted over to offer their tips. With her arms awkwardly raised overhead, Angel's muscles were screaming in agony, but she gamely attempted to follow along until the other three were choking back laughter.

"Thanks a lot," Angel grumbled, peering at her reflection. "It's not my fault I look like a mutant cross between Pippi Longstocking and Bozo the Clown."

She grimaced as some snickers escaped. "One of you will have to fix this mess."

As Katie obligingly moved forward, Angel's eye caught on Judd's and Cooper's reflected images in the mirror. Standing beside the barbecue, they were staring at the group of females. It could be that her hair disaster had snagged their attention, but when Angel glanced around her, she knew it wasn't the bad braid job.

It was the laughter. The lightness of the moment and the brightness in the faces of Lainey, Beth, and Katie.

Something warm waved through Angel, almost pride, almost . . . well, almost belonging. It was nice.

The mood carried into dinner. At a glass-topped table beneath a market umbrella, Lainey and Beth relived bad-hair experiments of the past and razzed Cooper about the George Michael look he'd affected once upon a time.

Angel drew back in mock horror from the man sitting beside her. "*George Michael?* As in 'I-will-be-your-preacher-teacher' George Michael?"

He crossed his arms over his chest and raised an eyebrow. "Are you telling me you're proud of your Madonna phase?"

"How did you—" She caught herself and lifted her chin. Fibbed. "She was *never* my role model."

"Liar." He leaned closer, his voice lowering for her ears only. "Which was it? The scruffy street girl, the blond bombshell? Were you *Erotica* or *Like a Virgin*?"

When a sweet little shiver ran down her back, Angel suddenly remembered she'd forgotten about Lainey's misapprehension. She'd also forgotten how dark his greeny-brown eyes turned when he was talking sexy, how his thick lashes made them even more like a deep, hot night in Big Sur. Hot night, hot skin, hot man.

Dragging her mind back, she cleared her throat. "I told you, I never dressed like Madonna."

"But she dressed as a boy," Katie piped up. "When she was in third grade she pretended to be a boy."

The words dropped like an unwelcome blanket over the table. All heads turned toward Angel. All eyes.

The camaraderie of the evening dissolved and Angel felt like the outsider again. The one who didn't belong in the family.

"Maybe Angel doesn't like to talk about that, Katydid," Cooper put in gently.

"Oh. I . . ." Katie's face flushed.

Angel jumped into the awkward moment, trying to save the girl from embarrassment. "No, no. It's fine. As a matter of fact, I have the funniest story about my first and only boy sleepover." She briefly sketched out why she'd impersonated a boy for Lainey, Beth, and Judd, then launched into the account of a backyard sleepover with three other boys that had morphed into a pissing contest.

A real pissing contest.

Beth's mouth dropped. "What did you do?"

It had been panic time then, but Angel could laugh about it now. "I made them all turn around and then I grabbed an almost-full can of soda and slowly let it dribble to the ground." She tilted her empty hand to demonstrate. "I knew I didn't have a prayer for the distance record, but I won the titles for volume and flow control hands down."

Instead of laughing, or at the very least smiling, the group around the table sat silent for a moment. Then Lainey stood and directed Katie to start clearing the table. Judd and Beth followed suit. When Angel moved to help, Cooper snagged her hand and held her back.

As the others trailed toward the kitchen, she made a face at Cooper and rose awkwardly to her feet. "Guess I shouldn't leave my day job for a stint as a stand-up comedian."

Instead of answering, he rose too and pulled her into his arms. "You're killing me, kid." His voice was gruff. "You're killing me."

"That's not good," she said into his shirt. Like Katie, he smelled a little of chlorine too. Angel thought of his strong, sure hands slicing through the water. She felt those hands on her now, strong and sure on her too. Looking into his face, she resisted wrapping her arms around his neck. "*This* probably isn't good either."

Then movement caught her eye. It was Lainey, coming toward them. In a rush, Angel recalled that wrongheaded matchmaking notion again and pushed off from Cooper's chest, stumbling backward toward the edge of the pool.

"Watch out," he cautioned sharply.

Angel caught her balance and planted her heels into the flagstone deck. "I'm fine. Fine."

Lainey continued toward them, glancing over her shoulder as she reached Cooper. "I need to talk to you," she said, lowering her voice. "Away from Katie."

Angel instantly started to edge away. "Um, maybe I should—"

Cooper shot her a look. "Don't go anywhere."

"But—"

"It's okay, Angel," Lainey said. "I trust you."

Oh God, Angel thought, a premonition tickling the back of her neck. But she didn't move.

"It's about . . . about Stephen. When I was going through his papers, I found something this afternoon." Lainey hugged herself, rubbing her arms with the palms of her hands. "I'm not certain, but I think . . . I think he might have had another family."

"A *what*?" Cooper said.

Angel wanted to run. She wanted to run away, faster and farther than she ever had. She wanted to go back to the day she'd decided to investigate Stephen Whitney and she wanted to decide to let sleeping dogs—dead dogs, she thought hysterically—lie. She inched back.

Lainey tucked her thumbs into the bend of her elbows and sighed. "I don't know. You'll have to look at what I've found. It was in a batch of old papers. It's a half-sheet, divided in the middle. *Stay,* he wrote on one side, *Go* on the other. Stephen often made decisions that way. You know, reasons to do something, reasons not to do something."

Cooper's voice was quiet. "So?"

"On the *Go* side is written *art* and *freedom.* On the *Stay* side it says *Michelle* and—" She hesitated.

"And?" Cooper prodded.

Angel held her breath.

Lainey took one, hesitated again. *"Our daughter."*

As the two words aimed for her heart, Angel tried backing away from them. But they pierced her all the same, just as she realized there was nothing beneath her feet. And then there was water.

Over her head.

She instinctively thrashed. The sky was still light and she fought toward it, even as her full skirt wound around her legs like a noose. Her nose cleared the surface, then her mouth. She gulped air and water.

She slid back into the deep water and wished for the hundredth time she'd had a father who'd taught her to swim.

Chapter 15

His mood at a boiling point, Cooper dragged Angel down the path from the Whitney house to the retreat. She kept trying to escape his grasp, but he ignored the resistance.

She cleared her throat.

He ignored that as well, too preoccupied with controlling his reaction to what had nearly happened.

"I didn't get the chance to tell Lainey she shouldn't worry," Angel said.

Her voice was breathless, but he didn't slow down and he still didn't speak.

"About . . . uh, about there being another wife," Angel continued between pants. "If that were the case, the press would have sniffed it out years ago."

At the moment, Cooper didn't care if his late brother-in-law had more wives than the King of Siam.

"But why don't I"—she heaved in a breath—"why don't I look into it for her?"

"Don't bother," he replied roughly. "I'll get someone at the firm to do it."

She stopped.

He tugged on her arm, but before she had a chance to start moving again, he swung around to face her. "We were laughing, damn it," he ground out, unable to contain himself any longer. "We were laughing and waiting for you to come back up."

"It's not—"

"And then you did, and then you went back under again. I was sure you'd swim to the steps, but instead you . . . you . . . Goddamn it, you *floundered*."

It was nearing dark, but even in the twilight he could see her wince. "I know it wasn't a pretty sight, but—"

"Pretty!" His muscles went rigid. "Damn it, you stopped my heart!"

She winced again. "Hey, I'm sorry."

Searching for control, he jerked his gaze skyward, staring at the black shadows of the trees and the first stars that were playing hide-and-seek with their branches. His breath was moving in and out of his chest heavily, but it wasn't due to exertion or medical emergency. It was fear.

Fear.

Fuck it.

He released her wrist, only to grab her by the shoulders and give her a little shake. "Life is too precious for a stupid stunt like that." His voice was hard. "Do you understand?"

"You know it wasn't a 'stunt,'" she said quietly. "I told you once you pulled me out. I can't swim."

Once he pulled her out. Closing his eyes, he relived the moments all over again. Standing on the pool deck, chuckling with Lainey. Watching Angel rise up, suck air, sink back down.

He hadn't worried right away, though she hadn't swum toward the edge right away and she didn't resurface. A couple of moments passed. Then it had hit him, a sucker punch that had cramped his stomach into a knot of icy, shocking fear. *Drown—*

—ing. Before the thought was complete, he was in the pool. From there it was memory flashes. His hand wrapped around her braid. Her pale face breaking the surface of the water. That first gasp of her breath. Water streaming from his forearms and her sodden skirt as he carried her up the steps and out of the pool.

Lainey had rushed over with towels. He'd wrapped Angel in them even as she'd coughed. He'd held her on his lap until she'd subsided to wheezing and then to normal breathing.

Five minutes after that, he'd pulled her toward Tranquility at a near run.

"God." He shook her again, mad at her, mad at himself, outraged at fate in a way that he hadn't been in months. Cupping her face with his palms, he tilted her gaze to his. "Why didn't you tell me you can't swim?"

"It never came up in conversation."

The answer was reasonable.

No, damn it, it wasn't. In a perfect world, he was supposed to know those kinds of things about her. It was unexplainable, unsayable, but he knew, *knew*, that he was supposed to know that Angel couldn't swim. He was the one she should tell that to. Her weaknesses, her fears, her scars—from scraped knees to wounded feelings—were for him to catalog and for him to console.

He dropped his hands and spun away from her. "You were in the hot tub that night. It was dangerous for you to be there alone."

"But I wasn't alone. You were there too."

She was trying to be reasonable again, when the time for reason was long past. Instead of arguing with her, though, he took her hand, gently this time, gently, and led her the rest of the way through the trees to his cottage.

At the door, he stopped. His hand brushed over her head, down the braid that was still wet to the touch. The night was so warm that she'd insisted on wearing home her damp skirt. It clung to her thighs, then frothed outward at the hem where it had already dried. She looked like a mermaid, he thought.

He almost laughed at himself. A mermaid. An angel.

At turns, she was either a siren beckoning him to his destruction or the one who would greet him once that destruction was wrought.

Sighing, he gave up the internal struggle that he'd been waging since the morning he'd opened his eyes to find her gone from his bed.

"I can't let you go." At her little start of surprise, he smiled, then amended his statement. "I can't let you go tonight. You know that, don't you?"

The dark had completely descended now, but he could clearly see her face in the glow of the small light fixture beside his door. She was still pale, and the milky light leeched the color from her eyes too.

"I don't think that's a—"

"For God's sake, it was never a good idea." But he had to touch her, hold her, assure himself her skin was warm all night long. "We both know that too, right?"

Closing her eyes, she nodded. Her long lashes were a smudge of darkness against her cheeks and he wanted to run his tongue along their tickly edge.

He thought she swayed toward him, or he told himself she did. Bowing to strong impulse again, he swung her into his arms, carrying her into his cottage just as he'd carried her out of the pool.

She laid her head against his shoulder like a tired child—he remembered Katie doing the same—and protectiveness, tenderness welled up inside him. This was the same, tough, wannabe boy who'd held her own with other third graders. This was the same woman who'd braved the spartan retreat and tofu three meals a day for the sake of a story. This was the same sexy beauty who had given him another taste of life.

He strode into his bedroom and sat them both on the edge of his bed, then reached for her braid, unwrapping the band and then unweaving her hair. He combed his fingers through the wet length, spreading it across her shoulders.

She shivered.

"Are you cold?" he whispered.

"Worried." She glanced at the glowing bedside lamp. "Will you turn off the light?"

Reaching over, he thumbed it off, then found her face in the dark. He didn't want her to worry, damn it, he wanted her warmth, he wanted her close. So he kissed her cheek, her temple, the top of her head, his chest aching as it hadn't since the surgery that had split open his ribs.

"It's only sex," he said against her ear, knowing the words would ease her mind. "Nothing a material girl like yourself should be concerned about."

She laughed, her stiff shoulders easing. "I don't know, George. I've always been a bit hazy on which way you batted. . . ."

At that, he pushed her onto the bed and followed her down. She spread her legs to make a place for him and he rubbed himself against her. "Speaking of bats . . ."

She groaned. "You flatter yourself, buddy."

He grinned down at her. "That's me, your buddy." His mouth found hers and he kissed her, soft and gentle. Persuasive. When he lifted his head he heard the little catch in her breath.

He wanted as much as he could get from her in the time they had left. "Tell your buddy your secrets, Angel."

Beneath him, she stiffened for an instant, then relaxed. "I don't have any secrets."

He brushed her hair away from her forehead. "Yes, you do. But I don't mind finding them out for myself."

His mouth trailed down her neck, and he licked across the pulse at her throat. He tasted warmth, building desire, the clean tang of pool water that made his heart slam for a moment before he shoved the memory, the fear, away.

She was here with him now. Safe in his arms.

"Your secrets, sweetheart," he murmured. "Last chance."

Beneath him, she moved sinuously. "Why don't you get naked?"

"I don't need to be naked for what I want," he replied. If he got naked too soon, he might not find out the answers he was after.

She went very still. "What's that? What do you want?"

"What I want"—he rose onto his elbows—"is you." His hands cupped her face, and he followed the curve of her bottom lashes with his thumbs. "Tell me, Angel. Did someone hurt you during sex?"

She stiffened again. "Of course not. No one could hurt me."

He rolled his eyes at her knee-jerk denial. "What was I thinking? Who could hurt *you*, of all people?" But he believed her. It wasn't sex that had hurt her, not when she could flame in his arms.

"Then what happened?" he asked, distracting her by outlining her pretty mouth with his forefinger. "Why did you stop expecting to find pleasure in bed?"

"You make me sound . . ."

"Like a pessimist?"

Instead of answering, she pulled his head down to hers. Then she kissed him, slanting her mouth to make it deep. He drew away quickly, though, needing to know how her mind worked before he lost his. "Why, Angel? Why did you give up on being satisfied in bed?"

She frowned at him. "I've never been able to get the timing right, okay? And it hurt—" Breaking off, she shook her head. "Not hurt, just left me wanting when I tried so hard to get there and couldn't."

"So you stopped wanting."

"I want you." Her hands sank into his hair and she

brought him to her again. Their mouths met, and this time she made it hot and wild before he could stop her.

Cooper wrenched back, breathing hard. She was so beautiful, with her lips reddened from his. "How could any man do that? Leave you unsatisfied?"

She huffed out a sigh, obviously frustrated with his persistence. "I don't think they ever knew," she said. "I faked it."

"Angel . . ." He didn't know who to commiserate with, the poor bastards who hadn't seen through her pretense, or Angel, who'd sacrificed her sexuality to save their egos.

"It's the timing," she murmured, her forehead pleating. "You know, it happened with you too."

He stilled. "'It'? You didn't fake it with me."

She smiled. "No. But I still didn't get it exactly right. Not the way it's supposed to be, anyhow. I can't get the timing for that man-on-top, woman on bottom dual explosion."

"The way it's supposed to be," he repeated. It was suddenly clear to him. She might be twenty-seven years old, but he guessed her partners had been few, far between, and *young*. Christ, any man with a little experience under his belt knew—

"Let me kiss you again, Cooper." She tried pulling his head down, and when that didn't work, she lifted her mouth toward his. "Let me kiss you."

He pushed her back against the pillows. "Sex isn't supposed to be a certain way, Angel."

"I read *Esquire* and *Maxim*," she said defensively. "I know there's more than missionary, but—"

"Then let me show you where the missionaries and the 'dual explosion' contingent have it all wrong."

He didn't think she was listening to him. Her hands speared through his hair again, tugged. "Kiss me."

He hesitated, staring at her face, at the delicate construction of her bones, at the froth of gilt hair spilling over the pillow. Young men would have been careful with an angel. Cautious. Afraid of shocking someone who looked so innocent.

They wouldn't have pushed her past her comfort zone to be truly intimate with her.

God, he was thirty-five years old and he'd had her panting and demanding and *he'd* never completely undressed her either.

She pouted. "Kiss me."

"Oh, I will," he promised.

Then he rolled off her to slowly unbutton her sleeveless top and peel it off. Her breath caught when he released the catch on her bra, so he put his mouth on hers to divert her attention as he pushed both garments away.

Then he slid down her body, kissing the spot between her breasts, below her breasts. The skirt had a drawstring at the waist. One pull and the full fabric slid easily down her legs. He sat up and tugged her sandals off, then looked at her pale body spread across his bed.

"Pretty," he said.

She seemed frozen by her near nudity. When he reached for her panties, she made a little sound of protest, but he ignored it, drawing the silky fabric past the light curls at the apex of her thighs.

"Shh." He dropped them over the side of the bed.

Staring down at her nakedness, he slowly moved his hand to stroke her nearest flank. "Last chance, sweetheart. Your secrets."

"I told you." She flinched as his finger trailed across the sensitive skin at the inside of her hipbone. "I don't *have* any secrets."

He let his fingers wander closer to the triangle created by her tightly clenched thighs.

She was trembling at his touch. "What are you doing?"

His eyes had grown accustomed to the dark. Between her legs, her soft curls were so pale that they couldn't hide the contours of the flesh they covered. It made it easy to place his forefinger directly at the high point of the line that separated her skin.

She jumped. Then her body settled again, her thighs an inch apart. "Cooper . . ."

He smiled, pressed deeper into the opening so that his fingertip was wedged between the twin, hot softness of her flesh. Just below the pad of his forefinger, her clitoris was rising to meet his touch.

"Cooper."

"Hmm?" He didn't move, letting her get used to his touch. "This is kind of . . . kind of . . ."

His eyebrows rose. "Painful?"

"No."

"Distasteful?"

"No."

"This is what I want. Please, Angel." Already, her body was unfurling to his touch, her flesh softening more. He flicked his finger over the hard, tight nub, felt, rather than heard, her breath catch again.

"See how good it can be when we do this one at a

time?" he asked, playing in her slippery heat, rubbing his thumb over her. "One of us giving, one of us taking?"

She swallowed a little moan and closed her eyes.

"Isn't it good?"

Oh God, he felt her body getting hotter. She was wet, opening for him. She canted her hips just the tiniest bit, just enough to make it easier for him to glide down the slide of her wet flesh and pierce her with two fingers.

She gasped, then grabbed his shirt, trying to force him against her.

With his free hand, he loosened her fingers. "Say it's good," he prompted, teasing her by moving his hand slowly, not in and out, but around.

Her hips lifted a little and her eyes closed again. "It's good, it's—" she broke off when he slid a third finger inside her, "*So* good."

He gently slid his hand from her body, then settled over her, lying between her legs again, his elbows on either side of her head. "See? Sex isn't supposed to be a certain way, Angel."

"Kiss me," she demanded.

"I will," he swore to her again. "I'll kiss every inch of you."

With her nude and heating up in his arms, he made good on his promise. He started slow, unwilling to rush her, but determined to have it all. He floated his tongue along the tender skin of her neck, he tickled her collarbone with the tip of it, he drew her nipples into his mouth and sucked until she was twisting beneath him.

"Cooper, Cooper, *please*." She lifted her hips against his. "Take off your clothes."

"Soon." He licked each nipple once more, then let

his mouth explore the underside of her breasts. His breath was harsh, his blood was burning, but he wasn't going to end this until she knew how many ways sex should be.

His mouth cruised over her flat belly, through the wispy hair at her thighs. He roughly pushed her legs apart, positioned himself to feast on her.

"Cooper!" There was a thread of panic in her voice. Her fingers yanked at his hair.

He glanced at her, ignoring the way her knees squeezed against his shoulders. "This is what I want," he said.

"No." She was trying to scoot back. "This isn't . . . this isn't the way—"

"This is one of the ways." He held her hips steady, and he could feel her femoral pulses drumming against his thumbs. "You're not afraid, are you?"

She hesitated. "Yes."

It shocked the hell out of him that she admitted it. "No, *this* doesn't scare you."

Her eyes were wide. "Yes, yes, it does."

Oh, Angel. "Then close your eyes, baby, and count to ten. If at eleven you want me to stop, I will."

Her body was stiff as he bent his head. When he touched her creamy softness with his tongue, she jerked, her fingers pulling on his hair again. But he knew she hadn't started counting yet, knew she would never get to eleven, because as he continued to stroke her, taste her, enjoy her, her body lifted toward him.

Her legs, which had been pressing hard against his shoulders, relaxed. Now he could hold her open and take her in. He found every secret, his heart pounding with each one of her moans, his blood burning and his body aching as the sweetness of her arousal filled his mouth.

And it was all the sweeter because it was an intimacy that he'd demanded, and that he'd made her surrender.

He felt the tension of orgasm building in her body, her muscles were shaking with it, and then he latched onto the most sensitive part of her and drew the pleasure from her, for her, commanding every tremor, every cry.

When he moved away from her, she was sprawled across the sheets, her limbs as he'd left them, open to him. It was the most beautiful, the most vulnerable he'd ever seen her. It ratcheted his own desire two more turns, and he had to force himself to breathe slowly as he quickly undressed. Then he repositioned himself between her opened legs again.

She moaned. "Cooper."

Her resistance was weak, his determination strong, and it was so damn easy to recoil her arousal, just by circling his tongue in his now-favorite territory. She was on the edge again in minutes, trusting him to take her to pleasure.

When he felt her give that trust, he lifted his head and quickly turned her body and pulled her onto her knees. "That's one way sex can be," he said hoarsely. "Here's another."

He thrust, hard, into the hot, wet glove of her.

She moaned.

He thrust once more, his climax approaching fast and furious. With one hand he braced himself against the mattress, with the other he found her clitoris again.

She was pushing back against his hips, gasping, as he drove himself into her. Not cautious, not careful, his mind not on innocence, but intimacy.

When she came, he continued thrusting, reveling in the way her body shook against his. It was her last tremor, her final moan that triggered his own climax. Sliding his hand up to her belly, he pressed her body tightly against his, hoping she was feeling what she did to him, hoping she would find pleasure in the pleasure she brought to him.

When he fell against the mattress, finally sated, she wiggled out from under him and placed a tender kiss upon his mouth. Then she sighed. "Okay, okay. I admit it. The missionaries have nothing on you."

He had only enough energy to smile.

She found his discarded T-shirt, pulled it on, then curled against his chest like a seashell on the sand. They were both drifting into sleep when a thought suddenly struck him. "Angel?"

"Mmm."

He smiled against her hair, satisfied with the smug, drowsy note in her voice. "When you said you used to fake it . . . well, how can you fake something you've never felt before?"

She stirred, snuggling her cheek into the hollow of his shoulder. He kissed her hair. "Baby?"

"I never said I hadn't felt one," she answered sleepily.

"Huh?"

She chuckled. "Cooper. And you think you know women." She rubbed her face against his bare skin. "I wasn't kidding about the vibrator, silly."

Chapter 16

Judd was crouching beside the rosemary bush outside Tranquility House's kitchen door when a bright voice sounded behind him.

"There you are!"

Beth's tanned, slender feet strolled into his field of vision. She wore leather thongs that buckled below the ankle. Directly below where that diamond-and-platinum anklet seemed to maliciously wink at him in the early morning sunlight.

"You haven't been by since that day in the tower, so I thought I'd come to you." She thrust a mug of steaming coffee under his nose. "If anyone asks, I'll swear it's decaf."

He slowly stood, looking down at what he carried in the hammock he'd made with his T-shirt instead of looking at her. He'd played the strong, silent rock in her life and he was afraid she'd see how close Mr. Calm, Cool, and Collected was to fracturing.

"What do you have there?" she asked. "More feral kittens?" Before he could move away, she was pulling at his shirt to get a better look. She bent lower, and the ends of her shiny black hair swung forward. Judd stared at the soft skin at the nape of her neck.

Distracted, he didn't notice when she first moved her hand. He had to wrench away so the arching, angry-kitten claws that had already done a number on him wouldn't mar her smooth skin. The abrupt action turned the squirming creatures into bundles of desperate, climbing fur. By the time he had them under control again, he had even more scratches on his arm. The stinging pain on his belly told him they'd probably nailed him a couple of times there too.

But at least he had an excuse to turn away from Beth. In the kitchen, he deposited the wild kittens inside the box he'd readied and then headed for the infirmary.

Beth dogged his footsteps, but he pretended not to notice. He even managed to shut the heavy door in her face.

But the damn thing didn't have a lock. Within a heartbeat she was inside too, with the door shut again and her back leaning against it. "I have to tell you everything," she said.

Judd swung away to rummage through a drawer. He knew enough, damn it. Enough to upset his calm, enough to upset his sense of balance, enough to make him want to dig Whitney up with his bare hands and kill him all over again.

He found the bottle of antiseptic and grabbed a couple of gauze pads. His fingers fumbled on the screwtop of the bottle.

"Let me do that," Beth said.

Before he could refuse, she grabbed it from him. "Sit down." She pointed to the corner of the desk.

"Give me your hand."

He stupidly held out his right one. The one that had made it through the kitten rescue and subsequent tangle without a scratch. Shaking her head at him, Beth took up his left one herself.

Then she slapped a hydrogen-peroxide-soaked pad on the scratches across its top. He sucked in a breath, and his gaze jumped to her face.

"There," she said. "Now I have your attention."

He raised his eyebrows in casual inquiry.

"I have to tell you," she said again. "You need to know everything."

He winced. It hurt like hell to know what he already did. Any more and his emotions might explode into words. Actions. Mistakes. He might lose everything he'd come to the Sur to find—tranquility, peace.

Real, authentic friendship.

But with Beth's hand clinging to his, he didn't have much choice but to listen.

"When he first came to the Sur," she started, "Lainey and I were around twelve years old. You know how it is here, everybody knows everybody. We all assumed he was just passing through like most artists. By the time we were seniors in high school though, Stephen was still in the Sur and starting to get national attention."

She soaked another pad with peroxide and daubed at the smaller scratches on his wrist. He wanted to flinch, away from the sting, away from her words, but he held himself still. *I'm a rock.*

"Then my father died. We needed money. Cooper was in college and trying to keep the retreat going. When Stephen asked about renting one of the cottages on a long-term basis, we were glad. I was glad, because I had a big crush on him."

Judd could picture her at eighteen, long-legged and beautiful. Stephen would have noticed, he would have noticed both girls.

"Not long after he moved to Tranquility, I . . . I imagined he was in love with me. I was certain he would ask *me* to marry him. But, of course, it was Lainey he married."

Judd closed his eyes, then forced himself to reach for pencil and paper. BOTH OF YOU?

She knew what he meant by the brief question. "Yes, I think at first he did flirt with us both. And then I ran into him at the cove a few times, just like Lainey described. But he never called me by name there, so when they announced their engagement, I thought . . . I thought he must have mistaken me for her."

The lead of his pencil gouged the paper. YOU THOUGHT HIM INNOCENT?

She abruptly turned away, then dropped the used gauze in the garbage can and recapped the bottle. "Until recently, until what Lainey said the other day about him never making that kind of error, I did think the times before their marriage weren't his fault. If I blamed anyone, I blamed myself for not realizing the one he loved wasn't me."

But the bastard had been two-timing both girls. The anger was gathering inside Judd again. Gallons of vitriol, rising fast. Stephen had been a grown man and Beth was a girl of eighteen when he'd played games with her heart.

"After they married, I had no good excuse for having an affair with him." Beth's voice was hoarse. "No excuse except that *I* wanted to be his wife. *I* wanted to be the one he chose."

Judd found himself reaching out to her, but she flinched away.

"I think I was a little crazy after their wedding. My father had died, my mother didn't seem ready to live, my sister had married the man I loved. Everything I did, I did for me, with no thought of the consequences. When Lainey announced her pregnancy, though I hadn't told anyone, including Stephen, I was already into my third month. I was so smug, because *I* would have his baby first."

Judd gripped the edge of the desk. What the *hell* had Whitney been doing? What had he been thinking?

Beth looked up, her eyes dull. "The miscarriage was the antidote to that craziness. I woke up to what I might have done to my family, to my *sister*. I told Stephen about losing our baby and I also told him our . . . intimate relationship was ended. And ever since, I've been . . ."

DOING PENANCE? Judd rose from the desk to shove the paper at her.

She gave a helpless shrug. "It hasn't worked. Because isn't guilt supposed to lessen with atonement?"

He could only shrug.

"But I know I need to move on." In a weary gesture, she swiped her hair off her face. "And I think maybe I can find my way past this if . . ."

He saw her swallow hard, then she stepped up to stand directly in front of him. "Judd, you're the most levelheaded and self-aware person I've ever met. The wisest. I really respect your spirituality. I respect you."

Out of nowhere, a sense of foreboding descended, its vibrations seeping deep into his bones. Judd instinctively backed up, only to slam into the solid metal desk.

"It would give me some perspective on the whole thing, some sense of relief, if I thought you understood. If I thought . . ." Her voice went hoarse. "Judd. Please. Can you—can you forgive me?"

Forgive her?

Forgive her?

The rage he felt toward Stephen flared, rising stronger than ever before. Judd tried to swallow it, tried to keep it inside just as he'd kept all his words inside for the last five years, but it only made the feeling build faster, stronger. Forgive her!

Under another volcanic surge of pressure, the rock that was supposed to be Judd cracked. Emotion rolled out of him in waves of acid heat, melting everything in its path.

His arms shot out and he wrapped them around Beth. He yanked her against him, holding her slender weight to his chest as if she were the cork that he needed to prevent the flow of his feelings.

Her head jerked up and he saw shock in her eyes.

God, it only made him madder.

Years of silence hadn't made him smarter, though, because he didn't try to soothe her. He'd been the comfortable friend for years. The silent partner in their relationship.

And he could no longer hold back communication.

He bent his head and pressed his mouth to hers.

God, God.

The taste. Her taste. Elegant. Restrained.

Bittersweet, because he wanted to taste her passion, her elemental self, and she was standing wooden and unyielding in his arms, her lips politely pressed to his as if he were another art patron and it was just another day at another Whitney show.

He wasn't even sure her heart was beating.

He needed to make her feel. Feel for him.

Angling his head, he attacked her mouth this time, willing her lips to soften. He shoved his hand beneath the silky little sweater she wore and cupped her breast.

That's when he felt her react.

She gasped, and he moved in with his tongue. It was hot inside her mouth, and he explored, touching her smooth teeth and the ridged roof of her mouth. Finally, he flicked her tongue with his. They weren't comforting strokes, but ones that teased, incited, demanded that she duel with him. Fight.

A needy sound came from the back of her throat.

A sound that set spark to dry brush. Judd flamed. He ran his mouth over her face, trying to take it all in, trying to taste every pore of her creamy flesh. His kisses slid down her neck and then he dropped to his knees at her feet.

It was there that tenderness caught up with him. His breathing slowed, his movements slowed. *Oh, Beth.* There were so many things he wanted to tell her body with his. There were so many places he wanted to stroke, to kiss, to tongue.

But first, first was here. His hands shaking, he pushed up her sweater to get to her pants. Despite the quiver in his fingers, he was able to work the button and slowly slide down the zipper. He wasn't certain either of them was breathing as he pushed the edges away to bare her skin.

There, three inches above her bikini panties and two inches below her navel, was her *tan tien*, the gathering place of her *chi*. He leaned toward her, toward the skin over her *tan tien*, toward the skin over the place where she'd also cradled a baby she'd loved and lost. Opening his hot, wet mouth, he buried his face against her, marking her with a last, fierce, deliberate kiss. Making her his.

Then, gentling his lips, he worked them inch by inch over the smooth fragrant flesh of her abdomen, while his hands ran up and down the back of her legs. Her fingers speared his hair and he shuddered, even as he still caressed her, kissed her, healed her with every loving thought, with every soft touch. One hand encountered her warm, slender ankle. He caressed it too, until his fingertips brushed the cold, snaky surface of the platinum chain she wore.

Stephen's chain.

Rage renewed, Judd curled his fingers under and tore it away.

Beth gasped and stumbled back.

He stared up at her. He'd never seen her rumpled, and here she was half-dressed, her hair messy, her face flushed. His possessive kiss had left a red blotch on her belly.

"Why?" Her slender fingers touched there, then touched her mouth. "Why did you kiss me?"

Judd rose. He should talk to her now. Let the feelings out. Say the words, take the chance, open his mouth, open his heart. But a five-year-old habit becomes an ingrained habit, and he hesitated.

Only to discover that the words were frozen inside of him. And even as he was looking at her and thinking she was never more beautiful, he was incredibly relieved that his feelings were locked away. After all, the secret of his love was safe, *he* was safe—if he didn't break his silence.

"Tell me," she said, her voice low but demanding, "tell me why you kissed me."

The levelheaded, self-aware, spiritual Judd could only lift his hand and let it fall. But he was wise enough to be unsurprised when at that she fumbled with her clothes, then rushed out of the room.

He looked down at the anklet in his hand, the diamond-encrusted *E* dangling from one end.

Five years before, he'd been a smooth, fast talker. He'd used that ability to make money and to make friends, but then one day he'd seen that he also used the talk to skate the surface of life and the surface of relationships—even his own marriage.

He'd left the Silicon Valley with some foolish, romantic notion of finding an authentic life. Of listening instead of talking, of living instead of skating, of finding real truth instead of making one up to fill the yawning emptiness that no number of wealthy clients and hours on the job could ever seem to do.

And he'd found something, all right. He'd found out that it had taken him five years to learn the simplest truth of all. Taoism, Buddhism, Native American spiritualism, none had really changed him. He wasn't willing to risk, to delve deep, to be authentic.

He'd turned quiet because talk had been so shallow. But hell, so was silence, if the person who'd stopped talking still refused to give another more than the surface of himself.

He glanced back down at the dangling anklet in his hands. News flash, folks: Ripping away the chains didn't make one free.

Angel was on the path leading to the Tranquility dining room when she caught sight of Beth rushing toward her. Clothes wrinkled, hair flying around her head, the other woman appeared upset, if not downright panicked.

"Beth!" she called out. "What's the matter?"

The other woman paused, and Angel saw her suck in a breath and straighten her spine in an obvious attempt to regain her usual composure. But then she gave up the struggle and, with a frantic shake of her head, brushed past.

Angel forced herself to walk on. Whatever was wrong with Cooper's sister was none of her business, right? But then she found herself spinning back to follow.

It was the reporter in her, Angel decided, that was insisting she trail Beth along the path leading to the cove's secret entrance. Her intuition was ringing alarm bells, just as it did whenever Cooper's sister was nearby.

It wasn't as if she were coming to care about Beth.

She didn't take a personal interest in the members of Cooper's family, just as she didn't take—much—of a personal interest in Cooper himself. Why, when she'd woken at dawn and found herself plastered against his body, she'd instantly detached without waking him, her brain clamoring for separation.

For distance. For objectivity. For all those good, girl-reporter qualities that she'd aspired to since she was twelve years old.

Of course, she shouldn't have gone to bed with him again, but there was no use crying over great sex. Anyway, she and Cooper had both been unnerved the night before. Cooper because he'd had to rescue her, and Angel because of Lainey's discovery of a possible Whitney daughter. But in the light of day, Angel realized that Lainey's find posed little actual risk to her secret. Tracking down this unidentified daughter would be impossible unless someone knew the facts that Angel did.

After all, her parents had never married. And though Stephen Whitney's name was on her original birth certificate, both her mother's and her own name had been legally changed years and years ago.

Angel hurried through the tunnel and emerged on the other side, blinking against the sun's bright reflection off the sand. There wasn't a distraught woman in sight. Not even a calm one. It was as if Beth had vanished.

Frowning, Angel spun a 360. The cove was formed by granite into a solid U-shape, its ends protruding into the Pacific. The battering ocean had broken them down, leaving chunks of crumbling rock that the waves usually dashed against in dramatic, foamy-white geysers.

But today the tide was lower than she'd seen before, and the sea quieter. If Beth timed it right, could she have scrambled over one of the projections and into an adjacent cove?

To see, Angel wandered close to the wave line and mounted the rocks on her left. Usually covered by water, they were slippery with green stuff, and she put a hand down to steady herself. Something spongy and shell-encrusted sucked at her fingers and she shrieked, jerking back.

"Damn it!" an exasperated voice yelled from behind her. "Do you need a keeper?"

Angel froze. Cooper's exasperated voice. She tried for a casual glance over her shoulder, but looking at him made her suddenly, stomach-clenching serious. He was striding in her direction, with rumpled hair and in rumpled jeans, his chest and feet bare.

He's the keeper. The one I want to keep.

The notion tried to settle into her chest, but she hauled in a huge breath so there wasn't any room for it.

He came to a halt below her. "Get down," he ordered, holding up his hand.

She shook her head. "I'm looking for Beth. I followed her to the beach and then she disappeared."

"You can't make it over the rocks," he said, glowering at her. "You have to wade around."

"Oh."

He snapped his outstretched fingers. "Come on. Get down."

Ignoring his hand, Angel leaped for the sand. She stumbled on landing, but managed to find her balance before Cooper reached her. Without a word, she started toward the incoming waves.

"Where the hell are you going now?" he ground out.

"To wade around. I want to find Beth."

"No!"

At the vehement command, Angel stopped and looked back at his angry, dark eyes. "What's the matter with you?"

He speared a hand through his hair. "Have you forgotten you can't swim?"

"Wade, you said. I can wade." She didn't want to think about swimming, about drowning, about the relief she'd felt the night before when his arms had come around her in the pool. She couldn't let him get his arms around her again, that's for sure, because she didn't want to start depending on their warmth. On his strength.

"No, Angel." His body was tensed, as if he were ready to charge her if he had to.

"But Beth—"

"Knows what she's doing. Don't go near the water." He raked his hair with his hand again, and softened his voice. "Damn it, Angel, don't. Please."

"Okay, fine." She retreated from the incoming waves,

though she stayed well clear of him. "But I assure you, I'm usually perfectly safe around the water."

"*Usually* being the operative word."

She hated the way he pointed that out. "I don't need a man to—"

"I don't like feeling scared."

She grimaced. "You made that pretty clear last night."

"I'm referring to this morning."

She lifted her arms from her sides. "I'm off the rocks and away from the water already!"

"No, I mean when I woke up and you weren't in my bed."

Angel swallowed. Did he mean he'd missed her?

At the idea, a traitorous warmth tried to steal through her, tried to make her soft. So she tossed her head and pooh-poohed the comment with an offhand gesture. "Oh, sure. It's terrifying to have a whole big bed all to yourself."

He let that go, only to narrow his gaze at her. "Why *do* you keep running out on me, Angel? Just exactly what's scaring you?"

"What kind of question is that?" She stifled a little flurry of panic and waved her arms around to indicate their surroundings. "Look at it out here! It's too beautiful a day for questions like that."

But he refused to be sidetracked. "Come on, Angel, I want an answer," he insisted softly, stalking closer. "What's scaring you? Say the first thing that comes into your head."

She turned away from him, but the answers tumbled into her mind anyway.

Weakness. *You.*

You breaking my heart.

With a shake of her head, she pushed those thoughts aside to make room for annoyance. Cooper was playing question games with her, lawyer games, power games. Clearly, as a man, he hadn't appreciated waking up alone. He hadn't liked being the one left behind. She'd "scared" him? Hah. More likely she'd bruised his ego.

In preparation for telling him just that, she took a deep breath and spun to face him again. But the words dried in her mouth as she was smacked right between the eyes by the amazing spectacle of the scenery behind him.

On a day-to-day basis, the natural beauty of Big Sur was nearly unfathomable in its majesty, so her mind had taken to relegating it to travel-poster or movie-backdrop status. But now it had her attention, and she saw it, *really* saw it.

Over Cooper's shoulders, the green-covered mountains appeared close enough to touch, their sheer faces dropping to meet cascading beige hills. From there, the hills rolled gently to the staggered, jagged granite cliffsides that plunged toward the roiling ocean. It was yet another hot day, and the sun was already fading the sky to a pale blue, while striking gold in the sand at her feet and finding pockets of silver in the grayish ocean.

It was incredible. Awe-inspiring.

She blinked, sucked in a breath, blinked again. It was still all there, still so incredible and awe-inspiring. She remembered the day she'd sat with Katie on one of those staggered promontories, and how insignificant she'd felt in the vastness of the natural beauty.

"Maybe I'm afraid of this," she murmured.

Startled to hear the words spoken aloud and alarmed by what she might have revealed, she tried covering up the gaffe. Shoving her hands in the pockets of her white jeans, she made herself saunter toward Cooper. "If I was afraid of anything, that is."

He shook his head. "Which you're not."

She grinned; she had to. "Which I'm not."

Sighing, he shook his head again. "You are one tough nut to crack."

"No. Just tough."

"Angel . . ." He reached out for her.

She jerked back. Then, embarrassed by her jumpiness, she leaned closer to jab him playfully in the stomach. "But how about you, big guy? How about you tell me *your* scariest moment ever? Taking the bar? Defending your first client?" She wiggled her eyebrows. "Your first kiss?"

There was a little bubble of silence, then he caught her gaze, held it.

She felt a tremor in her chest.

"Really, Angel?" There was another little silence in which he watched her closely, too closely. "You really want to know the scariest moment in my life?"

Her heart trembled again, but her head said, *Bluff, bluff, bluff!* "Sure."

"It was when my father died." His eyes never left her face.

Angel's feet scraped backward in the sand. No fair,

no fair. She'd been trying to ease them past this second-morning awkwardness! She was working on reestablishing a nice, impersonal distance. Cooper should be thanking her for that.

"We were alone in the Lucias. Our first father-son camping trip after his heart attack. The doctor had declared him hale and hearty, but he collapsed the very first night."

Oh God. She shook her head, holding out her hands to halt him. "It's too private . . . too personal . . ."

Cooper spoke right over her, his voice rough and implacable. "I couldn't leave him alone to get help, he didn't want me to. Instead, he gave me the Evelyn Woods speed course on becoming the man of the family. He told me where all the financial records were. He told me to take care of my mom and my sisters. He told me to always do the right thing."

"No, no." Angel shook her head again. "I don't want to hear—"

"I was holding his hand when he died. I didn't leave him until his skin turned cold."

"—any more." Though it was too late, she repeated herself. "I don't want to hear any more."

"Well, why the hell not?" Cooper demanded, his expresson tightening. "Why *don't* you want to know?"

"I—"

"Is it because you're not interested unless I'm the source for some article? If it won't grab your readers, then you don't want the story? Is that why you've left me, twice now, to wake up alone?"

He advanced on her, his eyes dark, hard. "This morning when you weren't there, I flashed on a vision of you at the bottom of Lainey's pool. And yeah, it scared the hell out of me, Angel. But now, now I'm just pissed."

She scuttled farther back, desperate to get away, yet just as desperate not to appear that she was.

He moved in for the attack, grabbing her at the elbows to hold her still. "That *is* it, isn't it? You're comfortable when the relationship is reporter-to-subject, aren't you? But not any other way. Not person-to-person." His fingers tightened on her arms. "Not woman-to-man."

It took every ounce of will she had to keep her face expressionless. She stared at him, willing nothing, *nothing* to show in her eyes. Not hurt. For sure, not hurt.

But, oh God, he *had* hurt her.

He was breathing hard, the scar on his chest rising and falling, rising and falling. "What the hell am I doing?" he muttered, dropping his hands.

Angel took an instant step back.

He winced. "Sorry. I'm sorry. I have no right . . . no right at all."

To be on the safe side, she retreated another foot.

He winced again. "Don't worry, I'm going."

And he did. She watched him disappear through the tunnel with eyes so dry they burned. Her throat was dry too, as if in the last few minutes the life had been leached out of her. As if she were a stalk of September weed that had been desiccated by the merciless sun.

She dropped to the sand and buried her head against her knees. Now would be a good time for a stiff wind to rise and blow her away. Let it pick her up and toss her somewhere in the eddies over the vast Lucias or send her along the jet stream that pulled across the Pacific.

It wouldn't matter if she disappeared. No one would care, because she didn't allow them to get that close. While Cooper might not think he *had* a right, he *was* right about her. Person-to-person, woman-to-man, she failed. She was fine as a professional, but when a relationship was *personal*—then she shut down, shut off.

It was a mechanism to keep her safe . . . and that kept her alone.

"Angel."

Her head jerked up. Cooper was on the sand behind her, pulling her onto his lap and into his arms. The bare skin of his shoulder was warm against her face and smelled like his bed had when she'd walked away that morning—like clean sheets and sunshine, with a tangy note of sex.

"You're back," she said, too surprised to wiggle away.

"I didn't really want to leave you." He rubbed his cheek against the top of her head and her hair caught in his morning stubble. It was the only part of herself that she allowed to cling to him. "I couldn't leave you."

She stilled, but inside her, inside her chest, something moved. It twisted, or maybe it untwisted, no telling exactly which. "W-what did you say?"

He shifted to cup her face in his hands. "God help me," he whispered, looking into her eyes, "I couldn't leave you."

Angel stared at him, feeling dizzy and breathless and totally unlike her usual cautious, tough self. Eons passed as she tried to figure out what was happening to her.

"Cooper, let's go back," she finally said, because there wasn't enough time in the world to separate and identify the emotions building inside and there was something more urgent. "Let's go back to your place. I . . . want your arms around me."

I need your arms around me.

His fingers tightened on her face for an instant, then they slid to her hands to tug her to her feet. In the next moment he'd pulled her against him in a warm, strong embrace. She leaned into him, reveling in the feel of his heart beating against her cheek.

"What are we doing?" he murmured. "What the hell are we doing?"

It was clear he didn't expect an answer, which was good. Very good. Because Angel had no idea what Cooper was doing—and she could only hope that *she* wasn't falling in love.

Chapter 17

The walk back to the retreat didn't smooth out Angel's mood or clear up her confusion. She only knew that her pulse was racing and she couldn't rid herself of that dizzy, breathless feeling. As they came within sight of the Tranquility common building, she spotted a strange group of men at the same instant one of the men spotted them.

"Hey, Coop!" the guy yelled.

Angel nearly jumped from her skin. The surprise of the loud voice in the usual silence shot a burst of adrenaline into her already overloaded system.

"Coop, over here!" The man waved his arms.

Grimacing, Cooper slanted her a glance. "The workers are here to erect the tents for the art show. They'll expect my help."

She nodded jerkily, relief and disappointment adding to the emotional cocktail inside of her.

He released her hand and cupped his palms around her face again. "Are you going to be all right?"

She nodded again.

"You said you wanted me."

Her head shook in immediate denial. "I'll be fine. Just fine." On second thought, she clearly needed something other than Cooper right now. What she needed was to quash the odd idea that she was in danger of falling in love with him.

"I'll see you later, then." He bent his head and touched his mouth to hers. Soft and tender, the kiss on top of the weird jitters made her woozy. When he ended it and let go of her, she wobbled.

He laid a steadying hand on her shoulder. "Okay?"

No. Her heart continued to wobble inside her chest. But she managed a carefree smile, slipping straight into her habit of bravado-under-stress. "Of course."

He strode off, then suddenly spun back.

She wished he hadn't caught her looking after him.

"Was that you whistling?" he asked.

Her eyes widened and she shoved her hands in her pockets. "I don't know what you're talking about."

She only whistled when she was uncertain or frightened. That wasn't the problem here. Flashing him her best no-worries smile, she made it a point to be the one to turn away first, and hoped she looked dignified and cool as she scurried toward her cottage and her expected return to sanity.

She was halfway there when the silence was interrupted again. "Girl!" an elderly female voice said. "Girl, over here!"

Angel's head turned toward the sound. In the door

of the cottage she'd just passed she recognized one of the retreatants.

"Can I help you, ma'am?" Angel called out, retracing her steps. The white-haired woman beckoned her nearer with one hand, while the other gripped a heavy staff in arthritic-looking fingers.

The lady beckoned Angel closer still.

With an inward shrug, she followed the elderly woman inside her cottage. Maybe the old gal needed help moving or reaching something.

When the door was shut behind them, the lady turned to Angel. "Sit down, girl. Sit down."

Staying where she was, Angel frowned. "Is there something I can do for you, ma'am?" She wasn't up to a social call.

"I'm Mrs. Withers." Gesturing to one easy chair, she lowered herself into another. "I heard you're a reporter."

Not knowing quite what else to do, she nodded and perched on the edge of the indicated seat. "My name is Angel Buchanan. I write for *West Coast* magazine."

"Well, if you're writing about Tranquility House," the old woman asserted. "The person you should be talking to is *me*."

Angel opened her mouth to correct the impression, then hesitated. Was there really some all-fired hurry to leave? The alternative to killing some time with Mrs. Withers was staring at her own four walls and worrying about whether or not she was edging toward being in love with Cooper.

Which she wasn't. She couldn't be. Why would *he* be the one after all these years?

And since that was exactly what she didn't want to

dwell upon, she focused on the older lady. "You know the retreat well?" she asked.

"Know it well! I've been visiting here every September for the past forty years."

Forty years! Angel's nerves were calming already. That many memories should keep both of them occupied for quite a while. "Tell me about it."

But as the old woman began to reminisce, Angel's mind refused to follow the conversation. She was aware of *hmm*ing and *umm*ing at sufficient intervals, but the busiest of her brain cells remained preoccupied with Cooper.

She *couldn't* be anywhere close to falling in love with him!

She couldn't be in love with anyone. Giving over her heart was something she'd been inoculated against a lifetime ago. When envisioning her future, she'd seen her life running along the lines of her editor's at the magazine. Jane had friends, work, a good, full life without a commitment from a man. That sounded fine to Angel, because nobody knew better than she how falling in love could only lead to disappointment—at the low end of the scale—or actual danger.

In between those extremes was heartache, unfaithfulness, abandonment. Suppressing a little shudder, she tore her attention back to Mrs. Withers.

"And they were such a lovely couple," the woman was saying. "They married in September, you know, right on the cliffs. I was there."

Angel blinked. "I'm sorry, who was the lovely couple?"

"Edie and John."

The names rang a bell, thanks to Cara's piles of research. "Oh," Angel said, nodding. "His parents." She felt herself flushing. "I mean the parents of Cooper, Beth, and Lainey."

"That's right." The old woman nodded. "They doted on those children."

Lucky for them.

"But they doted on each other even more. Edie fell apart when John died. I thought that would be the end of Tranquility House."

"Really?" Angel's mind spun back to Cooper and the beach, of how he'd told her of his father's death in that hard, cool voice. Of how he'd accused her of not wanting to get that personal with him.

Bull's-eye.

No, no! He just didn't understand that she was being *realistic*. What they had was chemistry. Incredible sex. A mutual interest in bad food choices. But nothing more! "Their" song was that ridiculous "Hakuna Matata," remember?

". . . that boy was tireless, though. Nineteen years old, going to college, working a job in town, working on the weekends at Tranquility to keep it running."

"Mmm." Angel nodded. So Cooper was hardworking. Smart. She'd known that from the start. There was absolutely no reason for him to be anything more to her than a fond memory of some pleasant sex.

"Edie, though . . . well . . ."

Angel snatched at the name to refocus the conversation. "Yes, Edie." She leaned forward in her chair. "Tell me more about Edie."

Mrs. Withers sighed. "There are some women who can't make it without a man."

Angel nodded. "I know just the kind you mean." *And remember you don't want to be one of them!*

"I was married for thirty years myself, and I still miss Charlie, but I was always an independent sort." There was a lively gleam in her eye. "After he passed on, I enjoyed myself. Still enjoy myself."

"Good for you," Angel said, nodding.

But then the old lady clasped both hands on her staff and sighed again. "Not that I haven't been lonely. Very lonely at times."

Angel's stomach squeezed. She thought about her too-quiet apartment that she filled with the noise of the news channels. She thought of Tom Jones, the neighbor's fickle cat that was often the only living creature she touched in the course of a day. "Well, I'm, uh . . ."

Mrs. Withers shook herself. "We were talking about Edie, though. She wasn't the same after John was gone. Pined for him, I think. Not many years later, she caught a cold that turned into pneumonia. I heard she hardly tried to fight it off."

Angel *tsk*ed. "The perils of love."

"The children were devastated, of course. But again, it was Cooper who stepped in and handled all the details."

"He's good at those."

Mrs. Withers nodded. "And more, he gave those girls the support they needed. He was there whenever they wanted a shoulder to cry on or to lean on. Lainey was already married and mother to darling Katie, but that artist husband of hers was usually locked in his tower with his canvases and his paints. Cooper is the one who has always been there for the women in his family."

That artist. Angel picked out those two words and tried forgetting the rest. She should ask Mrs. Withers more about "that artist." That's why she was at Tranquility, remember? To learn more about Stephen Whitney. To find out the truth.

The truth.

Cooper is the one who has always been there for the women in his family.

Image after image shuffled through her mind. Cooper coming for Katie at the memorial. Walking with his arm around his sister at the cliffside service. Rushing to Beth's aid when she'd been crying later that day. Sunset dates with his niece. Tending Lainey's garden. Back flips into the pool.

Why would Angel be in danger of falling in love with a man like that?

Hah. Hah hah hah.

The joke was on her. She wasn't in danger of falling in love with Cooper after all.

She already *was* in love with him.

As it neared sunset, Cooper's arms and shoulders ached from the unfamiliar lifting and holding required to erect the two huge tents. Though the crew had welcomed his help, he could have left them to the job hours before.

Instead, he'd used the work as an excuse to avoid

Angel and as an opportunity to kick his own ass to hell and back.

When he'd woken that morning and found her gone again, he *had* flashed on her floating toward the bottom of the pool. The idea ripping at him, he'd run from the cottage with a panicked need to make sure she was safe.

Judd had told him he'd seen her head toward the cove, but even in the short time it took to locate her, Cooper had worked himself into a state. A stupid, stupid state that was a potent combination of anxiety and anger.

So he'd attacked Angel for finding it so easy to walk away from him, when walking away from him was the very thing he wanted her to be able to do.

Damn it! Damn him.

Checking his watch, he decided he had another good excuse to stall before facing her again. It was almost time for his usual evening meet with Katie. Maybe the sunset would provide the solution to how he could cool things off with Angel.

But when he arrived at his and Katie's special spot, there was a blond head beside the dark one of his niece. They sat side by side, the soft breeze lifting their hair away from their shoulders and mingling the curly yellow and straight brown strands.

He was going to lose them both.

The weight of it slammed heavily into him. He stumbled on a rock, sending dirt and pebbles tumbling. Katie's and Angel's heads jerked around.

He tried to smile. "Sorry. I didn't mean to startle you."

The corners of Angel's mouth lifted and fell and she started to rise. "I . . . I was just leaving."

"Don't go." Why did the wrong words keep coming out of his mouth? "I . . . uh . . . uh . . ." Hell, he sounded as nervous as she looked.

She bit her bottom lip. "I don't want to intrude."

Cooper took his place on the other side of his niece. "We don't mind, do we, Katydid?" He wrapped his arm around the girl's shoulders and made himself look at Angel over her head. "After all, this is . . . what? Your second-to-the-last Big Sur sunset? We'll share it with you."

Angel hesitated a long moment, then she nodded, her eyes cooling, her expression now composed. Not a single nerve showing. "That's right. I'll be leaving right after the art show."

If she'd expected to do any different after his earlier demand for her to get "personal" with him, if she'd expected he'd ask her to stay longer, there was not a hint of it in her manner. Relieved, he took the bottle of sparkling water Katie held toward him and swallowed half in one gulp.

Then he looked down at his niece. "And how was your day, miss?"

"Fine."

Her wooden expression was an uncomfortable echo of Angel's. He *knew* there was a wealth of emotion beneath Katie's emotionless face. Did that mean there was trouble brewing behind Angel's calm eyes too?

Disquieted again, Cooper stared out at the fiery orange sun sliding inexorably down the slope of the afternoon sky. It was moving so quickly now, he thought, the day passing so fast. Like his life.

"I was just telling Katie about San Francisco," Angel put in. "That I can't wait to get back."

San Francisco. Maybe he should have returned to his firm after recovering from the surgery. Maybe he should have gone back to the city and burned out like a candle, doing what he loved best. But instead, he'd come here, hoping to secure the future of Tranquility House and his family as well as he could.

Watch out for your mother and sisters, his father had said that night in the mountains. Cooper was holding himself to that promise as long as possible.

Closing his eyes, he reminded himself that it had seemed like a fine idea to die in the Sur. Here, compared to the permanence of the mountains, the unceasing movement of the Pacific, the infinite horizon, his life was nothing.

He'd hoped that would make the idea of his dying feel like nothing too. He'd hoped to find acceptance.

He was still hoping, damn it.

"Uncle Cooper?"

Startled, he opened his eyes and looked down at Katie. "What is it?"

"The sun's gone. And you're cold, Uncle Cooper. You're shivering."

The wind had kicked up, and Katie's and Angel's hair was swirling around their heads, twining yellow and brown in a pretty dance that had him staring.

Angel jumped to her feet and put her hand on his shoulder. "Cooper?"

Her fingers were warm. He didn't stop himself from covering them with his cold ones. Just for the moment, just for now, he needed her heat.

Her eyebrows drew together in a frown. "You *are* freezing."

He avoided her concern by shifting his gaze to the ocean. He stared out across the endless water toward the distant horizon and the sunless sky. It was beautiful, he thought, even though another day was gone.

The wind and the waves roared in his ears. His chest expanded on a breath of briny air, and he could taste seaweed and salt and pine on his tongue. Yes, it was still so very beautiful, even with the sunset a thing past.

It hit him then. The sun was gone, but the world wasn't. Its light was gone, but this moment wasn't. Its heat was gone, but the warmth of Angel's hand wasn't.

And I'm not gone either.

Sudden optimism flooding through him, he squeezed her fingers and smiled up at her. "You ready to go back? It's getting late, sweetheart, and we have things to do."

"What?"

"You know," he said, his voice going husky. "*Things to do.*"

The startled giggle on his other side reminded him that Katie was still with them. He glanced at his niece and winked. "*Adult* things, squirt, so get lost."

"Cooper!" Angel sounded mortified. "What's the matter with you?"

He grinned at her, because he thought she might get mad if he laughed. But God, he felt like it. He felt like laughing, grinning, smiling, because there was no point in worrying about the future when having Angel in his arms once more sounded so simple and so right. So not yet finished.

He didn't let go of her hand, even when they came within sight of his place and Angel tried tugging it back. "You never answered my question back there," she said. "What's going on?"

Once again, smiling was easy, because he had all the answers now.

"We've been thinking too much." He ushered her toward his front door.

"We've been worrying too much." He pushed her over the threshold.

"And not living," he said against her mouth, "not living enough in the moment."

Her skin was sleek and hot against his cool flesh. She was wet where he was hard. Her mouth fit against his, his body fit inside hers. Just another of nature's incredible beauties.

There was no future.

There was only now.

Though not yet dawn, the art exhibition tent was as bright as noon, thanks to the track lighting spilling onto the paneled walls. Beth tore a strip of brown wrapping paper off another painting. They'd returned from the framer—who'd worked feverishly to get them finished as a special favor—the day before and she was going to hang them quickly, then go.

Leave the Sur.

Her hands were shaking, but she told herself it was lack of sleep, not fear of everything she was about to do.

Leave her home.

Leave her family.

For once and for all, breaking the chains of the past, of the secrets, and of the silence that had kept her half-living for too long.

Steeling herself, she tore at the wrapping again, revealing another cherubic child. Without allowing herself to look at the image itself, she reassessed the painting's size, making sure it would show to advantage on the panel she'd selected. Then she mounted the ladder.

As she reached upward, she heard footsteps. Her little start of surprise set the ladder rocking, but then its movement abruptly stilled. From behind her, hands—one still marked by long scratches—wrapped two of the ladder's legs to steady it.

There was nothing to steady her pulse, so Beth just ignored its jumping. She went about the task of hanging the picture on the silk-covered panel as if Judd weren't there. Then she took her time adjusting it to hang perfectly straight.

But the fussing only made her pulse more jumpy, so she finally forced her hands away and took a step down the ladder.

The back of her calf brushed him and she jerked again.

"Get out of my way," she said through her teeth.

He didn't move.

She shot him a glance over her shoulder. He looked as steady, as calm, as *silent* as always. "You're in my way."

He was. He stood between her and freedom. He was a piece of the why she'd stayed too long already.

Now when she moved, he stepped to the side, leaving only one hand on the ladder. She stared at it, at the scratches that had started to heal, at new scratches the kittens must have given him since.

"Will you take Shaft for me?" she asked abruptly.

He blinked. Frowned.

"I'm leaving. I need someone to care for Shaft."

Judd's hand released the ladder and fell to his side. His gaze stayed trained on her face as if he were trying to read her mind. For years, she'd thought he could. Somehow, anyway, through shared smiles and laughter, her chatter and his cryptic notes, he'd become her foundation, her sounding board, her best friend.

She sucked in a shallow breath, her chest too tight for a deeper one. "I can't stay for the show. I can't watch people stroll through my secrets and my shame."

Judd looked away, leaving her to wonder what he was thinking. She'd never been able to read *his* mind. Sure, they'd always managed to communicate, but he'd only let her in so far, so deep. Though Judd's calm silence had always been attractive to her, such a contrast to Stephen's nearly manic self-absorption, it had left her feeling selfish at times.

She took from Judd and never gave.

Just like Stephen had taken from her, from Lainey too. Knowing him, he'd probably egotistically rationalized his behavior as the demands of his muse. Or the passions of the artistic mind.

Not that he hadn't been charming about it. Not that

he hadn't possessed a talent for finding and connecting to the soft center of people's hearts. But now that he was gone she was seeing him—and what she'd done with him—so much more clearly.

Grabbing up the next painting, she viciously tore at the paper covering. The last time she'd felt this kind of anger, she'd been walking down the aisle toward the man she loved—as her sister's maid of honor. But the feeling was surfacing again, fighting its way through the layers of shame and blame she'd tried to suffocate it with. With another rip, she worked the painting free.

She instantly averted her eyes from the blond baby depicted on the canvas. Determined to get on with the job, she forced her gaze around the room, searching for a likely spot.

A likely spot among painting after painting of *her* baby. Blond, like Stephen. His blue eyes. There wasn't even a hint of her features in those of the child depicted over and over and over.

"How could he?" It was already warm outside and it was even hotter in the tent. Or maybe it was her mood, her rage, finally becoming something she was releasing from her soul. "How could he have married my sister and have an affair with me? How could he have made us both pregnant? How could he paint our baby like this, with such . . . such *love,* when she was already gone?"

Judd hadn't moved. He stared at her, silent.

She stalked toward him, seething. "I lived half a life as penance for my mistakes. I stayed to watch Stephen, to make sure he didn't take advantage of Lainey or some other woman again. I stayed because I love my sister and my niece. I also stayed because—"

She'd be damned if she'd tell Judd *that*. "But I'm done settling for half, for living on guilt and a friendship that only goes so far."

She whirled, made it one step. He caught her arm. She wrenched it free, then turned on him again.

"Why did you kiss me?" she demanded. "Why?"

He looked at her, his expression as helpless, as silent, as when she'd asked him that question the day before.

She laughed, and it was so short and bitter that it felt like a sob. "Go ahead, keep it to yourself. But I'm not keeping my secrets anymore. Not one. Not one more hour."

Resolved to face up to everything, though, she took a last, long inspection of the paintings of the child. Her stomach instinctively cramped, steeling against the pain of what was lost.

Funny, though. When she looked, really looked, it was hard to equate them with loss. The canvases were beautiful, really beautiful, the child in them vital and alive.

They weren't her child, she thought suddenly. They were Stephen's imagination, his artistic gift, and that warm part of his heart that was undeniable, despite his flaws.

Then she glanced at Judd's stoic face and her grief resurged. She ran out without saying goodbye.

Judd stared after Beth. What had she said? That she wasn't going to keep her secrets any longer? Oh God.

Oh God. He'd been so stunned by the idea of her leaving that he'd almost missed it.

Taking off after her at a run, when he burst through the tent entrance he smacked straight into Angel. They grabbed each other to keep their balance.

Her hair, her face, was a pale smudge in the dark gray of early dawn. "The world just keeps tilting on me," she muttered.

The odd rawness of her voice gave him pause. He tightened his grasp on her and looked into her face.

As if sensing his question, she met his gaze squarely. "I couldn't help but overhear. All of it."

Without even thinking, Judd spoke. "I don't know what to do." His voice was gritty, too low, too harsh. "I love her."

"You're asking me? Well, this is what I always say." Angel closed her eyes. "The truth. Once you have the whole story, you gotta tell the truth."

Chapter 18

Judd found Beth in her kitchen. He didn't bother ringing the bell or even knocking. Instead, he walked around to her back door and let himself inside.

And then stood looking at her, tongue-tied.

He still didn't know what to do. Nothing in the religions and philosophies he'd studied provided a suitable guide to this moment.

She glanced up at him from her place at the table. There was a smudge of dust on her cheek, her bangs were hanging messily in her eyes, and he realized she was wearing a T-shirt with a rip in the shoulder seam. He gaped, because except for the time he'd kissed her, he'd never, not once, seen Beth in less-than-perfect order.

Then he looked around the kitchen, surprised again by the dirty dishes in the sink, the long, wide smear of something—peanut butter?—on the usually pristine countertop, the quarter inch of scorching coffee in the bottom of the pot.

He stepped over to unplug the coffee machine and caught sight of Shaft peering cautiously around the corner from the hallway. Their eyes met, and they spoke to each other in the way that dumb animals—males—can do. *Don't look at me,* the creature clearly said. *I'm not gonna try to reason with her. Shaft may be "the cat that won't cop out when there's danger all about," but he was a character in a movie. . . . I'm a real cat, and a neutered one at that.*

Judd turned back to Beth. She was bent over the table, her pen racing across a sheet of paper.

He stepped closer, alarm twisting his gut again. He'd heard right. She was writing a letter to Lainey.

To get Beth's attention, he shuffled his feet. When that didn't work, he rattled an empty chair. When she continued to ignore him, he finally resorted to snatching the pen from her hand.

She didn't even blink. Instead, she grabbed for another pen on the tabletop, at the same instant that he reached for the stack of notepaper beside it. Their fingertips brushed.

They both jerked back.

They both bent over their pieces of paper.

Judd slid his note her way.

Without a beat, Beth swept it off the table.

It fluttered to the floor, even as her pen continued forming word after word of her letter to her sister. Retaining a tight hold on his calm, Judd grimly plucked another blank sheet off the table. Penned another line.

Watched again as she dismissed his thoughts with a wave of her hand.

On his third failed attempt, she spoke without looking at him. "Don't bother anymore. I won't read it."

Judd closed his eyes. *Be calm. Find balance.* He tried losing himself in the quiet of the room, settling his mind to its original state of purity and clarity—Zen. But his anxious heartbeats boomed in his ears, his harsh breaths ripped through the silence, the clock on the kitchen wall loudly ticked off the seconds of this last chance.

His mouth moved, once, twice. "You'll listen, then."

Her head jolted up at the rusty sound of his voice. She stared at him.

He held up his finger. "One thing. I have just one thing to tell you."

Her gaze jumped away from his. "It's too late. I gave you chances to talk about . . . about us. But you wouldn't, couldn't."

"Not us." He shoved back his chair, knelt at her feet, and put his hands over hers. "More important than us."

She tried to pull away from him, but he held fast. As a stockbroker he'd given advice thousands upon thousands of times. He'd made his clients money, enabled them to buy luxurious lifestyles and the most expensive of toys. But when his prize client—and best friend—the one he'd made millions for, committed suicide, Judd had woken up to the fact that all his talk and all his trading had never bought a cent's-worth of happiness.

From that moment on, he'd vowed never to advise

anyone again. He'd started listening instead. But now he had to break that vow.

"You can't tell Lainey." It was as concise as he could make it.

Beth jerked back in surprise. "Lainey? This is about Lainey? You're breaking your silence of five years for *Lainey*?"

"Yes."

Her face paled. "For Lainey?" she whispered.

"Yes."

She turned her head away from him. "No—"

"This is your secret to bear, Beth. I won't let you hurt your sister by telling the truth."

Her eyes closed, Beth was shaking her head. "No, no, no, no."

"It's not right, not fair, to free yourself by burdening her."

One tear squeezed from between Beth's lashes and rolled down her face. He followed it with his gaze, pretending it was his hand, his mouth, caressing her cheek.

"So I'm the wrong one again," she said dully. "The bad twin."

"If you tell, yes."

"No!" She wrenched her hands from his and jumped out of her chair. "Who the hell are you?" she yelled at him. "Who the hell are you to tell me what I should do?"

And there it was, the question he'd feared. It was the one he knew would come up the instant he opened his mouth. When he was Judd Sterling, noble guru, Silent

Man of Mystery, he'd always hoped he stood a chance against the "Artist of the Heart."

But now she'd know he was a fake. She would know there was nothing deep beneath his silence.

"Who am I?" His throat tried to hold back the words, but he forced them out. "I *was* a golf-obsessed, NASDAQ-addicted Wall Street trader who didn't know he was burned out until he buried his best friend and then his marriage. Your ordinary asshole."

Crossing her arms over her chest, Beth turned her back on him. "And now?"

"Now . . ." Surrendering, he sighed. "Now I'm still ordinary. I'm just your ordinary forty-something guy trying to figure out the fucking meaning of life."

Her back still to him, she walked to the sink to stare out the window. "Yet you've managed to figure out I can't tell Lainey." She said the words slowly, coldly.

"Beth." She was turning his heart inside out again and it hurt so damn much. "It's your cross to bear."

"It hurts me. You don't care how much it hurts me."

He closed his eyes. *You don't know how much I care about you.* But still, he couldn't say it. "I wish . . . I want . . ."

Her shoulders stiffened as he got to his feet. When he stepped up behind her, she pressed her belly against the countertop. "You've said your piece. Now go away."

But there was a wealth of pain in her voice and however ordinary he was, he couldn't leave her without trying to do something about it.

"Let me help," he said, lifting his hand to gently

stroke her hair. "I know you would never forgive yourself if you hurt your sister again, Beth. *That* would be heavier than what you're carrying now. But I'm still your friend. So tell *me* your secrets, tell me how and when it hurts, and I'll be here to make it better if I can."

She stilled. "What?"

"You'll only hurt yourself more if you hurt Lainey too."

Her head slowly turned toward him. They were close, so close that she had to tip back her head to look into his eyes. "You don't want me to tell . . . for me?"

He nodded, puzzled as to where the surprise was.

"For me," she said again, as if she had to be sure. "Not Lainey. You broke your silence for *me*."

He nodded another time.

She ran her gaze over his face. "I . . ." The word drifted away and she looked down at the countertop. "Why, Judd? I need to know why."

Why? She'd asked him that before. *Why did you kiss me? Why?*

All the old reasons for silence were still there. What wisdom had he really gained in the past five years? He'd never had more than a superficial relationship with anyone, even his so-called best friend. Could he do differently with Beth?

But he already had.

Would she let him get that close?

But she already had.

Could he win the heart that had been bruised for so long?

"Why, Judd?" Beth whispered again.

He had to try. Yet still, the words were difficult. He looked around for something to write with, but retrieving paper and pen meant leaving her side. So he made do.

In the smear of peanut butter on the countertop, Judd traced three symbols: I♡U.

Beth stared at them a moment, then turned so that her body was flush against his. There was something on her face—hope, joy, wonder? "You love me?"

Yes. He gathered her against him, holding her fiercely as he meant to for the rest of his life. Later he'd find his voice again and tell her everything, all his secrets included. He'd tell her how he came to Tranquility House and then stayed, not because he found himself in silence or yoga or tai chi or tofu. *I stayed because I found you.*

"You love me." She declared it this time.

He smiled against her hair. Whispered against her cheek. "More than words can say."

It was midmorning when Angel left her cottage, feeling drained. Flexing her cramped fingers, she headed for the common building. Cooper had to be wondering what happened to her. She'd slipped out of his bed at dawn, planning to retrieve her jar of contraband instant coffee and then slip right back in beside him. But then she'd heard Beth and Judd, and *what* she'd heard had sent her to her own place for more than coffee.

She drew in a deep breath, and the hot, dry air

sucked the moisture from her mouth. An image of a frosty glass of diet Pepsi bloomed in her mind to hover at its edge like an oasis. Lord, she missed them: diet Pepsis, manicures, lattes, honking horns. Deadlines, idiot copy editors, her byline, bold and strong in her favorite Helvetica font.

She wanted to go home.

Oh, she wanted to forget about the past three weeks.

"Hey!" A big hand grabbed her arm, spun her around. "I thought we had a deal about you not running out on me." Cooper towered over her, looking mildly harassed and monumentally gorgeous. Her heart tried to curl in on itself.

She wanted to forget about him.

But how could she, how could she ever, when he suddenly grabbed her by both elbows and hauled her up to his mouth? She lifted her face toward his kiss, letting it blot everything from her mind but its sweet, hot passion.

Pressing her body against his, she angled her head, silently begging him to make it go on and on.

"Damn!" His expression bemused, he set her back on her feet. "What good deed did I do to deserve that?"

She crowded closer to him, twining her arms around his neck. "Let's go back to bed." They could turn out the lights, draw the drapes, and pretend they were the only ones in the world.

He cocked an eyebrow and gently pushed her hair off her face. "It was *you* who got up for dawn patrol."

"Let's pretend I didn't." Rising on her toes, she kissed the scratchy underside of his chin. "Let's start again where we left off."

He smiled, toying with one of the curls at her temple. "Sounds tempting. But I can't—"

"I need you," she whispered, trying not to sound as desperate as she felt. If time couldn't run backward, then it would just have to stand still.

"Angel—"

"Cooper." She opened her eyes wide, trying to appear as fragile and innocent as everyone always thought her. Her bottom lip trembled. "Didn't you hear me?" She'd wheedle if she had to. Beg. "I *need* you." The words were getting easier to say.

He laughed. "You had me worried for a minute there." As he pulled away from her, he swatted her behind. "But Angel Buchanan doesn't need anybody, I know that."

She stared at him. "But . . ."

He gave her another swat. "Come on, honey. The fact of the matter is, the fun stuff will have to wait until tonight. Right now, I need *you*."

He was several steps ahead before he seemed to notice she wasn't with him. He turned around. "Well, come on. We've got a lot to do since Judd took Beth away."

"Away?" She hurried forward. "Away where?"

"Judd has a condo in Pebble Beach." Grinning, Cooper wiggled his eyebrows. "They're taking a few days off."

Angel blinked. "Now?"

"They left fifteen minutes ago. And no time like the present, is what I say."

The present. Angel's footsteps faltered and she thought longingly of the future. When she was back in

San Francisco, and all that was here—and what she'd have to decide to do about it—was behind her.

"So we're in charge of Tranquility," Cooper continued.

She stopped again. "*We?*"

"Shh, shh." Cooper grabbed her hand and made a big play of scouting about the deserted path. "Remember, we have to set a good example."

"I'm still unclear as to why 'we' are involved here." But she let him pull her forward.

He glanced down, his face unreadable. "Because . . . because I have to be and I want you with me. Good enough?"

It was good enough to end her objections. She didn't know what to tell him, what to tell *herself* when he said something like that.

So she helped him dismantle the breakfast buffet. She help him assemble the lunch buffet, then dismantled that too. They didn't have time for anything but a glass of ice water before they started the whole routine all over again for dinner. They weren't alone as they worked, because retreatants were in and out of the common building the entire afternoon.

Angel not only blessed their busy-ness, but for the first time she blessed the rule of silence. Thanks to it, she could work beside Cooper all day without the fear of spilling any of her secrets . . . including her feelings for him.

The feelings that were a queasy mix of sadness, longing, and love. Revealing them would only make their last hours together awkward and uncomfortable. She wanted him to be able to look back on their final night together with fondness.

At last, the dinner dishes were put away and the countertops clean. In the dining room, Angel dropped onto one of the picnic benches and rested her head on her bent arms. The area was deserted, so she risked a groan. "I think I have tofu underneath my fingernails."

"Poor baby." He walked over to stroke his hand over her hair. "But don't get too comfortable. We have one last thing to do."

"You go ahead. I'll sleep here."

"I promise it won't take long." His hand ran down the back of her hair again. "And then we'll go to bed."

There was a husky promise in his voice that she couldn't deny. And she couldn't deny *herself* one more night with him either.

He must have seen the eagerness in her eyes, because his laugh was low and smug as he drew her up from her seat to lead her outside and into the starlight. But when he turned toward the exhibition tents, Angel balked. "What are you doing?"

Without pausing, he swept her forward, then swept her through the flapped opening of the tent that housed the paintings. "Beth made me promise to give it a check."

Angel heard a click, then the interior was lit.

Just as it had been that morning, predawn, when she'd learned—

Her thoughts evaporated as her gaze roamed the inside of the tent. She'd glimpsed the paintings a week ago, but she'd avoided taking a good look at them. Now they were framed and mounted on huge, vanilla-colored, silk-covered panels. The panels were suspended at slight angles from a series of beams that also supported tracked lighting that strategically spotlighted the framed canvases.

Against the neutral background, the glowing, almost otherworldly Whitney colors leaped out at her.

The children—no, child—did too.

It was clear to her that on every canvas was the same child, a girl, depicted at different ages. There were two or three images of a fat-cheeked baby, but the rest showed her at five, at seven, at nine. Angel flashed back to the gallery in San Luis Obispo and her stomach clenched. Was this the absent child from the "missing children" series?

Was this—

"Angel?"

Her head whipped toward Cooper. "What? What?"

"You seem . . ." He studied her face. "I don't know."

She managed to smile, to shrug, to tell herself the paintings weren't what she thought. "I'm okay." Nothing, not even these paintings, would ruin her last night with Cooper.

He nodded, then scanned the room. "Everything looks fine for tomorrow. The brothers at the monastery will send a van for the retreatants before breakfast. Lainey will do her traditional thing and drive into Carmel to greet the guests and ride back in the first bus. Sometime after the retreat clears out and well before the first bus arrives at one, the caterers will show up. Once the show is over—"

"I'll be heading back to San Francisco." She didn't know what made her say it. To test him?

He stilled, then slowly turned toward her. "I guess you will."

And if it had been a test, the one failing it was Angel. "It's hot in here," she mumbled.

"Then let's go." Hesitating, he looked around at the paintings again. "You know, there's something familiar about the child."

Angel swallowed. "Cooper." He couldn't make the connection between her and Stephen Whitney. Not now. Not tonight, their last night. "Coo—"

"Uncle Cooper!"

They both swung toward Katie's voice. She peeked in the tent opening. "Here you are," she said. "I was looking for you."

"What do you need, Katydid?"

"Whoa." The girl was looking past Cooper, her eyes moving from one framed painting to another. "I . . . I didn't really pay much attention when Mom showed them to me before."

Cooper strolled toward her. "You okay, sweetheart?"

Katie swallowed. "Who . . . who is she?"

"I don't know," her uncle said.

Angel felt a pang of sympathy as she watched the teenager's face change from curiosity to unhappiness to a frozen nonexpression. "He never painted me," Katie said.

Cooper betrayed no emotion except love. He smiled at his niece, hugging her close to him with one arm. "Ah, Katydid. You know what he always said when you badgered him about that. Your dad swore he couldn't come close to the beauty nature—and your mother—had already created."

With that, he guided her out of the tent. Angel silently trailed them, listening to him redirect the conversation to the hot day, the hot night, then to the fact that Judd had called and asked Katie to retrieve the kittens from his cottage and take them back to her house.

When the little animals had been rounded up and placed in a plastic kennel for the trip, Cooper glanced at Katie and then told Angel he would walk his niece home.

"I'll hurry back," he whispered as he passed her. "Wait for me in bed."

Angel went back to her own cottage for a cool shower. Studiously ignoring the little desk and what was sitting there, she re-dressed. Then, carrying her nightgown and robe, she walked out into the still, warm air.

She slipped through Cooper's door and minutes later slipped into her nightgown and into his bed. Leaning back against the pillows, she pushed her troubles from her head and promised herself to create a last night he'd never forget.

Cooper strode down the path through the guest cottages on the way toward his own. And Angel. If she'd disobeyed instructions and wasn't in his bed *this* time, he was going to forget good manners and good sense and go after her.

This was their last night.

He pushed the ache of that thought away and focused instead on the anticipation. Already his body was growing heavy. He could almost feel her velvet skin against his palms, the weight of her—

"Cooper!"

He started. His head jerked right. "Mrs. Withers? Is everything okay?"

The small light outside her door turned her white hair a flat yellow. "I heard something."

"Heard something?" He walked closer. "An animal?"

"A hum."

"A hum?" He frowned, then he laughed, a little embarrassed. He'd been singing "Hakuna Matata" in his head. "I'm sorry. That was me. I hum when I'm, uh . . ." Happy. He was *happy*? "It's a habit."

"Not that kind of hum," she corrected. "An *electronic* hum, from that writer's cottage. Miss Buchanan's." Her finger pointed in the direction of Angel's place.

"Oh. Well. Ah." A hum?

A hum. In the next instant, his mind spun back to something Angel had said the first night she'd arrived. And *then* it spun away on an image of her and that vibrator she'd claimed to have with her.

Feeling his face flush hot, he cleared his throat and dragged his attention back to Mrs. Withers. "When, uh, when exactly did you notice this hum?"

"Just a few minutes ago, when I passed by her cottage on my walk before bed. You better go do something about it. There are rules, after all."

"Sure, yes. Rules, Mrs. Withers." Cooper stumbled backward, almost landing on his ass when he tripped over a root. "I'll take care of it."

He nearly ran to Angel's, his pulse pumping. Did she have something special up her sleeve for their last night? A surprise? On that thought, he knocked once, then turned the knob. She knew he would come looking for her.

But the cottage was empty of Angel, he realized with disappointment. Her desk wasn't empty, though. Her laptop computer was sitting there, its screen dark, but still humming away.

Brat. Smiling to himself, he recalled that he'd returned all her electronic stuff days ago, when he thought she was leaving the first time. She'd never reminded him to take it away again.

Reaching the desk, he stretched out a finger and ran it over the computer's black plastic casing. In his house in San Francisco's Twin Peaks, he had a similar model. This close, the computer's hum was very loud, almost a buzz.

He swallowed a laugh, because that's what listening to the noise was giving him. A buzz. It brought back to him the intoxication of work, of research, of the word of the law. God, he'd loved it. God, he missed it.

Still stroking the computer, Cooper closed his eyes. He'd confessed it to Angel and it was true—he was idealistic. Whether it was because of his dad's last words to him—*always do the right thing*—or because an overdeveloped sense of justice had overdeveloped into a championship of the needy, his work had fascinated him.

Tomorrow, when Angel left, he'd lose the only other thing that had ever fascinated him as much.

God, no!

His hand jerked as he rejected the thought. His fingers must have brushed a key, because the computer emitted a tiny electronic burp and the screen burst to life, filled with words.

Words that jumped out at him. "Stephen Whitney," "my father," "abandonment," "adultery."

Cooper paged through the entire document.

Betrayal.

Chapter 19

Angel couldn't let it end like this.

The longer she waited alone in Cooper's bed, the more certain she was of that. And she was certain that the night was hot, too hot for even the light nightgown she wore. Not too much for the warm temperature, but too much between her and Cooper.

In defiance of her usually modest nature, tonight she had to be closer to him. She had to be skin-to-skin from the very first instant.

Determined to have that, she drew the flimsy fabric over her head and dropped it to the floor. Then she sat up against the pillows, buck-naked beneath the sheet. Her pulse was racing and so was her mind—racing over all her previous objections to involvement with men, racing through all the reasons that *he* was too good to walk away from.

Yet Cooper hadn't seemed the least concerned about

her imminent departure. He wasn't making plans for them to be together once he returned to San Francisco and his law firm. Why?

Because, perhaps, *his* heart wasn't involved like hers.

But despite the evidence, she was beginning to doubt that. Hadn't he said *I want you with me* that morning? He'd want her with him tomorrow too. Next week. Next month. She knew it deep in her heart, deep in the place where she'd found her love for him.

So why would he let her walk?

Because *Angel Buchanan doesn't need anybody.* He'd said that too.

He was letting go because she'd never let *him* see how much she needed to be held.

The sound of the cottage door opening made her jump. Angel's hands started to shake and she tried to control it by squeezing them together. But then she unlaced her fingers and let them rest, trembling, on her sheet-covered lap. Hadn't she decided that hiding her vulnerability to him would only get her a goodbye?

His footsteps came toward the bedroom, thudding slow and steady against the tiled floors. When he reached the doorway, she leaned over and switched on the small bedside lamp. "There you are," she said. "I—I've been thinking about you."

She felt his gaze touch her face, flick down to her bare shoulders and then to the sheet tucked over her breasts. "Oh yeah?"

She swallowed, the dark note in his voice sounding like a warning. But no! That was her fear talking. "Yeah," she echoed, trying to smile as she patted the place beside her. "I missed you."

Instead of taking her up on her invitation, he leaned against the doorjamb. The lamplight was only strong enough to glance off his cheekbones and his chin, leaving the rest of his face in deep shadow.

He looked different—leaner, darker, harder.

Cursing her knee-jerk defenses again, she tried to suppress the shiver snaking down her back. Seeing a villain on every street corner had kept her safe . . . but it had kept her alone too. She didn't want that anymore.

"I'm trying to change," she blurted out.

He didn't move. "Is that right?"

There was tension in the room, the air was crackling with it, but she couldn't tell if it was something separate from the sexual awareness and the emotional upheaval that were so tangled up inside of her. "I, uh, I want to be honest with you."

"Sounds promising."

Her stomach knotted. Did she detect a remoteness in his voice or was it just her suspicious nature imagining the worst?

She thought of Cooper with Katie, with his sisters, the way he supported them, touched them, dispensing easy affection and genuine love. She remembered the warmth in his eyes when he'd looked at her earlier that day. *I want you with me.*

There was nothing to be frightened of, not with Cooper. He wouldn't hurt her.

"I'm waiting," he reminded her. "What was it you said? You wanted to tell me something . . . or was it show me something?"

Show him something! Yes. Her heart. How much she loved him. The future they could have together. "Show you something," she agreed.

"Sounds even more promising. Why don't you drop the sheet?"

She blinked. "What?"

"Drop the sheet. It's nearly up to your ears. You're acting like I've never seen you before."

"Well . . . I . . ." Heat bloomed on her skin. Surely he realized she wasn't the most natural nudist in the world. But it was symbolic, wasn't it, laying bare her heart?

Edging away from the circle of lamplight cast across the bed, she took a deep breath and let the sheet slide. It slithered over the top slope of her breasts, caught briefly on her nipples, fell to her waist.

The night air was warm, she knew it was, but her revealed flesh prickled with a million goosebumps. Her nipples tightened in a rush, contracting to hard, aching points. She dug her fingers into the covers to stop from throwing her arms over herself.

"Pretty," Cooper said. "Now let's see the rest."

The tone of his voice plucked at her stretched nerves. There was sex in the rawness of it, an edge that was exciting. Disquieting.

"You trust me, don't you?"

She did. And she was willing to do whatever it took to demonstrate that. Taking a breath, she made another surreptitious move away from the lamplight. Then she shoved the sheet to her ankles.

The overhead light blazed on.

Angel froze, paralyzed by the sudden brightness. "Wha—?" Her hands grabbed for the covers.

But he had them quicker, and with a jerk, whipped them off the bed and threw them onto the floor. "How does it feel?" he asked, his voice hoarse. "How do you like being exposed?"

Angel rolled, but he was faster again. Before she could fling herself from the bed, he was on it too, holding her shoulders to the pillows. "What are you doing?" Her voice sounded unnatural. Weak.

"I'm letting you know how it feels to have your flaws laid bare to the light." His gaze flicked down her naked body. "Not that I can find any on the outside."

She tried to get up again, but he pushed her back onto the pillows. "What's your problem, Cooper?" she demanded.

"My 'problem' is *you*. The *real* you."

Oh God. She sagged against the cushy feathers, wishing she could believe this was a nightmare. "What . . . what do you know?"

"I believe it's finally the truth, the whole truth, and nothing but the truth. I was in your cottage. I read the story on your laptop."

Stomach rolling, Angel closed her eyes and nodded. "It's true," she said, forcing the words from her tight throat and dry mouth. "All true."

"Did you think you could get away with it? Waltz in here on a lie and then waltz out with our secrets?"

She didn't know what she'd thought. Or rather, she'd been deliberately *not* thinking ever since she'd taken her fingers off the keyboard that morning. After overhearing Beth, she'd run to her laptop and written her exposé of Stephen Whitney in a white-hot, righteous heat. She'd written it in pain and she'd written it in anger. For all of them.

"So you're Stephen's daughter."

Angel opened her eyes and met Cooper's cold gaze. She reached for the anger again, trying to grab for it with both hands. Anger had always been there for her. It had been her protection too. "Yes, I'm his daughter."

"And the rest of it . . . ?"

"I found out this morning. Beth was talking to Judd, and she said—"

Angel broke off as Cooper shot up from the bed. "I don't want to hear it," he ground out.

"All right." She swallowed hard, refusing to give in and wrap her arms around her nakedness.

"I don't want to see you again either."

"All right."

He grabbed her robe from the nearby chair and tossed it at her. "Here."

She shoved her arms through the sleeves, then wrapped it securely around her body as if it could hold her composure together too. Though she knew the temperature hadn't changed, the night suddenly felt as cold as Cooper's eyes, and she shivered as her bare feet touched the tile.

He leaned against a long dresser, watching her. "Now get out. Get the hell out."

She shivered again. "Don't worry, I'm going back to San Francisco."

He sucked in a harsh breath, looked away. "In the morning. I don't want you on that road in the dark."

"Hah." With a huge leap of imagination, the sound

she made could be called a laugh. "You're still the protector of the innocent and weak?"

He shot her a look. "I've always known you're neither, believe me. But promise you won't leave until it's light."

"You'd take my word?"

"If you give it."

A strange calm was descending on Angel, as if this were a dream. Maybe she could pretend the past three weeks weren't real. Later, if any memories popped up to plague her, certainly she could banish them with the same disdain that Cooper was using to banish her.

"All right," she said. "I'll wait until morning."

His hands were braced on the dresser behind him. As she hurried past, the skirt of her floor-length robe brushed his leg.

He flinched. "We took you into our lives. You betrayed us."

In the doorway, Angel paused, trying to deflect her hurt. "Well, there you go," she finally said. "Now *you* know how *that* feels." Then she squared her shoulders and moved on.

The next morning, Cooper stood in the retreat's gravel parking lot and helped the last of the guests into the monastery's van, then waved it off. The morning was another hot one, blazing hot, with a stiff, dry wind that was waving the pine branches and rattling the leaves in the oak trees.

As he turned to walk back to the retreat, his gaze found Angel's car, lingered. Stacked in the backseat, he recognized the suitcases he'd trundled to her cottage that first night.

Despite everything, he almost smiled at that memory, remembering her chatter, her dismay upon seeing her utilitarian accommodations, the way she'd tried to protect her hairdryer from confiscation.

If only he could turn time back. He'd been wanting to do that since the very first chest pain, of course, but now he found himself wanting to return to a time that was *after* the heart attacks and the surgery.

But before he'd discovered Angel Buchanan's true colors.

Identity.

Whatever.

He heard footsteps on the gravel and turned. There was Angel, her hair kicked up by the wind and floating around her shoulders, her heaven-blue eyes wary. As their gazes met, her feet faltered. She stared at him too, and he swore he heard a sound, the quick *ftthht* of a striking match. The very air seemed to catch fire.

With a jerky movement, she broke their gazes and beelined for her car as if he weren't there. He told himself to ignore the combustion too. His feet scraping on the gravel, he strode off in the opposite direction. All the goodbye necessary had already been said. Right?

Right. He didn't want to have any more to do with her. He didn't want to spend any more time near her.

Then, he might remember how she burned in his arms. Then, he might remember how she made him laugh. Then, he might remember that his bastard brother-in-law had left her to run, fearing for her life.

His fingers curling into fists, he spun around again. He watched as she stowed her laptop and briefcase in the passenger seat, then slammed the door. In tight-fitting black pants and a matching sleeveless top, black high-heeled sandals on her feet, she was city-chic.

He stalked toward her, his imagination placing her on a San Francisco sidewalk. He'd recognize that gilt hair from fifty paces, and he'd hurry through the crowd to catch her. In his mind's eye, he saw himself grip his briefcase tighter and jog around strolling tourists and the business types slowed by the cell phones against their ears.

There were a million details in his head, the complexities of his current court case, the back-to-back filing dates that could give an attorney fits, the ever-present organizational decisions of co-owning a law firm. But when he glimpsed Angel, their heavy weight lifted. When he was near enough to smell her sophisticated fragrance, his world brightened. His perspective righted itself—living first, work second—when he touched her shoulder.

Now she whirled to face him, and imagination and reality collided. Damn it! What was wrong with him? Why had he allowed himself this close to her again? This was the woman who had taken advantage of him and his family.

Anger rekindled inside him and he stoked it, adding piece after piece of evidence against her. She'd betrayed him. She'd betrayed his family. That story she'd written would wreak financial and emotional havoc that he might not live to see righted.

This wasn't the city. He wasn't a practicing lawyer any longer. And Angel wasn't the light of his life. She was leaving whatever was left of it.

But he had one more item to take up with her first.

Staring at Cooper towering over her, Angel steadied herself by gripping the open passenger door. Her heart wouldn't calm, though, so she sucked in a hasty breath. The air tasted faintly of smoke, thanks, she guessed, to the anger burning in his dark eyes.

"What do you want?" she asked, hanging tight to her poise. He wasn't going to see her sweat. Hurt. Cry.

He would *never* see her cry.

With the wind blowing his hair off his face, Cooper shoved his hands in his front pockets and regarded her coolly. "Call me dense, but it didn't occur to me until a moment ago what was behind all this. I think I have it now, though. Stephen's attorney is John Abbott of Baker & Abbott in Monterey. He'll require proof of your claim. I assume you have a birth certificate listing Stephen as your father. However, you'll still need to submit to a DNA test."

Angel blinked. "A DNA test?"

"I'm certain Abbott won't recommend Lainey giving you any kind of financial settlement without one. I know I won't."

"You think I want a 'settlement'?" For the first time since she'd finished writing the story on Stephen Whitney, Angel felt her fury rise again. "You think I came here for his *money*?"

Cooper's gaze didn't move off her face. "Why else?"

"I came here for the truth," she said hotly. "The world was ready to canonize him and I wanted to see which Stephen Whitney was for real."

"And what did you find out?"

She looked down at her laptop resting on the passenger seat. On the floor below it was her satchel-style briefcase, yawning open and bristling with notepads and the manila folders of research that Cara had accumulated for her. More papers and files were stacked beside it.

What *had* she found out?

Shaking her head, she closed her eyes. "He was a loving father . . . and he wasn't. He was a loving husband . . . and he wasn't." Her eyes opened. "He was a fake."

"Harsh, coming from someone who arrived here under false pretenses herself."

That made her bristle. "I did not. I *am* a professional journalist."

"And it was as a journalist that you were asking your questions and digging into our lives?" Cooper leaned closer. "What did you really want to know, Angel?"

Though she backed away from him so that she was plastered against the hot car door, she refused to look away from his face. "When I was twelve years old I wanted to be Bob Woodward, and I've worked my butt off to be the kind of reporter who uncovers the whole story and doesn't hesitate to tell it. What does it matter that Stephen Whitney was my father? I know how to be objective."

"Objective?" Though Cooper's voice was still cold

and controlled, it had a furious edge that stung like a fresh cut. "Is that what you call making friends with my family, with my niece?"

"Your family? I don't ca—" Angel broke off as the breeze shifted, blowing a hank of hair over her mouth. But she did care about them, despite her best intentions. It had been so easy to slide into Cooper's little family circle.

A circle where Angel didn't belong.

She wasn't surprised that he was so angry with her. He'd do anything to protect the ones he loved.

"And what about sleeping with me?" he demanded now. "Would you call that being objective too, or was that merely the sacrifice the 'whole story' was worth?"

Angel felt herself flinch.

Story-whore. In journalism school, that's what they'd called women who had sex with a source.

"It wasn't like that," she whispered.

"Yeah? Then what *was* it like, Angel? Because I'd sure as hell like to know."

But there was nothing she could say. No way to make him understand.

"It's time for me to go." She started to turn from him, thinking only of getting away, and getting away fast. "Past time."

But a glance at his expression had her freezing again. It was tight, set, yet beneath the anger she suddenly thought . . . she suddenly wondered . . . she suddenly worried that there was—pain.

She'd hurt Cooper.

Her stomach fell. No. *No.*

Yes. *Yes.* A woman who'd spent a lifetime hiding her wounds could spot them in another easily. It was what she'd sensed in Beth too.

"Cooper." She stepped toward him, put her hand on his arm.

The wind whipped his hair across his face as he pulled away from her touch. "Goodbye, Angel."

"No!"

He turned his back.

She almost let him go. But then she remembered. This was Cooper! Cooper wasn't like other men. He wasn't the kind of man who was looking for an excuse to leave her. That was why she'd fallen in love with him, wasn't it? Cooper would give her another chance, if she only had the courage to ask for it.

"Cooper!" When he kept walking, she put her heart into her voice. "Cooper, please!"

He paused, then slowly turned around.

Of course Cooper would turn around. He was such a good man. She *could* tell him what was in her heart, she told herself. She could trust him.

Swallowing hard, she gave herself one last chance to chicken out. But Angel Buchanan had never been a coward.

"Please," she said softly, beckoning him to her. "Please come here." She knew exactly how to make her point. "I have something for you."

In the few seconds it took for him to return, her pulse rate leaped to thrum at a new, dizzying level. There was a half-panicked, half-excited whine in her ears and when he was standing in front of her, she thought she would probably talk too loud. But she went ahead anyway. "Hold out your arms."

"Angel—"

"Hold out your arms."

Looking wary, he obeyed.

Angel bent into her car and pulled a handful of files and papers from the floor, then shoved them at Cooper.

"What are you doing?" He grabbed at them, then grabbed at the next stack she dumped on top of the first. "What the hell are you doing?"

She didn't speak, but instead kept piling on the papers, notepads, and files—all that represented her story on Stephen Whitney. Finally, when they reached his neck and the floor of her car and her briefcase were both empty, she brushed her palms together.

"There," she said, looking at him expectantly. Her pulse was still beating, *tat-tat-tat-tat-tat-tat-tat-tat-tat*.

"There?" he echoed.

She wiped her damp palms on her pants and nodded at the tall stack. "There. Now you know."

His expression impatient, he shifted, struggling to keep control of the messy pile in his arms. "No. I don't know."

The whine in her head edged up a notch and she had to lick her lips, the air was so much hotter and dryer than the hot, dry state it had been minutes before. How else could she tell him?

Inspiration struck. She bent inside the car again and whipped her laptop computer from the seat. With a little flourish, she slid it to the top of Cooper's stack. It wobbled, then wobbled again, forcing him to brace it with his chin.

Damn it, Angel." With his jaw against the precarious pile, he had to speak through clenched teeth. "What the hell do you mean by this?"

She swallowed, then gestured at what he was holding. "It's . . . it's not obvious?"

He glared at her. "No. I'm afraid you'll have to spell it out for me."

Spell it out. Lay it on the line. Bare her heart. Expose her vulnerability.

Show him he could be—God, that he was—her weakness.

Her whole body trembled. She gripped her fingers together and braced against the car to keep herself upright. "I . . ."

She had to swallow, remind herself that Angel Buchanan was no sissy, then start over. The wind blew her hair across her eyes and she pulled it away to meet his gaze. "I choose you."

He frowned. "What kind of bullshit is this?"

"None, none at all." She was speaking too fast, but it seemed to come easier that way. "I choose *you*. Not the story. Not the truth. They're not important."

"You don't believe that."

"Not usually," she admitted. "Not when ignoring the truth protects the wrong people. Not when leaving the truth buried means that more people get hurt. But this time . . ."

This time the truth would only hurt. Closing her eyes, Angel wondered how many other times she'd plunged ahead with her story, with her own interests, without conducting the litmus test of pain first. Wasn't that what Stephen Whitney had done all those years ago?

She opened her eyes and looked straight into Cooper's. "This time it's the story or it's you. And I choose you." Just as she'd wanted to be chosen by her father all those years ago. "The story is not worth losing you."

His body tensed. "What? *What?*"

With an explosive movement, he dropped the pile of papers and the laptop onto the hood of her car. She didn't even wince when her computer slid off the tall stack and landed upside down.

Then he grabbed her by the shoulders. "Now what the hell are you talking about?"

Her hands waved. "You. Choose. Whatever. You know." It was pure babble again, pure protect-herself babble.

"I don't know."

It was easier if she closed her eyes. "When you come back to San Francisco . . ." It was easier, too, to talk about it as some future thing. "I want us to, um, be together when you come back to San Francisco, Cooper. I think we . . . I think we have something together. Something, uh, very special."

It was a lame finish, but her heart was pounding so hard and he had yet to say a word. She let her eyes open partway.

He was staring at her, a strange—forbidding?—expression on his face. She had to be wrong about that. Of course she was wrong about that.

"What exactly are you saying, Angel?"

"If I'd known you'd be so slow, maybe I'd feel . . ." She tried to laugh. The forced sound fizzled out. This moment wasn't about funny. She knew that. It was about truth. *Her* truth.

"Cooper . . . I . . ." The breeze suddenly died, as if the whole world were waiting for her to say the words. "I'm in love with you."

His hands dropped and he jerked back. At the same instant, a gust of the renewed wind tugged at the papers sitting on her car. It caught a handful, and then another, sending them skittering across the hood and then into the air.

"No." His eyes flickered to them, then flicked back to her. His voice was harsh and his face grim. "No, you don't love me. You can't. I'm never going back to San Francisco."

"Of course you are." She'd surprised him, she thought, swallowing her panic. He wanted her to love him. He loved her back! "When Lainey and Katie are settled, you'll—"

"I'm dying."

Her flesh flashed from hot to icy. "What?" she whispered. It was that whine, her speeding pulse, something about the day that made everything sound strange to her ears. He was lying, he'd said. Or sighing, buying, frying. Yeah, frying. "It *is* very hot," she said desperately.

"I'm dying."

"Dying?" The idea was so ridiculous she could hardly reply. "No, no, you told me your doctor said you were fine."

"The doctors told my father he was fine, too. And

then he was dead of his second heart attack within twelve months. I've already had my second heart attack, Angel. How much time do you suppose I have left?"

"That's silly—"

"My time's borrowed, sweetheart. Every day, every minute, every breath, borrowed."

"But—"

"The stats will back me up."

Give her a stat and she'd find a way to beat the crap out of it. "But—"

"So don't tell me you love me."

The wind picked up again, and another gust buffeted them, then another, wrapping her hair around her face. By the time she'd pulled it out of her eyes, the air was swirling with papers. She saw a half-sheet fly by with her messy handwriting on it, then an article from *Health* magazine she'd copied at the library in San Luis Obispo fluttered past. Her reflexes must have been as desperate as her mood, because she made a miraculous grab.

She held the paper up to Cooper's face, rattling it beneath his nose. "I did my research on heart attacks. I know that with the right . . ."

But he was already shaking his head. "Listen to me, honey. This is for you. I didn't—don't—want us to get any closer because I saw what happened to my mother. How my father's death sucked the life out of *her*. I wouldn't wish that on you. On anybody."

Honey. He'd called her *honey*. Hope reined back Angel's alarm. "I'll take the chance, Cooper."

A light smack hit her back, then her legs. It took Angel a moment to realize it was more of the unleashed paper from the pile on her car. Then the wind flared again, more sheets joining the flurry, some scattering at their feet, others dancing at their ankles. When a photocopy of a Whitney painting blew between her and Cooper, she batted it away to move in on him. "Think, Cooper. Think of what we could have."

Her hand reached to touch him, but he stepped away, shaking his head again. "No, *no*."

"Cooper," she tried again, laying it all out now. "I'm in *love* with you."

"And I won't love you back." His eyes had turned from greeny-brown to inky-dark. "Ever."

A paper slapped against her face. Then another landed against her chest, the wind keeping it pressed tight to her heart. Angel didn't move it, glad for even that flimsy protection.

Because she believed him. Oh Lord, she couldn't look into that set face of his and *not* believe him.

"Why?" Her voice came out sounding thin and lost. Young. But she didn't have the energy to strengthen it, she only had what it took to ask the question that had always lived in the darkest, scariest corner of her mind. "Am I . . . am I so unlovable, then?"

Cooper staggered back. "No, God, no."

The papers were whirling and twirling around them now, blowing across the parking lot, blowing against her car, blowing against their bodies. But through the tornado they stared at each other.

Cooper scrubbed his face with his hands. "Angel, Angel, I don't . . . I can't . . ." He scrubbed again, then looked at her once more, his expression somewhere between sadness and pity.

"Let me tell you what my father said as he lay dying in my arms." Cooper's voice was calm, so calm. "I was asking him to fight, to hold on, even though I could see how much pain he was in." He glanced away. "I *know* how much pain that was, now."

He took a breath, then met her gaze again. "He used the final moments of his life to give me advice. And the last thing he said was that it wouldn't hurt so badly to die if he didn't love my mother so very much."

Angel shook her head. "Are you telling me that you . . . that you decided not to love anyone?"

"Yes."

"You'd turn your back on what we could have? You'd turn your back on me?"

"Yes," Cooper said gently. "*For* you."

Angel tried making sense of what he'd just said. He was rejecting her for her own good?

"I don't believe you!" She was suddenly furious. And determined to get at him. She launched toward him, batting papers out of the air on her way. "I don't believe a word you say!"

He grabbed her wrists before she could strangle him. "What the hell's the matter with you?"

She twisted her arms, trying to get away from his grasp so she could give him the death he so richly deserved. "You're not doing anything for *me*! This is for you, damn you!"

"I don't—"

"Don't you hear yourself? You're *afraid* to love me. It makes it so much easier for you not to."

He dropped her wrists and looked away. "Shut up, Angel. You don't know what you're talking about."

She laughed. "Oh yes, yes, I do. Because you're just like him. Loving someone only when it's *easy*, when it's *convenient*. You're another one, just like him."

His hand snaked out so fast she didn't see him move. One moment she was an arm's length away, the next he'd snagged the hem of her top and had her hauled up against his chest. Papers had been caught between them, and they made a crackling sound, like flames.

His gaze was flaming too, and trained on her. "Maybe you're right, Angel, maybe you are. I'm human, damn it."

"Human, or just plain *male*?" Angel spit out. "I should have known better than to trust someone from your half of the species."

His eyes narrowed. "Well, then, you should know this too. You might call yourself Bob Woodward, but from here you look a lot more like Lois Lane. And believe me, baby, you're looking in the wrong place for your Mr. Perfect. Superman is in the pages of a comic book, not Big Sur."

Angel's car peeled out of the parking lot and onto the narrow road leading away from the retreat. Sick at how things had ended between them, Cooper watched her dust rise in the air, bargaining with himself. He'd move as soon as the drone of her car engine no longer reached his ears.

But as it grew fainter, then fainter, he made a new deal. When that lingering dust finally settled, that's when he'd make himself return to the solitude of the retreat. He was still waiting when he thought he heard her car turn back.

Yes, the sound of the engine was definitely coming closer.

He looked around the parking lot, strewn with the mess of her papers. She wanted them. Or at the very least, her laptop.

But when she'd sped off, the small black machine had skated along the hood of the car, then smashed to the ground. Hell. With his toe, he tried pushing the scattered pieces of metal and plastic into a neater heap, but then he gave up and decided to escape to the retreat. He wasn't up to another explosive confrontation.

His head lifted as the revving car engine sounded closer. Too close. *She's driving too fast,* he thought angrily. He wasn't going to get out of the parking lot before she was back in it. *The damn fool will hurt herself.*

His foot jerked, messing the nice little pile he'd made. Then her car came careening into the lot straight for him. As he leaped back to save himself, her front tire ran over the remains of the laptop. The car stopped with a jerk and the combined power of the wind and the airstream she created picked up a mass of papers, throwing them high into the air again.

They rained like confetti over his head as she threw open her car door.

"For God's sake, Angel." He went ahead and shouted at her because he was so fucking tired of everything. "I was hoping to survive at least until lunchtime. What the hell are you doing now?"

From behind the steering wheel, she swallowed, her eyes wide. "Fire! There's a fire."

He leaped toward her. "What? Where?"

She made a vague gesture behind her. "There. Back there."

"Get out of the seat," he said, trying to pull her from the car. "Let me go see."

"No, no. You can't. It's burning on both sides of the road. Moving fast, and moving right this way."

Chapter 20

Cooper's gaze shot from Angel to the road behind her. The dust hadn't settled because it wasn't dust.

Smoke. It was smoke. Now that his wits were focused, he could see it, smell it. Fire had been a constant threat all summer, and it was the worst of the punishments that nature could mete out to the Sur. Flash floods and mudslides were bad enough, but thanks to tricky winds and inaccessible canyons, a small grass fire could quickly become a conflagration.

"How close?" He was already turning, running for the path that led up to the retreat. "How close?" he yelled again over his shoulder.

Angel caught up to him, breathing hard. "Bad at distances," she answered. "Halfway to the highway?"

Only half a mile away. Okay, okay. *Think, Jones, think.* Beth and Judd were safely away. Lainey was nearing

Carmel by now. The retreatants were with the brothers. Then, with a vicious bite, fear struck.

"Katie!" He stopped short and grabbed Angel by the shoulders. "Katie's alone at her house."

Angel gasped. "Oh my God."

"Quick, Angel, think. Which way is the fire moving?"

She was trembling beneath his hands. "Southwest. It was coming from the south and moving toward the ocean. Toward us."

The Whitney house was north, a greater distance from the fire, but the phone at Tranquility was much closer.

"Listen," he said to Angel. "Since we can't use the road, you need to take the shortcut—the walking path—to Katie. I'll go down to the retreat, call in the fire, then come to you two."

"No!" She grabbed his forearms. "We stay together."

Shaking his head, he pulled free of her. "We're all better off if I call it in right away." He shoved her in the direction of the Whitney house. "Go. Go!"

She stumbled back, then stayed rooted to the ground. "No, Cooper. Don't. Don't leave me."

Ignoring the husky break in her voice—*Am I so unlovable, then?*—he forced himself to shove her again, making his voice hard. "You're leaving *me*, all right? You're leaving me to help Katie."

She shook her head. "I won't."

The smell of fire was thickening the air. It dried his eyes, irritated the inside of his nose. "Angel, you've got to do this." He worked to keep the alarm out of his voice. "For Katie. Please."

"Katie." The name finally seemed to pierce Angel's

stubbornness. She sucked in a breath, glanced at the path behind her, then met his gaze. "For Katie."

Without another look back, he turned and tore toward the retreat. It would take Angel three times longer to get to his niece, even if she ran. By then he would have called the emergency number and be making his way to them both.

Unless he was trapped by the fire.

Angel approached the Whitney front door at a run and thumped both fists against it. "Katie!" She pushed her hair off her forehead, the skin sticky and tight from the sweat that had dried instantly in the arid atmosphere. Her fists thumped again. "Katie!"

The door opened, releasing a cold wash of air. Katie stared at Angel, round-eyed. "You're here."

"Fire." She'd left her breath somewhere back on the path, Angel decided. "Cooper."

Katie nodded. "He called from the retreat and said you were coming."

"He's all right, then?" Angel clutched the doorjamb, her legs weak with relief.

"He said to wait for him here, but if we get worried to take the car and head north." She lifted her hand to show a set of car keys dangling from her fingers.

Drawing in a deep breath, Angel stepped inside and shut the door behind her. "Yes, we'll wait for him." She deliberately slowed her words, hoping to sound resolute and calm. "He won't be long."

But staying calm was like trying to keep still while the hot breath of a monster was blowing on the back of her neck. For Katie's sake, though, she calmly took a seat beside the window in the living room to keep watch for Cooper. As the minutes ticked by and Angel couldn't hide her trembling any longer, she casually directed the girl to go upstairs. "Gather what you need for an overnight stay, just in case Cooper thinks we should leave."

Katie threw her a frightened look, but Angel pretended not to see it. The last thing she wanted to deal with right now was anyone else's fear. She was having enough trouble controlling her own.

She looked out the window. *Where's Cooper?*

He shouldn't be more than twenty minutes behind her, even allowing for a couple of phone calls. Hadn't she already been sitting here for at least that long? It had to be twenty-five minutes. Thirty. Eternity.

I'm dying.

Inside her head, she heard him saying the words, she saw that implacable expression on his face. But he wasn't dying, he wasn't! And she couldn't think about that now. She couldn't think about him telling her he'd never love her.

"Angel!"

She jumped from her seat as Katie yelled her name again and came running down the stairs. "What? What?"

"Outside." Katie grabbed her arm and pulled her through the kitchen and out the doors to the pool area. "Look."

It was snowing. Oh God, not snowflakes, but flakes of ash. They swooped down, driven by a wind that was blowing from the south. From Tranquility.

Like flower petals, the ash was softly falling and settling everywhere—on the flagstone patio, on the market umbrellas and chaise lounges, on the square-cut hedges, the potted, blooming geraniums, even on the surface of the pool. It was drifting into their hair too. Angel tried brushing it out of Katie's even as another flurry drifted over them, dumping more ash on the poolhouse roof and dusting the pines ringing one side of the patio.

"What do we do?" Katie said, sounding small and lost. Sounding like a little girl.

Katie *was* a little girl. Angel's stomach clenched at the thought, but she spun away from the teen's white face and wide eyes. "We water stuff down," she replied, cool and matter-of-fact.

She had no idea how effective it might be, but they had to do *something*. Hadn't she watched news footage of people fighting fires hundreds of times? They always watered stuff down. "Where's a hose?"

When the girl only stood there, Angel sharpened her voice. *"Where's a hose?"*

Katie still didn't move. "I want my mom." Her arms wrapped around herself. "I want my mom."

Angel didn't like the panic on the girl's face or the tears in her voice. "We have to keep it together, Katie."

"I want my mom," she said again. "Let's go to my mom."

Angel shook her head, eyeing the ash raining down and the widening cloud of smoke moving their way. "We're waiting for Cooper, remember?"

Katie's eyes filled with tears.

At the sight of them, Angel's anxiety tripled. "Don't cry, for pity's sake. Don't cry." What could she say to calm the kid's fears? "We'll wait a little longer. If he still isn't here, maybe . . . maybe you can take the car yourself."

The instant the words left her mouth, she regretted them. Of course she couldn't let Katie leave alone.

But before Angel could take them back, the girl broke. She dropped to the ground, sobbing. "Can't drive," she choked out. "My dad . . . my dad . . . promised to teach me soon." Her whole body shook with more wrenching sobs as she drew her knees to her chest and buried her face against them.

Helpless, Angel stared down at her. What was she supposed to do now? She sucked at this kind of emotion! This was person-to-person stuff. Personal.

Tears made her uncomfortable. Worse, they made her feel out of control.

She hunkered beside Katie and awkwardly patted her shoulder. "We, uh, we have to be strong now." She remembered her mother saying that, every time they moved to a new apartment, new town, new country. "Now's not a good time to fall apart."

"My daddy . . . where's my daddy?"

The girl's wail was one of grief, of anguish, of fear, Angel thought, gritting her teeth so hard her jaw ached. It was every emotion Katie had bottled up since her father's death.

Their father's death.

Katie suddenly looked up, pinning Angel with a tear-drenched gaze. "Where is he?" Then her face crumpled again and another wash of tears ran down her cheeks. "He's supposed to save me."

He's supposed to save me.

Angel froze. It was as if the words were wrenched straight from Angel's childhood. Straight from that deepest, darkest corner of her heart. But she wasn't going to cry about it. Hell, no.

Instead, squaring her shoulders, she grabbed Katie and pulled her close. "We'll be all right," she said, her voice strong. Emphatic. "We're okay."

"I want my daddy," Katie sobbed against her neck.

Yeah, well, join the club, Angel thought, resentment toward Stephen Whitney piling on top of the ever-simmering anger. He'd deserted both of them. Her arms tightened around Katie. "We don't need a man to save us. We don't need anyone."

Katie looked up, her expression tragic. "But I loved him," she answered. "I loved him."

Why? Angel wanted to shout at the girl. *What did he ever do for you?*

But he'd been a real father to Katie, Angel knew that. He'd painted clouds on her bedroom ceiling and probably taught her to swim and to ride a bike and would have taught her to drive. He'd likely played toddler games with her too, throwing her up in the air, telling her to flap her wings. *Fly, angel, fly!* he'd probably called out as he tossed her. And then, as she fell, he'd saved her, catching her in his arms, to rub his cheek against her blond curls.

And the little girl had giggled and given her daddy dozens and dozens of angel kisses all over his face, until he'd laughed his deep daddy-laugh and begged her to stop.

"Did he . . . did he used to throw you up and catch you?" Angel whispered, her eyes strangely stinging.

Katie shook her head. "Don't remember."

But I do.

She remembered the flying angel game now, and other games, jacks and Old Maid and a board game with candy characters. She remembered a paint-splattered hand turning the pages of a picture book. She remembered being held in the curve of his arm and leaning against him, falling asleep to the sound of his voice rumbling in his chest.

What had happened? Why had he left her, why hadn't he come when she needed him?

She was never going to know the whole story.

But as Angel's arms tightened around her half-sister, she realized those answers didn't matter so much anymore. He hadn't been a superhero. Like all men, like all *humans,* male and female alike, he'd made mistakes, he'd made errors of judgment, he'd caused other people pain. But he was gone now.

With an odd sense of calm, she lifted her face skyward and watched the ashes continue to fall around them, on them, onto her cheeks. Her wet cheeks.

Amazed, Angel put her hand up to her face, and then she brought it away, staring down at the muddy concoction of ash and tears on her fingertips. She was crying.

Crying.

But not because she was weak.

Not because once upon a time some man had done her wrong.

She was crying in relief, she was crying while a quiet sort of peace entered her heart.

She was crying because she remembered now, because she knew, without a doubt, that her father had loved her.

Cooper had made the necessary phone calls without a hitch. The first-aid kit and the survival blankets had been right where he'd expected. After stuffing a water bottle in the front pocket of his jeans, he started after Angel, thinking he might be able to catch up to her before she reached Katie.

But somewhere between the retreat and the Whitney compound, bad luck and hell caught up with Cooper. One minute he was traveling through hot, but fairly clear air, and then the next he was engulfed in a drift of ash. Tiny embers blew down with it, looking like fireflies at dusk.

But he plowed forward, hoping he could outdistance the fire at his back, hoping the strong offshore wind would blow the flames straight toward the sea instead of letting the fire creep northward. But as he neared the halfway point on the shortcut to the Whitney house, the point where the trail was pinched between a steep incline and the V-point of a deep canyon, he saw flames crest the hill above him.

Then, worse, one of the "fireflies" landed at the bottom of the deep fissure below, igniting the dry brush.

Shit! If the wind shifted, blowing onshore, that little tuft of burning bush could become a firestorm that would race up the gorge at a hundred miles an hour. Cooper stumbled on a root and fell to his knees, his gaze fixed on the fire that was crackling and building below him. The air filled with smoke, drifting up from below and billowing down from the fire above him.

Abandoning the blankets and the first-aid kit, he stripped of his shirt and tied it over his mouth to filter the soot. Then he pushed to his feet. *Keep going,* he commanded himself, as he tripped again. *Keep moving.*

The wind shifted, swirling ashes, blowing another hot blast of thick smoke over him. He blinked rapidly, trying to get a clearer view of what was in front of him. But the smoke was huddled around him now, trying to cut off every breath, every step.

Cooper shook his head, willing himself to think clearly, see clearly. Glancing back, he wondered if the fire behind him had already burned all the way to the ocean. Burned out. If so, turning back toward the retreat was a better bet than proceeding forward.

Don't leave me. He heard Angel's voice in his head, saw Katie's precious face in his mind's eye. He'd promised to come to them. They were counting on him, though he hoped to God they'd already taken the car and gotten out.

The smoke blanketed him now. He couldn't see in front of him, behind him, around him. Was the fire moving faster, roaring down, roaring up?

It was hard to think. Hard to breathe. He was dizzy and his boots must be filled with cement. His chest felt so heavy. A dreaded heaviness.

If he died, would an angel find him in all this gray, sooty darkness?

No, his mind responded groggily. He'd never see Angel again.

The thought cleared his mind like a shot of pure oxygen. Oh God, oh God. He'd never see her again. He wanted to scream in frustration at fire and fate and his own stupidity. He was never going to see her again, and she'd never know how happy she'd made him.

Would someone else take his place in Angel's life? Of course, because she wasn't the least bit unlovable. But now he'd never get the chance to tell her she was right, that he'd let her drive away hoping to save *himself,* not to save her.

But, damn it, it hadn't worked. He'd half-known it then, and the truth was glaringly obvious now. He loved her. He was in love with her.

But he'd been right too, he thought, as he stumbled again and fell painfully to his knees: It hurt so much more to die when he had so much more to lose.

Katie saw the flames first. Angel and she were still beside the pool, still holding each other, when she suddenly clutched Angel tighter. Angel followed her pointing finger to the high, weedy hill behind the house. Fire was burning along its edge.

Swiping at her wet face, Angel jumped to her feet, dragging Katie up too. If the fire took a downward turn, there was nothing between them and it, because first it would cut off the road leading to safety. Then they'd be trapped, and she didn't think the small stand of pines clustered by the pool area, or the tamed vegetation around the house, or even the house itself would prove much of a deterrent.

"Give me the keys," she said. "Let's get to the car."

Surely Cooper would arrive any second.

Angel ran another quick, assessing eye over the situation. Okay, perhaps the manicured landscaping around the house might slow down or divert flames. If it didn't, the outsides of the tower, house, and poolhouse were constructed with at least some unburnable stone. If she had to make a guess at their point of vulnerability, it was that stand of eight or ten pines behind the poolhouse. If those went up, who knew what would go next?

Yes, it was time to get out.

But as Katie dug the ring of keys from the pocket of her shorts, over her shoulder Angel saw the flames start racing down the hillside. Terror spiked inside her, shooting from her belly to pierce her heart.

It looked as if it was too late for all of them.

Cooper's shallow breaths sounded harsh in his own ears as he struggled once more to his feet. He moved doggedly through the smoke, one foot at a time, one more desperate half-breath at a time.

The air was so dark around him, he had no idea if he was going away from fire or toward it. Every second might be his last.

A grimmer death than the one he'd faced on an ambulance gurney and then in the operating room. A much less peaceful death than he'd imagined when he'd moved back to the Sur a year ago.

He tried to work up some sense of outrage about that to fuel his forward movement, but it took too much energy.

A gust of cool wind suddenly buffeted him, clearing the smoke. Ahead was Lainey's house, he could see it! There was the front door and the curving driveway. The back of the house and the pool area weren't visible from here, but all looked well.

His gaze focused on the intact beauty of it, he managed to stumble forward a few more steps. Then his mind registered the presence of the car on the drive.

Katie and Angel were still there.

His feet sped up. He was running, sucking in smoke-filled air. With a jerk, he undid the fabric from around his mouth and nose and pressed on. *Katie and Angel were just ahead!*

Then his heart slammed once against his chest, then jerked back like a shotgun cocking. *Oh God. Oh God.* He could see more now. Fire had creeped up and was now running down the hill behind the house. The advancing flames were heading right for it.

He picked up his speed, the smoky oxygen burning in his lungs, the weight of good intentions and horrifying regrets riding like beasts on his back. The path took a bend, putting the house out of sight, and he felt his heart stutter again, that shotgun jerk.

He wondered if now was his moment to die.

If it might not be better that way.

But he was alive, still moving, as the front of the house came back into sight. Though he couldn't see from here what had happened behind the place, it appeared as if the ice plant and other flame-retardant landscaping had done its job. From what he could see, the fire must have swept around the property, then swept on, burning harmlessly out as it traveled down the near-barren cliff to the ocean. With a final press of speed, Cooper reached the Whitney front door.

It swung open to his hand, but no one answered his hoarse cries. He ran through the living room and into the kitchen, then glanced out the French doors, froze.

And in the next instant found himself on the pool deck, staring across the patio at the tall, still-smoking, but completely torched matchsticks that had once been flourishing pines. They would have gone up like Christmas trees in one of those public service spots produced by the SF Fire Department. Hot and fast.

His eyes moved to the charred top of the hedge he'd trimmed last week, the fried fringe on one striped umbrella, the blackened surface of the pool, and then, barely discernible, the—

—bodies at the bottom.

He didn't need air or energy or even will to dive into the water. Operating on pure anguish, he wrapped his arms around what he found there and shot to the surface.

Waist-high in murky pool water, he was in possession of two females, their hair, faces, and clothing smeared with a sticky, ashy concoction. But they were moving. Alive.

Thank God! Gloriously alive.

In his right arm, Katie hiccuped, wheezed. In his left, Angel started coughing, stopped, started coughing again.

Then she looked at Cooper, her blue eyes red-rimmed but startling in her blackened face. "You almost gave me a heart attack."

He grinned at her—what else was there to do? "That makes two of us."

"Three," Katie added. "We didn't see you were here because of the ash on top of the pool."

Still holding them tightly, he slogged toward the steps. "What the hell were you two doing in the water?"

Angel started coughing again, so Katie answered. "Getting away from the fire. When we couldn't leave by car and it looked as if the pines would catch, Angel decided we'd be safe from the heat and flames there. We came up for air when we had to, but we weren't sure if it had completely passed through yet."

Cooper's heart did a milder echo of that double-jerk again and he collapsed on the top step of the pool, taking his niece and Angel with him. They pressed close, his arms still over their shoulders.

"Thank God you're all right," he said, kissing Katie's cheek. "Thank God." He turned to kiss Angel but then hesitated, bowled over by a fresh wave of horror. "You can't swim."

"Shallow end," she said, her voice hoarse. She sucked in a breath. "But I confess I'm pretty happy to see you."

They were silent as the smoky air became clearer and clearer and their breathing became easier and easier. Katie dropped her head onto his shoulder. "It was hot, when the pines caught. Really hot."

His stomach churned, though he tried to hide it from her. "I imagine so. But you were okay in the water?"

"I dragged Angel to the middle," she said, "and I held on to her tight because she told me she can't swim."

Imagining it only made his stomach worse. He cleared his throat, reminding himself they were here with him, and safe. "What made you think of the pool?" he managed to ask Angel.

Her voice was still hoarse. "Read about it in *Woman's*

Day magazine. A lady saved herself, her dog, and twelve place settings of heirloom Lenox."

"Yeah?" He ran his hand over Angel's wavy, now almost inky hair. "Well, then, I guess you two didn't need a hero after all."

"Oh, Angel said you'd come for us," Katie put in. "She was positive about that."

"She was?"

Katie nodded. "But we saved ourselves, Uncle Cooper. I think . . . I think my dad would be proud of me."

Though he was looking at his niece, he caressed Angel's wet hair again. "I'm certain of it, Katydid. I'm certain he's very proud."

Again, a few minutes passed in silence as they caught their breath, caught up to the knowledge that they'd survived. But then the phone started pealing from inside the house. They looked at each other.

"Mom," Katie said with certainty, jumping up with the young's incredible powers of recovery. "I'll go tell her we're okay."

That left Cooper alone with Angel. He took her by the shoulders and turned her to him. "*Are* you okay, sweetheart?"

"I was worried about you," she whispered.

"Hey, I was coming. Nothing was going to stop me." He tried to smile. "Katie said you were certain of that."

She nodded. "I had faith in you. But I didn't want or need you to play the hero. Not a superhuman one, anyway."

He lifted her chin with his hand, looking into those heavenly eyes in the dirty, to-hell-and-back face. He'd almost lost her and now he couldn't bear to waste another instant of this second chance. "What about wanting and needing a very human, very frail man who's in love with you?"

Her eyes widened and her lower lip trembled. He saw her swallow. "Frail of heart?"

"Faint of heart, maybe." He couldn't get enough of looking at her. "But I've taken a lesson from you and toughened up. After surviving that fire, I figure I've proved to myself I have another thirty years or so in me."

Her lip firmed and her spine steeled. God, how he loved every noncompromising, soldier-in-an-angel's-disguise inch of her.

"I won't settle for less than fifty, even if that means we both eat tofu," she said.

She was too precious to lose. He smiled. "For that sacrifice, then fifty it is, as long as you promise to be beside me."

As if a dam burst, she sagged into his arms, a wash of tears brimming over her bottom eyelids to run down her face.

"What's this?" he said, concern clawing at him again. "Are you hurt somewhere?" He ran his hands over her shoulders, down her arms.

She shook her head, more tears washing her face clean. "More like . . . more like I'm healed."

And as their lips met, Cooper thought, *That makes two of us.*

* * *

As sweet as these new, committed kisses were, Angel could tell that Cooper was as exhausted as she. So she insisted on pulling out of his embrace and walked over to grab a couple of towels that were hanging, unscathed, on hooks against the side of the poolhouse. The pines behind the structure looked like something out of Armageddon, but its paint had merely blistered.

The pool itself had proved their sanctuary, she thought, looking over her shoulder. Her eyes narrowed, something about it suddenly striking her as . . . odd. She'd noted the two-sided, mirror-image shape before, but hadn't really thought much about it.

"It looks like a pair of wings," she said to Cooper, who was coming toward her. She gestured at the pool. "It's shaped like wings."

He glanced over his shoulder, then took both towels and tenderly wrapped one around her. The other he slung over his neck before pulling her into his arms again.

"What were you saying?" His mouth moved against hers.

"The pool."

"Oh yeah." He lifted his head and looked over his shoulder again. "It's in the shape of Stephen's *W*—the one he used to sign the paintings. But you're right. Upside down, it looks like wings."

Angel wings.

Angel. She'd never quite understood why she'd selected that name for herself when her mother and she had emerged from hiding. But now she thought of that memory again—*Fly, angel, fly!*—and smiled.

Then she pressed her cheek against the steady thump of Cooper's heart. In her time of most dire need, maybe both of the only men she'd ever loved had come to her rescue after all.

Epilogue

Angel hurried through the crowd in the bar at the Ça Va Restaurant, heading without hesitation to the corner, where she knew her husband would be waiting at their table. *Her* husband. *Their* table.

The thoughts put a smug smile on her face as she slid onto the stool opposite him. "Sorry, sorry, I know I'm late."

He captured her hand, squeezed. "I thought we had a deal. We both agreed we wouldn't get caught up in overtime."

"Uh-huh. I know." Her customary glass of wine was sitting on the tabletop in front of her, but she ignored it. Instead, she slipped her hand from Cooper's to unfasten the buttons of her trenchcoat.

He half-rose. "Do you want me to hang that—?"

She was already shaking her head. "Thanks, but not

quite yet." There were a few things she wanted to say first.

But apparently Cooper had a few things he wanted to say too. He captured her hand again. "Angel, I'm not kidding about the overtime. You've been exhausted the past two weeks."

"I know, but—"

"All work and no play makes a dull wife."

She rolled her eyes. "Considering we spent last weekend lazing around Tranquility, rousing ourselves only to indulge in activities I defy you to describe as 'dull,' I think I'm not going to worry."

He grinned. "It was great, wasn't it?"

She smiled back at him. "Yeah," she said softly. "It was great."

The retreat had survived the fire nine months before, with some damage. All the cottages had been spared, though the common building had burned to the ground. It was rebuilt now, with a fancy kitchen that Angel thought was a terrible shame to waste on organic, vegetarian cuisine. Judd and Beth had completely taken over the running of the retreat and planned to be married there in August.

Angel couldn't imagine waiting to be Cooper's wife for that long, though it was he who had insisted they marry right away. And insisted they move back to San Francisco. And insisted he start back to work at his firm.

She snitched his bottle of Perrier off the tabletop and took a long swig, checking him out from the corner of her eye. He didn't appear exhausted in the least. She thought marriage was good for him. And after today, no one could say she wasn't doing her part to get him home every night at a decent hour.

"So what are you smiling about, Mona Lisa?" he asked suspiciously.

She batted her lashes at him, all innocence, wanting to hold on to this last secret between them for as long as she could. "I don't know what you're talking about." To stall the inevitable cross-examination, she let her gaze wander to the television hanging over the bar.

Her eyes widened and her heart rocked inside her chest.

"What? What is it?" Cooper said. "Are you all right?"

"I—I—" Her attention still on the screen, tears filled her eyes.

Cooper's voice sharpened. "Angel. Honey. What's the matter?" He glanced over his shoulder, trying to figure out the cause of her distress.

"Th-the TV," she managed to choke out, even as two fat tears plopped onto her cheeks. Then two more.

"Something on the TV?" His head whipped around again even as he passed his handkerchief to her. "Did I miss something? It's a commercial."

The handkerchief that was stemming the next little flood of tears muffled her voice. "It's a *Hallmark* commercial. You know, the one where the sisters are shopping together."

Cooper stared at her, obviously baffled. "Is this about Katie?"

Angel shook her head, as another wave of tender emotion pulled at her heart. *She had a sister!* It still amazed and delighted her. Cooper's entire family now knew that Angel was Stephen Whitney's daughter. They'd accepted her apology and her bare-bones explanation that she and her father had lost touch over the years and that after his death she'd been reluctant to claim kinship.

But she happily claimed it now. Their trial by fire had created a strong bond between her and her half-sister. Katie would spend the month of July with them in San Francisco, and Angel couldn't wait. There was all sorts of fun shopping that needed to be done—

"Damn it, you're getting all weepy again! What the hell is going on?"

Angel blinked, realizing that not only had she drifted off on one of those daydreams she was so prone to lately, but that Cooper was right and she was tearing up again too. Wiping her eyes with the handkerchief, she decided to take pity on the man and put an end to his ignorance.

With a determined sniff and an only slightly watery smile, she stood up and met his gaze. "I have something to tell you."

"What?" An expression of such concerned alarm crossed over his face that her throat closed up with emotion. *He cares about me. He loves me.*

With words beyond her now, she told him the only way she could. Shimmying her shoulders, Angel let her trenchcoat slide off and fall to the barstool. Now she stood in front of him wearing only her brand-new dress—the one she'd been shopping for that afternoon when she'd realized she was running late. With her arms held out, she executed a half-decent pirouette.

Confusion joining the concern on his face, Cooper continued looking at her, his gaze running from her head to her high-heeled pumps. "Angel, I'm lost. What is it?"

She managed another watery smile and waved her arms to indicate the full, pale blue-and-pink garment.

He blinked. "Something about the dress? Well, it does look several sizes too big for you, but is it really worth crying about?"

Angel shook her head, not knowing whether to laugh or to cry some more. Swallowing the big knot in her throat, she stepped up and put her hands on either side of the face of the man she adored. "It's a *maternity* dress, Cooper. I know it's early, *way* early, but I couldn't resist."

His jaw dropped and Angel's happiness was suddenly edged with a little panic. They hadn't planned the pregnancy, not exactly, but the minute she'd suspected, she'd been thrilled. To have a husband, a family, *their* baby.

"I've thought it all through," she said quickly. "I can work part-time, and we have two spare bedrooms. The one across from our room would be perfect." She'd been planning how to decorate it. Soft yellows and cool vanilla. In a place of prominence, she'd hang the one Whitney canvas she owned, the only one that had survived the fire—a painting of a gilt-haired infant that was rendered with all the tender love of a father.

The new father-to-be in front of her blinked rapidly a few times, then reached up to take her hands in his. He held them, linked, against his heart. "You're pregnant?"

"Confirmed by the doctor today." It still wasn't clear what Cooper thought about it. "I hope you're not—"

"I'm going to be a father?"

There was an elated note in his voice that made her smile. That made fresh tears spring to her eyes. Hormones, she thought. She'd read a long article about them in *Maternity* magazine. "Yes, my love, you're going to be a father."

"Oh God." He pulled her into his arms, holding her gently against him. "Oh God, Angel. I—I never thought I'd feel this way."

She looked up into his face. "I never thought I'd feel this way either." She'd never thought she could love anyone so much, let alone love so much the idea of having his child.

A grin broke across his face. He laughed out loud, then turned to the group at the next table, slapping a complete stranger on the back. "Hey, guess what? We're going to be parents!"

After a moment of surprise, the people smiled and congratulated them. They even lifted their glasses in a toast, and Cooper, in turn, lifted his Perrier bottle. "To my wife, who has given me everything worth living for!"

Angel teared up again. "Darn hormones," she muttered. But unwilling to be outdone, she regained enough control to swipe the bottle from Cooper's hand.

Raising it, she caught Cooper's gaze with hers. "To my husband and my love," she declared to the entire room, "who is . . . who is one of the good guys!"

It felt like just the right thing to say.

The world should know the truth about men like this.